The Best
AMERICAN
SHORT
STORIES
2025

GUEST EDITORS OF THE BEST AMERICAN SHORT STORIES

1978 TED SOLOTAROFF
1979 JOYCE CAROL OATES
1980 STANLEY ELKIN
1981 HORTENSE CALISHER
1982 JOHN GARDNER
1983 ANNE TYLER
1984 JOHN UPDIKE
1985 GAIL GODWIN
1986 RAYMOND CARVER
1987 ANN BEATTIE
1988 MARK HELPRIN
1989 MARGARET ATWOOD
1990 RICHARD FORD
1991 ALICE ADAMS
1992 ROBERT STONE
1993 LOUISE ERDRICH
1994 TOBIAS WOLFF
1995 JANE SMILEY
1996 JOHN EDGAR WIDEMAN
1997 E. ANNIE PROULX
1998 GARRISON KEILLOR
1999 AMY TAN
2000 E. L. DOCTOROW
2001 BARBARA KINGSOLVER
2002 SUE MILLER
2003 WALTER MOSLEY
2004 LORRIE MOORE
2005 MICHAEL CHABON
2006 ANN PATCHETT
2007 STEPHEN KING
2008 SALMAN RUSHDIE
2009 ALICE SEBOLD
2010 RICHARD RUSSO
2011 GERALDINE BROOKS
2012 TOM PERROTTA
2013 ELIZABETH STROUT
2014 JENNIFER EGAN
2015 T. C. BOYLE

2016 JUNOT DÍAZ
2017 MEG WOLITZER
2018 ROXANE GAY
2019 ANTHONY DOERR
2020 CURTIS SITTENFELD
2021 JESMYN WARD
2022 ANDREW SEAN GREER
2023 MIN JIN LEE
2024 LAUREN GROFF
2025 CELESTE NG

The Best AMERICAN SHORT STORIES® 2025

Selected from U.S. and Canadian Magazines
by CELESTE NG
with NICOLE A. LAMY

With an Introduction by
CELESTE NG

MARINER BOOKS
New York   Boston

hc.com

FIRST EDITION

ISSN 0067-6233
ISBN 978-0-06-339980-8
ISBN 978-0-06-339984-6 (SIMULTANEOUS HARDCOVER EDITION)

25 26 27 28 29 LBC 6 5 4 3 2

Contents

Foreword

IN THE SPRING of eighth grade I got an A minus on the longest writing assignment of my thirteen-year-old life—analyses of nine short stories along with mini biographies of their authors. My English teacher was a firm, but benevolent, grammarian dedicated to great stories and vibrant tunics. Despite a grade that would mortify contemporary overachieving middle schoolers, I was proud of that A minus (I still am!). Even more significantly, the short story project marked the first time that my private reading life mingled a little with my school life. The reading I did away from school—in my bed, at the beach, in cars, on rocks in the woods—always had two settings, mine and the book's: grains of sand are still stuck in the binding of my first copy of *Little Women*, though the March sisters did not live at the beach; the spruce and balsam of the Nova Scotia coast merged in my mind with the Murrys' woods while I read *A Wrinkle in Time* by the light of a kerosene lamp in my family's tent. But, until the short story project of eighth grade, the books I devoured for pleasure everywhere else didn't seem connected to what teachers assigned me in the classroom.

At home I had already started a *Best American Short Stories* collection. The top row of my bookshelf was lined with a mix of paperbacks and hardcover editions—the pages dotted with foxing, most of which I scored from my town library's annual sale ($1 for hardcovers, 50 cents for paperbacks). Held in early June, book sale day was one of my favorite days of the year. I would arrive early and overstuff paper grocery bags, which inevitably ripped on my walk home until I wised up one year and brought pillowcases to carry my haul. Though I came to love the form immoderately, my initial reliance on short fiction anthologies was statistical: More authors per book meant I had better odds of discovering more, new (to me) writers.

During my first year as series editor of *The Best American Short Stories*, every day has felt like library book sale day. Though now I've upgraded to tote bags full of short stories, which I carry to the beach and cafés, to my children's baseball games and their cello lessons. Even if they have led me to ignore my family on occasion, the stories have been excellent company; when I have felt despair about the direction of our country, the fiction I read this year helped me make more sense of the world than real life was able to provide.

For most of this year's reading, I relied on the deluge of magazines—some forwarded from PO Box to PO Box, others passed through the HarperCollins New York office, and more still that arrived through email—to lead me to writers whose work I have loved for decades and to fall for writers whose work I had never read. I'm so grateful to the dedicated editors at those magazines—most of whom have other jobs, too!—for publishing so many artful, moving, hilarious, always surprising stories.

Beyond keeping up with my magazine mail, I also left time to explore other literary corners both digital and analog. An electric story would usually spark an online pursuit; following writers' digital publication trails led me to other stories they published during the year and to small digital journals publishing vibrant work. Sometimes I realized that the story I read was part of a novel, which meant I couldn't consider it for *The Best American Short Stories*, but I'd file away the title and author and a brief summary in a bear-in-mind document, which I keep close at hand. During slow mail weeks, when I worried that I might be missing out on stories, I haunted bookstores near home—

Porter Square Books and Harvard Bookstore. I added visits to Parnassus Books in Nashville and the Regulator Bookshop in Durham, North Carolina, to my vacation itineraries to look for any magazines that hadn't made their way to me.

After all the gathering, reading, and piling, sorting, and rereading of stories, I loaded up my favorites in reusable grocery bags, in three different batches, to hand off to Celeste Ng, who has been an excellent partner for this project. She's a swift reader with reassuringly sound judgment. Better still, her grounded nature belies not just her willingness, but her eagerness to be transported by all genres, perspectives, styles, and flights of imagination.

Among the discoveries I made in the worn volumes I bought at my childhood library sale was the work of William Saroyan, whose stories I included in my epic eighth grade project. First published in *Story* magazine, then included in the 1935 edition of *The Best American Short Stories* and reprinted in *The Best American Short Stories of the Century*, edited by John Updike and Katrina Kenison, Saroyan's "Resurrection of a Life" reads, thematically and stylistically, like a twenty-first–century story.

As the narrative drifts between third and first person within a shifting chronology, a man both remembers and then relives his days as a ten-year-old selling newspapers on the streets, shouting the headlines that announce the destruction and casualties of the war—WWI—in Europe. Throughout the impressionistic narrative the boy expresses horror at the war and a contemptuous fascination with the rich, while his family relies on discarded bread to survive. Despite personal and social strife, the boy's perspective is shaped by his visceral connection to the movies. After he is overwhelmed by a flood of images—terrifying, erotic, and atmospheric—he emerges from the theater, "insane with the passion to live," which pretty much nails how I felt after reading thousands of stories over the past year.

To the readers of these stories—I hope you make discoveries that help you make sense of the world.

To the writers of the stories—which are full of urgency and grace—thank you.

To the editors of literary magazines—please keep sending me your stories for consideration. I've loved reading them.

The Best American Short Stories
Mariner Books
ATTN: Maya Horn
HarperCollins Publishers
195 Broadway, 23rd Floor
New York, NY 10007
thebestamericanshortstories@gmail.com

NICOLE A. LAMY

Introduction

I HAVE AN embarrassing confession. I've been reading *The Best American Short Stories* for several decades—since I was about fourteen or fifteen—but until now, I don't think I have ever read the introductions to a single one of them. I was always in a hurry to get to the good stuff, which is to say: the stories.

I wish I could blame this on being an impatient teenager, but the truth is that I still feel the same impulse today. *I picked up this book because I wanted to read stories, not some boring introduction!*

So now I find myself in the awkward position of writing something I fully expect readers to skip—and honestly, I can't even blame them. Every day there are more demands on our attention, more dazzling distractions, more outrages that hurt our hearts. Why take the time to read fiction at all—short stories, no less—let alone an introduction?

If you're truly itching to flip ahead, I feel you, and here's all you really need to know:

Read these stories. They're all great in very different ways. They'll make you laugh and possibly cry and maybe even think differently about the world from now on.

Now, for those of you still reading, let me tell you a little about the stories in this volume, why I chose them, and why I think they—and stories in general—matter more than ever today. And then we can all get to the good stuff.

*

You have probably heard claims that the short story is dead, that no one writes or publishes them anymore. I'm happy to report that is extremely untrue. Hundreds, if not thousands, of short stories are published every year, in print and online—everywhere from long-established mainstream journals like *The New Yorker* and *The Atlantic* to literary journals like *The Georgia Review* and *Granta* to relative newcomers like *The Drift* and *Joyland*. Nicole Lamy, the indefatigable series editor, read absolutely every story published in 2024 that she could get her hands on. From all those stories, she selected a hundred and twenty-six that she passed on to me, and my job was to select the best twenty.

Every one of the stories I read was objectively excellent, and every one of their writers is someone you should be watching if you like good fiction. (You can find a list of all of them, and where they were published, at the end of this volume, and I hope you'll go and seek them out.) Most of the stories were by writers who were new to me, and I chose not to Google any of them before reading. As I read, I sorted the stories into three big piles: Yes, No, and Maybe. Then I read them again, moving pieces from one pile to another, re-reading and re-sorting to narrow down to the twenty that I felt were the best.

A quick disclaimer here: I agonized over the term *best* a lot at the beginning. What did it mean to pick the *best* stories? What standard was I supposed to be comparing them to? *Was* there even a single standard, when the stories were all so different and had different aims? Should I think of it like a dog show, where every dog is judged not against the other dogs but against the specific standards for their own particular breed: *This corgi is more corgi-like than that Dalmatian is Dalmatian-like—so therefore the corgi wins, even if I don't particularly care for corgis?* (For the record, I actually love corgis.) Or should I try to select a representative cross-section of the wide range of stories out there? If a story was beautifully done but simply not to my taste, should I put it in?

Insert about six more paragraphs of similar questions here.

Once I started reading, though, all these questions melted away. Because *best* is inherently subjective, and that's kind of the whole point. Each year, *The Best American Short Stories* is guest-edited by a different writer precisely *because* we want their particular opinion on which stories stood out. We don't want some algorithm-determined list of stories based on some allegedly objective set of criteria—we want a specific, subjective person's specific, subjective take.

So let me tell you about what I personally like in a story, my own idiosyncratic tastes in fiction that guided these selections. I'm not sure I could have articulated all this before I started, but as I read those hundred and twenty-ish stories, I noticed the following patterns:

First and foremost, the story had to grab me. Sometimes this meant an unforgettable premise, or a propulsive plot, or characters so fully drawn that I felt I would know them if I met them on the street. Sometimes it was charm, or humor, or an unexpected twist. The stories that ended up in the Yes pile were ones I couldn't get out of my head, that I kept thinking about days or even weeks after reading them. The best comparison I can find is that it's a lot like falling in love: You either have chemistry, or you don't, and often it defies rational explanation.

Second, the story had to feel complete. I don't mean that everything gets resolved at the end; some of my favorite short stories of all time end ambiguously. But I wanted a sense that the writer had considered the story holistically, that every choice had been made deliberately, and that all the pieces fit together, even if every corner of the picture wasn't fully revealed. And by the time I reached the last line, I needed to understand something more about the situation than I did at the start. To continue the jigsaw puzzle metaphor, enough of the picture had to emerge by the end to give a clear sense of the whole. There might still be gaps, but I needed to know enough so that I could imagine what might fill them—and those gaps had to feel like an invitation rather than a withholding.

Third, the language in the story had to be of the very highest caliber. If a piece didn't have sentences that startled or surprised me, or images that took my breath away with their absolute rightness, it usually didn't make the cut. (This is one of my own personal biases, and what can I say? I love a writer who seems fully in control of their language, the way a virtuoso is fully in control of their instrument.)

And finally, to make it to the Yes pile, stories had to have heft, another hard-to-define term. They didn't have to be serious or sad—two of the criticisms most often leveled at literary fiction. In fact, quite a few of the pieces in the Yes pile made me laugh out loud. But I had to feel that this story and these characters were deeply important to the author, not just a thought experiment or a whim. I wanted the sense that the author wrote this story because they *had* to, that the story was following them like a ghost, tapping them insistently on the shoulder, moving the furniture and rattling the walls, demanding to be told. I also tend to gravitate toward stories that are in conversation with big topics, whether that means our current moment or broad-reaching and eternal themes. Going back to that jigsaw puzzle analogy one more time, the picture that emerges has to show me something significant, something that feels worth looking at closely. In my read, the very best stories engage with more than just the purely personal, and this is what turns a good story into a great story.

I didn't go into this process looking for any particular topics or ideas, but certain themes seemed to be on the minds of writers in 2024, because they kept coming up again and again. Call it the zeitgeist, or just something in the water. So it's interesting to look at the selected stories as a group—along with the other hundred-plus stories that I read—to see what if anything they might say about the current state of short fiction, and what they might say about the current state of America right now, too.

It might feel a little strange to look to fiction—made-up stories about (usually) made-up people—for any kind of insight into the actual world. At the moment I'm writing this introduction, March 2025, I'm quite pessimistic about the state of our country, to put it extremely mildly. We are experiencing curtailments of our civil liberties and threats to our very democracy that, if they were portrayed in a short story, would cause most readers to dismiss the story as "unrealistic." So maybe, when we live in unrealistic times, the unrealness of fiction can actually provide a useful distance, allowing us to see our own times more clearly.

In this year's volume, you'll find stories about trying to survive (figuratively) in a harsh world; you'll also find stories about trying to survive (quite literally) in a harsh world. More than a few of the stories I read could be described as dystopian. Some touched on COVID-19 specifically, or referred to epidemics imaginary or unspecified; others added to the growing literature of "cli-fi," in which characters grapple with the ongoing, often catastrophic effects of climate change. Survival—both how it might be possible, and what's even worth keeping—is clearly on the minds of many writers these days.

This also feels like a time of increasing distances: the six-foot physical distances once imposed by COVID-19, the yawning psychological distances between the two ends of the political spectrum, the metaphysical distances developing as ever more of our lives is lived online—the list goes on and on. So it makes sense that many of this year's stories grappled with isolation and grief and the longing for reconciliation; many focused on attempts to reunite with people lost to distance, to estrangement, or to death. These are eternal themes, of course, but in our ever more–divided times, writers are increasingly examining that sense of loss and alienation.

But it isn't all gloom and doom. There are also many stories here about the flip side of isolation, about unexpected moments of connection and the possibilities of tenderness and understanding. For me, these stories read not as escapism or naïve optimism, but as convincing and much-needed expressions of faith: faith that we can hold on to our humanity even in dark times, faith that interpersonal connection is not only possible but lasting and redemptive. Other stories look at moments of reckoning, when long-simmering situations finally reach a boil—with results that are sometimes devastating, sometimes hilarious, sometimes darkly satisfying. In the past few months especially—as the level of chaos and injustice around us seems to increase exponentially, with no comeuppance in sight—these stories felt almost cathartic, offering a reminder that all bills, eventually, come due.

Many of the stories ultimately fit into several of these categories; I'll let you decide for yourself which ones belong where. Whatever you make of them, though—love them or hate them—thank you for reading. Reading fiction matters immensely, especially right now.

This is surely not news to you, but we're living in an era of disinformation, in which knowingly false stories—or to put it more bluntly, lies—are purposefully deployed to manipulate others, usually for the benefit of a select few. 2024 is hardly the first year this has happened (and sadly, it surely won't be the last), but this past year we've seen incredibly clearly the real-world effects disinformation can have. I'm reluctant to repeat any of the complete falsehoods that have spread on social media and in the real world alike, often from people in positions of power, but I suspect I don't need to give you examples. If you lived through this year, and the past few years, you already know that the space between reality and fantasy has become increasingly blurred in many people's minds—and to many, the distinction may not even feel important anymore.

So why should we still read fiction in a time of lies? If "alternative facts" are running rampant, isn't the antidote (real) facts, rather than made-up stories? Aren't made-up stories part of how we got into this mess?

Facts and verifiable data are immensely important—and I'm deeply grateful to those who work to counter false claims with real information. But I'd also argue that that's only one front in the battle. Research shows, again and again, that a single personal story is more likely to change a person's mind than any amount of statistics.

Obviously, this doesn't mean that when you read a story, you'll suddenly find yourself in agreement with its characters or author—stories are not magic spells, and I'm not saying that just reading short stories will save the world, either. But stories build our empathy by asking us to imagine what it's like to be in someone else's position, thinking their thoughts and feeling their feelings. Unlike disinformation, a short story tells you up front that it is fiction, and when you know it's all just pretend, you're often more willing to play along: *Okay, sure, I'll step into this world, it's just fifteen or twenty pages, and it's all pretend anyway* . . . It's like taking a weekend trip to a place you've never been and aren't sure if you'll like, but hey—it's only a weekend, right?

At the end, though—assuming the story's done its job—this made-up story will have allowed you to access an emotional truth. Facts may tap politely at the prefrontal cortex, appealing to your rational brain, but fiction snakes its way into your limbic system and nests deep in your emotions. By skirting all the rational barriers we hunker behind, sometimes fiction can reach us in a more visceral way. And in doing so, short stories in particular can act like little tuning forks, helping us to clarify our own values—then allowing us to bring ourselves into alignment with what we believe. In a time when our values are being tested daily, it's hard to think of anything more important.

I want to end by telling you just one thing about each of this year's stories that's stuck with me, one particular note that each of these little tuning forks struck for me.* The notes that they strike for you may be different—or maybe some won't resonate with you at all. That's okay! One of the joys of this anthology is that every story in it is different, and every year's anthology is different from every other year's; there's a huge diversity of stories out there. At this time—in which the very word *diversity* has become a target—it feels especially important to remember this: Diversity means there's a place for everyone, and everyone can find something that speaks to them. I hope you find something that speaks to you, whether in this volume or elsewhere.

"Dominion," by Lauren Acampora, is a feat of double consciousness: While reading it, I understood both the main character's questionable decisions *and* his many biases and limitations. It's a tricky thing to achieve—and the story is funny, to boot.

"Take Me to Kirkland," by Sarah Anderson, takes what could

---

* At the beginning of this essay, I told you that I'd never read any of the introductions to these anthologies. When it came time to write this piece, I went to the library, like a student cramming for a final, and read the introductions to the past fifteen years' anthologies. So immense thanks to those previous editors for providing examples of what an introduction might be, and particular thanks to Curtis Sittenfeld, whose introduction to *BASS 2020* gave me the inspiration for this section.

have been a cliché—a lost friendship—and transforms it into an achingly beautiful exploration of love, mortality, and regret. I will never look at Costco the same way.

"What Would I Do for You, What Would You Do for Me?" by Emma Binder, is deceptively quiet but fizzes with tension under the surface, and I especially loved that it offered the possibility of gentleness for characters that we often only see in pain or as victims.

"Abject Naturalism," by Sarah Braunstein, gracefully subverted my expectations about safety and strangers and human nature and makes a powerful argument that grace and joy and connection can still be found in this world.

"Unfathomably Deep," by Sophie Madeline Dess, starts as a bleakly funny story of obsession and shapeshifts into an exploration of the never-ending spiral of grief. Also! That ending! It still surprises me.

"Maritza and Carmen," by Lyn Di Iorio, poses big questions about whether it's ever possible to reconcile the disparate parts of oneself: motherhood with independence, your present self with your past self, the person you wish you could be with the person you fear you actually are.

"Gray, Cotton, White Lace Edges," by Isabelle Fang, manages to be many different things at once—a hilariously believable depiction of reality TV, a coming-of-age story, a complex portrayal of the many different forms love can take—with exquisite grace.

"Time of the Preacher," by Bret Anthony Johnston, captures something about the COVID-19 pandemic better than anything else I've seen: the deep desire to protect the ones we love from harm while realizing, in our hearts, that this is impossible.

"Underwater," by Hannah Kingsley-Ma, is not only one of the funniest stories I've read in ages, its renderings of interpersonal dynamics and the absurdities of human nature are lancet-sharp.

"Drapetomania," by William Lohier, seems like a simple "high-concept" story at first, but the historical footnote at its heart (Google "drapetomania" after you read it) elevates it to a meditation about the legacies of slavery and the complexities of being Black in America.

"The Clean-Out," by Yasmin Adele Majeed, slowly and expertly unravels what goes unsaid across generations—and asks whether withholding stories can sometimes be an act of kindness.

"Seven Stories About Tammy," by Elizabeth McCracken, paints a portrait of a complicated family with the concision of a short story and the depth of a novel, and makes it look easy.

"Till It and Keep It," by Carrie R. Moore, transcends the "cli-fi" genre by weaving a nuanced story about sisterhood and the narrow, nebulous border between being safe and being trapped.

"Angelo," by Andrew Porter, depicts the end of many things—a love affair, an artist's dreams, childhood—with exquisite sensitivity and tenderness, but what makes it memorable for me is that it's also about how those same things somehow endure.

"Yellow Tulips," by Nathan Curtis Roberts, looks back on the days of social distancing and slowly, almost imperceptibly, lays bare the many attendant losses of empathy that we are still continuing to discover.

"Third Room," by Julian Robles, hooked me with its strangeness but stayed with me because of its haunting (yet comic) depiction of isolation and loneliness. I still can't say I know what it means, but I *can* tell you I'm still thinking about it.

"The Masterclass," by William Pei Shih, purposely held me at arm's length—then suddenly, expertly, yanked me close to show me a flash of the white-hot emotion at its core.

"What About This," by Justin Taylor, has a voice like none I've ever read before: a relentless engine of a voice propelling this story into the distance and leaving just a Doppler echo behind.

"Aishwarya Rai," by Sanjana Thakur, begins like science fiction but spirals out from its premise to become a profound reflection on the complexities of mother-daughter relationships.

"An Early Departure," by Jessica Treadway, is just nine pages long, but it's also one of the most powerful stories I've seen about motherhood—and it isn't even about a mother.

And now, finally finally finally finally finally: Here is the good stuff.

CELESTE NG

The Best
AMERICAN
SHORT
STORIES
2025

Dominion

FROM *New England Review*

ROY FOUND A stack of letters on the counter. He lifted the first one, heavy with crayon, and studied its clumsy drawing of a blue-striped tiger with ears like a rabbit.

"They're from Piper's school," Marilyn said, clipping across the kitchen in a spangled white skirt-suit. Another woman might look tawdry in such an ensemble, but his wife carried it off like a duchess.

"Where are you going? I forget."

"Luncheon for the hospital. We're asking Lucinda Bette-Gilman to join the board."

"Ah."

Roy rifled through the letters, some two dozen, each with an inept artistic rendering of Molly. Only one differed, clearly typed by a parent: *While we appreciate your good intention in visiting our child's school with an animal ambassador as impressive as Molly, we're concerned by the practice of keeping wild creatures captive—*

"Marilyn!" Roy called out, but she was already gone. He wanted to write back immediately, tell these crabs that Molly was a rescue from a circus in Peru, thank you very much, where she'd been subjected to cramped and squalid conditions before Roy squired her to a three-acre habitat of her own—a tiger's paradise, more savannah than enclosure. He took out paper and pencil but was too indignant to form words.

What mattered, he reminded himself, was that the school visit had been an unmitigated success, and not just in his opinion, but as corroborated by the teachers' and children's obvious glee. Some of the students had been ill-behaved, of course, pushing ahead of the others, reaching to touch Molly without permission. The class, as Roy had feared, had been a motley little crew, a microcosm of the wider district's demographic makeup. Roy remained perplexed by Shannon's decision to send Piper to public school when there was a panoply of private and Christian academies at her disposal. It was doubtful that his granddaughter would gain any special benefit from "diversity" in this rawest sense of the word, this bestiary of scrappily dressed, minimally groomed children. Roy had been struck by one girl in particular whose hair looked like it had never been combed. And the boy, whom the teacher addressed as Chance, with his eggy, buzz-cut head, had flailed toward Molly with motions so spastic he thought the child might be mentally challenged. Amidst these classmates, Piper had stood out, highbred and luminous in her blue smocked dress and hair bow, serenely awaiting instruction.

And Molly had been the politest of guests, a perfect doll. Roy had crouched beside her while Luis held her chain, and she had patiently allowed the kindergartners to stroke her flank. There was no need for the school staff to know that they'd put a low dosage of sedative in her food that morning, just to be on the safe side. Molly didn't really need it, but Marilyn had thought it was a good idea, and he hadn't argued.

Roy had lunch with the flamingos, on the bench near the lagoon. After so many years of eating at his desk, it was a sweet reward to relax with his steak sandwich and his flamboyance of birds. He watched Diego scatter pigment-enhancing food pellets as they paced in their weird way, back and forth in unison like distracted women. Roy hadn't wanted birds at first, but when the opportunity for Caribbean flamingos came up—this most striking subtype with deep coral feathers—he couldn't resist. Up close, they were gawky and beady-eyed, honking obnoxiously, but at a distance they were art.

After his sandwich, Roy stopped at the serval enclosure, where Vanessa and Sienna lounged under a wooden table. Vanessa approached with her slow, fluid gait and extended her neck for a chin rub. When Hobo emerged from his den box, Roy threw a rubber mouse to him. He never tired of these cats, their long lines and breathtaking speed, their astounding vertical springs. He loved their oversized bat ears and their cloudy gray eyes like agate marbles, glamorously outlined in black.

Throwing the muddy mouse, Roy felt the pleasant emptiness he experienced only with his animals. It must be akin to Zen bliss, the way the yogis thought of it. After leaving the corporate world, he'd finally found a role he could joyfully fulfill, and which he'd wholly earned. Finally, he was making up all those hours of lost daylight: four decades of bureaucracy and conflict. He'd never really warmed to management, even though he'd excelled at it. He'd always found personnel too slippery and hard to pin down. But management was a necessary evil that came with any position of power. And power was something he'd pursued instinctively, adopted easily, worn like a calfskin glove.

It was amusing to think that so much hustle had ultimately led to spending his days like a farmer. When he and Marilyn attended black-tie galas, when they were photographed for the society pages, it tickled Roy to know that just hours earlier he'd been hand-feeding a beef shank to a tiger or helping to midwife a camel birth.

Salvador joined him in the serval enclosure with a bucket of chicken legs. The cats pounced on the meat before it hit the ground.

"Yes, sir. Yes, ma'am," Salvador chuckled to the cats. "That's good food."

Roy found himself laughing, too. The truth was that he enjoyed his property staff more than his peers in black tie. The people he hired to maintain the property and care for the animals were fine people, steered by other desires. The concept of ambition—of success for success's sake—was foreign to them. Satisfied by the simple things the natural world provided, they were unaware of or indifferent to the higher calibers of human pleasures. Roy might have envied this plain contentment, but he understood he was designed differently. His enjoyment of these animals, this life, was necessarily contingent on all that had come before, the challenges he'd met with his own brain power. He enjoyed the animals because he'd worked to obtain them. But unequal as they were, he and his staff were happy together in this Eden. Roy was pleased to share the humor of watching a capybara waddle into the lagoon. Marilyn took delight in the animals, too—especially the camels, whose faces she loved, full of comedy and tragedy. She divined profound feeling in their soft, long-lashed eyes. She was, ironically, the keeper of the household ledger. In a funny swap, she was the manager now, and Roy the irresponsible one in need of reining in. When he'd wanted to build a dolphinarium, Marilyn had unequivocally told him no.

When she came home, Roy was on the hammock near the kudus. She'd changed out of her luncheon armor into jeans and boots, a loose white blouse. She'd kept her earrings in and still looked like a glamour queen as she perched on the neighboring hammock.

"I was thinking," Roy said, "that since Piper's class enjoyed meeting Molly so much at school, maybe we should invite them to come visit the property. Maybe they could take a field trip here, to see where the animals live and how well we take care of them."

He wouldn't tell her about the disparaging letter, which he'd already shredded and stuffed in the trash. Its logic was so misguided, so asinine, that he'd decided to withhold the satisfaction that a response might give the author.

Marilyn raised a brow. "That's a lot of children, Roy."

"Yes, and we have a lot of land. I've been thinking we should make our property more accessible to the public. I mean, what's it all for, if not to share? We should be proud of what we're doing for these animals. People should know. We should be taking the lead in the community, helping to grow awareness about conservation."

"You sound like a CEO."

Roy laughed and swung in the hammock, waiting for more. Marilyn would have an opinion; she always did. He'd learned, the hard way, to heed it.

"Well," Marilyn finally said, opening the folds of her hammock and rolling herself in. "I think it's a very nice thought. Why don't we go ahead and talk to the school."

Roy smiled up to the sky above, a jolly blue canopy sheltering everything he loved.

The school was, in fact, amenable to the idea, and plans were made for a field trip in April. When they spoke to Shannon, she confessed that Piper was already crowing to her friends about it.

"Of course she's proud," Roy said. "Not every little girl's grandparents have their own zoo."

Sadly, the visit would only be for half a day. It would be challenging to wedge a guided tour into such a short window. The acreage alone was impossible for six-year-old legs. Roy would have to omit entire sections of the property and consider the proximity of enclosures. A visit to the red pandas, which he considered mandatory, would preclude seeing the binturongs. He'd have to choose between the mongooses and the anteaters, the bandicoots and wombats.

But whatever the children saw would be more than they'd have seen otherwise. He'd introduce them to Honey the kinkajou, and maybe let one of them hold her. That alone would be worth the bus trip. If this visit went well, maybe they could offer it to other grades, other schools. It could be a merging of their passions, for children and animals. Perhaps they could even open the property to the general public, at least on occasion. They might hire extra staff to serve as docents. It would be the ultimate charitable gesture, beyond any board membership or monetary donation Roy could dream of—cementing his legacy as a committed citizen and public servant.

Marilyn had already carved her own niche in the philanthropic world. She was a powerhouse: chairwoman of the children's hospital and on the boards of the pediatric cancer center and women's shelter. She put her spiritual beliefs into practice in a way few could match. This inspired Roy, too, to contribute to the betterment of the planet. He'd made a point of seeking out rare animals for his menagerie, some critically endangered. It was an ingenious way to leverage his achievements into preservation of the Lord's creations. More than one local article had referred to the property as an "ark," but Roy preferred to think of it as an invocation of the World to Come, this peaceable kingdom of his. *Be fruitful and multiply and fill the earth and subdue it; and have dominion over the fish of the sea and over the birds of the air and over every living thing that moves upon the earth.* His favorite lines from Genesis: engraved on the stone plaque he'd commissioned for the entrance gate.

Marilyn had wanted to offer a lunch buffet for the kindergartners, but the school declined, citing food allergies and liability. It went against every fiber of Marilyn's being to not provide refreshments, but even her proposal of lemonade and cookies was rejected. The class would only have two hours to spend at the property, the principal explained, before the bus would return to the school for lunch. And as it happened, a fundraising event for the women's shelter sprung up on the morning of the field trip. Marilyn was disappointed that she wouldn't be there to see their granddaughter, to watch the classmates' faces when they first arrived, but she brushed it off. "Have fun, and hug Piper for me," she said, and went out in her peach suit and pearls.

Roy opted for a chambray shirt, clean jeans, and his Lucchese ostrich boots. It was still early, so he popped into the lemur enclosure to see the new baby—the first born into their care—which Marilyn had named Marvel. Roy took the little goblin in his hands and examined its big new eyes, its exquisite ears. How could he have shared a planet for so long with this species without ever seeing one, holding one? The pressure of claws in the flesh of his palms shot a ray of pleasure over his skin. He released the baby lemur onto a branch, where it clung and turned to look at him. It truly was a marvel, the two of them gazing at each other with mutual surprise.

Roy felt elevated as he hiked out to the entrance gate to greet the bus. The gate itself was custom wrought iron tipped with elephant heads that, according to his daughter Shannon, looked decapitated. She'd been less than supportive of his enterprise, this grand dream of his golden years. When he purchased the property, she'd referred to it as a "vanity farm." Roy supposed it was typical for children to never fully forgive their parents. There was no harsher judge than a child.

Shannon had been a teenager when the oil spill happened. He'd been a new CEO at the time, and although it was only ten million gallons, not historically significant by any stretch, it had been blown out of all proportion by the media. Marilyn had advised him to get out in front of the press—in this case, more was better, she said: more details, more regret—but Roy had dismissed this. Why would he participate in his own demonization? To his mind, when events occurred that were beyond the public's understanding, the public needed a villain, and he happened to be the one in the dunking booth. The ensuing PR disaster had nearly submarined his career. The photographs of dead fish and oil-slicked birds had dominated the news for weeks. There was something pornographic, he thought, about the public's fixation on these images. Eventually the news moved on to other outrages, but in retrospect Roy saw that Marilyn had been right. He should have done the interviews right away. He should have offered an extravagant apology, provided all the esoteric numbers and timelines without being asked. It was harder to tar and feather a man who stepped out naked in front of you.

It had been a terrible time, but what had hurt the most was that, while he was being savaged by the media, Shannon had stopped speaking to him. She became a member of the Sierra Club and plastered stickers on her bedroom door. Marilyn had reprimanded her for this, but Roy's relationship with his daughter was never the same afterward. In the interest of civility, he'd curbed the urge to point out her hypocrisy—all the years she'd benefited from his oil earnings, sleeping in a four-poster bed in Nearwater, attending Cranbury Academy, hosting friends at catered pool parties. He knew the truth would only anger her. Shannon had always perversely pinpointed whatever was lacking. As a girl, she'd harassed them for a puppy, the only request they'd ever refused. Raising a child was hard enough; Marilyn didn't want to think about pets.

These animals, of course, were different. They weren't pets, they were Roy's prizes—each bringing its own distinct charm.

The money he'd so meticulously saved over the years, living beneath his means, he was now spending rapturously. At his age, there was a sense of racing against the clock, to pack in all the enjoyment he could. When a new animal became available, he didn't hesitate. What was he waiting for? There was no telling when the bad checkup might come, the bad biopsy. It was impossible to know what might happen to his wealth after death, with the tax laws always changing. He was confident there'd be plenty left over for Shannon and Piper, but even if there wasn't, his son-in-law was a successful psychiatrist, thank the Lord, and they'd be all right.

When the school bus finally lumbered up to the gate, he buzzed it in. He jogged alongside, waving, as it made its way down the driveway past the flamingo lagoon. When the children clambered out, Piper ran to Roy, and he lifted her in his arms, catching her special scent of crayons and vanilla. His own daughter hadn't smelled of anything so sweet, that he remembered. The teacher smiled at them. There were other adults, too: parent volunteers. Shannon, evidently, wasn't one of them.

Together, the adults corralled the kindergartners into a line. There was the awful boy again, Chance, in constant motion. There was the girl with brambled hair. Roy noticed several others from less conscientious families, in a skull-and-bones T-shirt, bedazzled tank top, trousers with no belt.

The children paraded under the tamarind trees, where the golden lion tamarins were already approaching. The first to peer down—to delighted squeals—was, of course, Lucifer. As the branches shook, the children scanned for the blazing orange manes, the compact faces, the bright black eyes peering down at them, and Roy dropped a few factual nuggets. Tamarins usually gave birth to twins, and they were the only monkeys without prehensile tails. Deforestation in Brazil had destroyed their habitat and endangered the species. The monkeys chirped obliviously, and the children chirped back.

Next, Roy showed off his staff. It was important that the children and adults see this team of dedicated professionals. He didn't know which child belonged to the crank who wrote the letter, but he hoped that this child was paying attention. The staff of five had congregated as instructed, near the main outbuilding where the feed and supplies were kept. They described their responsibilities as caretakers, and the teacher and parents made sounds of appreciation and respect.

After this, the staff was free to disperse. Roy wanted to guide the tour himself. He brought the class to see the adorable red pandas, lemurs, and bandicoots.

"This is Oliver, a bandicoot from Australia," Roy announced cheerily, holding the small marsupial. "He was rescued when he was just a baby, after being attacked by a housecat."

When he noticed the children shuffling in place, glancing around, he tried to be more interactive. "Who knows where Australia is?"

The children looked a little stunned, but then a boy's hand shot up. "My dad went there for work once."

"Ah! Yes, well, Australia is far away, in the Pacific Ocean. Bandicoots are almost extinct there. We take good care of Oliver, and we try to help him and Guinevere have babies, so there can be more bandicoots in the world."

The children giggled, and Roy caught a concerned glance from the teacher, as if afraid Roy might go into a lesson on mating. He moved on quickly, making time to say hello to their old tiger pal Molly before going to see the African servals.

Peering through the chainlink fencing of the serval pen, the kids took a moment to find them. Hobo was probably in his den box. Roy pointed to Sienna, in her habitual place beneath the table, and to Vanessa, who was pacing at the far end of the enclosure, looking tense but unusually beautiful.

"These three sweeties were rescued from the basement of someone's house, where they were being kept as pets," Roy told the kids. "Now, let me ask you. Do these animals look like they belong in a basement?"

The children shook their heads. One of them chirped, "No!"

"No, they sure don't! These critters need room to roam. When we got them, they were overweight and out of shape."

The children tittered, although he hadn't meant to be funny. He tried to put a serious note into his voice and spoke in short sentences that he hoped kindergartners would understand.

"So, let's see. Servals are native to Africa. They have the biggest ears and the longest legs of any cat. Their big ears help them hear prey they can't even see. Ancient Egyptians worshiped the serval, did you know that? I bet you can see why. Aren't they elegant?"

The children nodded. They were enchanted, he could tell, just like he was. Vanessa sashayed back and forth, strutting for them. Her neck was long and slender, like that of an African princess, he thought, stacked high with beads.

"Sometimes they're called giraffe cats. Can you guess why? They're smart, too," Roy said, feeling a swell of pride. "They can even learn to open doors."

Vanessa stopped pacing and stood at attention, her ears turned toward the group. She seemed to be assessing them, considering something in her cool, sphinx-like brain.

It all happened in a millisecond. Roy saw the cat's eyes focus, and in an instant, she had covered thirty feet and thrust her foreleg through the chainlink fence. There was a scream. It took a moment to connect the outthrust leg with that sound. Roy stood paralyzed as a woman gripped the cat's patterned foreleg and dislodged its claws from a little girl's chest. Finally, Vanessa retracted her leg back through the fence and stared crossly for another moment before stalking off to join Sienna beneath the table.

The children were shrieking now. The teacher knelt beside the little girl whose shirt was blossoming red. Roy watched as the teacher lifted her own skirt and pressed it to the wound. Another woman was dialing on her cell phone. It occurred to Roy that the girl was actually hurt, that an ambulance would come, that they would need to stop the bleeding. He herded these thoughts together until his fingers understood the need to unbutton his own shirt. He knelt beside the teacher and took over the stanching. The little girl stared mutely as Roy pressed the chambray to her chest. She had blond pigtails, pale eyelashes, downy hairs at her temple. Blood seeped through the fabric onto Roy's hand. He was dimly aware of resembling some sort of saint, bare-chested in the dirt, administering to this child.

In the corner of his eye, he saw his granddaughter clinging to her teacher, crying.

When Marilyn's heels came tapping over the marble entryway, Roy was lying on the daybed with an arm over his face. He hadn't called to tell her what happened; it wouldn't have made sense to disturb her during her event, and he wanted to be alone for a while. Seeing her now in the living room, in her unassailable salmon suit, he felt strangely guilty. Like a naughty child. He exhaled loudly through his mouth.

"How'd it go?" she began, then paused. "What's wrong?"

When he told her, she was apoplectic. She turned in a circle, flapping her hands, fluttering her fingers.

"Marilyn—"

"We have to go see her," she shouted. "What are you even doing here? We should be at the hospital."

Roy nodded, bobbing his head wordlessly. He hadn't thought of that. It hadn't occurred to him, not for a moment, to follow the ambulance. After it had gone, after the school bus had pulled away with its load of distraught children and chaperones, Roy had stood alone in the driveway. There was a roiling feeling inside his chest, like a terrible machine. He'd stood for a long time, listening to the chirps of the tamarins and the brays of the flamingos, before he was able to move.

Marilyn was silent on the drive to the children's hospital. Roy couldn't tell if she was upset about the girl, or angry with him. As they pulled onto the highway, he said quietly, "The girl's name is Layla."

Marilyn didn't respond.

"Is she a friend of Piper's?" he asked.

"I don't know," Marilyn said. "I've never heard that name before." There was an unmistakable chill in his wife's voice that he felt at the base of his spine.

They left the car with the valet, and Roy followed Marilyn to the front desk of the children's hospital. As they moved toward the elevator, they received glances. It was possible that people recognized them, whether for honor or notoriety. Or perhaps they just looked like people of importance in their carriage and manner of dress.

When they found the room on the sixth floor, Roy took a breath and held it. He let Marilyn enter first. Roy's pulse was skittish, a flush of heat prickling his skin. He saw the hospital bed and the tiny girl nested in it. He was struck right away by her plainness. In the midst of the emergency, she'd seemed prettier, more vibrant. Now she looked wan and dull, her eyes downcast. Both of her parents were there, chairs pulled to the side of the bed as in a crèche. Another child sat beside them—a boy of eleven or twelve, in stained sweatpants—probably an older brother. Marilyn went directly to them, bless her heart. She didn't wait for them to stand but leaned down to hug each of them in turn. Roy watched her embrace the strangers: the bald father with a derelict patch of hair beneath his lip, the peroxide-blond mother, the greasy brother.

Roy stood back, near the doorway, for perhaps a moment too long. It took an effort to shift from observer to participant, to step forward and shake the father's hand. The man stood halfway, meeting Roy's eyes briefly, and dropped back into the chair. Roy noticed the blurred tattoos on his forearm. Next, Roy put a hand on the mother's shoulder in a gesture that he prayed was appropriate. Marilyn was behaving as if Roy wasn't even in the room, having already turned to the little girl.

It was clear, just looking at her, that the girl was going to be okay. There was some injury, of course, but nothing awful. He heard the mother say that she was all stitched up, but she'd have the scar forever. The little girl said a few things, but she spoke so quietly, Roy couldn't make them out. Marilyn nodded and smiled and held the girl's hand. Truly, his wife had a magical way with children. Roy saw the mother's face soften. Here was a woman who never would have met Marilyn had it not been for this freak incident, whose life never would have intersected with theirs. He saw the dark roots at her scalp, noticed the cheap quality of her blouse, a mass-produced sort of tie-dye print.

Roy watched his wife interact with these people. He saw the brightening of their faces. It was no wonder Marilyn hauled in the donations. Roy didn't want to stare, but he couldn't keep his eyes from tracking back to the little girl in the hospital bed, the tiny gown patterned with cartoon characters. She looked back at him, and their eyes caught. When she blinked, he was reminded of Marvel, the baby lemur, whose enormous eyes were designed for seeing at night, watching for predators. Those eyes, like these, were all color and membrane. Nothing in the world could be softer, more vulnerable.

So many ugly contraptions surrounded the girl. There was no visible evidence of her injury, but Roy remembered the blood. There might be a hideous mess beneath the cheery fabric of that gown, a railroad junction of stitches. The child's big eyes seemed to never blink as she looked at him. His own eyes blinked, instead, and he felt a creeping itch in his armpits. This happened, sometimes, when he perspired. But he couldn't scratch—not here in front of everyone. An itch was beginning inside his pants, too, near his crotch.

"Why do you keep wild animals?"

The voice didn't come from the hospital bed, but from the boy, who'd been silent until now. Roy turned.

"Pardon?" he said.

"I said, why do you keep wild animals?" The boy's frame was slight like his sister's, but his features were blunter, his mouth a tight dash. The recrimination in the question was plain, and his gray gaze hit Roy like a rock, momentarily knocking the breath from him.

"Well," he began. "Most of them some of them are rescued." He felt strangely weakened by this boy's glare, unsteady on his feet. He wished he could sit, but there were no unoccupied chairs. He'd never been prone to nerves in front of an audience, even whole auditoriums full of shareholders, but now it was difficult to form a sentence. "We take care of them," he managed.

"Wild animals are dangerous," the boy said loudly.

"Jordan," the father said.

"But I think he knows that," the boy continued, not breaking eye contact. "It's not news."

Roy hoped the father would intervene again, bring his son to heel. No child should be allowed to speak this way to adults.

But perhaps it was folly to expect such decorum from people like these.

"Roy." Marilyn turned to him with an expectant white smile. Before he could think of what to say, the brother had risen to his feet. As the boy stood facing him, Roy was surprised by his height. He wasn't eleven or twelve, as he'd thought, but maybe closer to fifteen. Hostility lay flat across his coarse-featured face, and Roy could glimpse the rough man he'd become.

"*This* is news, though," the boy said, his voice lowering to a growl as he gestured to his sister in bed. "And I'm sure people would want to know about it."

As these words registered, Roy felt a stab of true fear. A malevolent energy radiated from this boy's body. He understood that the boy could, and would, strike him to the ground. A lost memory rippled through him, of arguments with Shannon when she was young. She'd gotten so revved up with righteous disagreement, hitting back against his calm logic, fanning herself into a red fury. Those arguments would end when Shannon would abruptly shut down, trembling with fists clenched, and retreat to her room. Now, Roy was confronted with a person utterly unlike his daughter. Whereas the anger and ardor in Shannon's eyes had betrayed a wounded heart, this boy's gaze held cold violence.

"Jordan," the father said again, uselessly.

"We can discuss some things later, I think," Marilyn interceded in a soothing voice. "We don't want to upset your sister now, I'm sure."

The boy held his bitter gaze on Roy. Suddenly, he pitched forward, and Roy took an automatic step back. He cringed involuntarily, awaiting a blow. As his eyes squeezed, he felt a sensation, a wet explosion on his forehead. For a long moment, he levitated in place, a disembodied entity. The roaring blood in his ears was a wall of white noise. It equaled silence. He felt that a spell had been cast, a judgment rendered, and that he had vanished. The boy had erased him like a witch in a fairy tale.

A hospital machine beeped. He returned to his body. "Excuse me," he muttered, and spun out of the room.

He was corporeal again, physically huge as he strode through the hallway, past the nurses' station to the visitors' bathroom. Once he'd locked the door, he rubbed his face with a paper towel, then he wet another paper towel and sponged it again. Still, he felt the wet spot like a brand on his forehead. And there was also the itch, vexing his armpits and crotch. He unbuttoned his shirt and rubbed the paper towel under his arms, then lowered his pants and rubbed there. Finally, he dropped the paper to the floor and scratched with his fingernails. The itch seemed to be spreading all over his body. Roy sat on the toilet between the handicap bars and scratched. He scratched with abandon, but relief was fleeting. He scratched until his skin turned red and raw and beads of blood appeared.

On the car ride home, Marilyn said that, despite the older brother's performance, she didn't think the parents would sue. They were tired. The father did long-haul trucking, and the mother was a nursing-home aide. They seemed to understand life's exigencies, and they were grateful to the Foxes for their visit and to the children's hospital for its superior care. Marilyn had told them that she and Roy would absolutely cover the girl's medical expenses and offer a generous gratuity to cover the cost of the family's trauma.

The skin of Roy's underarms stung when he turned the steering wheel, and an unpleasant hammering persisted in his chest. "That boy spat on me," he said.

Marilyn looked at him. "What?"

"You saw it. He spat in my face."

"No, he didn't. I didn't see that at all. What are you talking about?"

Roy glanced at her. He felt the color rise to his cheeks. "He did. I felt it."

"Well, I don't think so, Roy," his wife stated. "You're imagining things."

"I know what I felt."

Marilyn was quiet. Roy had come to a full stop behind a line of merging cars on the highway, and she waited until they were moving again before speaking. "Whatever the case," she said, "we need to do the right thing."

The heat remained in Roy's face. He knew without looking in the rearview mirror that his face was red. Perhaps it would always be red now.

"Of course," he answered his wife. "Of course, we'll cover their expenses and whatever else they need." He took a deep breath, which failed to cool his face. "Also," he added, "maybe we should invite the little girl back when she's better, for a private tour of the property." He paused. "In fact, let's invite the whole family."

Marilyn surveyed him, but he was unable to read her look.

"I mean, I don't want that little girl to be afraid of animals now," he said. "It's important that she comes back. I want her brother to come, too. I can look past what he did. I'll forgive it. They're children, and I'm a grown man. What's important is that both these children learn to appreciate the animals' true characters. I don't know what made Vanessa do what she did. Maybe she thought the girl was a toy, or a playmate."

Marilyn stared through the windshield. The traffic had merged into a congested single lane because of a stretch of road work. There were so many cars in front of them, inching along the highway. There were always so many cars. Roy disliked driving more than ever, disliked the traffic that seemed to never cease, that seemed to crowd him deliberately. With each passing day, he felt less inclined to leave his property.

"But really," he continued, "it's the least we can do, to invite her back. Maybe, if they're interested, she or her brother could have their birthday party with us."

Roy glanced at Marilyn, whose eyes were now closed. He didn't press the matter. It had been a difficult day, and they could talk later.

As they drove out of the city and into their greening domain, Roy found his mind returning to an invitation he'd received to join the board of a young oil company. He'd turned it down reflexively weeks ago, but now he wondered if it wasn't something to consider. It might not be a bad idea to keep one foot in the private sector. There might be a certain comfort, a sense of continued relevance in being with people who valued his expertise, especially junior executives like these. It might be invigorating to rejoin the pack, so to speak. It might even be good to be at a conference table again, the kind of long sleek table where he'd captured some of his life's best moments, drawn some of his canniest plans. Back then, with rows of colleagues looking toward him, awaiting command, he'd known his own nature and exerted it. This, he now realized, was what he'd been missing in retirement. It hadn't occurred to him before this very minute. When they got home, he'd tell Marilyn his thoughts, and he'd call Pavo Oil in the morning to see if the invitation still stood.

At last, they pulled up to their gate, and Roy pressed the button that instructed the iron doors to swing inward. The row of elephant heads receded in orderly welcome. The car drove through, its tires purring over gravel, down the row of tamarind trees. The gnarled branches laced overhead, wrinkled pods dangling—and like that they left behind the barbaric world with all its howling demands. This was home, a sanctuary in the truest sense of the word. Roy's heart eased back to a steady rhythm. All around them, miraculous creations. The flamingos in the distance like so many fresh brushstrokes. The camels, his grave dignitaries. The monkeys chirping merrily, scrambling through the branches, swinging down in bright numbers to greet him.

Take Me to Kirkland

FROM *Joyland*

WHEN CHLOE CALLED me in the car that Wednesday on the way to Costco, my boyfriend Damian and I were arguing about whether or not we would be willing to swallow a goldfish for money. "You have no concept of how the real world works," he said. "That's pretty fucking pejorative," I was saying, as my phone lit up with that stupid picture of Chloe's stupid face, filtered to have giant eyes and little deer ears and white deer freckles on the forehead. She always acted like her filtered selfies were ironic, but I knew she only took them because she thought they made her look hot.

I was surprised that Chloe was calling. We hadn't spoken in almost two months, for a few reasons. The first was that she had new friends now, the girls she waitressed with three nights a week at the Longhorn Steakhouse. The one Chloe liked the most, Kayla, had a pierced nipple. Chloe showed me a picture after the first time they hung out. I didn't know that an areola could be that big. I checked Chloe's face out of the corner of my eye and could tell I was supposed to not make a big deal about it. "Nice," I said. "Isn't it so pretty?" she said. "Yeah," I said. "I like that it's silver."

The second reason was that I had been spending more time with Damian, who Chloe said had too much body hair and a weird sense of humor. When I was honest with myself I kind of understood where she was coming from. Damian could be a real piece of shit sometimes and he was four years older than us which, at our current ages, many people found distasteful. But there were some really good things about him. The best thing was that every Wednesday after he finished work at the local Toyota dealership, he picked me up and took me to Costco even though he didn't like doing it. He knew it was important to me, and I always bought him one of the quarter-pound Kirkland Signature Beef hot dogs afterward. People really underestimate the power of positive reinforcement.

When I was a kid, I used to think that Kirkland was a real place. Around that time I had learned the word *isthmus* and in my head some wires crossed and the two became connected. Kirkland was an in-between place, a land bridge pressed on all sides by the sea, maybe not a nation, but a city-state at least. What mattered was its spirit of abundance. Rolls of paper towels long enough to drape round your whole body, absorbent and bridal, taquitos by the dozen as long and thick as a man's arm, mayonnaise in gallon buckets like thick white paint. My parents weren't interested in correcting my misconceptions about anything, so they just let me believe it. They loved going to Costco as much as I did. We went there on rainy Saturdays the way other families go to the movies.

Kirkland was the first of many misunderstandings in my life. For a while I thought that Bon Jovi's first name was Bon, and once that got cleared up, I thought that was how Al Gore worked too. Like, he had another first name. John Al Gore, or Peter maybe. No one updated me on the pronunciation of *indictment,* or *soldering.*

In second grade we had to write a poem about what *home* meant to us and I wrote about Kirkland. The teacher didn't know what to make of it because it was actually kind of good, but she was also worried about me. Everyone else had written about their nanna's kitchen or some other site of a cherished family tradition.

The thing was, she wasn't our real teacher. She was the teacher they brought in when they fired our real teacher, Ms.

Klein, after she had made us play this months-long game where we had a classroom economy and if we got too poor we became homeless and she took away our desks. Frankly, I didn't mind the game. I started with nothing but then had moderate success selling braided plastic friendship bracelets. Eventually I made enough that I got my desk back, sitting in a chair overlooking the Floor Kids and privately considering becoming fiscally conservative.

Chloe was in my class that year, but we weren't really friends. She was terrible at the game, refusing to sell her hot dog eraser even when she started losing all her pencils to debt collectors. But she actually seemed happy on the floor. Sometimes she stretched out on her belly to do her work, gently kicking her feet in the air. Weird, I thought, how she didn't even try. The only time I remember talking to her that year was when I gave her one of my shiny plastic bracelets for free. She had just lost her favorite crayon, Cerulean, and I felt bad about it and offered her one on impulse. "I don't have anything to trade," she said. "I know," I said. She gave one of her quick scrunched-face smiles. "Thanks. You can borrow my hot dog eraser sometime, if you want." "Thanks," I said, but I never did.

My parents thought the whole thing was funny. Nothing like the School of Hard Knocks, my dad always said when I complained about something, rapping his knuckles on the spot just above my ear. But when other kids told their parents, those parents felt that it wasn't age appropriate.

The final straw was actually not the game. It was when Ms. Klein told us she lived on an ostrich farm and that if all of our parents had her over for dinner by spring break she would take us there, but then didn't hold up her end of the deal. That was the disappointment of a lifetime. All year I had been learning facts about ostriches, staying up late looking at pictures of their long, gummy lips. And when no one was around, running with long strides and high knees, my eyes as wide as they could go.

The bait-and-switch around the ostriches also sucked because the dinner at my house was pretty awkward. I had told my parents it was for extra credit in the World Around Me unit for social studies and that without it I might fail, a fact they did not question. "Make sure she doesn't block the driveway," was all my father said, one of the great concerns of his life even though he never left the house after 6 p.m.

Ms. Klein didn't warn us that she was vegetarian, so that night she could only eat the string beans and my mom always puts a lot of butter on them, more than most people find appropriate. On top of that, my older brother Raymond was visiting from New York City and he can be kind of a wild card. The way my mom describes Raymond is that he is a "free spirit" who "cobbles together a living" through cat sitting and transcribing, but she doesn't see how that could possibly be enough in the most expensive city in the country so he probably supplements that income by selling drugs. Hopefully mind-enhancing instead of life-ruining, like psychedelics. That part she told me when she was drunk on a new pear martini recipe she was trying out. She's always looking for ways to improve upon the martini.

At dinner Raymond wouldn't stop talking about his current transcribing project, a documentary about an alien encounter a bunch of school kids had in Zimbabwe in the 1990s. "Lots of the kids went on to become addicts and go crazy," he said. He'd been helping with the documentary for years, but every time they got close to releasing it one of the witnesses would withdraw consent.

Ms. Klein did not seem interested in any of it. She had barely touched her string beans, and the butter was starting to congeal. To transition the conversation, my mom asked her how I was doing in the classroom, but she didn't have much to say about that either.

My dad jumped in then, talking about his belief that everyone's essence can be categorized on an x-y axis of hard or soft and mouse or lizard, and explaining which US presidents were which. "JFK—soft lizard," he said. "Andrew Jackson—hard mouse."

"Taft?" Raymond asked, like we hadn't heard all of this before.

"Good question, son," my father said. "Also a hard mouse. And if we're ever going to stop climate change, you better believe a hard mouse in the White House is what it's going to take."

While he spoke, Ms. Klein kept her eyes down and pressed a green bean hard against her plate as if to wring the excess butter from it, and I recited facts to keep myself calm. An ostrich will hiss when it gets angry. An ostrich, lacking teeth, must swallow pebbles to grind its food. Contrary to popular belief, an ostrich does not bury its head in the sand to avoid predators; she is merely adjusting her eggs. An ostrich is not helpless. An ostrich can kill you with just one kick.

Chloe and I met again when we were eleven, in July, when her family moved into the split-level one street over from mine. We had been in different classes every year since second grade and I hadn't really thought about her. But that summer there she was, sitting on the curb across from our mailbox when I went outside to check if my mom's *Cosmopolitan* magazine had been delivered so that I could read it first and then put it back in with the next day's mail. "No mail on Sundays," she said from behind me. I had forgotten what day it was.

I couldn't decide if the girl in front of me, this new Chloe, was hotter than me or not. Her legs were shorter but her tits were bigger, and I had a bad feeling that her face was better than mine. I wanted her to whisper something in my ear. I wanted to cut her hair off. I wanted to watch her suck a slice of lemon and spit the little seeds into my hand one by one.

Chloe considered me too, pausing on my legs. "I live over there now," she said finally, pointing. "Do you like trampolines?"

"Cool," I said. "Yeah."

"Come with me," she said. Her ass cheeks peeked out from her jean shorts, two pimply little half moons.

She took me to the pharmacy down the street to shoplift laxatives, and cough syrup as an afterthought. We passed the bottle back and forth the whole way home and then lay down on the trampoline in her backyard. The trampoline was covered in gravel and twigs and dead leaf fragments, so once we were high we took turns pulling out the pieces that were tangled up in each other's hair. The syrup left gritty little particles of something on our tongues and made our breath thick and sweet, our thoughts scattering like fistfuls of pennies in a fountain.

Chloe told me that her daddy had worked in underwater search and rescue for fifteen years, getting dead people out of their drowned cars. Once, he reached into a sunken sedan for four skeletons and a burst of little catfish swam out. When Chloe was born, he moved her and her mother to the driest place he could find, which was here. I could see why he did that. Chloe had that long, long hair that would float up all around her face like seaweed, collarbones that silt would settle into. There are girls you should never let swim.

All the rest of that summer we told our parents we were going to the park and rode our bikes to the public pool, where Chloe was forbidden to go. She didn't know how to swim but she loved to stand in the water up to her chest, eyes closed. Every so often she would ask me to hold her hands so she could duck her head under. Sometimes she stayed down there so long it scared me and I would start to tug her upward but she wouldn't let me until she was ready. "68 seconds!" she said when she finally came up, gasping. Her record was 99, but we agreed to call it 100.

We could do that for hours, me sitting and watching her from the side, trying to turn the pages of my magazines without getting them wet and puckered, our skin so tight with sun it felt like we might crack open, overripe. Then we went back to my house to wait for her hair to dry and her fingers to unprune, for her body to erase the evidence.

In the months before Chloe and I officially stopped talking, I remember thinking that it felt like I was stuck watching her underwater from above, the shape of her always shifting. It used to be Chloe who drove me to Costco every Wednesday in my mom's car from the time she got her license right up until the summer before our senior year, when she got the job at the Longhorn. I thought maybe once the school year had started she would start showing up again, but she never did, so I asked Damian instead. I would not be her obligation.

You can make yourself fall in and out of love with people pretty easily, I've found, if you have a strong sense of narrative arc and choose the right moments.

To make myself love Damian less, I thought about how when

we argued he called it "budding heads," like we were pushing up through the earth and unfurling, spitting mud. How I had discovered that he was throwing every used condom he'd told me he'd take care of out the window of his car, the very window he never let me roll down at speeds over 40 mph because of fuel efficiency. I imagined him reaching for a flash of orange and opening his wet mouth.

To make myself love Damian more, I thought about how he looked in the mechanic onesie he wore to work, gray with the name Dennis stitched on the pocket. As Dennis, Damian was extremely lovable. I also considered how he promised that as soon as I turned eighteen in a few months, he'd take me and Chloe to get our first tattoos. I'd known what I wanted for a long time. I wanted mine to say, "Give up the ghost," with a small tasteful representation of a spirit. Not a Halloween-style ghost, something more subtle, with spidery lines that made me look thin and fragile by association.

It's something my nanna used to say to me. She hated everyone in her nursing home, and when someone especially frail or demented or whatever shuffled by she would shake her head with disgust and say, "Some people don't know when to give up the ghost." She said it a lot, and it really stuck with me. Give up the ghost. It doesn't make a lot of sense, but it also makes perfect sense, and I like how it's from the Bible but also about machines.

And that was the third reason I wasn't talking to Chloe. It was partly her new friends and it was partly Damian but it was mostly because two weeks earlier, Kayla and the other girls had taken Chloe to get her first tattoo from their friend Rocco, who didn't care that she was underaged, and gave her a shot of whiskey before and after. She showed it to me the next morning at school. A little ghost outline on the small of her back. That's why I pressed Ignore on her call.

Inside the Costco, Damian kept trailing me, breathing down my neck. I tried to peruse the inflatables section. There, I am always reminded that we live in the golden age of inflatables. Bounce houses and paddle boards and full-size hot tubs. You can put air inside of anything these days. "We don't need a water slide,"

Damian said, in response to no one. "You bought that last time," he said when I stopped in front of a multipack of cropped pastel tank tops, the kind you can never have enough of.

"Respectfully," I said, "I would like you to leave me the fuck alone now." I left him sulking in the Personal Care aisle, where a man was reading carefully through the ingredients on a twenty-pack of deodorant. He seemed to be checking each individual stick, like any one of them might have a hidden carcinogen snuck in.

I paced up and down the cereal aisle looking at the massive, colorful boxes stacked perfectly like Tetris blocks, then went to the dairy section to get some air. The hum of the giant fridges and the cold they gave off soothed me. The rows and rows of matronly round jugs, color-coded by fat content. I opened one of the huge doors to watch the fog creep over the glass until no one could see my face, drew a C in the condensation. Then I turned to face the blast of freezing air, leaned in to rest my forehead against a sweating jug of 2%, and closed my eyes.

The moment was broken suddenly by the sound of footsteps. From in front of me, not behind. I opened my eyes and saw one of the jugs at my waist move. A pair of hands reaching toward me through the shelves. A man crouched on the other side. I heard myself start to scream. The hands jerked backward and the milk fell forward. "Hey," he shouted. "Hey! Stop!" The jug hit my stomach and then the floor, burst on impact.

I turned and ran. While I was running I realized that the man was probably just restocking the milk, just doing his job. But I couldn't stop, heart pounding, adrenaline still coursing through me. By the time I had slowed myself down, I was back in the inflatables, breathing hard through my nose, trying to shake the unnameable bad feeling. Panic and embarrassment and a gut-level sense that something was wrong. And I thought about Chloe. I was sure she would've known immediately what the hands were doing. She wouldn't have run away. She wouldn't have made a scene. Next to the kiddie pools I took a deep breath and tried to call her back, but it wouldn't go through. I never got very good service inside the Costco. It was one of my favorite things about it.

Damian was waiting for me by the exit with a signature Kirkland 100% beef hot dog as a peace offering. "Sixteen grams
of protein," he said as he handed it to me. He had a mind for
numbers, mostly nutrition facts. The sun was setting as we made
our way across the parking lot, silhouetting abandoned shopping carts and the wholesale gas pumps.

In the car on the way home, I rolled down the window, and
Damian rolled it back up. I asked him what he would do if I
died in an accident and came back to haunt him. "Could I still
touch you?" he said. "That is the stupidest question you possibly
could have asked," I said.

Late that night, I got a call from Chloe's mom. This time, I
picked up, realizing it was the longest I'd gone without talking
to her, too. "Is Chloe with you?" she asked.

"No," I said. "I haven't seen her."

"She didn't come home from her shift and it seems like her
phone is off." "Have you tried Kayla?" I said. "From the Longhorn?" Part of me, even then, was hoping she'd say, "Kayla who?"
but all she said was, "Yeah, the girls don't know either. They said
they're already home."

"I can text her," I said.

"Thanks, sweetie. Call me if you hear anything," she said, and
hung up.

One good thing about me is that I'm extremely adaptable. I can
adjust to new circumstances before they even happen. When
I start to sense a person pulling away from me, I immediately
imagine my life without them. The hobbies and TV shows I
could use to fill the time left by their absence. I could take up
fencing and win a scholarship to a fancy college, my breasts
smushed into hard white pancakes. I could commit to watching
every season of *The Sopranos* so people could finally stop telling me, "You should really watch *The Sopranos*." I could become
a dowser, follow my quivering rod for miles and miles until it
led me to an oasis in the middle of the desert that only I knew
about. I would bend down, cup my hands, and drink.

But I had not prepared myself for Chloe's disappearance,
which I found out about two days later on Instagram, through a

Find Chloe graphic that Kayla had made featuring a deer selfie, a new one I hadn't seen before. The last time anyone saw Chloe she was getting into a Toyota Corolla outside the Longhorn on the night that I'd ignored her call. Most people thought she ran away, but I wasn't so sure. She was always a girl who left, yes, but she was also a girl who came back.

Chloe's father didn't know what to do with himself after, no lakes to drag, no depths to dive, and neither did I. I'd figured that in a few months when I turned eighteen and got a better tattoo than her, I could finally forgive her, win her back from the steakhouse, promise to take her to the pool. I had not prepared myself for a world where I didn't get her back.

To try to make myself stop loving Chloe, I sifted through our moments, looking for a handful of them that could bend our narrative arc, or at least end it. The only thing I could come up with was the sight of that ugly black outline on her skin, glistening under the Saran Wrap, and the way she looked when I passed her silently in the hallway at school that last week, bony and distant. But other moments kept creeping in instead, things that made me love her more. Grape breath and her fingers working through my hair, the v of her legs and the o of her mouth when she jumped too high on the trampoline and scared herself, then did it again. The gasp when her hurricane body knocked me flat onto the nylon. "Sorry," she said, when I pointed at the slick red rug burn on my elbow, and then she licked it.

For the first two weeks after we realized she was gone, people kept asking me if I was ok, and I didn't really know but I thought I was, except that I was having a very hard time falling asleep. By the end of that first month, more and more I found myself on PornHub, which Damian introduced me to. I would start out watching really basic stuff but as the night wore on, things would escalate and eventually I would find myself watching a gangbang.

I was surprised to find that many of them are pretty lackluster. Those were my favorites, the ones no one seemed excited about, the men standing around waiting their turns and kind of looking off into the middle distance, tugging at themselves half-heartedly. One thing that annoyed me is the way events are always exaggerated in porn titles. Every video has to be some girl's first time doing something, and it's always a Huge Success. Just once I wanted an honest title. "Ashley Tries Her First Gangbang and Finds Out There's a Learning Curve." That I would like to see.

Porn helped me fall asleep that first month, but then in the middle of the night one night I saw a video called "You've Never Seen ROUGH SEX LIKE THIS BEFORE—Real Petite Teen," on the home screen. I was always curious what Real Petite Teens looked like, how different from me. Chloe and I used to spend hours researching the height and weight and bra size of celebrities on websites that described women in strange, stilted language like, "She possesses a taut figure, which, combined with her tall stature, compliments her semblance as a model!"

"Are you alone?" the robot voice droned before I could turn the volume down. The video started immediately, no exposition, and it was kind of grainy, but my stomach dropped because the girl in it looked just like Chloe, long hair wrapped up in some guy's fist, something familiar about the curve of her ass cheeks.

After that I stopped watching porn and started calling Raymond, who was always awake. At first he was surprised to hear from me but then I think he started to look forward to it. Recently there had been renewed interest in the alien encounter documentary. Sometimes he put me on speakerphone while he worked, so I could hear the testimonials too, a cat always yowling in the background.

"Do you believe them?" I asked him late one night, about three months after Chloe's disappearance, the posters of her face on telephone poles tearing loose at the corners. He paused, let the clip run out. "I don't know if what they say happened actually happened," he said. "But something did."

The one really good thing our bad teacher did before she got fired was let us raise ducklings in our classroom. First she brought in the eggs, and they sat in a big incubator on the windowsill, and sometimes she took us into the dark bathroom and held a light up behind an egg so it glowed pink like an eyelid and you could see the little duck curled up inside there.

After they hatched, we could sign up to take the ducks home for the weekend. There, we put them in our Barbie cars and held them too tightly in our hot little hands so they squirmed and fought against us and shit wet sticky puddles out of fear. One point of tension was that we all had an obvious favorite duck, the runt, and the only one that was brown. On Friday afternoons we took turns smushing our cheeks against her beak. "I'll miss you sooooo much, Coco," we said, and wept.

The Monday before spring break we shuffled into the classroom and found our teacher sitting at the desk with the blackboard empty behind her.

"Class," she said. "I have some hard news."

She wouldn't tell us whose house Coco had died at, but we all knew it was at the twins', Tiff and Tate. Tate had warts on his hands, and right before the Halloween parade Tiff had thrown up her cereal in our classroom, pink from strawberry milk.

The classroom fell into chaos. Tate wouldn't look up from his hands, and he kept denying that he knew anything more than we did, even when I got him alone during speech therapy. We were friends while we were sitting on the exercise balls in there, working on his r's and my s's. Or at least comrades. "You can tell me what happened," I said. "It's just me." He looked away and ate a large Tootsie Roll so slowly that he was unable to speak for the rest of the period.

After that, no classroom ever had ducks again. The next year the new teacher raised butterflies from chrysalises, which might have been exciting if no one knew ducklings had once been on the table. The chrysalises rocked and shivered close to their hatch date like twitching eyelids. When they finally emerged, a dark red liquid leaked out onto the white cotton floor of their nursery, like our mother's menstrual blood. "It isn't blood," the teacher said so many times that no one believed her. "It's completely normal."

The day Ms. Klein told us that Coco was dead, I wasn't sad because I was sure it wasn't true. Coco, I knew, had merely escaped, strayed too far and lost the path. Probably she was in Kirkland, doing her feeble little waddle through the smooth cropped grass of a golf course and into a manicured water feature with a giant fountain in the middle. Strong enough, now, to handle the currents it created.

What I'm trying to say is that sometimes, even now, when I can't sleep, I imagine all the places Chloe could be, her narrative arc climbing or flattening or starting its slow descent. The moments that have gathered to make up her life.

She is flying down the highway in that Toyota Corolla headed for the coast, some steakhouse at the beach where all the salt has to be mixed with yellowed grains of rice, where one day a busboy will come up behind her at the end of her shift as she's wiping down tables, point at the ghost on her skin, say, "What does it *mean?*"

Or she's in front of the red eye of a camera, straddling her fake stepdad and arching her back and moaning one more time, with feeling, and maybe for a second she wonders about the thousands of people who might see the video, and if one of them might be me.

Or she's in Kirkland, too, on the isthmus. Effortlessly thin, barefoot in a grove of trees, all of them lemon, all of them grown from seed. She is splashing out into the weed-choked waters where little by little she's teaching herself to swim, ducking beneath the surface and starting the slow count backward from 100, each number a bubble silver on her lips.

And some nights I'm sure she never left at all, not really. She's on the ostrich farm just outside of town, the one I never got to see. Each morning she flings open the barn doors to release the towering birds, a hiss in her throat, and all day she walks beside them in great clouds of dust searching for the perfect stone to swallow, some new way to have teeth.

EMMA BINDER

What Would I Do for You, What Would You Do for Me?

FROM *Michigan Quarterly Review*

AS CODY WALKS around Pearl Lake, he thinks these guys are crazy. It's March, almost fifty degrees, and three men are guarding the tip-ups in their ice-fishing holes, sitting on a melting lake without a care in the world. He used to see this every year when he was growing up in Iron River. Dark starbursts scar the lake where ice has melted and thinned, but some people seem to think that you can just wander around the bad parts, as if ice isn't all connected to itself. The men look like dozing bears in their seats, their small faces scorched pink from sunlight beaming off the ice.

For his part, if while Cody's ice-skating he hears that muffled shotgun sound of ice cracking apart, he's heading to shore. He's watched videos of how you're supposed to army crawl your way out of broken ice and it doesn't look like something he wants to do. This is his first time in Iron River since he was seventeen—he hasn't been home since his dad quietly kicked him out after graduation, since he left Wisconsin and moved to Chicago to live with Taylor and June. After that he got on T and moved with June to western Massachusetts, where they'd heard rural queers were living in communes and starting farms and living out some technicolor daydream of collectivism and love. It wasn't like that, exactly, but it was better than anywhere he'd been before.

He takes the western route around Pearl Lake, toward a rock-knuckled ATV trail that will loop him back home. He's been in Wisconsin for three days. Cody's here to help around the house while his dad is in the hospital, getting chemo, and he'll be around afterward, when his dad's nauseous and bedbound. When Cody first walked into his childhood home, he shivered at the smell of mildewed wood paneling, plastic vacuum bags, dusty curtains, and corn oil. That smell melted his heart. It brought back everything good: watching PBS with his sister on the carpeted living room floor, wriggling into musty snow pants in winter, leaning on his mom's shoulder in the kitchen before they left for church.

His sister, Molly, is the only person in his family he's stayed close with during the past seven years, and she's getting into town next week from Duluth. Molly has always had a way of acting as a translator between Cody and his parents, softening their words into something the other party could digest, if not understand.

Cody's cell phone pings; it's June, sending a video of their cat trying to claw up her sneaker.

Miss that demon, he writes back.

We miss you, June replies. *How's it going today?*

Unbearable, he types, then deletes it.

He unzips his coat, keeps walking. He's not sure what to say. It's been heavy, visiting his dad in the hospital and tiptoeing around his mom like a stranger. But Cody had missed his mom, that house, and his twin bed, still wrapped in the soft flannel sheets patterned with blue and green train engines that he fought his parents for. He never envisioned returning to Iron River because he didn't want to crave something he couldn't have. But now he has the corn oil, the old sheets. He has the golden desk lamp pooling on his midnight carpet, where he used to sit with his knees drawn up at night, listening to burned Pantera and Metallica CDs on his Walkman. He puts his phone back in his pocket without responding to June. The sun hikes higher, raking steam off the ice. Two of the three ice fishermen have packed up and begun lumbering toward shore.

Cody used to come to Pearl Lake when he was in high school

to fish and be alone, but sometimes Molly came with him. If it was empty at dusk, they built a fire on the lake's west side, where pines clothed the beach in green darkness. They tormented each other by pretending to see ghosts in the mist, trading urban legends about serial killers who lived in manholes and hunted teenage girls. They came home with splinters in their hands and sand in their socks. Out there, in the shadow of the woods with only himself or his sister, Cody had a body and it served an uncomplicated purpose. He was an animal among animals. He felt the clock of light in his blood.

Just one guy is left on the ice. Cody reaches the western beach, his sneakers slipping against wet sand. What's a couple bluegill worth, he thinks, watching the guy in his wool hat, head slumped forward. It occurs to Cody that maybe he's fallen asleep in his chair. Should he make a sound to wake him up? Cody looks away, trudges ahead. The guy's none of his business. People want to hang out on melting lakes, that's their problem. He looks back at the man. To Cody's relief, he's stretching now, beginning to stand.

The sun crests the pines east of the lake and climbs overhead, bearing down on the ice. In the distance the guy, who's tall and barrel-chested, takes off his jacket and hat and looks suddenly much smaller to Cody. He has a full beard and a floppy dark mat of hair. He briefly meets Cody's gaze, but Cody looks away. He knows better, at this point, than to wave at strange men in northern Wisconsin, whether it's his hometown or not.

His mom has been polite to him. He can't deny that. In the years he's been away, they've talked sporadically on the phone, but this is the first time he's been home since his dad kicked him out at seventeen—a period his mom calls *that whole business,* as if she had no part to play.

She's been making him dinner now, feeding him neighborly gossip: the Harts' teenage daughter got pregnant, the Markeseys had Mr. Pearson's truck towed after he parked only half a foot into their yard. Cody watches intricate, careworn lines play against her face. She's spent these years worrying, working late hours as an RN, praying at stoplights, deciding she doesn't need to say what she might say. When they watch TV together, Cody has caught her staring at him with tears in her eyes. She's going through something that involves him, but is private. He doesn't know whether the tears spring from happiness or distress, relief or pain.

Cody wants to tell his mom he's in love. In Massachusetts his friends just bought forty acres of land on a mountain in Leyden, where they're building cabins and community gardens. When he's not at work or home with June, Cody's learning about permaculture, seeding schedules, how to work a circular saw and cut rafters. Everyone who's armed with practical knowledge is primed to share it, ready to help everyone else make their homes, all these queers who spent so long merely surviving. In a world with so little to be optimistic about, Cody feels confoundingly optimistic about his own life, as if it's grown wide and spacious without him noticing. At the end of the day, he goes home to June, the curly-haired Craigslist roommate he crushed on as a young trans kid in Chicago, afraid of his own desire. When they started living together, he used to try not to think about her, shadow-boxing the weight of everything he wanted but didn't think he would ever have: love, family, peace. Why fantasize about being held by someone you think will never hold you? Why hurt yourself with a stupid, dogged dream? Since he was a kid, Cody tried to pretend he didn't need anyone, didn't want anything.

But now he has friends, a home, a place to feel safe. He has June. He wants to tell his mom that June is beautiful, smart, tough, and tender—and miraculously, she loves him back. He gets to be held. He's started to let himself want things, even when he feels his prior self rioting against him: *You want more than this? All this, which you don't even deserve?*

In Iron River, he feels shame digging into him like spurs. Its hooks are everywhere. His mom never brings him to the grocery store, even though she's got a bad shoulder and could use help getting bags to the car. All the pictures of him in the house are from when he was a little kid, before he got to middle school and started wearing boys' clothes. For the past three nights, he's fallen asleep staring at the blue and green trains printed on his sheets, thinking he might as well be dead.

Before he sees anything, Cody hears a muted sound like a far-off rubber hammer on wood. He looks up just in time to catch the man and his folding chair go through the ice up to his torso. The man shouts. He spreads his hands on either side of the ice and tries to shimmy himself free. For a moment he seems to succeed, but the ice breaks again and he plummets underwater, disappearing for a moment before he resurfaces and gasps.

Cody stands stock-still on shore, heart pounding.

"Swim!" he shouts. "Kick your legs!"

If he goes out onto the ice to try to help this man, he might fall through—and then where would they both be? Should he call someone? Who would get here in time? The man has braced his elbows back against the ice and is wriggling, trying to kick his way out.

"Spread your weight!" Cody shouts. "Don't stand up!" Without another thought, he begins to run out onto the ice. He treads lightly, as if running on hot coals. He can't stand on shore and do nothing.

When he gets to the man, Cody reaches down and grabs his arms and pulls him away from his ice trap. The man's joints are locked and he's heavy, but Cody's flooded with the strength of urgency.

In his soaking-wet clothes, the man kicks his way out of his hole, and they crawl back on all fours together, Cody talking to him all the while: *We're going back to land. We're almost there.* By the time they reach shore, the man's face is bone-white and his teeth are chattering like a snare drum. He collapses on the sand. Cody helps him out of his jacket, and then takes off his own thin canvas barn coat, wraps it uselessly around the freezing arms. He rubs the man's shoulders, something he's only seen in movies, to bring heat to the man's body and to have something to do with his own.

"I'm okay," the man mutters between chattering teeth. "I'm okay. I'm fine."

"You're shaking."

"I just need to get to my truck."

"Where is it?"

The man extends a shaky finger toward a path in the woods, which, Cody knows, stretches about a quarter mile before reaching a gravel parking lot.

"The fucking," the man says, struggling to spit out his words. "The fucking ice. Didn't look bad."

When they get to the truck—a lifted white Chevy, what June would call a Big Dick Truck—the man tries to unhook his keys from his belt loop, but his hands are trembling. Cody frees his keys for him, unlocks the driver's side door, and helps him into the seat, and then watches as it takes two, three tries of turning the key in the ignition for the engine to roar to life.

"I think you should go to the hospital," Cody calls over the grumbling engine. "I know where it is. I can drive."

The man shakes his head vigorously. "I'm fine," he says, even as Cody sees him shuddering forward against the steering wheel. His lips and fingers are white. "I'll warm up." Cody feels the warm air blasting through the vents, even from where he's standing outside the open door.

"You could have hypothermia. You should at least get out of those wet clothes."

"I'm okay." He shuts the door and peels away onto the gravel road. Cody watches the truck lurch forward, clipping a rock in the gravel lot on its way out. Not until the truck is out of view does Cody realize that the man is still wearing his own jacket—with his keys, wallet, and phone still in the pockets.

Almost two days pass before the man finds him, seemingly by chance. That morning over breakfast, Cody's mom brought out grade school pictures, which she's been keeping in the drawer below the kitchen telephone, as if she's wanted them close at hand. She smiled over the pictures at first, but then began to cry. It's enough to send him on a long, blistering walk. He's circling Pearl Lake again when he hears padding footsteps behind him and a voice calling, "Hey, buddy!"

Cody turns around.

"I've been looking for you," the man says, grinning. Cody recognizes his thick dark beard, his flannel shirt and wool cap. "In a town this small, I thought I knew everybody."

"I'm just visiting," Cody says.

"Well," the man says, clapping Cody on the shoulder. "I've got your jacket to give back to you. It's in my truck right now. Phone and wallet and everything's still in it."

"That's great. Turns out I need those things."

"Yeah, you got, like, twenty thousand text messages."

Cody bristles, thinking of the man reading his texts from June. They walk toward the truck together, up the same path they walked before. Along the way the man introduces himself: He's Greg Parham, works for Iron River Towing, lives just a mile and a half down the road from Pearl Lake. He must have fished on the lake a dozen times this month, in weather much the same as it was two days ago. Hasn't heard of anyone else falling through the ice. Just an odd thing, it was. Now that Cody can look at him calmly, he realizes that Greg looks familiar, and they're around the same age. Greg might be a little older, but probably his beard artificially ages him. They likely overlapped at school.

"What brings you to town?" Greg asks.

"Just visiting family. My parents live here."

"Oh yeah? You from here?"

"Yeah."

There's a long pause during which Cody's sure that Greg is trying to place him, trying to remember. But when Cody tells Greg his name, he shrugs.

"Doesn't ring a bell," Greg says.

When they get to the truck, Greg fishes Cody's jacket from the cab and claps him on the back again. "I'd like to buy you a beer. I want to pay you back for helping me out."

"Hey, it's okay," Cody says, patting down his jacket pockets. Everything's still there: phone, wallet, keys. "I just did what anyone would do."

"You'd really be doing *me* a favor," Greg says. "Making me feel better about the whole thing." He leans toward Cody as if about to confide something. "Truth be told, I feel a little embarrassed.

Never thought I'd end up in a fix like that. Woody's tonight, at seven?"

Cody makes some kind of gesture between a nod and a shrug. Greg grins. "All right, buddy. I'll see you there."

Cody has driven past Woody's a thousand times, but never gone inside. It's a gravel lot bar with a porch out front, neon flickering in the windows, and lifted trucks parked in a row outside. Before he goes inside, he sits in his mom's minivan and holds his phone, thinks about texting June, but decides not to. She's worried enough about him as it is.

He's borrowed his dad's flannel shirt and work pants for the occasion. The pants are too big for him; Cody poked holes in one of his dad's cheap belts with a Swiss Army knife to cinch them tight. These clothes don't fit his dad either, anymore, and they probably never will again. When Cody checked himself in his bedroom mirror, he almost laughed, thinking about how much his dad would hate to see him now. He would never allow Cody to rifle through his closet. But hopefully the clothes will shield Cody tonight, lend him the authority his dad used to possess, as one of those people who moved through the world unquestioned.

The bar is a wood-paneled room with booths and a pool table, clouded by a thin haze, even though no one seems to be smoking. There are dartboards and slot machines and one mounted television, airing a *Jeopardy* rerun. If he were here with his friends, Cody would feel at home.

He finds Greg Parham in a booth with two other men. They're both taller than Cody, one bearded and wearing flannel, and the other clean-shaven in a Realtree sweatshirt. "Buddy!" Greg says, standing up. He claps Cody on the shoulder and turns to his friends. "This is the guy who gave me a hand the other day."

Greg introduces the two men as Kevin and Nick. When Cody introduces himself, he thinks he sees their eyebrows lift a little. Even though he's been on T for years, he sometimes still gets clocked when he speaks. But the guys invite him to the table, make room for him in their booth. Greg immediately heads to the bar to buy Cody a beer, leaving him with Kevin and Nick.

"That's some story," Kevin says. "You dragged Greg out of the lake?"

"Not really," Cody says. "Just gave him a hand."

"We've been ragging him all day. Wish I'd been there to take a fucking video."

"It was pretty wild."

"Greg says you're visiting?" Nick asks. "Where from?"

"Massachusetts."

"That's a trek. What are you doing here?"

"Just visiting family."

All the while, Cody's trying not to look too hard at Kevin. They were in the same grade at Northwestern High School, even had biology and English class together. Cody doesn't remember their ever speaking to each other, but he saw Kevin's face in class on a daily basis, a little chubbier and smoother but unmistakably the same. Kevin played JV football and once got in trouble for keeping weed in his locker. He took Lacey Spencer to prom. Like most of the boys at school, he used to look through Cody like he was a ghost, which suited Cody just fine. Now, in his Packers cap and flannel shirt, Kevin looks like any other man in Iron River.

Cody tries to make small talk. It turns out Kevin works with Greg at Iron River Towing, while Nick grew up in Rhinelander but made his way to Iron River for a job in natural gas. Kevin's voice is loud, booming halfway across the crowded bar. Nick strikes Cody as a little softer, quick to break into a grin.

Greg comes back from the bar with both a beer and a shot for Cody.

"For saving my freaking life!" he says.

Cody takes the shot, sips the beer. Kevin starts re-hashing the lake story, which he's calling "Greg's Big Rescue." He tells Greg to re-enact it in the bar. Pretend he just fell through the ice and the pool table is shore. Cody shifts his eyes toward the door, thinking about how to leave. He wonders how long he's obliged to stay—one beer, a little more small talk. Then he can say he's got a sick dad, or early morning chores, and has to be getting home.

"Be honest," Kevin says to Cody. "Was Greg acting like a little bitch?"

"Well," Cody says. "It was really cold."

"Yeah, but did he act like a bitch about it?"

"I don't know, man."

"Thanks for having my back, bro," Greg says, gripping his shoulder. "I *was* cold."

Cody notices the dull sheen over Greg's eyes. It's not even eight o'clock, but he looks like he's already been drinking for a while.

"Just glad you're all right," Cody says.

"This guy grew up in the North Woods," Kevin says. "And doesn't even know how to read the ice." He looks at Cody. "Can you believe that?"

A prickly feeling worms up Cody's spine. He thinks that every time Kevin looks at him, it lasts a little too long.

"So you have family here," Kevin says. "Are you from the area?"

"Yeah."

"Northwestern?"

Cody nods.

"What year did you graduate?" Kevin asks.

"2011."

"That was my year." Kevin knits his brow. "You went to Northwestern High? How do I not remember you?"

Cody's heart beats steadily.

"I don't know. I was pretty quiet."

"Did you transfer in or something?" Cody shakes his head. "All four years? That's crazy."

Kevin keeps his eyes on Cody, head cocked.

"Jeez," Nick says, grinning. "No need to grill the guy."

"What's your last name?" Kevin says.

"Hartbrook."

"Cody Hartbrook," Kevin says slowly. "That does sound familiar."

Cody sips his drink. His mouth is dry. These men can't hurt him, he thinks. The bar is crowded, noise rushing in from all corners: Hank Jr. on the jukebox, booming laughter, cheers rising by the dartboard.

Greg smacks the table. "Pool? Cody, you in?"

"I should probably get going." He takes a long sip of his beer. It will look strange to these men if he leaves with a half-full drink.

"One round," Greg says. "Just so I can take some of your money."

"Yeah," Kevin says, getting up from the booth. "Then we'll let you leave."

Cody plays pool occasionally in Massachusetts, at a country bar called the Shutesbury Athletic Club, where his friend Joel works on Tuesdays. The bar is a little cinderblock bunker tucked in a gravel turnoff, nestled by pine trees. He and his friends go in a group. They put Dolly Parton on the jukebox, play pool and darts, and never keep score. Sometimes, if no one else comes in, Cody might climb up on the bar and lip-sync cheesy pop country. If he had his way, he and June would live in a backwoods hill town like Shutesbury, with one bar and one grocery store and wide-ranging stretches of green. But in most other rural places, he has to worry about whether people will clock him, and what they might feel motivated to do.

As Cody follows the men to the pool table, he realizes that no one knows he's here. He didn't tell June, and he told his mom he was just going for a nighttime drive. He wishes something would come on the jukebox that he loves, something to anchor him in his body.

Greg and Cody are on one team, Nick and Kevin on the other. Greg breaks at a weird angle, so the balls part only a few inches. When he straightens after shooting, he lists a little to one side.

"Jesus," Kevin says. "That was terrible."

They go clockwise then: Nick, Cody, Kevin. Kevin's a good player, which Cody could have predicted; he knows that men like that don't compete in public unless they're sure they'll win. Nick and Cody play at about the same weaker level, which is good, Cody thinks. He wants to be good enough to blend in, but not so good that he might beat Kevin and cause a problem.

"Greg, you fish a lot on Pearl Lake?" Cody says.

"Hell yeah!" Greg says. "I love fishing!"

"You are absolutely tanked, dude," Nick says.

"Me? No way." Greg shifts on his feet. He leans against the wall. "I got a strong man's blood. You fish?"

"Sometimes," Cody says. "Mostly fly-fishing."

"Nice!" Greg says. "Once I was out on the river, out by Wauzeka? I don't know if you know where that is?" Greg slouches against his pool cue, which he's braced against the floor with both hands, keeping him upright. "Caught a big fucking trout."

"Cool," Cody says. "That's awesome."

"I just can't get over it," Kevin interjects. He stands after taking his shot, which sends a striped ball into an unlikely corner pocket. "You graduated from Northwestern in 2011."

"Yeah." Cody takes another sip of his beer.

"I thought I knew everyone."

"I guess you didn't."

"Who were you friends with?"

"I mostly kept to myself."

"Clearly."

"Hey," Greg says. "Let the Cody Man take his shot already!"

Cody bends forward while the men watch him. He takes an uncharacteristically bad shot, sending the cue ball spinning at an angle into a corner pocket.

"Scratch," Kevin says.

Cody takes another sip of beer and heads to the bathroom. In a stall he begins to type a message to June on his phone.

I think I'm in trouble.

Then he deletes it. What does he know? And what could June possibly do, halfway across the country? If Molly were around, he would text her, but she doesn't get in until tomorrow morning. His mom would tell him it's late, she can't do anything to help. He has her van, after all.

Cody takes a deep breath and puts his phone in his pocket.

When he gets back to the pool table, Greg is sitting on the edge with his cue behind him, one eye shut, trying to make a backward shot. He shoots the cue and doesn't hit anything.

"That was your last chance," Kevin says.

"Fuck." Greg climbs off the table. "Hey, Cody! I'm sinking our game!"

"That's okay," Cody says.

"Sorry, man. This is the worst game I've ever played in my life."

"That's not true," Nick says, "by a long shot."

"Cody," Kevin says after he shoots. "Tell us about Massachusetts."

"I've never even *been* to Massachusetts!" Greg says.

"You live in Boston?" Nick asks.

Cody shakes his head. "Western Mass. It's more rural."

"Right, the fly-fishing," Kevin says. "What do you do out there? Don't tell me you're a Pats fan."

"I do some farming and restaurant work," Cody says. Then, without thinking, he says, "My girlfriend and I go hiking a lot."

Kevin nods, staring at him. "Nice. You guys live together?"

"Yeah."

"I been living with my girl for, I don't know. Two years? I love her to death," Kevin says. "But she's annoying as fuck sometimes."

"Amen, brother!" Greg shouts.

"Hey, remember when Melissa used to party with us?" Nick says. "Those were some *wild* times."

"Yeah," Kevin says. "Now all she wants to do is go to Target and talk about kids." He looks at Cody. "You guys think about that?"

"Having kids?"

Kevin nods.

"Not yet. We're still figuring stuff out."

Cody readies his cue for another shot. He and Greg still have four of their striped balls on the table, while Kevin and Nick have sunk all of theirs. After Cody shoots, it's Kevin's turn, and he sinks the eight ball.

"Good game," Cody says.

He shakes Nick's hand, then Kevin's. Greg is slouched in a chair in the corner with his cue at his feet, beer in hand.

"Another round?" Greg says.

"I should go. I got some stuff to do in the morning."

Kevin looks at his phone. "It's only nine."

"Yeah," Cody says.

He drinks the last of his beer, waves his goodbyes, and grabs his jacket from the booth. He feels Kevin's eyes boring into his back as he walks to the door, thinks he hears a burst of laughter from all three men behind him, and the paranoia digs in. But it's okay. He made it out. Passing through the front door, he feels as if he's entering a portal, releasing him from a frozen world into fresh air and life. The nighttime air is cool and biting. A heavyweight moon hangs overhead, casting the lot in white light.

As he walks through the gravel parking lot, he hears the door swing open, hears a burst of music and chatter from inside the bar.

He looks over his shoulder and sees Nick walking fast toward him.

Cody curses under his breath and begins walking faster.

"Cody," Nick says. "Wait up!"

Cody's mom's van sits all the way across the parking lot, in a dark pool of shadow beside a moldering pallet fence. He tucks his chin against his chest as he walks, rifling through his pocket for his keys.

"Hey!" Nick says again.

Cody speeds up. He hears Nick's footsteps landing faster behind him in response, quickening almost into a jog. Cody unlocks the van with a pacing heart, climbs into the driver's seat, and starts the ignition. Nick's knuckles rap against the window.

Cody has his foot on the brake, ready to shift into drive and peel out of the lot. But when he turns to look at Nick, he sees a lopsided grin on his face. Cody clears his throat, rolls down the window.

"Hey," Nick says, brow scrunched. "I was calling your name."

"Sorry, I didn't hear."

"I just wanted to thank you for helping Greg. Going onto the ice like that? I don't even know if I would have done it."

"Sure," Cody says, trying to steady his breath.

"No, I just keep thinking about it. I know Kevin was trying

to make a joke out of it. But Greg might be dead right now if it weren't for you. He's drunk all the fucking time."

Then, of all things, Nick reaches inside the van window and cups his hand around the back of Cody's neck. His hand is warm and slick with sweat. Cody freezes.

"Thank you, man," Nick says. "Thank you so much."

He squeezes Cody's neck once, then lets him go.

Cody drives out of the lot onto the dark country road, which will take him to his childhood home. The wide marbled moon spins like a plate. Distant deer flicker in the road. He slows down, realizing he's driving too fast. The last thing he needs is to get pulled over, take a hard turn, or kill something.

After a few minutes, he pulls into a stranger's dark driveway. He takes out his phone, thinks for a moment, and calls Molly.

"Hey, bro," she answers.

"Hey." Cody takes a breath and shuts off the headlights.

"What's up? When are you getting here?"

"Tomorrow, I keep telling you that. Everything okay?"

"Yeah. I'm just on my way to Mom and Dad's." He shuts off the engine. "Do you remember that kid we went to high school with, Kevin Graeber?"

"Kevin Graeber." Molly seems to search for a moment. "Totally. I was at a party once where Kevin threw up in the shower." She pauses. "Why do you ask?"

"I just saw him at a bar."

"He give you trouble or something?"

"No," Cody says. "Nothing like that."

They talk for a few more minutes. Cody feels his heartbeat level out, his breath slow: signs that he's returning to himself, that he's anchored, that he can see things as they are. After Molly assures him that she'll text when she's leaving tomorrow, he gets back on the road.

Before he goes home, he stops at Pearl Lake. He's driven this route a thousand times. Even after all these years, he could maneuver its dirt parking lot with his lights cut. He knows how minor, threadbare footpaths branch off the main trail to the water, bringing him to lesser-known beaches. He parks the van and takes one of these small paths to a spot where he and Molly used to go when they were in high school. He knows that different selves arise in different environments. He knows that when he's feeling safe, an easy, warm, funny, and shameless version of himself comes to the fore. He wants to be this person in Iron River—in the kitchen with his mom, at the dive bar, at the grocery store. This is the place he came from, whether he likes it or not. And even if he never returns, he'll either be haunted by what he yearns for, or spend the rest of his life trying to cleave himself from what he wants. Which doesn't work for anyone. This he knows.

Cody digs his heels into the cold sand. His body feels heavy and damp with sweat beneath his jacket, though it's cooling quickly in the late March air. The temperature still hovers below freezing at night. The lake is smooth and iced over, spidered with cracks. If Molly were here, he would start a fire with her and distract himself with memories and jokes until he was warm. As it is, Cody walks a few feet onto the frozen lake. He's thinking of the noise the ice made when it broke under Greg's weight, that dull, shotgun sound. The places where the ice cracked might still be weak, like fractures in a bone. But he wants to be brazen and unafraid, like any other man.

SARAH BRAUNSTEIN

Abject Naturalism

FROM *The New Yorker*

THE BABY'S FATHER left before the Cesarean incision had
fully healed, when it was still a raised red line, tender to the
touch, glistening with Vitamin E oil. Perfidy! This from a man
who'd once said he'd die without her, who'd written her piles
of letters after she'd rejected him, back in graduate school—
though graduate school makes it sound more serious than it
was. They'd gone to a university to become fiction writers. The
degree took two years. During this time, Toni slept with several
of her peers but not with the man who eventually became her
child's father. He left letters in her mailbox about how much
this pained him. But he was too odd, she thought, terribly in-
tense, with a work ethic that made her ashamed of her own and
a burrowing gaze that at once flattered and repelled. He was
skinny and had a ponytail. He carried a briefcase. He didn't die
for lack of her, despite what his letter warned.

It wasn't until a decade had passed, when she was working
as a waitress in a small New England city and had just broken
up with a bartender named Dusty, when she had given up writing, all early sense of specialness evaporated, that she decided
to reach out to him. He was happy to hear from her, her old
suitor said, thought about her sometimes, wondered how she
was. Was she still writing fiction? Now and then, she lied. He'd
always loved her prose style, he told her. He himself had two
novel drafts and was finishing a PhD in a city a few hours away.
The next weekend, she took a train.

*

The briefcase had become a rugged leather saddlebag. He'd grown into the weirdness, cut his hair and gained some weight, a humanizing softness. She found he was easier to talk to than he'd been when he was twenty-four. There was too much sex at first to get any writing done, but she hoped the urge might return. Being with him, she began to feel that little kick, a sensation in her wrists, her fingers, an idea that shows up first in her palms. It was hard to pinpoint where this urgency resided, or what use she might make of it. She worried that what she really wanted was to be adored—not to write but for him to tell her about what she'd written, to praise it, as he had done in school.

None of that happened, because she got pregnant, an accident that disrupted everything spectacularly. She expected shock, sure, but after the shock—something. Maybe she wanted to be swung around, have her belly kissed, but what he said was this: "I've always been so fond of you, but I never wanted to be a father."

"Fond? But I was your white whale. I was your Beatrice!"

She saw in his expression that she'd made a terrible mistake. All the years of rejecting him, and in the end he dashed. She hadn't wanted a baby in any conscious way, but the moment she saw the test result she knew—a drilling knowledge—she'd keep it. She could drop certain pretenses now. During her second trimester, she trained to become a phlebotomist. He put some money into an account, for college. He gave her some money, too, but not very much, because he didn't have very much. "If you do this, Toni, you're going to be on your own," he said, and she made him put it in writing.

When the baby was only a few weeks old, something lucky happened. A friend had a friend who was renting a cool apartment at the top of a hill in a newly hip part of their city. The friend had gotten into grad school and was moving to Chicago. Wasn't Toni always talking about finding a new place? Toni couldn't afford to buy a house, not in that hip neighborhood or anywhere, but the deal on the rent would let her live among the gentrifiers for a while, in this up-and-coming district overlooking the actual ocean.

Toni toured the apartment the next day, the baby in her car seat carrier, her Cesarean incision smarting but so subtly she could almost forget about it. The landlord was a bearded beatnik, a vestige of another era, who'd bought several ramshackle structures for a song in the sixties and liked to curate an assortment of interesting tenants. Like a rabbit warren, Toni thought, six small rooms, wide wooden floorboards, a tub on avian feet, porcelain sinks, and clanking radiators. Nothing was square or plumb, there was no dishwasher, but it was only three blocks to a coffee shop, another five to a wine bar called Moon Under Water, and one day, when the baby was older, they could walk together to the new elementary school, certified green and—because it served students from the housing project at the bottom of the hill, many of whom were immigrants or asylum seekers—impressively diverse.

She and the baby moved in, and she painted the rooms, and the years passed. She stopped doing blood draws, worked her way up to administrative management at the hospital. Her child qualified for Gifted and Talented, a letter that came in the mail said.

The child had been given the name Amalie, but a few months after she turned seven she said, in a grave, flinty, fully assured voice, "I want you to call me Nancy."

Toni refused. Even so, Amalie began to write "Nancy" on the top of her assignments at school. Her friends, even the teacher, began to call her by this wrong name. Amalie liked when people complied. But she was gentle about it, had a savvy sort of guilelessness, with her big eyes and long dark lashes that made Toni think of a cartoon llama. By nine, she was Amalie again. She was studious, quick to anger. She cut the tags out of every shirt. Hated anything nubby. Hated crumbs in the butter. She collected seedpods, which turned to dust on her dresser, and the carapaces of odd bugs.

One day, she said she was going out by herself. "I'm old enough," Amalie said. "I want to jog. Alone."

"No," Toni told her.

"I'm *ten*."

It was true, ten. Toni's heart seized whenever she said it—gruesome, how fast a decade could pass.

"I'll take you for a walk."

"Alone. And I want to jog. For the children." The students in the school district had been given digital wristbands that counted their steps; if one took a certain number of steps a day in America, a child in Africa would be given a tube of peanut paste. That hadn't sounded right, but a brochure affirmed it.

"It's the difference between life and death," Amalie said.

"That's not quite accurate."

"It is!" She waved the arm that wore the wristband, then tried another strategy: "It's safe. Lucien and Violet and Hollis are allowed."

All true. "You can't go past the firehouse."

"I know. I promise."

She allowed Toni to apply sunscreen to her face. Then Toni led her to the door and said, "Not past the firehouse. Come home in half an hour." Amalie nodded solemnly, tapped the face of her big black watch.

"Don't talk to anyone, all right?"

"Why would I talk to someone?"

She ran off, sprinting, as if she might be chased.

When it's your own baby, every loping shadow in every bush is a sociopath with a jar of baby teeth on his mantel. He lived in the perimeter of her thoughts, this man and his jar. But not really. Only sometimes. She had seen too many serial-killer movies. That bartender she'd dated, Dusty, had a library consisting mostly of books about the Zodiac Killer. She blamed Dusty, in part, for her paranoia, and she also blamed whomever Amalie's elementary school contracted with for picture day. When you ordered prints from that photography company, it sent you—gratis, like it or not—a demented little card with your child's face and address, which you were supposed to keep in your wallet and give to the media and the police if your kid disappeared.

It actually said this on the back of the card: *In the event of your child's disappearance . . .*

Twenty minutes passed. *I should not have let her go,* she thought. She is too curious. She has no father. No man has imprinted. She's vulnerable.

But she came back whole. A knock, and when Toni opened the door she found her daughter breathing heavily and standing next to a glossy black telescope on a tripod stand. "A man gave it to me," she said.

"A man?"

"It needs to be cleaned. We can see Saturn's rings!"

"Which man?"

"It needs a new—I forget the word." She wiped her brow. "He told me. He said to look on eBay. He said I could buy the part for cheap."

From the months in which she and Amalie's father had negotiated the end of their relationship, one conversation stood out. She was newly pregnant—not showing, but her waist was distended, her face puffy—and perhaps for this reason when he said, "I'm in love with another person," it was so jarring she saw actual stars in her peripheral vision. When she began to cry, he said, "Listen, no. I made that up. That's not true."

"It's not? Is there a woman?"

"No," he said. "Not really."

"No, or *not really?*"

"I don't want a family. I don't want a wife or a child. I want my central relationship to be with texts."

"Texts?"

"I need to organize my life around my work."

"You're in love with a book?"

"Not a book."

Soon, he got a teaching job at a prestigious university. Then he began to publish his novels. Toni read them in hardcover at the public library, in a room full of homeless people, the body odor amplifying her sense of punishment. She thought of the books as his ex-wives. He was prolific. No one who resembled

Toni or Amalie appeared in the pages. The novels had bold, handsome covers and often featured protagonists who were writers themselves. How did he get away with that? She had been told in school not to do that, to stop being so clever.

Amalie knew her father was an author. She spoke of him as an abstract, a concept—"my biological father"—as if she were the child of a sperm donor. She was not especially curious, not yet. But one day she would read his books. That was coming. Toni did not like to think about it. She didn't seek out his reviews, though she could read them without having a panic attack, if she happened upon them in the *Times* or in waiting-room magazines. She'd stopped Googling him long ago, after she read an article in their alumni magazine with the headline "The Author's Retreat: A Place for Plotting." His living room had wall-to-wall bookshelves, a giant window through which you could see a span of darkly pink extraplanetary sky, and Barcelona chairs. She felt immensely jealous. To be free of children is truly to be free, she knew that now.

She found the telescope guy on the street that ran parallel to theirs, Beckett Street. Amalie had pointed out where he lived. It was a solid square house, shabby but not dingy, a single-family. A small yard, no landscaping but a lone pot of geraniums on the front porch. When Amalie was at school, Toni went to confront him. *Confront* is too strong a word. She had a point to make.

A doorbell coated in rust. She knocked instead and he came to the door. Before he spoke, she could tell he was a local, one who would be displaced. He had a wide, ruddy, pleasant face. Mid- to late sixties. Gray-brown hair, white at the temples, and a pair of black glasses over his T-shirt collar, pulling it down so she could see his chest hair, silver and feathery.

"You gave my daughter a telescope—" she began.

"A telescope?" He raised a finger, tapped his lips. She thought he was going to deny it, but he said, "Annie? Emily?," and now she wished for a fake name.

"*Amalie.*"

He snapped his fingers. "Right, yes, Amalie. Did you get it to work? It needs a new—"

"What message are you sending her?"

He blinked.

"I'm sure you don't mean any harm. But consider the precedent." She spoke with effortful neutrality. "You sent her the message that it's safe to talk to men she doesn't know."

"Did I?"

"And it might have been safe in this case. That doesn't mean next time, or on the next street, it will be."

He took the glasses off his shirt, put them on. "I think you might have misunderstood. I was only setting out a bunch of trash on the curb. She skipped by. It was going to the dump, right? I told her she could take it or it was trash."

He spoke carefully but without condescension; she could hear years of smoking.

"I figured a kid her age might like a thing like that, you know? That's all I did. I'm not a predator."

She did not like that word: *skipped*. *Skipped*, *predator*, these words she didn't approve of, but then he smiled and she saw his crowded teeth, the white of bleaching products.

"Thirty seconds, I swear. Our whole interaction." He held up his right hand. She began to feel sheepish.

"It's my policy that you're dangerous," she told him. "Until I have evidence to the contrary. It's not personal. Do you have a daughter?"

"A niece."

"How old?"

"Grown. But she's fine. She works in security. I'm Marco."

"Toni."

"You want to come in? Cup of joe?"

She saw into the house behind him, plush red seventies-thick carpet, a couch with wooden armrests and yellow-daisy upholstery. She said she had to go to work. She'd be late. She was walking away but then turned back and said, "She was *jogging*, for the record. Amalie doesn't skip."

"Roger that," he said, saluting her.

She was paranoid. She was projecting. She met at the wine bar with her friends Lucy and Katherine, who were a decade older, and they told her she had overreacted, but she cut them off—"I know, I know, I'm crazy."

"*Not* crazy!" they said in unison, each stroking one of her hands, which lay flat on the table. She sat upright, like a person taking a pledge, like it was a deposition.

"Lots of mothers go through this," Katherine said, stroking. "When Sadie got boobs, it fucked me up. I wept in the changing room at Macy's."

Lucy said, "My sister had an actual breakdown when Coco got her period."

"Amalie's not going through puberty."

"Of course she is."

"A puberty of *will*," Toni said, and they told her it was the same thing, all of a piece. But Amalie was so little-girlish, her body concave and lithe in the way of a child. She didn't even need deodorant yet.

"It's happening," they promised her.

"I'm not afraid of her period."

"Boobs are triggering, too."

"They get those nubs."

"Pubes."

"Right, that's the order."

"You sound like perverts," Toni said, "worse than any man," and they laughed but she was not joking, there was something sick in this hypervigilance, hungry and wistful and canny and boundary-less—and suddenly she felt shame for how she had treated the telescope guy.

The next day, she dropped by again. She had only ten minutes to spare before she was due at work. Today, his T-shirt was gray. Salt-and-pepper shadow on his face, darkest on his chin. "I was rude," she said.

"It's understandable."

She looked hard at him. "You're too *nice*."

"You're a mother. That's how I see it. You're allowed to overreact."

She felt he'd accepted her apology before she'd fully made

it. She said it was true, yes, she'd overreacted, she was a single mom—but she wished she'd been allowed to apologize fully.

"Coffee?" He pantomimed a mug in his hand, a swig. She saw an agility in his body, lightness despite his size. "You want to apologize inside?"

"I'll be late to work."

He dropped the mug. "Where's that?"

"The hospital."

"Doctor?"

"Administration."

"Forms," he said sympathetically. "I don't envy you."

"They're not bad. I used to take people's blood."

"You prefer forms to blood?"

"The money's better."

He said he was retired. But once he'd built houses. "I messed up my back bad. A beam fell on me. Traction for three months. I sued a giant. Talk about forms."

"I'm sorry to hear that."

"It turned out okay." He made the rubbing gesture with his fingertips that meant money. He added, "I barely limp. I'm not addicted to pills. Only Tylenol, swear on my mother's grave. No one can believe it. Show a doctor at your hospital my X-ray. Tell him only Tylenol and see what he says. Or she. Tell me what she says."

Lightness in her chest when she drove away. John Lennon singing. In the middle of the night, he calls her name.

That night, she said to Amalie, "Never tell a man you don't know your name."

"What? I never would tell a man that."

"No, I mean never give your name to a man you don't know."

Amalie thought about it. She didn't speak.

Toni said, "Did you tell the man who gave you the telescope your name?"

"No."

"I think you did."

Amalie's expression didn't change. She turned her head to

the side, like a rabbit listening. Toni didn't say anything more—the weirdness of her syntax felt like warning enough.

A few days later, a package arrived. It was the telescope part. He had bought them a present—had figured out where they lived. It wouldn't have been hard. She held it, her heart beating in her neck. It had been a long time since she'd received mail from a man. This was just a piece of square plastic with an angled mirror, but it returned something to her. And then Amalie walked into the room and said, "I know I should have asked you first. You were in the shower. I found it on a website. It was easy. Just $4.99. I used your credit card."

Her credit card?

"Amalie! That's—that's—" The only word that came to mind was *criminal*. "That's not okay," she said, but the girl's face remained placid, indifferent, and so Toni said, "That's criminal, Amalie—*criminal*," and saw a flash of surprise.

This time, she had forty-five minutes before she had to go to work. He seemed surprised to see her. The white T-shirt again, and he was clean-shaven. He invited her in. His kitchen had an old linoleum floor, a white countertop speckled with inky gold. All the appliances were fifty years old except for the coffee machine, which was the kind that ruins the environment with its plastic pods. A Brooklynite would gut the kitchen in a second. They sat down in green molded-plastic chairs.

"You really had a fire under you," he said.

"I'm prone to worrying."

"You're suspicious. That's a good thing. My mother was never suspicious. Not a whit."

"A whit?" She liked that word.

"Not a crumb. It was different back then. I don't think our mothers worried so much."

He was brought up here, in this house, him and his sister and his mother. He could not imagine his mother tracking down a neighbor and yelling about danger.

"I didn't *yell*."

"You didn't."

"I hope I didn't."

"You didn't yell—*my* mother yelled. But she had to. She had no idea where I went. Who I talked to. We were all just let loose. All the neighborhood kids. We got back in time for dinner, mostly."

He handed her a bag of potato chips. She took a few.

"No camp, no programs. We were wild. Scrappy. Same exact place. Not too long ago."

She said it might as well be a different country now—the watching eyes, the schedules, the helmets and knee pads and consent forms.

When he got up to brew another cup, she saw evidence of the injury, but faintly; it was more a hitch than a limp. He moved gracefully, poured a mug of water into the machine's reservoir. He was tall, on the edge of burly, but had a way of gliding. She sat close enough to the fridge that she could read its magnets— there was one that said "A minute on the lips, a lifetime on the hips." It held a reminder card from the dentist. She read his last name. Now she could Google him. She felt sad that she could Google him. She wouldn't. She'd spare one person in her life.

That same day, driving to pick up Amalie from aftercare, Toni saw children playing in the street at the bottom of the hill. How had she failed to account for them, these dozens of children who parted to make way for her car? They rode their bikes in the streets, helmetless. Of course, Toni did not judge the parents. These families brought different traditions and practices. Many had fled true danger. But why had she not thought of them when she and Marco were talking?

Amalie's elementary school was diverse, dozens of languages spoken there, but the playground nearest their house was generally occupied by white children. Once, she'd asked Amalie, "Do the African children play by themselves at school?" Amalie considered the question for a good while. All she said was, "Halima is really annoying."

On the fifth night, Toni broke down and gave Amalie the telescope part. Amalie tried to install it, but it turned out that she'd purchased the wrong size—it was too big for the hole. "Serves you right," Toni said tenderly, and gave her a squeeze. Amalie was so disappointed she cried. She hardly ever cried. She looked so helpless, like a kid lost at a fair, shamed by the spectacle, adorable despite every intention. Toni measured the telescope several times, got her credit card, and ordered the correct part. She paid for expedited shipping.

"Three to five days?" the girl sniffled, and Toni said yes, three to five, and Amalie let her mother wipe her eyes, and let her do a French braid and tie a yellow ribbon at the end.

Later that night, Toni called Lucy and said, "I'm not going to Google the telescope guy."

"What if he's an offender?"

"He's not. I trust my gut."

She Googled him. His full name, city, and state. She found a White Pages listing with his address, which she already knew. An obituary for a woman who'd died a decade ago, who was perhaps his mother . . . yes, Helen Lorraine, survived by two children, Marco and Loretta, and a granddaughter. She was described as a homemaker and a long-standing member of a bridge club. Toni saw Marco's features in the woman's square, serious face. No crime, no red flag. She closed the computer. She imagined a group of boys roaming the neighborhood; she put them in clothes like they wore in *The Outsiders*, greaser gear, Levi's and dingy white T-shirts. Poor white boys. Working-class boys before they worked. It was classist to be turned on, she thought, but also not to be.

Now she had two hours until she had to be at work. This time, he brought them coffee in his living room. It had ancient carpeting and furniture, but the TV was new, as was his armchair. "A smart chair." He showed her the hidden panel—a hatch for power, USB, a dial for lumbar support. There was even a refrigerated compartment where one could store drinks. "From the manufacturer of those Japanese toilets. You know those toilets?"

She did. There was an elaborate toilet at Yosaku, her favorite restaurant in town; it caressed you with a stream of warm water, a sensation so much like urination that she felt dirtier for having pressed the button. He said he'd never tried sushi but he liked Japanese gadgets. Looking at them in magazines, knowing how they worked—he liked that. He was thinking of ordering a toilet for himself.

Toni said, "We ordered the telescope part. She can hardly wait." He smiled. He had an uncomplicated warmth to his face, like an elementary-school teacher. They drank more coffee and he served a sleeve of Ritz and told her about a kid called Tato, a friend back in the day, two streets over.

"What kind of name is that?"

"Short for Potato. His real name was Richard."

The neighborhood wonder. At nineteen, he went to Hollywood to try his luck and actually landed a part on a soap opera, a real part. Everyone followed the show vigilantly, all its twists, cheered whenever he came on-screen.

"The day after Thanksgiving, Tato died of a drug overdose in a shitty motel on Sunset Boulevard. Died in real life. Not on the show. Some of the guys kept watching anyway. They got hooked on it. 'Westerly.'" He hummed its theme song, which she vaguely recognized. She wanted to know who else didn't survive their adolescence. He shook his head.

"That's no talk for you," he said.

"I can take it."

He wanted to tell her—she could see a hunger to reminisce. She liked the way he told her the scary bits so calmly.

"There was Jimmy Tampuco. Overdosed in his basement. Your girl won't do drugs. I can tell she won't. Oh, and Sissy LaDuke. That was sad. She won the jump-rope contest in elementary school. She was drunk. That might make you feel better."

"Drunk in *elementary school?*"

"In the crash, later. Your girl won't drink. Amalie isn't like that."

"How do you know?"

"You can tell," he said. "She's—" He paused. "Clean. Maybe that's not the right way to say it." She pictured a white sheet on a clothesline, shuddering in the wind. She liked that he said it, even as she understood it was problematic, implying as it did that there could be dirty children. And what would make a child *dirty*? And whose fault would it be?

She let Amalie out on her own again. She didn't return with a gift this time, swore she hadn't spoken to a soul. Toni felt better, proud of herself for overcoming her paranoia. She let her out the next day, too. But that night something happened that scared her all over again. At two in the morning, Toni woke up, got up to pee. As a matter of habit, she poked her head into Amalie's bedroom, and saw her bed was empty. She searched the apartment, calling for her. Thought to call the police but could not find her phone. It was not on the nightstand. Or in her purse. She called louder, ran to the front door, saw Amalie in the yellow beam of a streetlight, in her tie-dyed nightgown, an arm stretched to the sky. She held an illuminated object in her hand, moved it as a person sways a lighter at a concert.

"What are you doing?"

Amalie spun, clutched the phone to her chest. "Don't be mad. It was free."

"I couldn't find you!"

An app, she explained. You held your phone to the night sky and it named all the stars for you. You looked at the sky through the screen, as if the phone were a window, and each star was labeled, and dotted lines connected the stars into constellations, which were labeled, too.

"But you can't leave the house in the middle of the night! You scared me, honey!"

"I was ten feet away," Amalie said steadily. She came to her, took her hand, said, "The app was free, Mama."

"You don't know who might be roaming around at night," Toni said, when she'd got Amalie back into bed, when she was sitting on the edge of the bed, tucking her in again.

Amalie said, "What do you mean? No one was out there. *Who* are you talking about?," and since that was not a question Toni could answer she began to name the things she would take away from the girl if she did not comply. Screen time. Jogging. The special magnifying box into which she put live bugs and her bloody scabs.

The sunroom next. He was showing her the house in this way, a cup of coffee in each spot. Wicker furniture with firm, pink-pastel cushions. A ceiling fan spun brown parchment blades. Looks exotic, he told her, but it came from Lowe's. A bookshelf contained spy thrillers and Stephen King. The Danielle Steels had been his mother's. He gazed at her in a way that was—well, that was loving. That word felt accurate. How would she explain that to Lucy and Katherine? She would tell them straight: He looks at me like he loves me. But they would burst out laughing, because she wouldn't be able to say it straight. From brain to mouth, in that nanosecond, it would become distorted with irony. She could only *think* it unironically. So she did. He looks at me like he loves me. She felt her cheeks grow warm. She could feel her heart in her ears, as if she'd plugged them. His mouth did not frighten her. Did she want to kiss it? Maybe not yet. But she would contentedly share a straw with him, or an apple.

She told him some more things about herself. She told him her childhood fantasy was to become a writer. She'd written stories on a secondhand typewriter about people who were way worse off than her, and on the basis of these she'd got a scholarship to the state university, and then to graduate school.

"What did you want to write?"

"Scary things."

"Like Stephen King?"

"Scarier."

"Than *that?*"

He looked at her like such a thing was not possible.

"A different kind of scary. Funny, too."

"Dark comedy?"

"I couldn't do it. I quit."

"Of course not," he said, chuckling. "You're a nice person." Then he said, "But why not?"

"I guess I didn't have the discipline. And I could never end things right."

"Huh."

"Amalie's father is a writer," she offered next, because then she wouldn't wonder anymore how much she would tell him. "He's famous. In certain circles, I guess. He's written many books. He's won awards. I met him in graduate school."

Marco did not look impressed by this or ask his name.

"Does he see her?" he wanted to know.

"He put money in an account for her college. I asked him to give up his parental rights."

"And he did it?"

"In a snap."

"A snap?"

She snapped her fingers.

"A fool," Marco said, thumped a fist like a judge's gavel on his broad thigh.

Marco told her he'd come close to having a kid. A long time ago. He'd been in love with a woman named Diane. She worked in a sandwich shop owned by her father. When he picked her up after a shift, she smelled like spicy meat. She had extremely long hair. Crystal Gayle hair. Did Toni know her? The old country singer? Hair nearly to the floor, long and straight, like a cape. Diane kept it in a braid at work, wrapped all around her head, kind of like a turban, because you couldn't let a customer find hair like that in a sandwich.

"Talk about a health-code violation. She washed it twice a month. It took twelve hours to dry. Hey, can you find me a picture of her? Of Crystal Gayle? I'd like to see her."

She called up a photograph of the country singer from the phone sitting on her lap. He looked at it for a while, then returned the phone and said, "We thought about having a kid. It was on the table. But she didn't want to. That's what she decided in the end. It was the right decision for her. I respect her for it."

Their stories had a kind of symmetry, were inversions of each other. That's what he was telling her. The room overlooked a fenced-in backyard. There was a hammock on a metal stand, an overgrown brick patio. The light was a deep, dappled green that made her eyelids and limbs grow heavy, a spontaneous fatigue like Dorothy in the field of poppies.

*

The newspapers began to speak of a housing crisis. Her landlord always swore he wouldn't raise the rent. "Not on you and
Amalie. Never would." One day, he added, "But when I die—
well, you're on your own, my friend."

"You can leave me this house in your will," she'd replied, a
joke, but his face got serious and he told her it was going to
his son. They both knew his son would sell to a developer or a
Brooklynite. Her landlord was getting older. He'd had a knee
replacement and might need to do a hip. It struck her, one day,
that she thought more about her landlord's health than about
her own parents'.

Young couples kept moving into the neighborhood. They
drove Subarus or Audis or Teslas or vintage, gas-guzzling
Mercedes-Benzes in white or butter yellow. "I work remotely,"
everyone said. Or "I'm a consultant," no further explanation, as
if she should know what that meant. Young chefs, screenwriters,
environmental lawyers, medical-marijuana growers, beer brew-
ers, everyone so exceedingly passionate, alert with creativity,
everyone—all of a sudden—younger than her. She felt like a
fraud in their company. She only dressed like a member of the
creative class.

Once, her imagination had been like a puppy that wanted
to lick everything. In college, she didn't go out on the weekends, preferring to stay in and write. Late at night, she would
read what she'd written to the girls who remained in the dorm,
who'd show her the goosebumps on their arms as proof of the
excellence of the story. She didn't get the same reception in her
MFA program. The first fiction she shared was about a girl who
shoplifts a box of tampons. It's meant to be a rite of passage,
but she gets caught and arrested and bleeds everywhere. The
story ends with the cops calling her mother. The girls in the
dorm would have had goosebumps. But her teacher stared at
the place where the ceiling met the wall, tapped his long fingers
on the table, and said, "There is so much writing that could be
good but isn't."

A long pause.

"Why is this?" he asked the class.

They guessed: Passive voice? Poor characterization? Disharmony between form and content?

"No," he said. "It's because it doesn't take responsibility for itself."

The new telescope part arrived, the right part. She hoped. Toni gave it to Amalie after dinner. The girl squealed and raced to the telescope, but she couldn't get it to fit. It seemed to be the correct size but it wouldn't slide in. They searched for a button, a lever, some trick. Went online. There were people on YouTube demonstrating every conceivable thing in the universe but not how to make this eyepiece fit in this telescope, and by then it was getting late.

"Time for bed, honey. We'll do it tomorrow."

"We're close. Please!" She had written a list of features of the night sky on a piece of notebook paper and held it up now, her forehead clenched. "Tomorrow, it's going to rain. Tomorrow, there's an eighty percent chance of rain."

"The sky isn't going anywhere, is it?"

Amalie began to cry but recovered quickly. She wiped her face with a handful of toilet paper, rubbed her eyes, and took stoic, heartbreaking breaths, like a businesswoman in a bathroom stall. Her restraint destroyed Toni. Amalie fell asleep with the tattered edge of her old security blanket gripped in her hand.

Toni would get her girl's telescope working. Wake her before dawn. That was the idea—to surprise her, wake her up, show her the sky. But she couldn't figure it out. She played with it for a while, drank a glass of wine, finally gave up.

Once not long ago Toni had a dream in which she was renting the same apartment but the other bedroom, Amalie's orange room, was an office full of IKEA furniture. No Amalie. She had not been born. The walls were white. The books in the office were arranged by color, a trend Toni scorned in waking life. That was the whole dream. She had woken flooded with dread. Amalie! On the nightstand, she'd spotted proof of the child's existence—a drawing the girl had recently done, a bird with a deformed beak. Evidently, Amalie had predicted her mother's critique, because upon giving her the drawing Amalie had said, "Its beak is *supposed* to be like that." She'd been reading about the animal deformities following Chernobyl. All kinds of deformities, she explained. "Weird beaks on the birds. Extra legs on deer. Twisty spines. Long necks. No necks."

"*No* necks?"

"Anything can go wrong," her daughter said brightly.

Now Toni turned on the bedside light. She looked at that bird drawing. The bird's beak was twisted in a way that made it seem like it would be difficult for it to eat. It had lopsided, querying eyes. Then Toni had an idea. If she thought about it too much, she wouldn't do it. She got out of bed. She left a note on the kitchen counter. "Ran an errand! Back shortly. Go back to sleep. love, Mom." Amalie wouldn't wake, hardly ever woke in the night. It would only be five minutes. Ten, tops. That episode in the street had been an anomaly.

She saw herself from above—a woman jogging. A woman in black leggings and a slouchy gray sweatshirt and no bra, holding a telescope out in front of her like a baby that is not her responsibility. Help. There were no lights on in his house. She'd hoped that he would be reading in bed or playing solitaire downstairs in the special chair, which had a removable desktop. Then she could say, I remembered you're a night owl. I saw a light.

In the darkness, her fist made a frightened sound. Finally, the light above her head came on. His face was reddish, cleanly shaved, his hair in surprising disarray and longer than she'd expected.

"Toni, you all right?"

"Hello, Marco. I'm fine. I'm really sorry to wake you. I need to get this thing to work. I can't get the new part in, and tomorrow it's going to rain. There's a storm coming."

He shook his head. He rubbed his right eye with the heel of his hand.

"You apologize too much."

He was wearing a blue velour robe. She could see the soft rise of his pectorals, the outline of his abdomen under the robe. He

looked at the telescope and frowned. Looked at the night sky.
He didn't look at her.

"Come in," he said finally. They didn't go far—just into the
foyer. He bent down, careful to keep his robe closed, and examined the telescope. There was a hidden button on the base.
"Here," he said. "Underneath. See?" The part slid in, easy as
pie, once you pushed this button. "Ta-da."

He stood, smiling. She felt suddenly embarrassed. She said, "I
hope you don't misunderstand."

"Misunderstand?"

"It's late."

He looked at her squarely.

"I just want to make Amalie happy. I want to surprise her before daybreak," she said.

"My doorstep, in the middle of the night. Don't misunderstand?"

"You gave it to her. Where was I supposed to go?"

He tightened his robe. "You want a cup, Toni?"

"I won't go back to sleep." She shook her head. "I should
go. She might wake up." But she was only a block away. Two
minutes. Less if she jogged. She had left the note. "One cup.
You have decaf?"

They sat together on the stoop, mugs in their hands. It felt
less rule-breaking on the stoop. She wasn't in a man's house,
only outside her own. They watched the spastic display of moths
in the streetlight. An upstairs light came on in the house across
the street. Light from these two sources fell onto Marco's face
like powder, softening his complexion. She admitted that she'd
Googled him.

"I'm flattered you did that. Not too newsworthy, you see."

"I read your mother's obituary."

"You did? I wrote that."

"It was lovely," she said softly. That wasn't quite true. She had
felt nothing of the woman's essence. But the writing was clear,
said what it meant, and that was more of a feat than anyone
realized.

"What about you, Toni? What would I find if I looked you up?"
She felt mildly disappointed that he hadn't. "Nada."

He leaned back, clasped his hands behind his head, so that his elbow lightly touched her shoulder. "Your parents are alive?"

"Nominally."

"I don't know what that means."

"They fight all day."

"Too bad," he said, bringing his hands back to his lap. "A shame."

In graduate school, she had written a story loosely based on her parents, in which a couple has to contend with a skunk in the basement—their failure to contain the animal leads them to pitch a tent in the backyard. The same teacher said the story suffered from abject naturalism. The plausible was described plausibly, credible things occurred in credible order. Toni felt this was the worst thing that could be said about a story, the worst way you could live a life.

Marco went on. "I'm dyslexic. That's why it took me so long to write the obituary. That's why I didn't graduate from high school. I could only read in a totally silent room, and then it was exhausting."

He pointed to the lit room on the second floor of the house across the street. "There," he said. "That room." The house they faced had a sporty Volvo in the driveway, an amazing garden, raised beds and trellises. He gestured to the telescope. "You should look, but from upstairs. We have to be higher. You can see the book titles."

"You can?"

"And their moles."

"Jesus, Marco."

"You don't approve?" He kept his eyes on the window. "I gave it away, anyhow."

"*That's* what you were using it for? Spying on your neighbors?"

He laughed. "What—you're allowed, but I'm not?"

What did he mean, *allowed*? She thought of her own girl, alone at home. She said, "You have a niece, Marco."

"I do."

"She works in security."

"She does."

She kissed him. First a peck, then deeper. He kissed her back.

He did not seem surprised to be kissing her, nor did he hesitate. Beneath the coffee, his mouth tasted pleasantly herbal. They brought the telescope upstairs. There was wainscoting in the bedroom. There were those old-fashioned on-off light switches, with two black buttons, one above the other, that make such a satisfying sound when you press them.

When she got home, she found Amalie in the exact same spot, drooling on her pillow. All that time, which felt enormous, like hours, had actually been fifty-two minutes.

She had put her eye to the telescope, allowed Marco to adjust it. The man across the street had been reading a book in bed, a slim light clamped to the headboard. He had curly blond hair. A person asleep next to him. A lump with black hair. Toni did not know if the lump was a man or a woman. The reading man occasionally, absently, rubbed his genitals. The book he was reading was called *Screenwriting*. That was it. Nothing else happened. The dullness of the scene, the abject naturalism, aroused her.

"This is what you do, Marco? Watch them?"

"Sometimes."

"And what else?"

"What else?"

The whole time, Amalie slept. Now Toni shook her shoulder until she sat up, still asleep. A hank of hair clung to the side of her mouth. She wasn't awake yet, her eyes strange and empty, like a ghost who would haunt this place when it became a condo, and Toni couldn't bear it, said, "Baby, baby, wake up." Amalie let herself be pulled up. Her nightgown was hitched into her white underpants. Toni pulled it down and pulled the hair from her mouth, led her into the hall. Only when she opened the front door, when cool air rushed at them and she saw the telescope standing in the street, pointing virtuously upward, did she really wake up.

"I fixed it."

Amalie made a sound. A joyful yowl, feline, so quick and piercing that something screeched back in alarm. Then she surged for the telescope, took it in her hands. She knew where everything was up there. Her patience was enormous. Her focus.

She was a polite kid, considerate—she didn't forget Toni.

"You want a turn?"

"Later, honey. Not now. You look now."

Toni felt strange. She'd sneaked out like a teenager and come home different, out of joint, as if she'd lost her virginity.

"I see a satellite," Amalie announced, but Toni's focus was earthbound. She was planning something in her head. She felt it all there, laid out. A structure she could borrow. A new sense of urgency.

"I see Mars."

"That's amazing, honey."

He would be another set of eyes. He would keep an eye. The moment she decided, she decided everything. Where she'd put her bureau, which room Amalie would get. Where Toni would set up a desk. Where she would try one more time. *Slow down*, she told herself, but then she thought, *Why should I slow down?* She had been too humble, too modest. The edges of the sky lightened. A seam appeared in the horizon, and they went inside. In the apartment, Amalie hugged Toni around the waist—hugged her hard, encircling her totally, the way she had as a toddler. She made a move to return to bed, but Toni took her wrist and said no.

"No?"

"Let's end the night in a doughnut shop."

"It's the morning already!"

But that was what Toni wanted. Like in graduate school. Like the early-morning diner after the first time you've been with someone. Coffee after a hookup. So that she could linger in this state, so that Amalie would remember it longer. They drove to the Christmas-themed doughnut shop off Exit 5 and Toni ordered half a dozen, what the hell, to celebrate.

"To celebrate? What are we celebrating?" They sat across from each other in a hard plastic yellow booth. On a shelf above them, several mechanical Santas were frozen in hip gyrations.

"You!" Toni said, lifting her coffee.

The girl made a doubtful face, blinked her red-rimmed eyes. There was still a faint indentation around her eye socket, from the telescope.

"You and the cosmos, honey. The sky. That's what."

"Oh," Amalie said, taking a large bite.

Toni allowed Amalie a few sips of coffee. Sugar granules sparkled on her cheeks. People came and went. Mostly old men.

Toni said, "We should thank the man who gave you the telescope."

"I thought I wasn't allowed to talk to him."

"I checked him out."

"You did? When?"

An elderly man in a stained shirt and green-tinted glasses—looking toward Amalie—smiled and pressed a button on a Santa across the room, the tallest Santa, who began to gyrate and sing. He was trying to please her, the only child in the place. Amalie winced like a woman with a hangover, looked out the window. The Santa crackled dementedly.

Toni said, "We should give him a doughnut."

"*Him?*"

She thought Toni meant the man who started up the Santa.

"Marco."

"Wait. Who's *that?*"

"The man who gave you the telescope. His name is Marco."

Amalie stopped eating. She blinked her long lashes.

"Why?"

"It would be nice."

Amalie thought about it. "A lemon," she said finally, looking into the box at the remaining doughnuts. Lemon were her least favorite. Then she tapped her watch, reminded her mother it was a school day. As they were leaving, she passed the man who had made the Santa dance, and he put his hand out, the way one does for a high five, a meaty palm, but Amalie sailed by, did not pause.

Amalie my anomaly, her mother thought. Good girl. Just like that. In the parking lot, a big black bird tore at a garbage bag. Empty cans skidded across the pavement. A storm was coming, like Amalie had said. They were stuffed to the gills with sugar and caffeine. The school nurse would call in two hours. By that point, Toni would have called in sick herself, would be home napping. But before the nap. Before Amalie throws up in the coatroom. While the sky is so lovely and strange and their glucose levels have not yet plummeted—she feels entitled to everything she wants. Ambition is ascendant. Danger everywhere, but it's not—look at that—in this story. In this story, no one lays a finger on any child. The wind lifts Amalie's hair. Toni lets her ride in the front seat. When she starts the car, the radio is already playing the right song, Freddie Mercury announcing a homicide, and they sing together, and it ends just when she pulls up to the school, as if God himself had set the needle down.

Unfathomably Deep

FROM *The Drift*

> I know indeed what evil I intend to do,
> But stronger than all my afterthoughts is my fury,
> Fury that brings upon mortals the greatest evils.
> —Euripides's *Medea*, 431 BCE

THREE MEN WERE supposed to spread me open, check me out. One of the men was late. The other two began without him. The room was hot and forbidding. As the men locked me in my stirrups, they told me their names, which now I've forgotten, but I do remember that one was blond, the other blonder. They were medical students. I played their patient. Together they shot me small smiles and then proceeded to probe.

When at last the late doctor arrived, his hair looked extremely black beside the blonds. "I'm Daniel," he said. "Sorry I'm late. It's *unseasonable* outside." He walked over to the exam table on which I was spread, where the blonds had also just begun apologizing—for Daniel's being late, and also for the sorry quality of Daniel's apology. Three young men, wearing white coats, looking deep into my body and expressing solemnities. I looked away. Then back at Daniel. *My god,* I thought.

Everyone asks me, Why him? What was it about him? I can't quite say. The way he said *unseasonable*. The efficiency of his beauty, its immediate implication of eternity. His eyes! Their slow pulses of anti-death. How his childhood—when his brows lifted—how his whole childhood erupted before me as something impossibly sweet and distant. How I'd have died to see it. His tiny teeth erupting through swollen gums. His hair after a bath, fresh smells of baby chick, or even butter. He also, I might add, looked very much like my sister's ex-boyfriend.

"Can I get that?" Daniel pointed to the speculum.

"We probed her already," blond said.

"But we all have to do it," Daniel said. "So."

"We don't," blonder said. "That's not part of the rules."

It was my job to intervene. Formally speaking, I was a GTA: a Gynecological Teaching Assistant. Really just a body lender for medical students. Their one task was to perform a partial gynecological exam on a pretend patient—me—who had pretend gynecological problems, which were the result of a pretend sex life, which was the result of a pretend desirability. I had a script and everything.

"It's okay, he can probe," I said to blond and blonder.

Daniel smiled at me. I shivered, died, came alive five times in a row. I noticed his eyes were huge, grape-green, with teeny seed-like pupils—all of which lent him a certain snack-time innocence.

"Great," Daniel said, beginning his examination.

Since I became a GTA, my view of doctors was typically of their jaw. Daniel's was sharp and clean-shaven. I had the urge to tell him I knew what it was like; my sister shaved my face once. Even though I was already hairless. My sister said it was like using a sword to cut foam, or like taking a rifle to an ant (and you could trust her on that: she was a gun-loving woman, always armed up). I looked at Daniel and sighed. Then I took my thought a little deeper. I imagined how, if I were lying beside him at night, his hairs might prick my ear, and how I'd attune myself to the offbeats of his aorta, how balletic I would be in mustering his sex.

"Do you feel any discomfort?" Daniel sat on the stool between my legs.

"None," I said. Then I remembered my script, cleared my throat. "I'm here today because I'm trying to get pregnant, have not succeeded, and want to make sure everything is okay, basically."

Daniel nodded. He held the speculum in one hand and spread the labia with the other, then directed the tool away from my urethral meatus, toward my coccyx, and proceeded to spread the blades. I stiffened.

"A baby," Daniel said, "that's wonderful." He looked up into the center of my forehead, as if it was the locus of fertility, expressing prophecies. "I am sure everything is okay."

Blond and blonder exchanged a look. Daniel was not supposed to say that. Warm assurances about being "okay" must never be uttered in a medical room. In fact, as my sister's doula once told me, medical rooms are designed specifically to keep those kinds of assurances at bay. All the steel tools and lacquered plastics are there to encourage a kind of physical-emotional nonstick. Daniel should've said, "Okay. Okay. I see. Let me just take a look around . . ." I'd have corrected him myself if it weren't for my own improbable and god-given certainty that Daniel was to be the love of my life. ("You're going to know he loves you," my sister had told me, "if he breaks you open right away.")

When the exam was over I gave blond and blonder medium marks and Daniel high ones. His grade sheet included his scanned ID, the details of which I copied onto my notepad: DANIEL DEMARCO; 519 EAST 79th STREET; Sex M; Height 5'-11'; Eyes GRN.

He was shorter than he looked. I considered including this point under the NOTABLE section of the grade sheet, but didn't. In fact, I mentioned nothing special about him at all. Nothing about his grape eyes and their luxe pulsations. Mostly because Ally, my supervisor, had already taken issue with what she called my *irrelevant insights.* Earlier that day, Ally'd stopped me in the hall and I'd found myself telling her that Utah (Ally's home state, as well as mine) ranks in the top five states for deaths by car crash, suicide, firearms, you name it. I told her she was lucky to have made it out of there alive.

"Thanks," she said. She looked at me like I was being extremely disarming, so I decided to confess to her right then that, yes, back in Utah I was actually an actress. I assured her I was significantly thinner back then. That my sister Danielle and I had starred in all the local shows. Or really my sister had starred. We were minor celebrities. "But I had to get out of there," I told her. "The winters scrape out your insides. I'm sure you understand." Ally nodded.

After I met Daniel—still hot off my chair—I bumped into Ally again in the hall. I suspected she might want to keep talking about Utah, even though I was over it. "Izzie." She gestured toward my grade sheet. "So, do you have any more points of confusion?" I considered. If I'm going to tell the story right, I should let you know: Ally was a little physically incongruous. I mean that she was very muscular but also chinless and rotund. And while I found this confusing, I did not mention it, because I knew my sister would have said something, and that felt like enough.

"Do you think I might get to play pregnant any time soon?" That's all I asked. Some of the girls got to play mothers-to-be. They got to gain a little weight. It looked super wholesome.

"We'll see," Ally said. She smacked her gum and handed me a wad of papers from her clipboard. "Here are your scripts for next week. And your schedule. For now, you're still trying."

I took the papers, and she thanked me. I watched her soften. "All in due time," she said. (She said it the way my sister used to say it, but when my sister said it she'd put my hand on top of hers as she rubbed her belly, like there was about to be some big movement she wanted us to feel.)

So that day with Daniel, was it love at first sight or something? That's what they ask me now. Make it make sense, they say. Was it some kind of fairy tale? I suppose it must have been. There was certainly a shift in me. My therapist said that I seemed to be nearing the end of my grief. That maybe I'd soon be healthily transposing the savage depth of my distress into love. That I might stop using the word *because* so much and realize some things don't have reasons. I might even grow calmer, or attain a certain cerebral delicacy—I might even return to my former state. And it's true that, thinking of Daniel, overall it was peace that I felt. In fact, it was a new, more violent peace, like the peace of a new religious convert, or the peace of a post-birth, oxytoxic surge. Anyway, it was an improvement.

Soon I saw that Daniel's rotation in mammary was coming up. It was his last mammary before moving to prenatal. I asked Ally to put me in a mammary every day over the following two weeks. I didn't tell her why. She agreed because there were always insufficient girls in mammary. The mammaries were endless hands fondling my softest spots, syncopated finger taps on my areolar complex, which gave me a smattering of bruises, some of them even puffy, like extra nipples. I prayed, throughout these sessions, that I'd be assigned to Daniel's team. Once, I got close. A young man walked in. Henry. Henry was Daniel-height. His jaw had similar dimensions. But Henry's stubble was riddled with bald patches. The baldness made me laugh.

(Have you ever worn a bald cap? In Utah, my sister wore a bald cap when playing Lear in *King Lear.* She came out of the dressing room looking raw, glistening. Seeing her, I laughed so hard I began to cry, which made her do the same, and we both got kicked out of rehearsal. "They wouldn't have kicked us out in New York," she said as she drove us home. Her bald cap was still on, her pseudo-skull beaming in the flinted Utah light. She said she felt smarter. It was like the bald cap was suction-cupping her intelligence. I put my hand on her head and pressed on the dewy rubber. By the next stop sign we were back in hysterics.)

"Do you need to get up?" Henry asked me. It's because I was sitting there in a giggle fit on the exam table. I said no to Henry. I straightened my arms, took a deep breath, controlled myself. If I were to get up he'd report me, Ally would dismiss me, and Daniel might never see me again. I thought: If Henry is a good student-doctor, he will notice the bruises across my chest. But Henry didn't mention the bruises. He pressed them, sending a drum line of pain to my anus. I bit my lip and thought only of Daniel's face. I thought of his ears. I thought of his open mouth. I would find him, I was sure.

And then, at last, a miracle: There was a disastrous dropout in the pregnancy cohort. Three girls dumped it mid-term. The GTA team was desperate. With warm, askance eyes Ally handed me a packet. In three days, I was to be four months pregnant for my next assigned group, the names of which read: APPLE,

DEMARCO, ZEAL. Say it again? I asked Ally. That's APPLE, DE-
MARCO, ZEAL.

I held my breath for seventy-two hours. My sister told me this
was a good tactic. She mostly saved it for the stage. She said the
trick to sustaining tension in a scene is to hold your breath as
the other actors speak. When you finally speak, whatever you
say will naturally sound urgent. It was a tactic she used when,
two months into her very real pregnancy, she was cast as Medea,
a woman who murders her own children in order to spite her
unfaithful husband. The director, a Utah native, did not like
the way my sister played this woman—he didn't like the breath-
holding, the righteousness. "You give her too much," he warned
her. "Remember: This is in*fant*icide. Medea kills her *child*ren.
This is *grue*some." My sister fought back. I watched as she stood
up and got personal, using words like *silly* and *troglodytic*. The
next day, the director gave a long lecture to the entire cast about
Euripides, about Greek culture and why we should understand
Medea's actions as reckless, immature, melodramatic—actions
with brutal, long-lasting consequences, in a series of equally if
not increasingly gruesome tales. "Good, well, I think we've covered a lot of ground," he said at the end of his speech. He said
it especially to my sister.

I felt my sister gather her nerve. Her drama was cosmic. Her
rebuttal ran for hours, with the brutal consequence that my sister was Medea no more.

My sister and I were sitting in the audience when, two weeks
later, her understudy played a more fretful, self-conscious Medea whose rage no one believed in. I remember waiting for my
sister to burst out, either in mockery or in helpless enthusiasm,
but instead—I can see her now—she sat still, with a quiet dignity,
her scarf wrapped tight around her neck, the tip of her nose
catching the fringe of stage light. She smiled, enjoying the sub-
dued performance before her. I watched her lips move faintly
as she mouthed Medea's lines: *You will have seen the bitter end of
my love.* When I asked her afterward about her understudy, she
said, "You know, the Medea we saw tonight was the damn best

that girl could do." She said it while holding her belly. I could tell she was practicing motherhood. "You know," she said again. "It was her goddamn best."

While I awaited my prenatal with Daniel (during which he'd feel for my milk ducts as they prepare for lactation), I imagined telling him this very story, and making sure he knew that, at other points, my sister was less diplomatic. That she stretched the spectrum of human experience. She could take the cruelest blow of fate as if it were mere wind, giving her direction. Or she could let a pinch, a prick, destroy her. Two days after *Medea*, I found her in the kitchen eating spoonfuls of peanut butter out of the jar, tears streaming down her face. "Hormones," she said. Daniel would have told her which ones; I'd have corrected him. "You know what?" She pointed a sharp, narrow finger at her developing belly. "We're gonna make this bitch the next Meryl Streep. Or the next fucking Uma Thurman, if she somehow gets your bones." She scraped the Skippy jar clean. I told her she looked more like Uma, and I more like Meryl. "Right now we're too fat to be either," she laughed. It was true. "In New York, they'll call us fattics. They'll tell us all about fatness and just how fat we are." She scraped and scraped. "They're not loving in New York. They're not gonna like us. You and I, Izzie, we would do anything for love. That's one thing about us. We'd do anything for love." This was the third boyfriend to dump her. "At least he called me depthless. He meant it nicely. But he doesn't even know what it means," she said. "It means literally unfathomable. I'm unfathomably deep." She put the empty jar down. "I hate that everyone's so fucking nice to me." But then she winked at me like, It's time for us to go.

On the day of my first prenatal, Daniel walked into the room. It was another unseasonably cold day, and I was desperate for Daniel to say so. But he didn't recognize me. Not because of my bruises, but because he refused to look at my face. He kept his head down. Still, even in this posture I could tell his beauty was undiminished. If anything he looked tan, although in a passive way, like he'd spent a fortnight under the fractured shade of some immaculate eucalyptus. The only thing that had changed was his medical team: He was no longer with the blonds, but rather with two women, one of whom was named Rebecca Apple. Rebecca went first. She was a genius. I knew this right away. Intelligence buzzed bright around her face. She had the gentle authority of a docent and walked me through my body like I was spread around a room.

Daniel nearly failed in comparison. He was too confident to be useful. He asked me no questions When it came time for the breast exam, he didn't press hard enough on my tissue. Had there been any swollen lymphs, he'd have missed them, and I'd have gone on to die.

I convinced myself he was shy. He couldn't engage in the tension we'd developed, because that would require action. And he couldn't act because that would require strength. And he was not strong because he was too eternally dumb for that. Around this time I started thinking (and I still think, even now): My god, it's gotta be so beautiful to be so dumb. To be born with such a stagnant little forever face. To be born so entitled to a certain eternity. It's gotta be like nothing just to live and live and live and live!

Anyway, yes, throughout the prenatal, Daniel checked me like I was just another patient. He attended only to my most basic needs. He answered my most fundamental questions. There were no more warm, misguided assurances. He began speaking to me with clinical perfection and yet—you might even say, therefore—I sensed him escaping me. Where did you go? I wanted to ask him. Daniel! I loved your prior idiocy. This new idiocy of complete composure and competence is darker, is not so good. My sister said: Over time, competence comes to replace personality. She said: Do not trust a professional man. Still, I held out hope for Daniel. I convinced myself there must be more of him—a depth in him. I dared myself to find it, perhaps even to create it.

Daniel's block. The length of the journey from my own apartment is not what I'd call prohibitive. I began visiting it weekly. He lived along the East River, but I didn't mind the smell. Early on in my visitations, a woman emerged from his building.

"Hi there," I said to her. She turned to face me. She was elderly. Each cheek a sheet of congealed milk. The dog she was walking took a sour pee. "Do you know if Daniel lives around here?" My sister had promised that eventually New York would come to feel like a small town, where everyone knew everyone. The woman shoved her hearing aid farther up her ear canal. I tried to look innocent. I took a deep breath, cradled my womb, and swayed in a way that was supposed to seem unconscious. The woman didn't notice. "If there's?" she asked. "A Danielle's around here?"

"Danielle!" I felt myself smiling. "Yes, that's my sister's name. They're very similar." I didn't explain to her that, of course, Danielle was still back in Utah, in eternity, because of being dead with the baby inside her, because that news could kill someone and this woman was near enough to death.

"Yes!" The woman echoed my enthusiasm. "Danielle's Consignment. Around the corner, on First. There's a sale."

"Oh, thank you," I said. I squatted down in a fetchingly laborious gesture and let her pup lick my fingers. "I love you!" I yelled at it.

That evening I waited until seven, watched the moon be cute with clouds. Daniel didn't come. I was not discouraged. Next time, I thought.

On my walk to the train, I was surprised to find Danielle's Consignment still open. I went in and bought myself a dress. It was pleated and had strawberries scattered all over. The fabric was stiff, almost crisp, but in my sleep it softened onto me.

Soon I had a Monday off. I had never workdayed Daniel's block before. I decided to try his street in the early morning.

It was chilly. I didn't mind. I headed for the esplanade, a cobblestoned walking path along the East River. Joggers passed me. I stood, breathing deep into my pelvic region, cradling the air in there. There was no real railing along the esplanade—just a squat ledge—so I bent way down and got all beglittered in sea spray. My hair whipped around my neck and across my mouth. For the first time in a long time I felt myself being beautiful. I licked the salt off my lips and listened to my stomach growl. A surge of warmth ran up my legs as my dress billowed riverward.

An hour passed. Another. I stood silent at the edge of the earth. Then, as you all know, I fell in. Not down into the water, but backward, into the steep ravine that's cracked up my brain. And then what happens is what has been happening ever since, where I'm down on the floor of neural matter, and my sister's there reminding me about hysterical strength, and how two girls on a farm nearby lifted a tractor off their father. And how, before that, over in Kanarraville, a mother lifted a car off her tot. How this mother had arms thin as wheat stalk, yet still she managed. She's holding forth in oracular fashion. She's telling me all about how nothing comes of nothing! I tell her okay, all right. I tell her to give me a second. I'm just waiting. I have time.

Eventually, I'm pretty sure I crawled back up my brain. The world rematerialized. The river regained its current, the wind its coercion.

And it's then, before I have even seen him—in that infinitesimal second between impression and cognition (that no-man's-land of perception, perhaps our only true reality)—that Daniel is before me. Or, rather, he's past me. He has run by. A red thermal shirt. Black shorts. Two white stripes down the side. My voice catches when I try to say his name, so I scream it. He glances back. Sees me. Keeps running. "Daniel!" I breathe deep and then gesture toward my womb, like, *remember?* You need to understand that I'm not sure what I meant, because in my brain there's this grisly collision of memory and prophecy taking place, and it's like I can hear it—the impact—but, I have to tell you, I don't think about it. I just sprint.

They ask me how a girl like me could do it. They're skeptical. They say I'm made of myth. But getting him into the river wasn't hard—I was larger, fuller than him. Plus, he was right where the ledge dips to knee-height. One solid drive into his side and we were submerged together. It was keeping him under that tested me. *Push*—I was my own counsel. And so I pushed. In the moments when my head breached the water I heard our splashing. But underwater all was velvet and muted. All of my sounds were internal. The way you can laugh deep inside yourself.

Soon, though, there was the elastic snap of Daniel's shoulders as he pulsed under my palms; his bulby body, his trapezius, where I sat as I wrapped my thighs tight around his neck. I squeezed harder and held steady as he tried to kick up. At one point, I got to press my nose into his hair, which had turned silky. I got to touch his jaw. I slipped my tongue into his ear, and got to touch all over his big, eternal head. It was everything I ever wanted. At last, my legs still latched, I felt his limbs shut down one by one. His whole body grew slack as a child's. Finally he became so heavy that I had to spread my legs. My sister kicked through me as I released him.

"It's twenty-three weeks, so it's a fat little eggplant," my sister said over the phone. She was driving back from her appointment, and I heard her grin spreading, the sound of her sucking a sour-apple Altoid, her scarf ruffling around her neck, her wipers clearing the snow. Over the last five months her baby had graduated from seed to blueberry to lemon to peach to pear. Now eggplant. What to make with an eggplant? I told her I could make a parmesan—"but without the cheese," we agreed. Our lactose intolerance would not be a problem once we are actresses in New York, where we'd buy cheesecakes and cannolis at vegan patisseries. Even though they'd cost bank. On the phone, I suggested we could always pawn the baby if we couldn't afford the sweets. She agreed. "Right. We can't afford to lose weight in New York," she said. "That'd be cliche." Her appointment ended at eleven. By then it was snowing. It was unseasonably cold. Later, on the news, they announced the pregnant woman was killed at "lunchtime." The local reporter shook her head and asked the news anchor, "The other driver—drunk by lunch?" The anchor didn't look into the camera; he stacked his script, cleared his throat, and said, "A gruesome event, folks . . ." Another throat-clearing, a glance toward the weatherman. "Only in Utah, where today it is unseasonably—"

LYN DI IORIO

Maritza and Carmen

FROM *The Georgia Review*

LATE ON A May night, with no more customers in the café, Juancho and Maritza sat in the marquesina, the carport which they used as a patio, soaking their feet in plastic basins filled with cool water. In the light, the leaves of the hibiscus shrubs behind the latticed wall made shadows that waved like little hands. The latticed concrete wall divided the carport from the house and yard next door. During the day the humidity in the carport was stifling, but Juancho loved being out here at night, when the air was sweet with the fragrance of tuberoses and the breeze cleansed his throat of the heavy oil smell of the kitchen. In their lawn chairs, with a little table between them, they faced the café's yard and its four trees: mango, avocado, jobo, and sweet lemon. When Maritza first showed up at the café, a year ago, she was unable to sit without jiggling her knee and vaping. She no longer did either. He knew that she too found herself soothed by the place: the chirping coquís and mole crickets, the tree branches rustling as if talking to each other. Now and then they heard the click-tap-click of fruit bats in the mango tree. Maritza had started growing tomatoes, okra, basil, anamú, and flowers on the far side of the yard. She could see them now from where she sat. In a few minutes, when her feet no longer pulsed from exhaustion, she would get up and water her plants.

Juancho was reading *El Nuevo Día*. Sometimes he read it on his laptop, but today he had a paper copy. He enjoyed its ink smell and how the paper crackled in his hands. It was like opening a present. He read an article about draft prospects for Matthew Lugo. Done with the sports section, he leafed back-to-front, his mind veering to what he wanted to cook tomorrow: plantains baked with a ground beef stuffing, called Pio Nono and named for Pope Pius IX, his mother told him when she first made it for him. With its rich sauce and candy-sweet plantains, the dish conveyed family comfort and criollo identity for Juancho, and he was excited for Maritza to taste it. He was still thinking of where to get yellow but not overripe plantains when an image caught his eye in the paper.

The woman in the photographs was dressed in a midnight-blue police uniform, had hair dyed reddish orange like a clown's, and a pillowy body cinched tight by her belt. Like her body, her face was much heavier than Maritza's. Carmen . . . ?? Not the same name, no, and her face was half-obscured by a police hat. But he recognized the smile that lit up those hazel eyes. It was Maritza, undoubtedly.

"¡Que rayos!" Juancho kicked the basin. Water splashed out on the concrete floor.

"¿Qué fue?" Maritza tilted her head.

Juancho's throat felt thick. He plucked his feet from the basin and squatted next to Maritza's lawn chair, pointing at the two pictures. She examined first the one of the policewoman being given a plaque by a police captain. The caption said that the woman's name was Officer Carmen Sandín de O'Farrell. She was being commended for rescuing victims of Hurricane Irma. In the second picture, she was dressed in the same uniform, with the same bizarre hair and body like a large pillow squeezed tight by a belt. Her arm was around a teenaged girl's waist: Taína O'Farrell. This was her daughter, the caption said, whom she had saved by *sacrificing herself heroically in Hurricane Maria.*

She had been fucked over by Hurricane Maria. Everybody had been, of course—many had lost whole houses and some had lost people they loved. But Maritza had lost herself.

Her self—her previous self. It was as distressing, in some

ways, to realize she had been in the police as it was to realize she had worn her hair like that. The turning point in her life had been her arrival in San Juan. She had told Juancho about her memory problem as soon as she applied for the cashier position, revealing that she called herself "Maritza" after her favorite rescuer, a young Nuyorican woman who had spotted her body under a door on the side of the road in Arecibo.

Her past life, while unyielding of so many details, pressed close, in a way that often made her feel breathless. It held shapes in dim light that revealed themselves stintingly: a colonial-style church with two red cupolas; a fountain in a Spanish-style plaza; uphill streets lined with empty buildings and almond trees clustered with pods like open mouths.

However, these were features of many northern and eastern island towns. Which was her town?

Still other shapes were obscured, moving in the darkness of waking dreams in which she would watch them, darker than the darkness around them. Those shapes moved stickily, as if a velvet sheet had been thrown over them and they were struggling to free themselves. Sometimes things slipped out from under the sticky sheet: a horse so skinny its ribs shone through its skin, an eyeless stone frog, a yellow ruler with the numbers and lines erased. These objects left her with a feeling of irritation; she understood that they symbolized her deprivation, yet they brought her no closer to recalling names and places.

She had been freed (at least her body had been taken out from under that door). But when she lay in bed and saw some of the shapes that slid from under the velvet sheet, she was afraid that she would again be covered by that sticky darkness.

Since she had met Juancho, however, she had built a nice life, managing the café and loving him, the veteran of one war and two failed marriages, with an adult son he had not a lot to say to. Juancho was gentle and laid back, his hair was silvery, his skin the color of light amber honey. He smelled like mint and sweet lemon and had a deep belly laugh. He was a good cook and a hard worker and they had fun in bed.

The shapes that struggled under the sticky velvet gave her

the feeling that her previous life was nowhere near as good as this one.

Maritza had forgotten names, including her own, but so many news stories about how Hurricane Maria made landfall allowed her to access her own impression of the moment of impact, different from what others described. For example, some reporters had compared the sound of the wind to a woman's endless screams. Maritza, on the other hand, remembered that, rather than blowing wind, Maria had endless inbreath, sucking up the sky's blue and the land's many greens until the entire world darkened to shades of charcoal, graphite, and ash. In the tomb-like darkness filled with the endless insuck of the wind and of tree branches breaking against the car she was driving, Maritza lost control of the wheel. The car moved under her, rolling in floodwater like a boat but enclosing her in tunnel-like darkness like a coffin.

There was the crackling noise of power lines pelting the coffin-boat-car.

The wind chewed up the glass of the windows and water exploded into the car. Still pitching forward, the car started to sink.

The car was never found. When asked by her rescuers in Arecibo, she couldn't recall the names of family members, although she did remember that her father had been a teacher and that he was dead. But she did not remember the name of the town where she grew up or where she had been living. She could not remember what her job was or whether she was married and had children or even what make of car she had been driving.

When it rained, Maritza tried Juancho's patience by opening all the louvered screened windows in his—now their—second-floor apartment, which overlooked the café. He didn't understand why someone who was so afraid of storms would open all the windows when it rained. It had to be the opposite; he tried getting her to internalize that.

"Yo sé, yo sé." She would look away, half-smiling, the fingers of one hand encircling her other wrist.

But the next time it rained, she'd do it again: open all the windows. With the rain hitting the stone-tiled floors like javelins, she would stand in the hallway as still as a statue. The hallway was dark and narrow and gave onto the bedrooms, the bathroom, and the living room. She would close the doors to all the rooms so that the hallway was the only space that stayed dry. As if they were playing a game, Juancho would close the windows. But once he did that, she'd glide away from the hallway and open the windows again. He'd have to mop up the floors and wipe down the walls after every storm. Otherwise, mold would creep along the walls almost instantly, like shadows.

He never saw Maritza so quiet as when she stood in the dark, closed-off hallway, with the rain spitting through the windows in the rest of the apartment, messing up his floors. She wasn't just petrified with fear. When it rained, she was just not there. He had touched her once when she stood behind the hall door. She looked through him. He looked behind him, and of course there was only the opposite wall of the hallway. The way that the strong rains made her disappear like that was why he stopped complaining about all the mopping he had to do.

"Does it make you remember what happened?" he asked one time when she was hiding out in the hallway during a rainstorm.

Standing still, her only movement was the swiveling of her eyes. "Juancho, the blue light! It filled the car." She held her hands out. "It hurt!" she said. When he put his hands on her forearms to steady her, she snatched them back.

He asked if it was lightning she remembered.

She didn't know. She couldn't remember whether the blue light appeared just before the car started its yawing movement in the floodwater or right after the world was drained of color.

She said her hands were burned and she let them fall into the water where they flopped around like fish. Burned fish.

She looked up from the newspaper. "Sandín." Her hand flew to her mouth. There seemed to be more yellow flecks than usual in her hazel eyes. "Ay, I remember. My uncle was mayor . . . of Vega Baja: Ángel Sandín. My father was Alejandro Sandín. I am of the Sandíns of Vega Baja."

"And your name is Carmen?"

She had a flash of a woman kissing her. The woman had called her "Carmencita." A woman with brown-purple eyes; silver-streaked black hair tied in a bun at the nape of the neck; yellowish sallow skin; and a dazzling smile, which she herself had inherited. Her mother was Carmen.

"Yes, Carmen. That was my name, I was named for Mami." But beyond her mother's face with its surprising eyes, objects receded and additional details about her mother did not come to her.

"And 'O'Farrell'? The article says that was your ex-husband's name," Juancho said. "He lives in the States. Do you remember him?"

"I don't remember him."

"He's a gringo, it seems."

She laughed.

"Why do you laugh?"

"Why take up time trying to remember a man I divorced? I have you."

"So, then I should call you Carmen?"

She looked at the picture of the woman with the unfortunate hair. "I like being Maritza with you. I feel more like Maritza."

Juancho was relieved, not because she did not remember the other man and did not seem to want to remember him, but because he also felt that the name Maritza suited her better than Carmen. The name Maritza seemed lighter, laid back, vivacious, not to mention sexy. There was something jagged and blunt about the woman in the photo.

"Then I will keep on calling you Maritza."

"My uniform is so tight in these pictures and I'm so chubby. And that dyed hair—like iodine! I don't remember *ever* wearing a uniform. Why would I join the police? I don't like the police, their questions and procedures. I don't remember having hair that ugly color. But this man in the hat . . ."

She put her finger on the picture of the man.

The captain's dress hat worn by the man was almost black, with gold-embroidered oak leaves on it. Flashy but so stiff it looked like an embalmed bird. He was a big-shouldered, bearded man, rather handsome.

"The man in the hat is Eduardo," Maritza said. "We were novios in high school. But I don't remember when he gave me this . . . prize . . . whatever it is. I don't remember working with him or for him. I remember when we were teenagers. I remember he married young."

Carmen (her former self) had loved Eduardo when he was a boy, but he married Alicia. Alicia had naturally red hair, unusual on the island. Was Carmen's hair so bleedingly red because she had tried to imitate Alicia? In the photograph, she couldn't help noticing, and hoped Juancho had not noticed, that Carmen was staring at Eduardo as if he was, as the island truism would have it, *the last Coca-Cola in the desert.*

Yes, she remembered, even as a teenager, she had been in a triangle with Eduardo and Alicia. She would wait for Eduardo to meet her in an abandoned shack near the Cibuco River. There was a mattress and an old oil lamp inside but no glass on the windows. At night there could be caculos, those large beetles that flew around in fast zigzags. They made a rattling noise before landing on your head.

Was the lust with which she gazed at Eduardo unrequited?

It was pretty obvious. While she stared at him, Eduardo was staring at the camera.

"What about this girl?" Juancho pointed at the picture of the policewoman with her arm around a teenaged girl. "Your daughter. Don't you remember your daughter?" Juancho sounded scandalized.

The teenager was lovely, with a heart-shaped face and a vampy widow's peak, large, heavy-lashed brown eyes, and plump lips. Unlike Carmen's, the girl's body was sensuous yet lithe in a sleeveless blue dress that accentuated her curves but did not cling to them.

"I don't remember her. But her smile is like mine, really it's better. ¡Que linda es!"

The article said that Carmen had resided with her daughter, first in the States, where the girl grew up, and later, for a year, in Vega Baja. While she could not place the girl in the context of Vega Baja, just reading that they'd lived in the States allowed her to half-remember: a house that smelled of firewood; a winter sky that went gray at 4 P.M.; the wonder of snow warming up the atmosphere and turning the sky pink and powdery; and the man with yellow hair and a lumpy, veined nose. The more he drank, the duller his eyes got. David was his name. She shuddered.

For some reason, it was her mother's face that came to her clearly now: the warmth of her mother's beautiful eyes, a curious shade like the center of oncidium orchids. Her mother was long dead, she now knew. Why did she not recall this stunning girl in the picture, who was very much alive, who was now applying to colleges? The girl was looking for the mother who had saved her, the article said. Her daughter. It seemed she had given life to the girl not once but twice.

"I remember Vega Baja now," Maritza said. "My town has beaches, rivers, and lagoons. The way some lakes are replete with fish, our lagoon and rivers are filled with caimans. People eat them. Their meat is dense but also flaky and buttery. Like a tarpon ate a chicken."

"Okay, I could make . . . uh, caiman, if you miss it. But the girl," he said. He looked worried, poor Juancho. He probably was thinking, *What else don't I know?* "The girl is named Taína. You named her that."

"So many people name their daughters that," Maritza said. "I can't understand why I didn't give her a more unique name. Why didn't I name her after a flower: 'Azucena' or 'Lirio' or even 'Amaryllis'? I don't remember much about her," she said.

He was puzzled that she seemed so placid. "Don't you remember giving birth to her?"

His cue helped her see a woman lying on a hospital bed, a doctor and a nurse next to the bed. The woman's eyes were closed, her face gray and slick with sweat.

"I think I had a fever and was sick when I had her," Maritza said.

But then she remembered that it was her own mother, Carmen, who'd had puerperal fever and that her mother had not been able to nurse baby Carmen because her milk was infected.

She decided not to tell him that she wasn't sure whether she'd had the fever or not, whether or not she was remembering her daughter's birth or just imposing the circumstance of her own. Eyes narrowed, arms crossed, Juancho seemed to be judging her. She blinked a few times, scratched her neck and started reading aloud:

Carmen Sandín de O'Farrell distinguished herself as a heroine of the hurricanes of 2017. In Hurricane Irma, she rescued townspeople whose homes had been flooded when the Cibuco River in Vega Baja overran its banks. Two weeks later, in Hurricane Maria she saved her daughter, Taína O'Farrell, and another adolescent named Pito Ávila, rescuing them from a shack near the Cibuco. Her daughter has been haunted by her mother's last moments when Sandín de O'Farrell opened the door to her police cruiser and tried to pull her daughter into it. The vermin-filled floodwater rose suddenly and took the car with Sandín de O'Farrell in it. Her body was one of hundreds never recovered. In a testament to a daughter's love, Taína O'Farrell has persisted in searching for her mother.

The words *haunted, tried to pull her daughter into it,* and *vermin-filled floodwater,* helped her see herself as Carmen, sitting in the car seat, braced against the rising water, heavy as cement yet also roiling with centipedes and squirmy things and swaying over the sill into the car.

Ah now, yes: The girl screamed at her—eyes narrow, mouth taking up her whole face—that she was a "¡bruta!"—a stupid woman.

What came to her then was not *Why did she call me that?* What struck her was that she had screamed the same thing to her own mother when she was a girl.

Her mother had turned away, frowning, brown-purple eyes lidded. Yes, she also had called her mother a "¡bruta!"—a stupid woman who had allowed a bad man into their home.

Her mother had slapped her hard, so hard her teeth cut into the inside of her cheek.

"Muchachita de mierda!" her mother, Carmen, screamed.

They were outside in a patio, the sun like an exploding chandelier. When the man she was afraid of walked out of the house, she couldn't see his face.

And then she knew that she had slapped her daughter too the day Maria came. Was that why her daughter called her a "bruta"? Her mother had never understood her—that much came to her. Perhaps, similarly, she had not really understood her daughter?

Her head hurt suddenly as if all at once she felt the impact of the slap she had given and the slap she had been given.

She got up from her chair and leaned against Juancho's shoulder and he held her. Something shone in the mango tree like an emerald shattering in the air. A colibrí—a hummingbird? She thought she should cry, and she tried to, but she couldn't get any tears out. Were there any in there?

He smiled at her, this nice fifty-one-year-old with silver hair and a tanned, surprisingly young and muscular face. He wore a white T-shirt that said I'M NOT YELLING, I'M PUERTO RICAN.

"Do you want to meet her . . . your daughter?" he asked.

Instead of responding, she left the marquesina and opened the screen door to the café. An old chalkboard held the menu scribbled in both Spanish and English. The white walls were lined with potted plants and laminated, wood-backed copies of silkscreens by the painter Luis Cajiga. The small square café tables were covered in plastic tablecloths patterned with fruit and flowers and topped with empty rum bottles. These held Maritza's own arrangements of azucenas—island tuberoses—and frangipanis. She pulled an azucena out of a bottle and held it to her nose. It smelled creamy and sweet, but its hollow stalk was already limp, its petals starting to brown on the edges.

She heard him come in behind her.

"The azucenas faded," she said. She went from table to table, removing the azucenas from the rum bottles.

"We should contact your daughter, Taína. She must miss you so much."

She didn't answer him. The word *daughter* floored her. Why did she not feel more motherly? She went to the last table. The half-length Cajiga reproduction hanging over it was the

Mujer con Sombrero Negro, a portrait of a beautiful woman with clay-brown skin wearing a large-brimmed black hat that was indistinguishable from the color of her hair. She wore a strapless dress. Her arms were held over her head just below the hat brim. One hand clasped her other upper arm so that her elbows framed her face. It looked like there was a big shadow floating over her head and the woman was holding the shadow aloft.

"We should tell her you are alive," Juancho said.

The shadow in the picture pressed down on the woman who nonetheless was preventing the shadow from crushing her. But also she was caressing the shadow.

"Yo sé," she said. Like she said when he told her that the windows must be shut, not opened, against the rain.

"When you see her, you will remember her completely," he said. "Everything will be fine." He tried to take her in his arms again, but she moved away. "You will remember."

She said nothing. She was not afraid that she would not remember more details. She was afraid that remembering would not make her feel anything different from what she felt now when she looked at the girl in the newspaper. She felt curiosity and she admired the girl's beauty. Maritza herself was not beautiful. To go by the pictures in the paper, her former self, Carmen, was close to ugly.

She was surprised that this lovely girl had come from her body but was outside in the world, feeling and doing things Maritza, such a different person clearly from this luminous young woman, could never feel or do. But Maritza did not feel love, and that was troubling. Even if you forgot so many other things, wasn't love something you remembered?

Juancho had been right that seeing the girl would make her remember more. The problem was that in the end it didn't help her remember as much as she would have liked. She wondered if that might be true, too, for the girl.

The girl stood in the marquesina and gave Maritza a hard-elbowed embrace that made Maritza's heart quicken. This was not some unknown girl but her daughter, Taína, Maritza reminded herself. Her hija. Hijita. Why couldn't she remember ever calling tenderly for her hijita? But she couldn't say, even think, that word *hija* much just now. *Taína* would have to do.

Taína's dark eyes, small perfect nose, thick eyebrows, and wide mouth in a heart-shaped face were different from Maritza's river-colored eyes, thin brows, flat nose, and thin lips. Taína had long, wavy, fine dark brown hair. Maritza's hair was thick and short and gray-streaked. But the wide, full-cheeked smile that lit up Taína's face mirrored the way Maritza smiled when she was happy. She was not smiling like that now. Maritza's smile was quite perfunctory.

Taína was voluptuous in her white eyelet blouse, ivory linen pants, and lavender high heels. Maritza, on the other hand, was thin and dressed in blue jeans and a retro green cotton blouse that accented her hazel eyes.

Juancho wore a guayabera, pressed pants, and oyster-colored wingtip oxfords, his best shoes, which he only wore on holidays. He introduced himself.

Right away, Taína asked how her mother and Juancho had met.

"There was a sign on the café door advertising a cashier position," Juancho said.

"How did you get to San Juan?" Taína asked Maritza.

"The clinic in Arecibo found a shelter for me," Maritza said. There was a pause. "It's hot," Maritza said. "We could go inside with the air-conditioning, although there are people in the café just now."

"I like it here with the trees," Taína said. "It's different from my apartment. Our apartment, I mean."

Maritza and Taína sat in the lawn chairs facing the trees in the yard. The mango tree was tall and queenly. It was in fruit, the fruit shaded in red, orange, and green, almost globular and ready to be picked. The sweet lemons were mottled green and yellow. The avocado and jobo trees were not in fruit. The leaves of the avocado tree were thick and shiny like patent leather.

Maritza was fascinated by how pretty Taína was. It was hard to recognize herself in these features except for the sudden smile that, like her own, had an effect like the sun sliding out from behind clouds.

"You are a beauty. You must have a boyfriend," Maritza said.

"There were two boys I'd been going out with when the storm hit, Mami." The girl smiled with Maritza's smile. "You loved one and kind of hated the other."

"Did you like the one I hated and hate the one I loved?"

"Ay, Mami, I liked them both, but I preferred kissing the one you hated." Taína laughed.

Mami this, Mami that—she was this strong-willed seventeen-year-old girl's mother! When she was seventeen, Maritza remembered, her own parents would sit behind the latticed balcony wall and watch her drive away with her friends. When she returned, at the time her parents had prescribed, they'd still be sitting behind the latticed wall, as if they'd never moved, watching as she got out of the car.

"Did I give you a curfew?" Maritza asked.

"You drove Felo and me everywhere. Felo was the one you liked. You hated Pito, but you didn't know I was seeing him too. Pito was the one I was with when you went looking for me . . ."

Maritza didn't remember these boys, the one she hated or the one she loved. It sounded like she'd been a little tedious as a mother. Maybe all this crushing of nuance was why her former self had liked police work. Although, it seemed to her now that her obsession with Eduardo must have made her follow him into the police force. She wondered if she'd had an affair with him.

Taína talked about how the apartment that they had lived in together had black mold after Maria. FEMA had taken six months to clean it up.

"Now, I'm back there, in my room, but I have a different bed. My old dresser with its mirror is gone. You were always telling me I shouldn't check myself out in the mirror so much. ¿Te acuerdas?"

Maritza shook her head, no. Carmen sounded so uptight.

"My new dresser doesn't have a mirror. I'm glad . . . I think you were right that I was vain."

Maritza, recalling that her own mother had told her the very same thing, suspected that she'd been jealous of her gorgeous daughter. Just as her own mother had been jealous of Carmen.

Juancho brought mango shakes in tall, thick glasses with straws and then left them.

Maritza and the girl sipped their mango shakes, which were as thick and cold and fragrant as ice cream. "Que rico." The girl sipped her shake through the straw like a slurpy. She had beautiful teeth. Maritza herself was missing her top back molars—something that a dentist she now saw said was an old situation. She wanted to ask the girl if she knew how she had lost her teeth but realized that might be too trivial a question. She found that most of the things she wanted to know were trivial. What had been her favorite dessert? Did she like dogs or cats better? Did she have a vibrator? Did she go to church every Sunday? Had she ever mentioned her obsession with Eduardo? Was the hideous red wig due to some envy of Eduardo's red-haired wife that she'd carried for decades? A downside to meeting her daughter was discovering that she had probably been a very boring person.

"Juancho is a wonderful cook," Maritza said absently.

Maritza noticed that the light pink hibiscuses behind the concrete lattice wall were now half-unfurled. Their pistils, just starting to show, looked like bottle brushes. The shadows the hibiscuses cast on the concrete floor looked like the faces of elves.

Taína herself looked like an elf, dark-haired, glowy-skinned, otherworldly.

Taína finished her shake and put her empty glass on the patio table. "Mami," Taína said, leaning forward, her eyes staring into Maritza's. Maritza blinked and looked away.

"Mami, I never knew . . ." Taína looked down. "What it was to really miss someone until you disappeared. I never felt so lonely. It wasn't like when you divorced Dad. It was like I lost a hand or a foot."

Maritza understood that Taína had rehearsed these words many times, probably too many times. Not because she didn't feel the right thing. Taína scratched her nose until it was red and Maritza then remembered the gesture. She understood that the girl was overwhelmed with sadness and Maritza felt a flicker of envy.

"I'm sorry," Taína said. "I was always trying to get away from you. And when you were gone, all I wanted was to get back to you, to . . ."

Maritza put a hand straight up. "Mira—"

"I missed you so much, Mami." Oh no, tears. How to respond? Should Maritza take her in her arms? *Take her, take her, hold her, soothe her.* But Maritza couldn't move.

Maritza tried again for tears that would at least express her own frustration. As so many times before, the tears would not come. Not because the feeling wasn't there. The feeling was there, but it was submerged.

Maritza nodded and moved her hand toward Taína and the girl reached out to touch her. Taína's hand was as warm as bread.

"I need to tell you, there is little that I remember . . ." Maritza had been about to say *little that I remember about you.* But that might devastate the girl.

Taína leaned forward in her lawn chair and touched Maritza's hand. "I thought maybe that's what happened. Because you didn't look for me. Either that or . . ."

"I died," Maritza said.

The girl nodded.

Carmen died, Maritza thought.

Her mother looked so different! She had been chubby and tired-looking, bossy and easily angered, evasive, always so on top of Taína and yet always disappearing, going on endless shift after shift or visiting homeless people in the town center. Secretive but explosive, her mother had liked to wear her police uniform even when she wasn't working. Her well-pressed uniform with its belt, holstered gun, taser, and tactical waterproof boots comprised her mother's only impressive outfit.

When she wasn't in uniform, however, her fashion choices had been regrettable. Her mother had worn cut-off shorts that showed her thick cellulite-ridden thighs or flowered house-dresses that made her look like a bedridden woman who watched soap operas all day. She had liked carrying elaborate raffia and crocheted purses and would put messy food in them, like the tomatoes she liked to eat whole as if they were apples, and which frequently got smashed, ruining the purses. Because her mother's hair was getting prematurely gray and not growing much, when she knew she'd be receiving the commendation for heroism, her mother had bought some wigs. She had become partial to wearing the wigs under her police hat. The wigs were annatto-red and curly. Taína wondered if she wore them because the police chief's wife had red hair. Unlike her police uniform, her mother's police hat was ridiculous. It was too broad at the crown and ostentatious with gold embroidery. Her mother was not responsible for choosing the hat, of course, but she often wore it with her shorts or housedresses like a sun hat.

Her mother had been talkative and disruptive, but this woman with the different name was quiet and reserved and thirty pounds thinner. Her jeans and top showed off her figure but were not too tight or vulgar. Taína could not believe how good this woman looked. How, well, sexual . . .

Her mother had insisted on divorcing Taína's father and bringing Taína to Vega Baja from New York. The buildings and houses that surrounded Vega Baja's central plaza had been abandoned long before Hurricane Maria. Named for Taína's granduncle, Ángel Sandín, who had been mayor and had helped pen the island's constitution, Vega Baja's high school had been rundown long before Taína and her mother even moved to the town. After Irma, black mold had seemed to creep like a living thing along the school hallways and up the walls, making it hard to breathe inside the school.

In Vega Baja, poor people lived on the side of the road and near the river in concrete boxes with old furniture and rusted car parts visible in their garages. The river had many turns like a snake. When it rained, the long snake slithered through the houses of the poor. Right after storms, caimans waddled out of the river, their jaws wide open, their teeth like stalactites and stalagmites, glistening wondrously.

Although she knew too well that they had come to the town because David O'Farrell had taken up with a woman only a year or two older than Taína, she was put off by the more backwater aspects of Vega Baja.

Unlike Taína, her mother, Carmen-now-Maritza, had thrived in Vega Baja by becoming a policewoman. In Hurricane Irma, she rescued people from houses overrun by the river. She even brought some people, mostly old women, home to sleep in

Taína's bed. For most of the two weeks between Irma and Maria, Taína had to sleep with her mother in the same bed. This was annoying, because Carmen honked and snored all night long. It interested Taína that, despite having been a charity case herself, Maritza, unlike Carmen, didn't look as if she went in for charity work.

Maritza also looked like she did not snore.

Taína's mother had been fearless, it was true. As the first rains of Maria started, her mother had tracked Taína and Taína's boyfriend, Pito, to a wooden shack near the Cibuco River. She had led them to her cruiser in the rain that fell like spears and the wind that dislodged, sucked up, and masticated everything in its path.

Her mother's cruiser slid away in the floodwater with her mother in it, and Taína and Pito ran for a cave that Taína knew of near the river. In the cave, they huddled on a rock shelf leading to an interior tunnel. They could so easily have drowned there, as so many did drown that day—in just that way—all over the island. Far too much water would have appeared, and they would have thought, *Ay, we can still get out of this* until the moment when they would have realized that they were done for. Floodwater rose in the cave and fist-size spiders, with gleaming legs like fork tines, crawled over Taína and Pito. At some point, Taína felt as if she had split off from herself and was watching from on high at the top of the cave as Pito hugged her. Taína covered his mouth with her hand so that the spiders wouldn't climb inside it. Their spiky legs stuck into her scalp as they crawled into her hair. There were so many spiders on their naked backs that, regarding herself and Pito from this impossible on-high perspective, the teenagers looked as if they wore some kind of mesh-like Gothy clothing with a spider motif.

But the spiders did not bite them. Taína realized that the spiders were sheltering on Pito and Taína, just as Pito and Taína in turn had sheltered on the rock shelf. As soon as she understood that, Taína came to and dropped back into a closer view of what was happening. She shushed Pito and knocked a few spiders off his back, hoping that the water would not rise higher than her chin because she didn't want to climb farther into the dark hole behind them, which no doubt led deeper into the network of caves in the hills.

But the water did rise and she and Pito slid into the hole. So did the spiders.

The sudden death of someone you think you hate as much as love can make you all at once become a more complex thinker. In the past eleven months, Taína had often thought of hateful things she had said to her mother. Said and done. She hardly regretted the feelings that had made her say and do those things. What she regretted was not expressing herself with nuance.

For instance, Taína had not been clear on the subject of Rafael. He was her mother's cousin. Taína had invited him to shelter with them the day before Maria was supposed to make landfall, but had not told her mother about it. Rafael was a middle-aged man with ash-dark skin and a graying buzzcut who lived in one of the concrete houses by the side of the road. Her mother had not told her that Rafael was their relative—one of her secrets—and when Taína found out she was mad about it.

But her mother had been right to shield her from Rafael, it turned out. Taína felt now she had a second chance. She wouldn't be a good daughter exactly. But she would certainly ask more questions. And she would be *nice*. She would say the *nice* things that she felt she had never said to her mother.

"I'm sorry I never told you how proud I was that you saved those people in Hurricane Irma," Taína said.

Her mother looked at her blankly.

"I know you don't remember, maybe," Taína continued. "But you were a hero. Everyone said so. I just . . . I didn't tell you I was proud. Because I . . ." She swallowed. "I was mad that you made us leave New York." Taína ran her fingers up and down her thighs. "I was a pendejita. You called me that a few times. Remember? You were right. I kind of was a pendejita."

Her mother's eyes finally became animated. Recognition. Maybe not completely of Taína.

"Angry, sí," Maritza said. "I remember you were angry. I remember you shouted at me. You shouted at me as we were getting into the car."

"We had a fight . . . earlier that day," Taína said. "About that guy, Rafael. We drove by his house every day. There was busted furniture and moldy mattresses in front. He kept animals in pens on both sides of the road, remember? They drowned too."

Her mother frowned. "What about horses?"

"He rented horses for riding, but they were too skinny." Taína sighed. "I didn't know he was your cousin. And you didn't tell me. I found out and I asked him to shelter with us. You got mad. It turned out he'd—he was a bad person—and that's why you kept him away."

"I remember my cousin Rafael." Maritza shook her head. "He touched me under my clothes when I was little. He told me he was allowed to do it. But I knew it wasn't right. I told my mother and my mother allowed him back in our house. Oh, it made me angry that she let him keep coming to the house." She was quiet a moment. "The things I remember most seem to be from when I was a girl."

"I'm sorry, Mami. I'm sorry I invited Rafael to shelter with us," Taína said. "I didn't know what he had done. You didn't want to tell me, and I understand that now."

"I remember him as a teenager, but not as a man," Maritza said.

"When he showed up, you took me into the kitchen and we didn't see that Rafael stole something from us. It was a stone pestle made by the Taínos, a real one. Do you remember?"

Her mother shook her head.

The girl shrugged. "It doesn't matter. But I loved it—Tío Ángel gave it to you. It was made of river rock. It looked like a skull face, and also like a frog's body. We were fighting and we didn't see him take it. And he left. Then you hit me because I had invited him without telling you. I was just . . ."

Taína massaged her left shoulder with her right hand. "I went off driving with my boyfriend even though the storm was coming. We went to the shack by the river." Taína looked tired. "We were stupid."

"That broken-down choza? I used to go there with Eduardo when I was young," Maritza said. As an afterthought, she added, "To have sex."

Taína stared at Maritza. Her mother, Carmen, would never have spoken like this, casually, without embarrassment about sex! Maritza's frankness was kind of cool, but also a little strange. Taína opened her mouth to say something, then brushed lint off her white pants.

Finally, Taína said, "The shack doesn't exist anymore." She did not have to say it was because of Maria. It seemed that almost everything was. She was tired of saying "Maria." *Maria, Maria, Maria, Maria, all the horrible sounds of the world in a single word.*

"So, you went there to have sex," Maritza said. "With Tito."

"Pito," Taína said.

"You went to have sex with Pito—"

"Don't you remember? You went looking for us because Maria was coming. Mami, you saved us."

The sound like trucks riding round and round the shack, about to run right through it. The girl naked on the bed, the boy fucking her fast and hard, the girl telling him to please slow down, her head turned to the side, eyes glazed.

That other boy touching her so long ago, touching her under her dress on her bed and her mother walking right by the room with the door slightly ajar. She pulled away from those hands that stabbed her like doctor's equipment. She went running after her mother and told her. Her mother had looked angry, but not at Rafael. Her mother shouted at *her.*

"I remember now that I didn't like Tito," Maritza said. "He lacked class."

"Pito." Taína smiled. "I broke up with him."

"It wasn't too bright going to have sex in the shack with the hurricane coming."

"Did you mostly forget Daddy too?" Taína asked.

But what she really wanted to know was why her mother seemed to remember these other people—her dead mother and Rafael, her asshole cousin—better than she remembered Taína.

Maritza didn't know how to answer, so she again touched her daughter's skin, warm with long-held sunlight.

"You didn't want to let Pito come in the cruiser with us," Taína finally said.

"What?"

"You pointed your taser at him and told him he couldn't come in the cruiser. That's why I yelled at you. I thought he would die if he didn't come with us. You were going to leave him there. Then a wave of water came and took you and the car."

The water that came into the cruiser was boiling with leeches and dead and dying things. A large rat, its body bloated but its eyes moving, looked into Carmen's eyes. Carmen kicked at the rat. The rat had bright, black, intelligent eyes, like a professor. It was still alive. She knew right away that, on top of the bad luck of being caught outside in the storm, this was extra bad, the way the rat seemed to be both alive and dead and looking so tenderly into her eyes.

She shouted at Taína to get in, but Taína pushed the boy ahead of her. Some of the wormy things from the water were clamped on the boy's naked body. Leeches covered his torso; a centipede was wrapped around his wrist; a lizard bit into an earlobe, hanging like an earring.

Not nearly as smart as the rat's, the boy's eyes were glazed over. Death was close.

Maritza-then-Carmen pointed her taser at the boy.

Her daughter, her own daughter, screamed and called her a "bruta" and slammed the cruiser door on her mother.

Yes, yes, the girl had slammed the door on her and a wave of water swept over the car, which filled with blue light and rolled away in the floodwater. And Carmen started her journey toward Maritza.

"That's what happened?" Maritza said. "The water came and took the car?"

Taína nodded.

"How did the door of the car close?" Maritza asked. It was a leading question, she knew.

"It stayed open. The water just took the car."

Maritza saw that the girl was not lying. Taína really did believe that. The girl did not remember that she herself had slammed the door of the car shut.

The girl had to believe it, of course. Maritza would not tell her otherwise. But then she'd always have to hold back this detail whenever she spoke to her daughter. How could she ever really talk to her?

Maritza remembered then what it was like to be a mother. It was shielding and protecting. Omitting things, even lying to protect the precious, but oh-so-difficult, child. The child that was part of you but also was becoming someone completely different and doing so in the blink of an eye. Much had to be— and clearly had been—sacrificed for this new person.

After the girl left, Juancho asked, "How did it go?"

"Taína is a nice girl, very intelligent. I have forgotten many things but now I remember a few more. In fact, she helped me remember the most important thing. On the other hand, she remembers almost everything but *not* the most important thing."

Maritza sucked in her lips and tilted her head, her eyes narrowed. "Because of that, I doubt that I will see her again."

Juancho stopped short, his jaw clenched; he clasped his hands, as if about to pray. "Don't be so drastic," he said. "You've only seen her once since that time, you can't make a decision like that so quickly." He shook his head.

"I didn't realize that she also had forgotten things that happened in Maria."

"Who has not?"

Maritza left the marquesina and went into the café.

Juancho followed her inside.

Egg-shaped lamps fitted to the sides of the walls provided a warm lemony light. While the air conditioning exhaled a slight smell of humidity, it made the interior cool and pleasant. A young woman, a customer who had quickly devoured her plate of crab-filled mofongo, had gotten up from her table and was examining the Cajiga reproductions as if she were in a gallery.

"Maritza, what is the most important thing?" Juancho said.

Maritza didn't respond.

"Tell me, what is it that you're afraid of?" he asked.

She was too ashamed to tell him. What she feared most was that perhaps it was that circumstances were the opposite of what they seemed. Perhaps it was not so much that she had loved her daughter and circumstances had made her forget. It could be that she had not loved her enough in the first place and it had been easy to let go.

Maritza bent over a cardboard box just inside the door and took out cuttings of white azucenas, purple alelís, and yellow bitter gourd flowers. She started putting the flowers in the rum bottles on the tables.

Despite being composed of the same flowers with the same colors, each posy of white, yellow, and purple flowers in its own bottle looked entirely different to her.

ISABELLE FANG

Gray, Cotton, White Lace Edges

FROM *McSweeney's*

ONCE EVENING HITS and preproduction officially wraps, May's in the bathroom slipping off her panties. She drops them into a Ziploc bag, then the Ziploc bag into a large envelope. She washes her hands. On the walk back to her desk, she passes Bridget and they smile goodbye. She adds today's note (Peach, Lace: googled pictures of the beaches in Honolulu) before sealing the envelope. She uses the prepaid postage because work's taken enough from May today; it's her turn. On the way home, she slides the envelope into a mailbox and texts Bill that it's on the way. At home, she rubs her eyes and opens her laptop. It's not until re-reading the flight confirmation for tomorrow, then refreshing her inbox twice, that she allows the workday to end. She peels off the rest of her clothes. She drags herself into the shower.

It wasn't always like this. May's panties used to come vacuum-sealed, tucked into boxes finished with ribbon. The ribbon always took too long to tie. More often than not, May needed a Christmas-gift-wrapping tutorial, to watch someone else's hands work through the motions first. This was back when May thought the packaging set her apart and she still had the instinct to work above her pay grade.

She started selling used panties her first year of film school, after a boy offered her one hundred dollars for her thong at a party. It was a bad joke that May escalated—she snatched the bill, slipped off her thong, offered it hanging from her index finger. The boy took her thong with a shaky hand and went on to use it in his freshman-year short film. As her life shifted over the years, May let the buyers dwindle, except for one. Bill has always been her favorite. He never requests anything too high-maintenance ("Wear them for five days so they smell just right"; "A few drops of period blood, don't leave anything gross"). He doesn't care if the panties are plain, lacy, or stained. He never haggles or hesitates over her pricing. His one request, always: "Please write down what you were doing while you were wearing them [☺ ♪]." Pre-Bill, May had always had the sneaking suspicion she'd be a better person if she journaled. But it was a habit she couldn't keep without someone on the other end, without stakes. Over the past six years, May's writing has condensed from full letters to field notes:

Blue, Cotton: Lunch with my mom
Pink, Boy Shorts: Laid in bed, ate a Hot Pocket
Lavender, Seamless: Got new boss coffee (splash of oat, 1/2 Splenda packet)
Black, Lace, G-String: Caught up with ex-boyfriend

For a while, May stopped daydreaming about her own life. Instead, she'd picture Bill: clumsy fingers tugging at a Christmas ribbon, ripping into shiny airtight plastic, a man lying in mountains of panties and paper. May never worries about posturing with Bill. He doesn't care if she lands the best entry-level job or moves the farthest from her hometown. Bill will read about May microwaving old Indian food while wearing a pair of baby-blue panties, and thank her for it. Maybe it's not a friendship, exactly, but it's the easiest relationship in May's life.

These days, May daydreams about earning Bridget's total trust. May can never picture the mechanics of it. Her chest stirs with the idea, with pride. Her hair's still wet while she's packing, dripping onto her laptop, shirts, bikini. Technically, May doesn't have enough experience to assist a producer on a show of this size. But it was the perfect storm: a new show that executives needed made fast and cheap, paired with Bridget, an eager producer who likes to mentor (and ran out of time to interview

more people). May falls asleep, grateful for all the infrastruc-
tural cracks and shortsighted decisions that led to her good
fortune. It's not the best job she's had, and far from the most
lucrative, but it has the shiniest contacts, the highest stakes. Tomorrow: her first business trip.

Bridget's waiting outside the airport, chewing on the straw of her
iced coffee and typing into her phone. She looks up just in time
to see May walk over. "Good morning! You excited?" Bridget
asks before hugging her. May apologizes for not arriving earlier,
but Bridget shrugs this off. She's forgiving that way. Once everyone's past security, May's body untenses.

At the gate, May gets a text. It's from Bill. *Thank you, these will
have to be my last pair. I can't buy from you anymore.* Before May can
process this, more typing: *But you mean a lot to me. Could we meet
for a goodbye dinner?* May re-reads Bill's texts, annoyed at him for
putting her in an uncomfortable position, annoyed at herself
for being sad about this ending. Bill adds that he'll pay and,
scout's honor, he only wants dinner. May doesn't know how to
say no, so instead she says she's traveling for work.

I'm gone for three months.

Where are you going?

North Carolina, then Hawaii.

That sounds nice. May hopes Bill will just fade out. But he goes
on. *You don't have to decide now. Go work, go enjoy. I'll still be here
when you get back, answer me then.*

The whole flight, May tries picturing herself at dinner with
Bill, but again she can't picture the mechanics of it. Imaginary
May won't walk to the table: Her legs become jelly or she just
stands in the doorway. Early on in their arrangement, Bill saw
they were in the same city and asked if they could ever meet.
May avoided it by saying she was too shy but maybe one day. Bill
was polite and told May not to worry about it, but May wonders
if this is him cashing in that one day now. She's unnerved that

something she built for most of her adult life is ending, and she wasn't even the one to end it. But she anchors herself in Bridget's snoring, the new people and responsibilities ahead of her.

In person, John's worse than advertised. During preproduction, he had been sad in a way that pushed past pity, mutated into something closer to sympathy. Most of John's slimy qualities (raving about his love of Asian women) were connected to a humanizing backstory (raised his kids alone after his Thai ex-wife left). But as he greets everyone, in a robe with his name stitched on the breast, they know they've miscalculated just how *much* John can be. May spots that his chest hair's been trimmed jaggedly, and even from three feet away she can smell him, a sugary-sweet bright blue (Arctic Freeze, Blue Raspberry, Fresh Glacier).

He thanks the producers and feigns surprise that anyone would find his love story worth documenting, despite the months he spent convincing production to pick him. But even though they're standing on his lawn today, they didn't pick John. They picked his nineteen-year-old fiancée from the Philippines, Ally. She's the perfect woman for viewers to hate (she uses John's credit card to pay for rent, skin care, dental work), yet still feel sympathy for (she's marrying fifty-three-year-old John).

In casting interviews, it was clear that Ally knew what people must think, but she laughed it off when probed by the producers. In a video of the two FaceTiming that John sent for casting, Ally kissed her webcam and said, "I love you!" Bridget dubbed it a "generic-brand I-love-you," meaning that based on the tone alone, Ally could've been saying she loved her dad, or a friend, or a celebrity. It lacked specificity, romance. For production, this sealed the deal.

They film a tour of John's home. He talks like it's *MTV Cribs*, like they're in a long-dead, simpler era of reality television. He still keeps a picture of his ex-wife on his nightstand, stacked on top of paperwork for Ally's K-1 visa, brain-dead to the optics. Instinctually, May pulls out her notebook, jots down the header "Beige, Seamless," and writes, "Toured a strange man's home." She remembers that Bill won't be buying anymore, and feels her face get hot. She scratches it all out and starts taking notes on the day's schedule.

May's own mother married young to leave. Her dad isn't quite like John, but to May, old men have a sameness: at least a little slimy, the same unoriginal tastes. May's parents left Taiwan together, but three years into their new life, May's father hired a babysitter. She showed up in jeans so low-rise that the zipper was only one inch long (at least this is how May's mother tells it). When the babysitter leaned over to hug May, she had a pink lace whale tail. May's father wasn't even there to see it. Still, this is when May's mother knew it was over.

May wants to call her mom now and remind herself that, in the end, her mom turned out fine. But her mom didn't move here all alone. And May's mom was twenty, not nineteen like Ally. There can be so much that happens in that year. On May's nineteenth birthday she went home for dinner with her mom. They finished the night with white wine and chocolate sheet cake. On May's twentieth birthday, her then boyfriend took her out for surf and turf he couldn't afford and then yelled at her for how he'd felt pressured to do so. May wrote about that night under the header "Red, Scalloped Lace."

At the airport, Ally doesn't look real at first; she's a blur running into John's arms. But then John grips Ally's arms and the meat of her bends to John's hands. Cameras adjust and Ally comes into focus: tan shoulders in a tank top, rainbow braces on her lower teeth, milia and sunspots across her cheeks. Ally still moves like a teenager, gangly limbs that she's never sure where to place. In an interview, Ally gushes that this was all she's daydreamed about for months. John asks if this is like she dreamed. "It's better."

But on the car ride home, Ally and John are already fighting. Later at night, recounting the day to a friend, May can't even remember what the fight was about, exactly. She can only retell the bones of it: John setting up a condition, Ally pushing back, John relenting but logging this in a list of grievances he started the morning he realized his ex-wife was gone.

The first pair of panties May sold Bill were Gray, Cotton, White Lace Edges. The day she wore them happened to be her last day of classes freshman year. She wrote about how bored she was, how she'd miss this, how she wasn't ready for much else. Her handwriting was small and uniform. It was just like taking real notes in class; to be diligent, studious. It was also just like when she first touched herself; to be excited, discreet.

When she read it back, she realized it was probably too chaste. So at the end, she made up a bit about actually touching herself. Then she spent ten minutes cutting and folding the letter into the shape of a heart, another touch she hoped would make it flirtier, racier. She tucked the heart into the folded panties. She mailed them on her way home for the summer.

John proposed to Ally spontaneously. "I woke up and her face was the first thing I saw. I knew this was how I wanted to start every single day, for the rest of our lives. I woke her up and proposed on the spot. She was confused but once she really woke up, she said, 'Of course!' I didn't even have a ring; I drew one on with a pen." Bridget asks what kind of diamond John drew onto Ally. "Diamond, solitaire."

Each morning, after Ally helps John shave, he redraws that engagement ring onto her finger. He's offered to buy her a real ring, but for now, Ally prefers this. "It's our tradition," she says, smiling. John kisses her hand before drawing a diamond across the thin hairs on Ally's knuckle.

John makes Ally breakfast the way his kids like it—two eggs sunny-side up, bacon extra crispy, buttered toast. Ally's not hungry, but she eats it all and thanks him. Later, while filming her confessional, Ally plays coy about her first night with John. She focuses instead on the morning: shaving John's stubble, the breakfast she didn't want, sharing a home.

Everyone's a professional; they film, they interview. But whenever anyone makes eye contact, they know they're all wondering the same thing: How could she love John, truly? Everyone counted on Ally's affection being more begrudging, formed around an understanding of the exchange. One camera guy, Dave, obsesses over a clip of Ally recounting how she used John's credit card to cover the extra cost of her rainbow braces. In the video, she flips her lower lip down to show off the braces, giggling. "She has no remorse; it's disgusting. I'm watching it again." A debate rages about whether Ally is hot enough to pull this off. Bridget tries cutting this talk short. It's gross and Ally *is* pulling it off, so what does it matter? Max, the producer most responsible for Ally, interjects that this matters plenty. "Audiences will wonder."

May wondered the same about herself when she first started selling panties. She drafted her site-bio and pricing fourteen times, numbering each version in a document. She borrowed a friend's ring light for the pictures and spent a whole Sunday getting the right shot. But once she posted, May found it didn't matter like she'd thought. The site was competitive, but most men bought at such a speed that they couldn't have thought twice about it.

Max has his assistant set up a Google Form to settle the debate. By a margin of just three votes, yes, Ally is hot enough to get away with it. What is "it," exactly? This is a whole other debate, one with too many possibilities for a clean vote. But they all know this show will scratch an itch, the kind that starts as a few irritated bumps before blossoming into a rash on an asshole.

"She loves him. In whatever way girls even love at nineteen, she loves him," May says. She sends the voice note to a friend, but it's not enough. She peeks into her shorts to check which panties she's wearing (Orange, Lace). She renders the day in field notes, ends with a question: "Do you remember what it was like to love at nineteen?"

When Bill received May's first letter, he circled the last paragraph, sent a picture of it to her, and asked, *Is this part true?* May was at dinner with childhood friends and had to excuse herself. In the bathroom, May paced, trying to decide how honest to be with him.

Yes. Why?

It doesn't sound like the rest of the letter.

I'm sorry, but I don't do refunds.

That's okay. I don't want one. I just thought I'd ask.

May stopped answering, too embarrassed, but Bill kept texting. At first to clarify, *It just didn't sound like you,* then to apologize, and apologize some more. By the third day, May was over her embarrassment and started to feel secondhand embarrassment for Bill. This was the first time May had tried picturing Bill, a man in his fifties, waiting by his phone like a teenager. At the end of the week, Bill placed another order and texted, *What I've been trying to say is that if that bit was a lie, you didn't have to do that for me. I wanted to read about your day. Your letter was very thoughtful.* [🌐 🗨 ✨]. May laughed to herself at how Bill sounded both like the fifty-something-year-old he was but also kind of like a fifteen-year-old girl. This was the most anyone had ever apologized to her. She wrote all this down in her next letter for him.

John has five kids. But only one matters, because only one still speaks to him, twenty-one-year-old Kate. The rest are collateral, backstory, faces to be blurred in post. Before Ally, Kate would visit every week for lunch. Since Ally, Kate's been downgraded to calls and texts. To the frustration of production, John and Ally fight about Kate at night, when the cameras are off. Bridget tried having John and Ally re-create their fight, but Ally refused. Bridget settles for the two doing separate interviews about it.

John's terrified of pushing Kate into meeting Ally. Whenever John talks about Kate, sweat gathers along his hairline and there's that bright blue smell again. In her interview, Ally says she didn't sacrifice her family only to be denied a new one. Still, John makes breakfast. But Ally doesn't eat; she cleans her braces and leaves for a walk. When John sees the leftover breakfast, he calls Kate. This, he won't let them film, he says, sequestering himself in his bathroom.

Thankfully, his mic is still on. "Yes, I know what I said before . . . I wouldn't ask if I had any real choice . . . Kate, please, I'll lose her . . . I'm not choosing anyone over anyone." Then, after a three-minute pause in which all hope seems to be lost, "Thank you, thank you, thank you."

Polka-Dot Hearts, White Lace Edges: Prepped appearance-release forms.

Kate's hesitating. John never told her about the TV part. May watches Bridget listen to Kate's worries. Bridget's eyebrows scrunch up in concern. That morning, while they touched base over coffee, Bridget told May she felt for Kate. "I can't imagine meeting my dad's girlfriend for the first time on TV like this." Without thinking, May overshared about her own father. "When I met his girlfriend, she lied and said she was twenty-three instead of twenty-two. As if that was better." Bridget's eyebrows scrunched up in the same way, before she ultimately laughed and rubbed May's back. May didn't need the comfort but relished that Bridget wanted to give it.

Now Bridget pulls May aside and whispers, "Talk to her. Don't push too hard but get her in there. You know what this is like." It's the first time Bridget has ever counted on May to solve a crisis. May, too nervous, doesn't jump into action. Bridget reads May's hesitation as an offense and adds, "Sorry, you know what I mean."

Bridget shoves a folded-up appearance-release form into May's back pocket, before sending her a few blocks away with Kate, to speak privately. They end up in the parking lot of a CVS. Kate leans against a brick wall and asks May to be honest. "How serious are they?"

May considers how honest to be. She decides to just recount footage: airport reunions, favorite breakfasts, ballpoint engagement rings.

"I need a second." Kate rubs the sides of her head, then starts pacing around the cars.

May met her own father's girlfriend when she was thirteen. It was Mother's Day but her dad insisted, and her mother relented so as not to seem bitter. Unbeknowst to May, they were using the day as a dry run, deciding if they were ready for children of their own. The girlfriend kept trying to hold May's hand whenever they crossed a street. Afterward, May knew it wasn't worth it (in this case, "it" being a relationship with her dad). Kate stops pacing and crouches in a handicapped parking space, her arms covering her head. "I don't know if I can go in there. I feel sick."

"You don't have to," May says and she almost means it too. May crouches down in front of Kate. "You don't even have to go back. I could call you an Uber and I'll tell everyone it's off." Kate takes her arms off her head. May continues, "But if you did go in and said whatever you needed to, everyone would understand. You wouldn't be the villain." May watches Kate's face for any change, and spots how Kate has her mother's eyes, the slope of her nose.

When Kate joins John and Ally, Bridget squeezes May's shoulder with pride. It feels undeserved, but still May basks in Bridget's silent praise. The dinner is as bad as production had hoped. Ally presses hard for Kate's approval, but Kate's not like her father, not as lonely.

After that first letter, May resolved never to lie to Bill again, never wanted to risk the embarrassment. But she never owned up to that first lie either. Bill responded to her letters in texts with follow-up questions: *How did class selection go?; Did he ever apologize about your 20th birthday?; How was the job interview?* May began writing about things she couldn't bring herself to tell the actual people in her life. Letters about classes she skipped, exes she shouldn't have gone back to, frustrating panty orders she dreaded filling.

Her friends would see May texting Bill and ask who she was talking to. May would lie and say her mom. She knew what her friends would say if they knew, make some joke or express concern about creeps, daddy issues. May often caught herself thinking the same thing. But when she thought about it more, her dynamic with Bill didn't feel like it compensated for anything about her dad, at least not consciously. Bill didn't occupy the same space in her mind. In May's mind, Bill was barely a real person. He was a place to house all her confessions, like a real journal.

*

On a sunny golf course, John vents to an old college buddy. It's their first time filming John and Ally apart for so long. May wonders what it's like for the crew at home with Ally, if it feels better to be on that side of it all. John's friend swings at the ball and says, "I don't see why you're doing this all over again."

"Doing what all over again?" John laughs.

"John." The friend drops his golf club, exasperated. "You know exactly what."

"Well, it's not the same. I'm older, wiser." John takes his swing. "I do worry she wants to go home. But I know the signs now. I can tell when someone's actually going to leave."

It's been ten days since Ally left the house, two since she left the bedroom for anything other than the bathroom. But, most important, there are only two weeks until their wedding in Hawaii and Ally refuses to go dress shopping. "It's too embarrassing. I don't have anyone to go with me." Ally pulls the duvet over her head. John sits next to the Ally-shaped lump and pets her. Dave films from the edge of the bed. Bridget and May watch from the doorway.

"You have me."

"That's not enough. I need friends; I need my mom."

"We can call her on FaceTime."

"No, she's asleep right now."

"This is ridiculous." John pulls the duvet off Ally. "You need to stop acting like we have all the time in the world. We have two weeks before Hawaii and only thirty days left on your visa." Ally wipes a tear from her eye but it smudges her ballpoint ring and leaves a black smear on her cheek. John throws the duvet onto the floor. "Get over yourself." John storms out, slamming the door behind him. Cameras follow John as he walks away, but May stays by the bedroom door. She hears Ally try to call her mom, the endless ringtone, the sniffling.

Once, on a random Tuesday, May received a gift from Bill. It arrived in a beat-up cardboard box, and for a split second, May was too scared to open it. This was always the thing about Bill; this was always the thing about most men in May's life. Bill was kind enough, but at the back of May's mind, there was this fleeting fear. Fear that Bill was about to prove not to be as kind as he seemed. May tore open the box before she could overthink it. Inside there was a plastic gumball and a note. "I saw these while in Japan on business and thought it was my turn to send you a pair." May twisted the gumball open and a plastic bag filled with panties fell out. They were sky blue with navy polka dots. May sent a picture of them to Bill and texted, *???*

Bill explained they were from a used-panty vending machine. *I think it's all fake though. I don't see how they could be real. Still, when I saw those machines, I thought of you.* When May didn't respond immediately, Bill added, *I know you're not Japanese.* May laughed; she knew he knew. Though she often got the sense he wished she was Japanese; most men that bought from May did.

I know you know lol.

It's just because they're "used" panties.

I got that. Thanks for returning the favor. Bill asked if sending her a gift was inappropriate. She answered no because this was ultimately funny to her. But it struck her that he asked if it was okay only after the fact. Then morbid curiosity got the best of her and she asked, *Did you buy yourself a pair too?*

Yes, but it wasn't the same.

The sky's so blue, it almost hurts May's eyes. She puts on her sunglasses and watches other tourists start their day. The air smells like sunscreen and coffee. "It's nice, huh?" Bridget says. May nods, still not believing they're really here. No fights were ever resolved, only shelved in favor of a beach wedding, toes in the sand on the walk into happily-ever-after. In the end, it was

decided that Ally would wear a white Forever 21 sundress down
the aisle. Bridget asked May to be up early today for a walking
meeting on the beach. "How are you liking the job?"
"I'm just trying to keep up," May admits.
"You're doing great."
"Thank you." There is a lull in the conversation when they
both consider if this is true.
"We should enjoy this morning, before things pick up again."
Bridget explains that John plans on surprising Ally with a real
engagement ring. He's being secretive and doesn't want anyone
on Ally's side of things to know. "He only told me last night. I
convinced him to let us film him buying the ring with minimal
crew."
On the car ride over to the jewelry store, everyone debates
how much John will spend on the ring, the guesses ranging from
fifty dollars all the way to fifty-five hundred dollars. A condition
only John and production know: Ally must sign an extensive
prenup. John already has one drawn up, has since even before
he met Ally and there existed only the idea of another Asian
bride who could run away with everything. When pressed on
when he plans on telling Ally, John always says the same thing:
"Soon. The prenup is a very intimate thing for me."
When Bridget, May, and the cameras arrive, they see that
John's already there. He greets them and ushers them into the
store like he owns the place. He even knows the jeweler, Sandy.
"John's been coming here forever," Sandy says in her interview.
It turns out that, like the prenup, the ring had been picked out
since before John met Ally. "Whenever he's here on vacation,
he'll stop by and check on his ring." John holds a real-life diamond solitaire ring up to the cameras.
He ends up spending thousands on the ring and two wedding bands. John tears up while he pays. Sandy congratulates
him. On the ride back, Dave says he's been doing the math on
how much John spends on Ally and it's insane. Bridget and May
share a look but say nothing.

John reserves a romantic dinner for himself and Ally. At the
bottom of Ally's glass is, finally, the real engagement ring. Ally

spots it as soon as she sits down, and she squeals. She chugs her champagne as John laughs. "It's beautiful," she says, cradling the ring in her palm.

John takes the ring and puts it on Ally's ring finger. Still holding her hand, John says, "I have something else for you too." From inside his suit jacket, John takes out his prenup and presses it into Ally's hand. Bridget and May, watching from the sidelines, look at each other in shock. He gives a speech about love and prenups. "For me to give in to our love, I need to protect myself."

"Stop." Ally tries refusing the papers, but John pulls at her wrist and her hand opens reflexively. "Why are you already thinking of divorce?"

"You know about my ex-wife." Ally's so quick, no one realizes what's happening until John's already soaked in his own champagne. Ally stumbles getting up from the table, but soon she's storming off, cameras tailing her. John wipes his face with a napkin but says nothing.

The next day, Ally meets with a lawyer Max arranged for her. Meanwhile, May watches John sit at the resort bar, recounting (again) the morning he realized his ex-wife had left. "The house was colder than usual and I just knew." Ally calls. John answers but doesn't say hello; he just puts her on speaker. Ally tells him the lawyer is saying not to sign. John doesn't say anything back. Ally says the prenup would leave her with nothing and asks John if he'd really do that to her. He hangs up on her. By the time Ally's back, John's booked a separate room for himself. Ally tries returning the prenup but he tells her to keep it and think on it. "I'll be waiting at the altar. Decide if you love me enough."

In her hotel room, May sifts through her bag and finds half a Splenda packet at the bottom from Bridget's morning coffee. May unfolds the packet and tips the rest of the Splenda into her mouth. She licks her teeth and scrolls through her texts. Tomorrow morning, everyone has to be up early to prepare for either a wedding or a breakup. People bet on which it'll be. Bridget asks May which way she's betting. Bill reaches out to say no pressure but he knows where he'd like to take her and links to the website of the steakhouse from May's awful twentieth birthday. May's equal parts touched and horrified that he remembered. She can't bring herself to answer anyone. Instead, she silences her notifications and organizes her clean clothes. May checks and the hotel pool is still open for another hour. She finds her bikini.

May doesn't see her at first. The water's too blue. May's eyes are too tired. There's just movement in the water, rippling forward. But then Ally's head bobs out of the water. May sits a few chairs away and tries to act natural, but she can't help staring. Ally climbs out of the pool and towels off before settling into a chair. It strikes May how young Ally looks. May wonders if she looked this young at nineteen. May remembers feeling older at the time, or at least wanting to be.

Ally turns and looks back at May. May panics until she realizes Ally doesn't recognize her. She realizes Ally has never seen her, not really. "Are you here on vacation?"

"Yes," May says. "What about you?"

"Yes, I'm on a long vacation."

"Where's home for you?"

"I'm from the Philippines." Ally wipes her face; her hands stay over her eyes, resting. May spots the remnants of the ring, a blotchy ink stain underneath the real thing. "I'm here with my fiancé. We're getting married."

"That's exciting, right?"

"Maybe. I'm not sure."

May knows Ally's looking for a stranger to open up to, but May doesn't think she can pretend to be a stranger for long. "Well," May says, "you could always run away." Ally laughs but May insists. "Lots of brides run away. My mom canceled her second wedding after she saw the groom pick his nose at the rehearsal dinner." Ally laughs more. May shrugs. "People have their reasons."

"No, I can't."

"You can." May leans in for emphasis and there's a change in Ally's face. Recognition, maybe. May pulls out her phone. "We could look at tickets to the Philippines. You could go and

I'll tell everyone it's off." But when she looks up, Ally's already walking away.

There was only one casting interview when Ally directly acknowledged what people must think of her. Max asked what her parents thought of her relationship with John. Ally rolled her eyes before answering, "They think what you're probably thinking right now."

May forgets to turn her notifications back on and sleeps through her alarm. She wakes up to nine missed calls from Bridget. Nobody can find Ally. When May races down to help search, Bridget freaks out. "Where have you been? Do you have any idea where she is?"

"I'm so sorry. I overslept. I have no idea," May says. Bridget looks at her with suspicion.

"Where have you been?"

"I really did just oversleep, I promise."

Bridget looks doubtful but says only, "Let me know if you hear anything." The whole afternoon, John waits—downing fruity cocktails and staring up the beach at vacationing families, honeymooners. The officiant leaves to tan and says to text him if it's ever time. John calls Kate but she doesn't pick up, though she does text him later. Bridget prompts John to read it aloud. "I can't. Let's just get lunch when you're back, okay?"

But then, as the sky goes orange, Ally appears. Instead of a bouquet, she holds the signed prenup. She walks down the sand aisle barefoot, puka-shell anklets on each leg. Her dress is like white crepe paper. Her makeup's faded from the day. She looks small. She looks beautiful. John's vows are flowery promises of endless love. Ally's vows are short, direct: "I promise to love you. I promise to stay." Ally kisses John "I do," just as day finishes becoming night.

In the warm glow of a family-friendly tiki bar, the crew digests the day. Dave says the film crews for Nat Geo TV can't interfere with the animals, "not even when otters rape each other or lions eat defective cubs." Everyone looks at him sideways, though no one has a rebuttal. They're all too tired. May has a Sex on the Beach, Bridget's treat; all the tension from the morning has dissipated now that the day's over. "I'm proud of you. I was worried, but you stuck it out." Bridget hugs May before leaving to speak with Max. Everyone is filing away into groups now, turning toward their own kind. Across the bar, a dad wipes burger grease off his kid's chin with a beach towel. May sips her drink and suddenly feels so, so hungry. She orders a burger, medium-rare.

May couldn't bring herself to throw the Japanese panties away. They ended up in a shoebox May uses for memories (stringy, faded friendship bracelets; novelty shot glasses; baby teeth). She always forgets about the box until she moves. With each new move, she looks through the box again, surprised by the panties, by Bill's note, by who she was back then.

The flight back and the ride home blur together, hours of May sitting in an old, worn seat, being jostled. She falls onto her bed, prepared to sleep the whole weekend, when Bill texts: *Are you home?* In the back of May's mind, there's that fear again. But there's also six years' worth of panties and letters that mutated into something like friendship. May still can't picture herself walking to the table. When she tries, she only sees Ally's toes in the sand.

Before she can overthink it, May texts, *Yes, just got home. Sorry, I know this is last minute, but can you meet me at the steakhouse around 7?* Bill's ecstatic; he thanks her over and over but May's not reading his texts anymore. She's getting ready. May showers in the hottest water possible so she comes out all pink and new. She has two cups of coffee. She packs her letters from the last three months. She does her makeup like it's a first date, because, well, it is.

She sees him first. Bill through the window: a slouch in a business-casual suit, tapping the table. She stares long enough for Bill to feel it and stare back. His eyes light up with recognition and May's pleased she still looks like the picture she sent him years ago. Bill's the only buyer to ever receive a photo with

May's face in it. Looking back, May shouldn't have sent it, but she was nineteen, not yet twenty.

They hug and May feels like the luckiest girl alive, because it's a real hug (not a grope, not a stab). "You look beautiful," Bill says, while pulling out May's chair for her. Dinner is wistful but formal, like catching up with your high school math teacher. There's a sense of *look how far we've come, how much has changed.* Bill apologizes again: "I'm still sorry about that first letter." May laughs but forgives him one last time. Then she decides to come clean. "You were right, you know; I did lie." Bill laughs. "How did you know I lied?"

Bill explains that over the years—years in which May would've been in middle and high school—Bill bought from so many girls that he gained a weird eye for these things. "Well, I forgive you. You were so young back then."

"Yeah, I was." May didn't mean for it to sound accusatory, but the fact of it hangs in the air, heavy. Bill looks away. By dessert, there's been enough wine and enough time has passed that May tells Bill theirs is the longest working relationship she's ever had. The longest relationship with any man, ever. He blushes, he laughs. "I'm just curious: Why won't you be buying from me anymore?"

"I finally met someone. She doesn't like my panty habit, and we just got serious." Bill flashes his left hand, the new wedding band. "Very serious." He laughs.

"No shit!" May pulls his hand closer to see. She feels the ring. "I was just at a wedding." There's a pause when May knows she's supposed to ask who the lucky lady is, but she decides she doesn't want to know. Whether his wife is like May, where she's from, how old she is—there are no good answers.

"I have something for you," Bill says, interrupting May's spiral.

"Oh, you really didn't have to."

Bill shoves a gift bag into May's hands. She smells it before she looks inside: fresh laundry. "I thought it was time." Inside the bag are all of them. Years of panties, neatly folded, tied up with ribbon from May's old packaging. Stacked and bound by rubber bands are all her letters. May picks up her journal, packed so densely it feels like a stack of business cards. May knows then that she can't give him her new letters, that time has passed. Bill launches into a goodbye speech, about the girl May was back then, how it's been a privilege to be part of her life. May nods, she smiles, but her head's still too far away, stuck at a beach wedding during sunset.

The workday ends. May showers yet again, she pours herself water to drink while sifting through her gifts. She finds the first pair, Gray, Cotton, White Lace Edges, just as she left them. She puts them on. Stacked at the top of all her letters is the very first one. Bill had refolded it into a lopsided heart. May can't bring herself to read it, but she slips the heart into her shoebox of memories. May finally lies in bed and closes her eyes. At the bottom of May's mind, a nineteen-year-old girl. If May got close enough, she could maybe feel the meat on her arms.

Time of the Preacher

FROM *Virginia Quarterly Review*

HOLLAND SPENT WEDNESDAY building a privacy fence for a tiresome academic couple in Barton Hills. Pressure-treated posts, horizontal cedar boards, stained and sealed, it was his third that week. He had another scheduled tomorrow, then a set of deck stairs on Friday, plus bids out on a tree house, a couple of pergolas, and too many fences to count. Now that everyone was marooned at home, they were dumping money into their yards, walling off their neighbors.

Holland was still getting acquainted with being in demand. He was forty-two, living in a gooseneck trailer out by the airport, divorced. He'd started Good Fences right before the world skidded to a stop. Well shit, he'd thought, and figured he'd soon be back working the paint counter at Home Depot. In those early months, when folks were only buying toilet paper and hand sanitizer, he occupied himself by building elaborate coops for the chickens he'd found pecking along the gravel shoulder of the interstate. Now almost a year in and the price of lumber near quadrupled, he turned away more jobs than he took.

While Holland was ripping cedar planks on his table saw in the Barton Hills front yard, a man stood on the opposite sidewalk trying to get his attention. When Holland finally clocked him, the man asked if he built skateboard ramps. "Wouldn't know where to start," Holland said with considerable relief. The man seemed skeptical, possibly insulted. He had two poodles on retractable leashes. *Liberals*, Holland thought.

When he finished the fence, he pinged the academics inside the house. He knotted his bandana around his nose and mouth despite knowing they probably wouldn't venture outside. Every aspect of the job had been negotiated by text. And like that, they appeared in the bay window, reminding Holland of meerkats. The husband pointed at the fence and pumped his fist like he'd sunk a difficult golf shot. Beside him, the wife laid her hands on her heart and mouthed, *Thank you.* Holland waved, then felt ridiculous for having raised his bandana. The husband made a show of brandishing his phone to send the payment. Holland set to loading his table saw into the truck bed and soon felt his own phone vibrating in his pocket. He used a leaf blower to clear sawdust from the manicured lawn.

It was January, warm even for Texas. The day's light was giving up. When he climbed into the truck, he fished out his phone to check traffic and found his screen stacked with notifications: the academics' payment, news alerts about case numbers and vaccine trials, a request for a bid on a patio deck, a message asking when he could start work on the tree house. Holland hardly registered any of it because there was also a text from Mandy, his ex-wife.

Snake at preachers. help?

It had been almost three years. He dragged his palms over his hair and his patchy beard, couldn't recall when he'd last trimmed either. A churn in his bowels. His thoughts firing too fast. He was tired and hungry and read the text again. He dropped the truck into gear.

Mandy had been the preacher's landlord for a decade; her parents owned rentals all over Austin and employed her to manage them. Before she and Holland went bust, he'd done the handyman work. The preacher's house was well south of the river, tucked back on a street with ditches instead of sidewalks. A few lots had never been developed, dense with twisted mesquite and waist-high bluestem grass. At night, deer stalked into the neighborhood to tear up gardens and tug clothes off the lines. The preacher had once told Holland about seeing a buck with a woman's red teddy hanging from its antlers. Holland could still readily summon the pride he'd felt upon refraining from a joke about racks.

Snakes didn't bother him. He liked catching them and feeling them slip from one hand to the other, as if he were letting out rope. He liked watching them vanish in the brush afterward, liked happening upon the sheaths of their shed skins, featherlight and lace soft. Mandy knew he was partial to them, which was undoubtedly why she'd invented the snake tonight. Driving toward the rental, Holland clocked a certain surprise that this was the first time she'd baited him like this, then beneath that, the deeper surprise that she'd stoop to invoking the preacher. Mandy wasn't a believer, exactly, but she wasn't a nonbeliever either, so whatever had occasioned the lie had her in a corner. When she'd contacted him a couple years back, she was just of a mind to start some static. They'd met at the Little Darlin' and fought about midterm elections, property taxes, their past transgressions. Holland gathered she was arguing with him because the stakes of arguing with her husband were too high. Mr. Tech Boom, Holland thought. Mr. Start-up.

Holland passed a food-truck court illuminated by a sagging canopy of string lights, then a bible church with a digital sign that read: TEXT YOUR PRAYER REQUESTS!!!! Rush hour traffic. Bleating horns. Cars blocking intersections. A mobile testing site had taken over the parking lot of a dead mall, and Holland got stuck behind the line of cars stretching out onto the street. He tried to fix his hair in the rearview mirror while waiting to change lanes. On the radio, hotheads debated stimulus checks and mask mandates. The sky purpled.

When he arrived, Mandy's Tesla was in the driveway where the preacher's hatchback should have been. The front door was open and spilling light onto a doormat: Bless This Mess. The scene had the upending air of aftermath. Like someone had fled. Like medics hadn't had time to close the door after wheeling the preacher out on a gurney. Holland's body flushed with the abrupt, radiating heat of panic. He parked behind the Tesla and bounded across the clumpy front yard, trying to remember the shortest route to the closest hospital.

But then Mandy appeared in the doorway, framed in light. Holland halted, embarrassed she'd caught him rushing. At the house less than a minute and he'd already lost ground. Mandy wore yoga pants, her favorite chambray shirt, a floral mask. She pointed to her face, somberly. He raised his bandana. "Those don't do squat," she said. "You'd be better off wearing a paper bag with eyeholes."

"I can turn around," he said. He sensed neighbors watching between window curtains. "I've got chickens to feed."

"Sorry," she said, regrouping. "I've had a day."

"Where's the preacher?" he said.

"Exactly," she said.

Holland followed Mandy through the house. It was all but cleared out, and yet smaller than he remembered, more cramped. The air smelled like the inside of a dust-bloated vacuum bag. In the den, the preacher's ratty leather recliner sat opposite the wall where a TV had been mounted; now only the stubble of protruding cables remained. A single wire hanger dangled in the coat closet. In the kitchen, cupboards were open, a can of peaches on one shelf, a box of instant rice on another. Mandy's sleek leather purse hung by its strap from a cabinet knob. The overhead lights were garish, the kind of despairing brightness Holland associated with police stations.

"He's under the fridge," Mandy said, and it took Holland a beat to understand. He'd already forgotten the pretense of the snake. And now he remembered how Mandy referred to all animals as males. He wondered if she was still in therapy.

"What color?" he asked.

"Brown," she said. She opened the back door and posted herself beside it, keeping distance. "Or gray. I didn't get the best look. I screamed and ran outside."

"Any black and white stripes on the tail? Any red or yellow?"

She lidded her eyes, a pantomime of recollection, then shook her head. "He's all the color of mud."

"That's the right answer," he said. He kneeled woodenly; his muscles had seized up on the drive. He used his phone's flash-

light to look at the bottom of the fridge: a plastic grille near
flush with the Saltillo tile.

"You smell like outside work," she said. "You could bottle it
and call it Eau de Labeur."

"You saw it go under here?" he said. "How big?"

"Brides would buy it for their husbands by the boatload," she
said. "You could retire early."

"I like my job," he said.

"Good for you," she said. "Good for fucking you."

The preacher—midsixties, eyebrows as wild and white as tooth-
brush bristles, the slightest suggestion of a lisp—had been two
weeks late on rent. He didn't use a cell phone and hadn't replied to emails. He usually paid early, so Mandy assumed his
payment had gotten lost in the mail or, with the world gone to
pot, he'd just lost track of the date. She waited another week.
She logged into her bank account to confirm *she* hadn't forgotten depositing his check. She did entertain the possibility
he'd gotten sick but talked herself out of it; Sunday services
had been online since March. And weren't preachers prone to
cautiousness? Preternaturally wise? Driving to the rental, she'd
rehearsed how to strike a disarming tone—*I near forgot my own
birthday this year! Who can remember anything right now? Not this
lady!* She stopped and bought the Bless This Mess doormat as an
excuse for dropping by. Even pulling into the empty driveway,
she told herself he'd started parking in the garage. She rang
the doorbell. Knocked. Checked her phone. Knocked again,
harder, with the heel of her fist. When she finally turned the
master key, she was already berating herself for not checking on
him sooner, already convinced she'd find him stiff on the floor.

"But, no," she said, pacing the kitchen. "The only things left
were that ugly-ass chair and the goddamned snake."

Holland was laboring to move the refrigerator. It was wedged
between the counter and hallway wall. Each side would only
scoot an inch at a time.

Mandy hopped up to sit on the kitchen island and started
swishing her feet like a girl on a pier. Still, she kept her distance.

She said, "So that's the situation. The world's on fire, and preachers are skipping out under cover of darkness."

"If you had to estimate the size of the snake, shoelace or belt or—"

"You don't find that, like, blasphemous?" she said. "That a man of God would just up and disappear, shafting his landlord? What's to keep me from logging into his Sunday sermon and outing him in the chat?"

"He's been in the wind for two weeks, maybe more. I guarantee he took more from the church than from you," Holland said. A kind of doubt was accruing form and ballast. "Right now I need to know how big of a snake I'm liable to find when we lift this fridge."

"Average size," she said.

"Average of what?" he said.

"He wasn't too big. Or small," she said. "Maybe on the smaller side. Maybe a youngster. He's probably not dangerous, but I don't want him making a guest appearance when I'm showing the house."

Holland was stretching over the counter to see behind the fridge. If there was a snake, and if Mandy had startled it, the most likely place to slither for shelter would be under the fridge. It wasn't impossible.

"Younger snakes are more dangerous," he said. "They can't control their venom. They shoot more in."

"Like I said, I didn't get a good look," she said.

Back in March, when it became clear the madness was only beginning, he'd expected Mandy to check in. Each day he thought: Tomorrow. Each week he talked himself out of calling. Borders closed. Field hospitals were set up. College students were throwing parties, trying to catch it, and Holland knew Mandy had rentals by the university. Before long he got spooked enough to drive out to the gated community on Bee Cave Road. If the gate wasn't open, he'd wait to tail a Land Rover in; the drivers never balked. The Good Fences logo on his truck made it easy for them to think he was building a gazebo for a neighbor's pool. He parked out by the stalled new constructions and watched

Mandy's house through field binoculars he'd ordered to sight planes and birds of prey. He listened to the radio, Willie and Waylon, and hotheads saying convention centers might be converted to morgues. Eventually, he spied her mulching a flowerbed while her husband cleaned their gutters. Occasionally he allowed himself to believe Mandy had done her own furtive wellness checks, but he knew better. He'd just about broken the habit of hoping to hear from her when she texted about the snake.

And now she was standing on the kitchen island, poised to tip the refrigerator back so Holland, sprawled on the tile, could see underneath. Her palms were flat against the freezer. He was actively avoiding looking up her chambray shirt.

From the floor, he said, "If I say, 'Drop it,' just let it go. Don't worry about me, I'll move."

"You already said that," she said. "Just tell me when to tilt it back. I feel like I'm being frisked."

"Okay," he said, bracing, ready to spring to his feet if he saw anything he didn't like.

"Okay, tilt? Or okay you'll tell me when?"

"Tilt," he said.

"Now?"

"Now," he said. "Yes. Go."

Dust bunnies and dead cockroaches. The bottom panel was solid sheet metal, nowhere for anything to slip in. Holland said, "You can let it down."

"He's gone?" she said. She lowered the fridge but stayed on the island. Like they were castaways and she'd sought higher ground in hopes of flagging a helicopter.

"You're sure it went under here?" he asked. "You're positive?"

"Hundred percent," she said.

Holland sidled between the counter and refrigerator, squeezed behind it. The space was so tight that his only option was to squat straight down, as if being lowered into a well, and graze his hand over the backside of the fridge near his boots. He shut his eyes to picture what he was touching: six tiny screws fastening a vented panel, the slits thin and tight. To slip inside, the snake would have to be the circumference of a drinking straw.

Assuming Holland could even remove the panel, he'd have no room to scramble if the snake struck. A rush of claustrophobia, a sense that the walls of the well were constricting, pressing in from every direction, that water was rising. His bandana made it hard to breathe.

"And there's zero chance of it being red and yellow?" he said, leaning back to rest his head against the wall, eyes shut. "I need you to be real certain on that count."

"I'd recognize a coral snake," she said. He heard her jump down from the island and pad in the opposite direction. "You think I'm dumb, but I'm not."

"I've never said that."

"You say it without saying it." Her voice had gotten louder, clearer, but also farther away. He envisioned her sitting on the threshold of the back door, unmasked, inhaling clean night air. She said, "That was always your method. You're an insult ventriloquist."

"I don't think you're dumb," he said, and it was true. He thought she was selfish and impatient and made a habit of grinding his heart into dust, but not dumb. She ran circles around salespeople, convinced judges to dismiss speeding tickets, and on a lark one summer, she learned passable Spanish by watching Mexican soap operas. Since the divorce, he'd measured every woman against her and enjoyed a surge of futile, misbegotten pride when each came up short.

"But then again," she said, "a preacher left me holding the bag, so maybe I am stu—"

"There's a vent," Holland interrupted, feigning discovery. "He might've gotten inside."

"That sneaky little shit," she said. "I knew it."

Holland opened his pocketknife and used the tip of the blade to loosen the screws. Tedious, halting work. The blade kept slipping, and it took concentration to find the slot again. He imagined Mandy scrolling through her phone, texting Mr. Start-up or searching for the wayward preacher. Chambray shirt, he thought. Yoga pants. How she believed brides would buy his bottled scent. He wanted to squirrel away every detail that would animate this evening in his recollection. He wanted Mandy to offer up something she missed about the old times. There was only the metallic hum of the refrigerator, the blood marching in his ears.

When he undid the final little screw, he held the panel in place. Sweat in the corners of his eyes, tracking through his whiskers. He reminded himself that Mandy had conjured the snake from thin air, that it was imaginary, a ploy. To what end, though? To call him an insult ventriloquist? With his shoulders lodged between the fridge and the wall, it seemed feasible he'd misjudged the situation, that he'd maybe never trusted her enough, and for that, he'd soon find himself inches from the dull gaze of a pit viper. He wiped his face on his sleeve.

He had to work to get eye level with the vents in the cramped space, finally rolling half onto his back, chin pressed to his chest like he'd fallen down a stairwell. His breath was coming quick and shallow. The image of the snake striking: the pink flash of its diamond-shaped mouth, the rifle-fire snap of its recoil. He could almost feel the slow boil of the venom in his veins. He slid the panel up slowly, incrementally. If he was lucky, he might be able to slam the edge back down like a guillotine. He was overcome with thirst, sandpaper in his throat. He considered refastening the panel and telling Mandy he'd been mistaken, the vents were too tight after all. When the panel was high enough for him to squint inside, what he saw reminded him of a glove compartment in an old Cadillac—black and spacious and empty. He closed his eyes, just then realizing he'd been forcing them open. He was sapped, awash in humiliating relief.

Now who's dumb. Now who's left holding the bag.

When Holland squeezed out from behind the fridge, he found himself alone. Now Mandy's purse lay on the island like a curled-up animal. She's snuck off to the bathroom, he figured. Or the preacher had returned, or her husband, and she'd intercepted him at the front door. He felt useless, besieged by the seasick awareness of standing alone in someone else's house. The urge to hide. To bolt. On his phone was a text from the Barton Hills woman saying she'd given his information to a neighbor who wanted a skateboard ramp. Holland deleted the thread. He listened for Mandy's voice, for a flushing toilet. He tried to think of anywhere else a snake might hide. He pulled down his bandana, then pushed and slid and rocked the fridge back into its place. Eventually he went out the back door, stepping down onto the rough concrete slab that served as a patio. The backyard was bigger than he recalled, and darker. The preacher had once told him that Mrs. Salazar, the sickle-backed widow in the corner house, had shot the streetlamp out with her husband's rifle because the light shone directly into her bedroom. Holland had repeated the story many times. He hoped she was still there, armed and ornery. The stars were splotchy and dim, the weak splatters of a near-empty can of spray paint. And yet there was light enough to see the yard had gone mostly to dirt. Either the deer had defeated it, or the preacher had never run the sprinklers Holland had installed.

"I left the door open in case he slithered out," Mandy said. Holland had to squint to find her under the live oak across the yard. She was in a folding lawn chair. "I'm sorry I abandoned you."

"Do what?"

"In the kitchen," she said, too quick, lest her apology evoke past disappearances. "I started feeling panic attack-y. I carry chill pills these days but left my purse inside."

"I can grab it," he said. Still in therapy, he thought. "Water too?"

"He took all the cups," she said. "I'm calmer now. I just keep thinking this is the end of the world. A snake in a house previously occupied by one of God's servants didn't exactly help."

"Maybe the snake was raptured too," he said.

"Or maybe I'm just mourning not making enough bad decisions when I had the chance."

Holland couldn't tell if she was hinting, setting a snare, or saying the first thing in her mind. His eyes were adjusting, and she was coming into focus. Maybe she'd undone a button at the top of her shirt. Years ago, when she'd started static about the midterm elections, they'd wound up at the Deluxe Inn.

"So far," he said, aiming to sound unfazed and open a door, "my worst decision has been adopting chickens somebody dumped out by the airport. It took me a day to catch them.

Brahma, they're called. Show chickens. Prize winners. They have feathers down to their toes. I guess their owners couldn't afford to feed them and couldn't bear to eat them."

"That's some depressing shit," she said.

"The chickens might disagree," he said.

"You built them a chicken mansion is my bet."

The stomach-jump of being known. He looked at his work boots in case he couldn't suppress a smile. He said, "Special chickens deserve special accommodations. They deserve towers connected by a covered bridge. They deserve ramps and balconies."

"And I bet you still make your spaghetti sandwiches," she said.

"Everything tastes better between two slices of bread," he said.

A flotilla of clouds skimmed over the sky from the east, pulled or pushed by secret wind. Then, the sucker punch of memory: a decade prior, another backyard, Mandy sitting in another lawn chair while he cut her hair. He'd never done such a thing and was convinced he'd botch the job, but they were trying to save money for—what? Just then he couldn't remember wanting anything beyond her. The next morning they drank their coffee outside and watched a wren deliver wispy clippings of Mandy's hair to its nest.

"Why did I cut your hair? What were we saving for?" he asked.

"Speaking of bad decisions," she said, but fondly. "I spent twice whatever we saved the next day at the beauty shop. I don't know what we wanted. I think you were mad about taxes."

"So you didn't lure me here for a haircut?" he said. "That's not the next bad decision."

"I lured you here to catch a snake. 'Comes with king cobra' isn't a selling point in today's market."

"If you'd actually seen a snake, you'd call the exterminator. Or your husband."

"Exterminators charge for their services, and Wade appreciates snakes less than I do," she said, then shuddered, as if hit by an arctic blast. "He moved so fast! I'm sure I'll have nightmares about him coming—"

"Up through the toilet when you're trying to pee," he said. "It'll never happen."

"And saying that will never be reassuring," she said.

"Snakes can't breathe under wat—"

Mandy started swiping tears from her cheeks. Then she just crumpled and was crying in her hands. Holland wanted to rush to her but knew she'd fumble for her mask and retreat across the yard. It wasn't a reality he'd be able to bear. He surveyed the dirt and rotting fence, then realized the haggard clouds had disappeared without his noticing. The murmur of faraway traffic.

"Fuck, Holland," she said. "I was already worried before I knew you were just wearing a bandana. Real masks aren't expensive. I'm sure they make sizes to fit libertarians."

"I'm getting by," he said. "I'm doing all right."

"I'm worried you'll get it, obviously, but also that you'll get it and not tell anyone," she said. "And by anyone, I mean me. You're all the way out in the sticks. You're all alone."

"You're really underestimating my chickens," he said. Insects trilled ceaselessly in the dark, a throbbing chorus he now realized he'd been hearing all along.

"You think you're protecting people, but really you're just scared," she said.

"Scared of what?"

"I never figured it out. If I had, maybe we wouldn't have parted the sheets."

"Things can be simple," he said. "Not everything needs figuring out. Not everything is a mystery that needs—"

"What I need is for you to swear you'll tell me if you get it."

"Scout's honor," he said, quick and easy. When she started crying again, he said, "I've got bottled water in the truck. I can fetch your purse and you can take a—"

"It's like everything was on a solid glacier for our entire lives," she said as she blotted her eyes with the cuffs of her shirt, "but now it's breaking apart and we're on our own little pieces of ice and floating away in different directions. Soon I'll be gone or everyone else will. I mean, if you can't count on a preacher to stick it out, who's left?"

"I am," he said. "I'm right here."

"You are," she said. "And you're sweet to rush over even if you think I'm lying about the snake."

"I want you to feel better," he said.

"Maybe I hallucinated him. Maybe mirages are a symptom they haven't announced yet. Maybe I *did* invent him to get you over here and seduce you one last time, but the shitty preacher took the bed. Who knows? Nothing feels true anymore."

The feeling was constant lately, fortitude being corroded from the inside out, but in her presence, he knew some things were still true. Like, he'd already spent a week in July coughing up blood, his sheets so sweat-sopped that he'd rolled onto the trailer floor but found no relief. Like, he was convinced that's where someone would eventually discover him, and he'd spent hours imagining Mandy getting the news but couldn't figure what he hoped her reaction would be. Like, he'd told himself that if he recovered, he'd vie for another chance, that he'd find a way to approach her without suspicion or wariness, that he'd suggest lighting out for Mexico or Canada, just them and the chickens, but now here they were and he was the same old coward.

"I have a drywall saw in my toolbox," he said.

"English, please."

"I can cut into that wall behind the fridge and look for the snake," he said. "No one'll know once it's pushed back."

Mandy leaned forward in the lawn chair, pondering something. A breeze expanded the branches of the live oak, as if the tree were drawing a great breath. A barred owl called from somewhere nearby: Who cooks for you? Who cooks for you?

"People need home offices right now," she said.

"English, please."

"I'll list it as having space for an office, and someone'll rent it, snake or no snake."

"Or I can cut in behind the bottom shelf of the pantry, which might flush him out the way he came in," Holland said. "If he's not there, we can take the house down to the studs until we find him."

"You're as stubborn as a scar," she said. "Maybe just help me drag that awful chair to the curb on our way out?"

And like that, the night was over. They listened to the owl for a while, then donned their masks and sulked into the house. For no reason beyond extending their time together, Holland dipped into each room as though doing one last pass for the snake. They tried a couple of different approaches at moving the recliner before pulling out the footrest and stretching the chair to its full length, which made negotiating the doorway disappointingly easy. Mandy carried the front end with her back to Holland. He was tempted to crack a social distancing joke, but instead suggested they hoist the chair into his truck bed in case the garbage collectors wouldn't take it. "I'll give it to the chickens," he said. "Or I'll leave it in the truck and put my feet up when I go fishing." Really, he just wanted to offer her a little more help, wanted that memory to ambush her at some point. Mandy thanked him and promised updates on the preacher. Holland promised to call if he got sick. They took a rain check on hugging goodbye and pledged to grab lunch when life returned to normal, the bald and courteous lies their parting required.

Holland reversed from the driveway, then she did, and he followed her to the stop sign. Even after the Tesla glided silently through its turn and her twin taillights faded, he lingered at the corner. He knew the chickens hadn't eaten since morning, knew he was due early at tomorrow's job site, knew she wouldn't text or hook a U-turn, but his boot stayed on the brake. No other cars on the road. The night pressed against the truck's windshield; the temperature was dropping. He needed to remember anything he'd said to make her smile, anything that might serve as a seed for some future encounter. His thoughts could gain no purchase. His turn signal clicked and clicked. The engine idled. The exhaust purled like smoke from a downed plane.

From behind trees and the darkest corners of the undeveloped lots, the deer watched the blinking red light. All twitching ears, flicking tails, delicate ankles. A buck nibbled delphinium, then, still chewing, raised his top-heavy head to scan the area and check on the red light. A doe scratched her neck with her hind foot. Then she froze. The buck's jaw locked. A tremor beneath their hooves, a rumbling motion somewhere. They swung their heads in unison toward the blinking light as it advanced slowly into the dark. In the truck bed, the old recliner jostled, swayed. There, deep under the seat's cushion, the snake—a copperhead, hungry, still gray at five months old—lay coiled and alert. The world was reverberating from every dark direction, a chaos that frightened and confused her, so she curled tighter, made herself smaller. She stared with unblinking eyes into nothingness. She flicked her tongue, trying to decipher the numberless threats in the cold air.

Underwater

FROM *The Drift*

WHAT A POOL it was, Sam thought. A special kind of pool. Very cold and salty. There was no chlorine in it, someone informed her. All saline. She took that to mean they were basically bathing, treating their various open wounds. She had been on vacation with her husband's family for exactly two days.

A frog was dying somewhere in the corner of the pool. A well-bred dog, genetically modified to have the personality of a teddy bear, pawed at the water hesitantly, struck with the expression of someone who has either witnessed or committed a crime. The previous night this same dog, Dotty, had been seized by an urge to hump one of Sam's Crocs, still affixed to her foot, and she had stood there frozen until her husband, also named Sam, kindly suggested she kick it to the side. So she had kicked the dog in front of the entire family, and the dog had issued a sharp and plaintive yelp—*you betray me?*—and Sam had profusely apologized, again and again and again, but no one present could get the sound of hurt out of their mind.

I can't believe you told me to do that! Sam wailed at her husband later, once they were alone.

I didn't tell you to do that, said her husband. I meant kick off the shoe. I didn't know I had to clarify not to kick the dog.

I kicked the dog, Sam said mournfully.

You did, he confirmed.

To be a Sam wed to another Sam was hugely embarrassing. But what could be done? Sometimes you just made an asshole out of yourself, falling in love with someone with the exact same name. Sam, said the judge who married them, do you take Sam to *blah blah blah*. Everybody laughed.

Everybody except Sam's mother. She did not think the sameness was funny and had in fact suggested that Sam take legal action.

What do you mean? said Sam.

Change yours, said her mother. Otherwise, it will make your mail too confusing.

Change it to what? asked Sam.

What about Naomi? Naomi is a nice name.

Then why didn't you name me that back when you had the chance? said Sam.

I didn't think of it then, said her mother. Things change.

Her mother wasn't entirely wrong. The problem with the matching names was that Sam's husband already had a twin—the owner of the genetically superior dog. The twin's name was Lizzy, a name that Sam found undignified for an adult. The sound of it conjured up images of roller skates, a downy kitten squealing in a bassinet. In reality, Lizzy was modern, shiny even: a woman in control of her own image. Not daftly pretty, but beautiful. Pink lips drawn on like a crayon. Dangerous looking ankles. Hers was an anxious, odorless kind of beauty, quietly protected. By what means and at what cost, Sam couldn't tell, even after all these years, but she detected a hardened effort in Lizzy's looks. This fascinated Sam as much as it threatened her. Every now and then Sam was suddenly beautiful, but on those days she felt that she had simply grabbed her attractiveness out of the sky, like loose bills in a radio contest.

Sam kept these thoughts private, ashamed of the underground river of jealousy that every now and then threatened to sweep her away. Seeing her husband and his twin sister interact made Sam feel insane; she wasn't sure whether she was perverted or they were. Which would be worse: if Sam was imagining a psychosexual dynamic that didn't actually exist, or if her husband was cultivating an intensely subtle psychosexual dynamic with his sibling that only Sam was smart and incisive enough to pick up on? She feared that the odds were against her being a perceptive genius. After all, she had grown up in a single-sex household. She had three sisters, a fact that others could convincingly argue had deformed her in more ways than she'd ever be aware of.

But the whole business of twins, she thought, was nothing short of witchcraft. What had they been doing while they were in there, swapping amniotic fluid in the womb, getting wasted and doing backflips whenever their mother ate maple syrup? Sam didn't like to think about it. When Lizzy called her brother—and during a typical week she called quite often—he always took the phone to another room, leaving Sam alone on the couch. She would be attempting to read a book or work on her computer, but really she was listening in on their muffled conversation: her husband's easy laugh, the cool note of his concern that she recognized as love.

Sam wasn't proud of the way she acted when Lizzy was around. Putting her hand conspicuously on her husband's knee as if to say to Lizzy, *I fuck your twin brother.* In the presence of her sister-in-law, Sam stomped about with an explorer's swagger, sticking her flag wherever she could. She employed the royal "we." She spoke loudly and sympathetically of her husband's small struggles, as if she was taking an oral exam on his emotional wellbeing: the boss who didn't listen to him enough, the friend who was mysteriously ailing, the mechanic she thought had disrespected him. Look how well I know him, she seemed to be saying. Look how well I care for him.

The vacation with the Woodruffs—twin sister Lizzy, parents Hugh and Elaine, a few rogue cousins—was controversial in Sam's own family. Her three sisters filed a formal complaint. An ethics board was assembled, a verdict reached: Sam was showing preferential treatment by taking time off work to attend this vacation instead of one with *them.* Her people.

You like them better than us, her sister Sarah had accused, one day when they were watching Sarah's toddler Arthur at the playground. Sarah was the oldest, first of their name, and Sam was third in line—the undecided middle.

Look at him! Sarah added, jabbing her finger toward her son, who sat dumbly in a patch of sand. Look at how much older he already is! You're missing it.

I'm not missing it, said Sam firmly. I'm right here. I'm with you all the time. I'm with your son all the time. I know the specific grunt he makes when he takes a shit in his pants behind your couch. I was the one who sat with you when you fed him just a smidge of peanut butter for the first time, in case his little throat closed up. God forbid I spend some time with Sam's family, which, don't forget, is a million times more normal than ours.

They spoil you, said Sarah, her arms crossed in displeasure.

What's wrong with that? said Sam. I don't ask them to.

Well, I spoil you, too, said Sarah. You don't say thank you. Then you pretend like it's so special when they treat you to something.

Because they don't make me feel bad about it, cried Sam.

I don't make you feel bad about it! Sarah cried back.

You don't even like me, Sarah, reminded Sam.

So much could be said for Sam's sisters: they had spirited dialogue, good jokes, grew up eating dinner at the dinner table, relatively minimal inherited trauma, no allergies to tree nuts or gluten, zero stints in rehab, only one had been divorced—and that had really been for the best. But under no circumstance did they ever go with the flow. In fact, they were salmon out to spawn, swimming upstream. Mouths open. Gulping.

When Sarah gave birth to Arthur, Sam and Maya and Allison had stood around his crib looking at his tiny anatomy and reassured one another that gender wasn't real. Sarah, initially apprehensive at the news of his assigned sex, had announced, with the sudden confidence of a conservative pundit, that she was a *Boy Mom*.

Gross, Sam had whispered to Maya. She wants to kiss him on the mouth.

Stop, Maya had said.

The other sisters had tried to protect Arthur from the UV rays of boyhood, but somehow it had crept under doorways and through slatted windows. Sam found herself reading to an

eager audience of one, usually library books about giant monster trucks dumping their big filthy loads. She and Sarah were
driving back from the grocery store, Arthur yawning in the back
seat, when Sam had asked Sarah if he had said anything funny
recently.

Um, said Sarah. He said he wanted to S-A-W my L-E-G-S in
H-A-L-F.

Excuse me? asked Sam.

He wanted to S-A-W my L-E-G-S in H-A-L-F, Sarah repeated.

Where did he learn about that? asked Sam.

I don't know, Sarah said. But then he said that after he
S-A-W-E-D me he wanted to put me on the back of a flatbed
truck, drive me into a tunnel underneath the water, and cover
me in C-E-M-E-N-T.

Damn, said Sam. What did you say?

I said that might hurt Mommy's feelings.

Sarah had warned the three of them when Arthur was still
an infant that he was his own person, made in his own image.
It was as if Sarah knew the dark thoughts brewing in her sisters'
minds: that they could change him if they wanted to, that they
could press down upon him and make him into a shape all their
own. No, Sarah had said, as if warding off a powerful spell. Arthur was who he was, who he wanted to be. Even if it meant him
sawing off her own two legs.

The house Sam's husband's parents had rented was an elegant,
big-windowed cottage in the Berkshires. Every morning, Sam
swam in the pool with her husband and Lizzy, while the air
was still and full of birdsong. They ate good bread and grilled
meat on the deck, took turns reading on the daybed in the afternoons, walked through the thick grass of the woods before
supper. At the end of every evening, Lizzy parted her dog's hair
(the dog had hair, not fur, signaling once more its genetic supe-
riority) to search for ticks. Sam did the same for Sam, and vice
versa. Everybody groomed each other like a bunch of chimps.
This was the stuff of a real family vacation. Yes, they were surrounded by the threat of crippling tick-borne disease, but they
weren't afraid—simply mindful. Practical.

The truth was that Sam liked to go on vacation with her in-laws because her husband relaxed into himself around them. She could almost see it: his whole body going slack. He was cheerful to begin with, but out in the world he could be mistaken for a serious person. Shyness wasn't the right way to describe it—it was more like he knew when to pause. But around his family, a simpler, genial humor descended on him, the practiced cynicism so common among their friends fading away with each day. Didn't the opposite happen in most families—in *normal* families? Weren't you supposed to have your hackles raised, the hair on the back of your neck prickling with the electric feeling of what was to come: the conversations veering inexorably toward wounding, the cracks of conflict widening into chasms? *That* was family. *That* was love. It was supposed to be hard.

It was hard between Sam and Sam, after all. From the outside, their relationship had moved smoothly, as if guided by wheels: a couple of years dating, a couple more living together, and then the proposal on a rare overseas vacation. And yet Sam often felt the hard edge of contrast between them: their expectations, their reactions. Sometimes, in an argument, she could see them wallowing in their respective personalities—her charging into battle, him cowering. In these moments, she felt the desire to slap her chest and shout, *Fight me, bitch!* If personality was the story of who you'd become, who told you that story in the first place? Your family, Sam thought. These people had steamrolled a path before Sam and Sam, and now whenever they considered making a family of their own, they found themselves walking down it as if it were the only available road.

Sam wondered if her husband's family had figured out something no one else in the world had, or if they were just supremely in denial about their own dysfunction. In her mind, she had always associated closeness with a certain level of difficulty. And yet here were these twins, all tangled up in one another, the proverbial umbilical cord wrapped around both their necks, and they didn't seem to be vexed in the slightest.

Once, Sam had practiced this theory on her husband, and he had replied matter-of-factly, No, we had our own umbilical cords. Twins don't share one.

I meant it metaphorically, she said.

I feel like the umbilical cord is already inherently a metaphor, he said. A direct line to your mother? That gives you all the nutrients you need? Blood? Oxygen? Life?

I'm dictating the metaphors here, said Sam.

Right, said her husband smoothly, burrowing his head into Sam's hair. What's a new way to say that my sister and I are fucked up?

You aren't fucked up, said Sam, pushing him away as he reached for her. That's what's fucked up.

Usually Sam loved how affectionate her husband was. He touched her whenever he could—her dangling foot, her roughened elbow. This could be sensual, but sometimes he reached for her breasts with an eagerness that made the dreaded phrase echo in her head: *Boy Mom.*

Historically, Sam had loved the part of dating someone when you first dug into the family stuff. It was like a vintage store full of garbage and one priceless purse. When meeting someone new, Sam always led with the fact of her sisters. She considered it the most salient detail of her life. She thought it made her sparkle. All those women! As if she had invented the concept of sisterhood. She didn't want to be competitive, but she had felt a little upstaged when Sam first told her he had a twin.

A twin brother? Sam had asked.

No, said her future husband. Sister.

Wow. What's that like?

What do you mean?

To have a sister when you're a brother, said Sam.

It isn't any kind of way. I think it all depends on who those two people are, you know?

I would think, said Sam, that it's kind of like having a mother wife.

Um, no, said her future husband. It's really nothing like that.

We shall see, thought Sam. *We shall see.*

One evening, Sam and the Woodruffs were lingering over a perfect summer meal: sliced tomatoes, boiled corn, oily pesto. Their plates were splattered with sea salt, green petrol, a seedy red. The twins were reminiscing about their last trip to the Berk-shires, back when they were in college.

Oh god, said Lizzy, that was when I was dating Ben.

I liked Ben, said Sam. He was a nice guy.

He wasn't that nice, Lizzy corrected. You always think my boy-friends are nice.

Maybe you have good taste in men, said Sam.

I obviously don't, said Lizzy.

I'll never forget you telling me about the way he kissed, said Sam.

You mean badly, said Lizzy.

You said it was somehow both too wet. And also too dry.

Both, said Lizzy.

Sam fidgeted in her seat while her sister-in-law spoke. How is that even possible? she asked.

He was a magician, her husband said. A magic man. Too wet and too dry.

Enough, said his mother. I'm losing my appetite.

We've already eaten, Lizzy noted.

Maybe it was your fault, said her brother.

Impossible, said Lizzy. I'm a good kisser. I've been told that before.

That same evening Sam felt possessed to ask her husband: Am I good a kisser? He laughed. She tugged at his waistband. But he claimed he was sleepy—and maybe he was. He fell asleep instantly, into the kind of deep, unbothered sleep that only the well-adjusted can achieve. Sam, agitated, read until it was late, listening to the soft huff of his snores. And then suddenly, her husband was sitting up. He began to scream. He screamed and screamed and screamed.

The sound activated the whole house. Everyone ran in, one after the other: Lizzy, Elaine, Hugh, the dog. Their urgency was almost cartoonish. Hugh had a golf club in his closed fist. Sam was trying to reach her husband through all the impenetrable screaming, asking him what was wrong, did something hurt? Who was this rigid, alert man in front of her? Where was the man who had spent all week so relaxed his body seemed nearly liquid? The new Sam's eyes were open but unfocused. He was wearing nothing but boxers. She scanned his body for signs of injury.

Sam, said Lizzy. Sam, can you hear me?

Sam was confused, but his thrashing slowed. He blinked hard and gasped.

You're okay, she said. Sitting on the edge of the bed, putting an authoritative hand on his shoulder. You're having a night terror.

Sam began to paw at his throat, as if he could feel the rawness from the outside.

What's that smell? said Hugh. The room was full of it: sulfuric springs, rotten fish.

I think it was Dotty, said Sam's mother. I think dogs do that sometimes when they're afraid.

Dotty was whimpering in the corner. Lizzy turned away from her brother to comfort the dog.

Whoa, said Sam. He kept tilting his head back and raising his eyebrows, as if he was slowly reinhabiting his body. That was crazy. Sorry, guys.

What happened? asked Sam. That was horrible. You were in pain?

Weird dream, I guess? said Sam. I don't even remember. Maybe it's just being in a new place. But I feel fine.

Look at Dad, laughed Lizzy, with his weapon of choice!

Listen, said Hugh, disgruntled, lowering the club to his side. At least I didn't express my anal glands.

Oh, we scared her, said Lizzy, patting Dotty. The sound you made scared her. You made an animal sound, Sam. You went someplace wild.

Sam couldn't fall asleep after all that trouble. She was convinced it would happen again—her husband's disembodied agony. She kept turning over and staring at him. But he slept through the night, something unnervingly close to a smile stretched across his face. He was still asleep when she woke up and headed toward the salt water pool.

Sam took up residence in one of the lounge chairs, a soggy paperback book by her side, a thriller in which a woman with a cataract turned out to be psychic. Sam neglected it in favor of her phone: a black, gleaming square that sent dire warnings about its own overheating. She felt a pathetic desperation when her device told her it was too hot to use, even though she was the one who had left it out in the sun.

Lizzy, too, was frequently on her phone. She kept it tucked at her hip, as if what she was texting was secret. And she frowned at the screen a lot in careful concentration when she was facing it, whereas Sam had the unfortunate habit of grinning whenever a message or notification came through, so that people frequently asked what she was smiling about. Nothing, Sam would report glumly, that's just the expression I make when I look at my phone.

Sam knew that Lizzy always had some suitor chasing her. The last time Sam had seen her, not so long ago, she'd been dating a man who made expensive bucket hats out of old lampshades. Would he be coming on the trip? Sam had asked her husband. Oh no, he informed her. That guy was long gone.

She's seeing someone new, he said. A woman named Eleanor.

Eleanor, said Sam.

I think Lizzy's pansexual, her husband said.

God, said Sam, please, it's only eleven in the morning.

That's not early.

It is always too early, said Sam, to be talking about your pansexual twin.

Okay.

Do you notice how beautiful she is? she asked.

Of course I do, he said. I've known her my whole life.

Hm.

Sam, do you realize that you're the one making it weird?

It's only weird if you acknowledge it being weird! she cried, with the unbearable satisfaction of a person proved right.

This is the start of a fight, he said. A long and terrible fight. Can't you see that?

No, she said. Yes. No. But also yes.

She had tried to complain about all of it to her little sister, Maya. But Maya was never sympathetic the way Sam wanted her to be.

Tell me again, Maya said. What's wrong with them being close?

I don't think I can be clearer, said Sam.

We're close, said Maya. All you ever do is tell people how close we all are.

But it's different.

Why?

Please, said Sam. It's obvious.

It's not, said Maya.

What are you trying to say?

I think Sam's right, said Maya. You're the one making it weird. I'm his *wife*.

My God, said Maya. Listen to yourself.

She tried her second-oldest sister, Allison, next. Sam could never figure out the time difference between the East Coast and France, where Allison had lived for the past five years. Or Sam chose not to. She called in the early evening, long past midnight for Allison.

Wha, said Allison sleepily.

Hi Du, said Sam.

Da, said Allison. Is something wrong? Why are you calling?

To chat, said Sam defensively.

Yeah, said Allison, but it's late.

It's not my fault that you live in France.

It is my fault, said Allison.

Correct, said Sam. It is your fault.

Okay, said Allison. Proceed.

Sam laid out her case. All the evidence she had gathered.

Sam, said Allison.

Yes, said Sam.

It's you.

Wrong.

You got it twisted, said Allison. It's not your fault, but you need to check in with yourself.

I'm checking in all the time.

Why do you do this? said Allison. It's like with our baby.

The sisters always referred to Arthur as "our" baby.

What do I do with our baby? asked Sam.

The way you gender things. You think all boys and girls kiss on the mouth. You say things like "kiss on the mouth."

I don't! said Sam.

You know how I know you're sick? said Allison.

How?

You married someone with the same name, said Allison.

We don't have control over these things, said Sam. Our minds. Their power.

Okay.

Lizzy's pansexual, said Sam.

So?

I just mean, I'm open-minded, said Sam.

You're not, said Allison. It's actually one of your worst qualities.

I can't listen to you, said Sam. You live in France. Twins probably kiss on the mouth there, too.

Do they kiss on the mouth? Sam and Lizzy?

Metaphorically speaking, said Sam.

Goodbye, said Allison.

Bon nut, said Sam.

Nuit, said Allison.

Over the years, Sam had figured out how to court Lizzy, just as she had figured out how to court her husband. She was careful to remember all the small grievances Lizzy held against her parents and to affirm Lizzy's retelling of collective memories. She had agreed to let Lizzy officiate her wedding. With her own sisters—the people she felt actually close to—it looked different. There was something so ancient in the way they collided. Cave-wall-painting ancient.

What if, Sam's husband once ventured. What if—

What if what? she said, her eyes slits.

What if it's the four of you. The weird ones. The way you fight isn't normal, is it?

Sam, said Sam.

Okay, said Sam.

The conversation ended there. That was the razor-sharp

power of sisters. People feared them. The collateral damage they were capable of inflicting, like a windstorm. Someone blowing down your whole damn house.

Normally on a vacation with the Woodruffs, Sam would've stayed near her husband, slinking off with him when she thought no one would notice. But that wasn't going to cut it this time. Sam had kicked Lizzy's dog that first night. And though it was an accident, a karmic stench seemed to trail the act. Lizzy loved her dog with the ferocity of someone who had a dog. She loved her dog very, very much. So Sam tried extra hard with Lizzy in the days that followed.

Let's take a stroll in the pool, she said the morning after Sam's episode.

Just the two of us? said Lizzy brightly.

Yes. Sam's still sleeping the screams off.

Okay, said Lizzy. That sounds nice. The early light was white, overcast. They lowered themselves into the pool, their shoulders up by their necks and their little T-rex arms at their sides, easing into the chill. The water flicked at their torsos, settling right above their pubic bones. Sam could track the faintest fur below Lizzy's taut belly button, noting her exceptionally clean bikini line. Sam's bush protruding from her own bathing suit looked like a wig a child might wear in a school play. It was errant and sideways. As they moved toward the deep end, Dotty ran along the perimeter of the pool, anxiously barking, her tail wagging.

Just get in, said Lizzy, patting the surface with her hand. With each splash Dotty barked louder.

She wants to be near me, explained Lizzy, shaking her head. She's obsessed with me.

That must feel good, said Sam.

Sure, laughed Lizzy. Who doesn't love to be loved the most?

A small inflatable raft drifted past them. Sam helped Lizzy position it right up against the lip of the pool, and Dotty tentatively eased her weight onto it, sinking each paw nervously into the soft squish of the plastic. The effort caused the raft to cleave from the cold concrete, and now the dog was fully marooned, an island unto herself. She let out bewildered yelps, silenced only by Lizzy's steady hand, guiding the raft. Finally, the dog could take the uneasy motion no longer and fell sideways into the water. She paddled furiously, yelping some more, her head craning desperately above the wobbling surface.

Oh please, said Lizzy, as the dog clambered up the pool steps and gave herself a hearty shake. What a drama queen! You know how to swim!

The night terror, said Sam cautiously, once calm had been restored. I've never seen Sam like that.

He used to get them occasionally when we were kids, said Lizzy. It's like, what happened to you as a child? But I know everything that happened to him as a child. And the worst thing was one time our parents said he couldn't go to Six Flags because our step-grandpa died.

What would you do when he screamed like that? Sam asked.

Well, the first time it scared the living shit out of me, said Lizzy. We had our own rooms, but we never slept in them. I would go to his room, or he would come to mine.

That's so sweet, Sam lied.

After the third or fourth terror, Lizzy said, I just started kicking him. Or pinching? Once I even bit him. Something to jolt him out of it. And then he'd be fine, his usual smiling self.

What a freak, said Sam.

Lizzy shrugged. The water stilled between them.

That's just like him, isn't it? said Sam. To wake up in the middle of the night screaming, and then two seconds later just pretend it never happened. That man wouldn't know his own feelings if they slapped him across the face. I guess that's what we're for.

I think he'd do okay without us, said Lizzy coolly.

Sam's husband emerged from the back patio, his face streaky with sunscreen. He must have applied it himself, a fate he was unaccustomed to. Someone was always reaching out to rub him, as if racing to do the honors. That trip, Sam had tried to make sure that she was the anointed attendant, lest he revert and ask his sister or mother, but then one afternoon he'd discovered a red plot of skin in the middle of his back, the ghostly white imprint of fingertips swiping at the edges, a clear record of her lack of follow-through.

Sam thought back through the six years she'd known the Woodruffs. Had she heard even one of them breathe a bad word about her husband? They might have rolled their eyes at him every once in a while, but nothing beyond that. No combat. It bothered her, like the pale scrim of sunscreen on her husband's face. He bent down at the edge of the deep end, hovering over the two of them as they treaded water like a pair of gigantic ducklings. Sam looped her hand around the hard egg of her husband's ankle. He staggered back to escape it, nearly stepping on Lizzy's dog, who skittered toward the grass.

Don't worry, said Sam, as her husband loosened himself from her grip. I wasn't going to pull you in.

The last outing of the trip was to a swimming hole that a second cousin had recommended. He lived in the area and would stop by the rental with his two young sons to swim in the pool. The boys were eight and ten, and they referred to Sam as Girl. Where's Girl? they would ask. They knew Lizzy's name. There was Lizzy, and then there was Girl. A strict, policed border existed between them. Girl was a precursor to Wife, thought Sam. She was pleased.

It was a relief to leave the rental house. The pool's four corners had begun to feel claustrophobic. Plus, Sam loved spots like this, had spent her childhood exploring them. Like all worthy swimming holes, this one required some light trespassing. They parked at the end of a private road and set off, Dotty running two steps ahead, regularly throwing her head back to make sure they were behind her. The two little boys were their guides. Like hunting dogs, the boys were trained to sniff out anything age inappropriate—every empty beer can and old yellowed condom. A swimming hole was the provenance of yahoos. Sam had seen one too many drunk dads attempt a poorly timed backflip into a cold river, or lose their shorts to a particularly strong current in an effort to chase down a bottle of Gatorade traveling downstream. But she also knew that you couldn't be a snob about spaces like this. They existed to be ungoverned, and if that attracted men who were prone to self-injury, so be it.

The little boys had sloping bellies, and the creases of their joints were covered in bug bites. When they spoke, they did so in short shouts—all HEY or WHAT or RARGH. WHERE IS GIRL? Lizzy's dog nosed their elbows every now and then, and they absent-mindedly petted her dirty fur. Together they made a pleasant tableau: wild things. The Woodruffs followed, their orthopedic water shoes sinking into the wet earth, Saran-Wrapped turkey sandwiches swinging about in a backpack.

As they walked, Sam could hear the distant echoes of other bathers: a hollow yelp from the top of a tall rock, the crash of a body as it hit the water. After a few minutes, they emerged at the top of a small waterfall. The water was green and scummy at the edges. There were little hot holes in the rocks where spiders spun their webs. Teenagers sunned themselves on the nearby granite shelf, eating tortilla chips and shouting at one another. Sam felt the relief of an obviously beautiful space. She instantly shimmied out of her shorts and into the water, which smelled faintly of runoff, but she didn't mind. She crawled to the ledge where the water cascaded down. There were rocks underneath, the current pulling tight around them.

Sam's husband swam toward her, with Lizzy behind him, and the three of them raised their voices to be heard over all the rushing water. Dotty, swept up in the feeling of the afternoon, approached with her tail wagging, a waterlogged stick hanging sideways out of her mouth. Sam's husband threw it a couple of feet and she swam after it, bringing it back. Sam herself threw it next. She had terrible aim—the stick landed right at the edge of the waterfall, then quickly sailed over. There was a moment of disbelief before Sam thought to scream after the dog. But her scream meant nothing: in a matter of seconds, Dotty, blinking and paddling, was gone, too.

It all happened so fast. Sam and Lizzy's parents were standing up, their books abandoned, craning their necks trying to look downstream, shouting after Dotty. Even the teenagers stopped talking, a hushed audience in the presence of desperation. Sam spun around with a splash, and came face to face with her husband and his twin. They were clutching one another, sobbing. Quiet then. And too much of it. Just the sound of the water, as they all strained to listen. But wait, couldn't Sam hear it? She thought she did. A twilight barking, equal parts joy and apprehension. Maybe that dog had gotten free. Maybe that dog was running right back. Couldn't her husband hear it, too? Didn't he know what was coming, to whom this dog belonged? The current was strong enough that if Sam wasn't careful, she would lose her footing. She bent down to readjust her stance, then righted herself.

WILLIAM LOHIER

Drapetomania

FROM *One Story*

I FIRST HEARD the running at school. Jackson had been fidgeting all week, though the rest of us pretended not to notice. He raised his hand for the bathroom, leaving us hunched over a midterm exam, and we heard footsteps circling the hall for the rest of the period. No one went to check on him. Even Ms. Price soldiered on, gripping the chalk so hard it snapped in half as she marked the time we had remaining.

Maybe we should have acted sooner, understood the danger when the first reports of manic running appeared on our timelines and newsfeeds. At first people thought it was a prank, some viral stunt for media attention. Parents started taking their kids' phones and petitions were circulated to ban the latest social media. We were two weeks into the semester when the first runners began to collapse. Interludes between classes were hashed out in fierce whispers as we huddled around videos of them, crumpled on the ground, coughing up blood.

Jackson didn't come to school the next day. During attendance Ms. Price stared at her clipboard, then at her students. She had everyone seated behind Jackson move up a row. We swallowed his absence and moved on to the next lesson.

Some lucky few were taken to hospitals in time to be resuscitated. From them it was discovered that while malnutrition, collapsed lungs, broken feet, and muscle breakdown could be treated, the running was terminal. As soon as they could move again, the runners were back on the road until they collapsed.

The class was silent for the rest of the week. Ms. Price gave us worksheets and we strained our ears each time sneakers squeaked past the classroom. Through a slow accumulation of news and hearsay, we began to realize that all of the victims of the manic running outbreak were Black. The next week Kasey was gone too. She didn't even ask to leave. She just stood and walked out of the classroom. Ms. Price let her go without pausing the lesson. We crowded around the window to watch her run down the gravel path from the school building. She stumbled once, kicking up stones, but momentum kept her on her feet.

I was rooting for her. Our desks were adjacent and she had bullied me at first, but before long we were sharing homework answers and cheating on tests together. I almost cheered when she regained her balance, as if I were watching one of my sister's track meets. Ashley pulled out her phone to record. She zoomed in on the body and exclaimed, "She running. Oh my god, y'all. She really running."

I imagined beaded braids clacking together with each footfall as the distance folded Kasey's silhouette into a comma. I stayed at the window as my classmates returned to their seats, wondering what her face looked like, if it was all scrunched and teary. Maybe running brought some relief and she looked up at the sky and felt free. Ms. Price cleared her throat and class continued, Kasey's desk yawning empty next to mine.

Mom made hot dogs for dinner that night. She sat my younger brother, TomTom, and me around the kitchen table and said we had to talk about what would happen if she died.

"Just in case," she said.

Without futures beyond torn muscles and broken feet, how many parents imagined their own deaths like a video clip on loop? We imagined ours too—the mania didn't recognize age, only bodies it could infiltrate and terrify.

Mom took me aside once the plates were dry and stacked. Outside, a runner circumscribed our block in a chatter of feet. We watched him through the window. It was snowing. He was wearing boots and the footprints he left behind made me think of the pictures in the news of the blisters, raw and angry, the trailing pale flaps of skin.

Mom worried a napkin until shreds fell to the floor like dandruff.

"Nina," she said, "you take care of your brother for me. You hear?"

I nodded. There was a brightness in her eyes that scared me.

That night I walked through dreams of ivy and an endless sky and woke to sirens and screams. The man running last night had died a few doors down. I walked past the mourners on my way to school and caught a glimpse of his lumpy bruised flesh as an EMT zipped him into a body bag.

It took weeks to become accustomed to the sound of my classmates running themselves to death. The empty seats in the back of the classroom swelled toward us like a gaping mouth.

Before long, there were cases in every major US city. Detroit and New York were the hardest hit, but Black neighborhoods all across the country were marked by the slap of feet against concrete. No one knew whether the running was caused by a virus or bacteria or if it was purely psychological. Cases in other countries were still rare, but the mania seemed to spread with each sensational news cycle. After the outbreak began to make headlines, runners were sought after by a range of companies for their potentially unregulatable labor potential. Delivery and transportation services, sports teams, farming and agriculture industries, even electric companies were interested in harnessing whatever specter could make Black people run nonstop, ostensibly of their own volition. TomTom sent me a black and gold ad posted by a pharmaceutical company offering $60,000 for runners in the early stages of mania. The prices decreased if they were nearing the end. For their profit margins, corporations were determined to extend the lives of runners for as long as possible, even if they eventually succumbed.

During Friday assembly, Principal Cartwright introduced a girl in the year above us, a senior named Jai who was reporting on the impact of manic running on our school for the local branch of a national radio station. She smiled and took wide landscape shots of the gym, the dingy wall mats and scuffed floors, and of my classmates, unusually demure, with an expensive looking camera. Jai was pretty. I had seen her before, but I wasn't the kind of girl she would notice. Her blazer clashed with her flowy pants. I rummaged through my backpack to hide my face when I felt the camera lens on me.

After the assembly, she came up to my locker. She smelled like raspberries and described her project as the "running beat." I liked how that sounded, like something from music. She had wide pretty eyes and her outfit was much more cohesive up close.

She asked about Demetria, my sister. She was a sprinter, our school's pride, and one of the earliest victims of the running disease. She had won the state championship last summer, a few weeks after she graduated. The starter hollered and waved his cap pistol at her when she kept running around the track, long after the race had ended. He tucked the pistol into his belt and stood in place and grabbed her waist when she ran by. She kicked and shouted. The crowd cheered as his pale arms lifted her from the ground. Her legs never stopped moving. Soon her body was lost in a swarm of medics, coaches, and security guards who strapped her into a gurney and carted her, thrashing, to an ambulance outside the stadium. That was the last time I saw her alive.

I asked Jai why they had assigned an Asian reporter if all the runners were Black.

She looked at me with a guilty half-grin and leaned in to explain in a hushed voice.

"My dad's from Japan but I live with my mom, who's Guyanese. I'm just an intern for the station, but they felt that someone from the community should lead the local coverage." She asked if she could shadow me for a day or two and profile me for the story. "You won't even know I'm here," she said. She took my hands in hers. They were cold but soft, and her short nails were painted a burnt orange. I looked at her eyeliner, her pretty upturned nose, and felt a twinge in my gut.

The doctors had blamed my sister's hysteria on exhaustion and stress and she stayed at the hospital that night. They called the next morning to tell us she had run off. They found her body in an alley over twenty-five miles away.

Girl Devon beelined past us toward the gym. I shut the locker and walked to my next class. Jai followed a few steps behind me.

It was soon determined that non-Black people were protected from the disease. After that, the headlines faded to particularly gruesome updates. Funding for research on the outbreak dried up and Black workers, running or not, were laid off by the thousands. All we could do was watch as manic running became a peculiarity of Black bodies. We grieved and waited and lived and grieved.

Two months after the first reported cases, the Governor ordered all predominantly Black schools to shut down until further notice. We took the news loudly.

"It's for your own safety," Principal Cartwright said, hushing the agitated gymnasium. "We must look out for each other, now more than ever."

Jai panned over us and zoomed in on the principal. I stared at my hands, flexing my fingers, lacing them together.

"I know this is a hard time for all of you," the principal said.

Someone coughed.

"But your futures are bright," she said. "You are the stewards of your generation. Remember that education is a guiding light. The learning journey you've begun here, which will continue for the rest of your lives, is key to our collective freedom. Be mindful. Don't take anything for granted—" A student leaned into one of the speakers and the principal's speech was drowned in feedback. I gathered my things.

After assembly, Jai walked over to me from the far side of the gym. She smelled different that day, like crushed flowers and spice, and her skin was so clear it glistened beneath the dingy gym lights. She took my hand and my face got warm. Together we dodged through the mass of bodies in pairs or trios, percolating gossip: who had already gone, who would catch the running bug next. The whispers floated up to the ceiling and gathered into an echoing cloud. Jai followed me to my locker and watched solemnly as I shoved textbooks into my bag.

She asked if I was really going to need them.

I paused. The textbook in my hands had an enormous gorilla on the front cover, holding a dandelion in an impossibly green jungle. It was Photoshopped to look like the gorilla was blowing the dandelion spores into the air, continuing the circle of life or something, but the gorilla just looked tired to me, like she was ready to go home and give up the modeling life for the real rainforest, damp and cruel. I grunted as I flung the textbook across the hallway. It clanged against the lockers opposite mine and thudded facedown on the dirty linoleum.

"I know das right!" Jai said. Her camera blinked red. With her free hand, she reached into my locker to grab my trig textbook and flung it down the hall with a shout. Its open pages rippled through the air as it somersaulted like an off-balance bird. I drew a sheaf of paper from my bag, the final for my Black excellence class, and threw it open against the ground. I ripped page after page into ragged white confetti. After a moment, Jai snapped the camcorder shut and joined me, gathering the discarded bio textbook and tearing glossy diagrams from the gorilla's grasp. We howled with laughter until we cried. I buried my face into her neck and sobbed, enveloped by the scent of wildflowers and tea.

We wiped our eyes and walked outside. She took my hand again as we went past the school gate.

"Let me come home with you," she said. "Now that schools are shutting down, I want to start documenting our lives from home."

Other kids flooded around us, between us, pushing us farther into the road. The teachers were the last to go, shepherding us out of the building. Some looked sad, others relieved; most wandered out in a daze. Principal Cartwright saluted us, then took off at a jog, clogs striking the concrete. I wondered whether months of watching the school disintegrate around her had somehow infected her as well or if she just wanted to get out quick, put distance between herself and us. Jai whistled low and dug her nails into her palm until the principal was out of sight. Then she pivoted back to me, and I watched her pupils widen as clouds passed over the sun.

"I'll have to ask my mom and my brother. You'd want to interview them too, right?"

"Whatever's easiest," she said. "Don't sweat it."

Mom came home late and laden with shopping bags. TomTom ran to greet her. In one hand she carried a Walmart survival kit: rope, first aid, a portable stove, water purification tablets. In the other she carried cans of soup and beans that clanked heavily in the bag as she rounded into the kitchen. She looked tired. I helped sort the cans and stowed the rope and stove before Tom-Tom took an interest.

"It was some madness in the ICU today," she told us at dinner. "Someone's been robbing folks out here. It's not enough to wait for the running to get us, they're hitting licks while they know we can't fight back."

"They probably didn't want us here to begin with," TomTom said. "In history we learned they used to use busses to—"

There was a knock at the door. Mom tensed and rested her hand on TomTom's, which tapped the rhythm of the bean cans. She glanced at the knives in a block on the counter.

"Anybody expecting company?"

The question hung taut in the air until I remembered and cursed under my breath.

"Yes, I am actually," I said. TomTom started scrolling on his phone. "This girl from my school. She's interning for a radio station and working on a project about the running. She asked if she could come over and feature us in her story."

Mom sighed and began to stack up plates. There was another knock and in the silence behind it we heard runners outside, two of them, footsteps just slightly misaligned. We all stood still until the sound faded to nothing.

"If you'd told me I would have made another plate," Mom said.

Everyone was surprised that Jai looked Asian. She played it off well, but I could tell she was annoyed that I had forgotten to tell them about her. Mom's face went dark when Jai offered her condolences for my sister. Jai asked if we had any family photo albums and whether she could look through some of my sister's belongings for the story. Mom looked her up and down and asked whether she would be able to contract the running mania.

"I'm not sure," Jai responded. "Asian Americans can't contract it, and my mom is from the Caribbean, but I was born here, so I guess I'll have to wait and see."

She ate quickly and took a few photos of us and of the house. When she was getting ready to leave, Mom looked out the window at the darkening sky and shook her head. "Stay the night. We have the space, and it's not safe out there anymore." Jai glanced at me and I nodded. "For anyone," Mom added.

We turned in early. Jai crashed on Demetria's empty bed in the room we used to share. She scribbled notes and snapped pictures of her trophies and athletic gear as I got ready for bed. A headache set in just as I lay down, and I could barely sleep all night for the pounding of feet.

When I woke up the next morning, Jai was steeping tea beside the stove. The kitchen smelled like lemon and honey and it blued in the rising light. Nobody else was awake yet. Nobody had reason to be except runners. She smiled at me without teeth and sipped from her steaming cup. Her lips were thin and almost blended into her skin as they stretched across her face.

"I'm going out," I told her.

"Where?" she asked.

I didn't answer. I noticed one of my sister's journals open on the kitchen counter beside her. When I met Jai's eyes they were already locked onto mine and I wondered what she saw. She was beautiful, bed-headed and calm, and the morning light startled her eyes into a brightness I hadn't seen before. Her gaze felt cool, like water trickling down my chest.

She nodded slowly. "Be careful," she said. "My boss told me that runners are being taken off the street, like vans will drive up next to people running and pull them inside. He thinks it's some kind of government testing program . . ." She trailed off.

I grimaced.

"Just . . . don't run . . . at least," she said.

I turned and left.

It was still early but the sun outside was harsh and prowling.

I walked and walked past empty houses and littered abandoned streets that gave way slowly to pristine, untrampled yards. I didn't know what I was looking for until I found it. A door, half hidden behind a wall of ivy. I had to crouch to get inside. It was dark, a safe place filled with stars where the light came through. I lay there and dozed and looked at the stars for hours.

When I got back that afternoon everyone was gathered around the TV. The reception was poor and the image kept flickering to static, but in flashes I saw huge plumes of smoke rising from a row of apartment buildings. Then the image jolted to a mess of black and white. Mom turned to me, her eyes wet.

"Fire," she whispered. "They're setting whole neighborhoods in town on fire."

Who "they" were was unclear. Black people tired of waiting for the running to come, frustrated with the country, the order of things, and raring to burn it all down before they went. Non-Blacks who saw the disease as their opportunity to get rid of us for good. The government. Whatever it was seemed to have caught on.

The TV snapped clear again. Someone had set the fires in the middle of the night. At least two hundred dead. They switched to an aerial view. Then static. Then an older Black woman in front of a house spewing flames. She wore a nightgown. Bangs curled out from under her headscarf and her eyes looked so tired. Her voice caught with the lungfuls of smoke she had probably inhaled. Then static. TomTom reached for Mom's hand.

"—investigation, although authorities suspect the fires were set intentionally." The news anchor's hair was glossy and she wore pearls around her neck. "Needless to say, this is a tragedy for a community already ravaged by the running epi—" Static again. Then a breaking news banner flashed bold and red across the screen. Reports of another fire, the anchor said, in another predominantly Black neighborhood. Smoke again, then static.

It continued like that for the rest of the afternoon. We all sat around the TV, watching as Black neighborhoods in every major city were eaten up. Smoke, static, fire, another tired dark face, static. Drones and helicopters collected footage of people streaming from the buildings, packing into cars or running from the ruin with all they could carry. The same anchor narrated it all. I noticed Jai putting another finger down every time the anchor said "tragedy." She stopped after she saw me looking. "We're leaving tomorrow morning," Mom said at dinner. "Until this is all over." TomTom started out of his chair, but Mom swiftly raised a hand and he sat, hunched over the table, staring into the scarred wood.

"We'll stay in a hotel for a few days, in a whiter area up north. It's just not safe here right now. We can come back and get more things when the fires have died down." TomTom's locs bounced as he shook his head and looked at each of us. His voice had just begun to drop.

"So that's it?" he said. "This is what they want, you know."

Mom opened her mouth to speak, then closed it again.

That night Jai got a call from her aunt and broke down into tears. It was her mother. She was missing. She had apparently started running just before the fires started and disappeared in the chaos that followed. I let Jai scoot into my bed after she wiped snot onto my sister's pillow. She leaned into me and rested her hand on mine. Her tears soaked my shirt as she sobbed, and I stroked her hair, wishing I could melt into the safety of a new body. Her hand was cool and smooth and heavy on mine, like stone.

"How are *you* holding up?" she asked eventually, blowing her nose. I couldn't open my mouth because I knew that once I unclenched my teeth, everything would come tumbling out. She made to speak again but more tears spilled out instead. I stared down the blackness of her throat and felt myself leaning toward it like a sapling toward the sun.

"I know, I know," I whispered. "Are you sure you don't want to go home? It sounds like your family needs you right now." After a moment Jai's hand left mine.

"I can't," she said. "It's the journalist in me." Her hair was black and smooth and glossy with oil. "I've never reported on a story like this before. It's changed me, going through this with you, and I think it will resonate with . . . with other people too.

And I can't go home, knowing that she's not there. I just want to stay here with you." She paused. "What about you, though?" In the dark, her recording device glowed. "What do you want out of all this?" I drew the blankets around us, wrapping us in the warmth of each other's bodies, and I thought of the room filled with stars.

"Clean air," I said. "And clean water. A body that belongs to me and to watch the sun rise every morning."

Jai hummed before she spoke. I could feel it where my shoulder met her chest. "You could make a change, if you wanted. Become a doctor or scientist and research what's behind this mess. Go into politics maybe. You'd make a good leader."

"Like you're a good journalist?" I pulled away from her and watched hurt darken her face. "Can you just be for real Jai? I don't want to lead. I don't want to do anything. I'm terrified all the time, and I just want us to be safe." I felt something expand in me, against the inside of my skin. She leaned away from me and the space between us felt hot and dense as lead. I kept on.

"I said you could stay here because I like you and . . . I wanted to get to know you and I don't know how much time any of us have left, but you don't care about me, or my family. You just want to know what my sister was like. I mean, you don't even look Black! I bet you think you can't even catch the virus."

Jai switched off the recording device and started crying again. I thought about Demetria, how much I missed her, how I'd give up Jai in a second to have her back.

"I care about you, Nina," she whispered.

She leaned back into me then, and we cried against each other in the darkness. Her nails were filed and square and massaged circles into my back that left the veins tingling beneath my skin. In the heat between us my anger softened into something molten. She smelled like my shampoo with something milk-sweet and human beneath it, and her mouth was hot and wet and close as she bore down on me like the sky. In the whispered dark, she told me she loved me and apologized until she ran out of breath, and I promised her that I would stay alive, that I wouldn't run. My body felt like the heaviest thing in the world.

We woke in an inferno. I couldn't breathe. Someone was shouting and the smoke alarm blared. TomTom banged through the door, a silhouette against the licking glow of flames. He shouted *Get out! Go!* His voice cracked. He'd gotten bigger—he was almost my height now. Jai coughed awake beside me. Her eyes gleamed. TomTom stared at us for a moment, then bolted from the doorway and I heard him shouting for Mom. I shoved a window open. The shadows our bodies cast on the walls flickered and danced.

I looked around my room again, wondering why someone would do this. Jai stared out the open door. Her face gleamed, constellated with beads of sweat. I was angry all of a sudden. I rushed across the room and slammed the door shut.

"We have to go," I said. In the dim, I could see the door smoldering. The smoke in the room made it hard to breathe.

Jai turned toward me. Her voice was soft. "This is hell," she said. "We're in hell."

I heard something groan and crash. We climbed out through the window. Outside, half of our block had been consumed. Bodies flooded the street.

Mom was waiting for us, barefoot in a nightgown, shivering in the road. I saw her stomach drop even before Jai and I reached her.

"Where's TomTom?" she said. I looked at the house. It looked back at me with cherry eyes that leaked smoke. "I'm going back in."

"Don't. Mom, you can't." I reached for Mom's hand. She shunted it aside. Her eyes were pits, dense and furrowed. They drank in the glow of the fires.

"I'm not losing another child, Nina. You stick together. I'll be back," she said. Her voice didn't waver. I wondered if she'd heard our conversation the night before. She shoved past us and ran back to the house. I started after her and Jai grabbed my arm.

"Not you too," she said. I started to cry. Jai was silent. The front door snapped shut behind Mom like a mouth. Just then, TomTom burst out the kitchen window with something tucked under his arm. He ran toward us and asked where Mom went. I shook my head. We all turned when we heard a scream. Through the window I saw something spinning in the fire. Then it ended. The house let out a sigh and the roof fell in, sending up an explosion of sparks. TomTom tightened his bleeding hands around what he'd rescued from the house—our sister's medals and a photo of our family—and wailed into the night. I tipped back my head and my voice spilled to join his.

I sat shotgun, next to Jai. She was the only one who could drive. My brother was in the back, occupied by his own shock and sorrow. I knew we were all looking at the same nothing. We drove north, where Mom said it would be safer. The mourning hush of miles slipping by was metered by TomTom's erratic tapping and twisting in his seatbelt. I stared out the window and cried, clutching the photo of our family like a lifebuoy. TomTom wore my sister's medals around his neck.

We drove all day and it rained that night, the kind of steamy drizzle that grays everything. I imagined embers somewhere being put to rest. We had to stop to buy sleeping pills for TomTom after he started kicking the seats. Too much longer and he would have opened the door and run off into the woods siding the highway. I didn't know what we were going to do with him. I didn't want to think about it.

Once night had fallen and TomTom was snoring against the window, I turned the radio on low. Jai glanced at me but said nothing. We hadn't talked about the night before. I didn't know if we would both live long enough to. I remembered my promise to her and regretted saying anything at all. I remembered what she had said, staring into the flames that ate our house and our family. *This is hell.* Staring down the bright path the headlights carved through the darkness, I believed her.

We listened. A gravelly voice recapped the fires. Jai swiftly changed the station. A voice so polished it sparkled shaped words like *epidemic* and *immunizations*. After a few moments, I realized they were talking about an offshoot of running mania that might have infected some non-Black people. It was contained in Oregon for the moment, and there were few if any confirmed cases, but I could still hear an edge in the host's voice.

Jai switched stations again. She flexed her fingers before reaching for the dial and her joints cracked. I could tell driving was wearing on her. The channel was staticky and the voice was gruff, the words sank like stones in a river. I turned up the volume. We had only stopped twice after getting on the road, once for a pee-break and TomTom's pills, and a second time for a quick dinner from a McDonald's drive-through. We emerged from the trees as the highway cut across a reservoir. Dark waters stretched around us. Jai slowed and opened the windows. The radio voice spread out over the water.

Runners, they were saying. Hundreds, thousands of runners, as many as there are stars in the sky. They kept calling it different things, a stampede, a marathon, an exodus, and I understood the inadequacy of language to describe what was happening. What do you call a people running for their lives?

We stopped at a motel a few miles later. Jai was exhausted. She was barely coherent as we checked in and collapsed into bed the moment we stepped inside. I laid TomTom beside her then downed some sleeping pills with water from the sink. My face was hollow and my eyes were like red-ringed mouths. We slept.

The world was still there when I woke up. I shrugged on a sweater and slipped on my shoes and stepped outside. I let out a shuddering breath as the cool and blue shocked me into awareness. I hadn't been alone since I went out the day of the first fires. I wondered if the room was still there, behind the drifting vines, or if it had been burned with the rest.

I sighed and sat on the curb of the parking lot in front of our door, searching the sky. I could make out the Big Dipper and a few other stars, weak, scattered in a giant nothing. I would give anything to lie beneath new and gentle skies. I stood and walked out to the road. A car whooshed past.

Gravel crunched behind me. It was Jai. I didn't know what woke her but she still looked tired. She stood beside me and together we listened to the night. I wished she were closer and longed for her warmth, remembering when I thought hers was the only safe body I knew.

"TomTom doesn't have much time left." She looked at me and I looked for the moon through the trees. "He was kicking in his sleep. He'll probably be up soon, and if he starts running I don't know if he'll stop."

I found the moon, half hidden, low on the horizon. It would be dawn soon. A new day and unimaginable horrors. I wanted to be somewhere else. Anywhere but where I was. It was a feeling I knew I had known before. Something fugitive, like catastrophe, like living in a world that has already ended. Something jolted in me.

I stood. I imagined the sun breaking, just below the horizon. When it rose, its burning shards would fall to the earth and set everything aflame. Something darted past me. TomTom. Jai sprang to her feet. We ran after him. I was so tired. I desperately wanted to rest. My mother and sister were gone and no one was left to hold me. It was then that I noticed the earth, speaking.

It shuddered and rumbled and moaned. Beyond TomTom's lithe back I could see only a weltering sliver of sun. Runners, I realized. I edged into a sprint. The motel and the moon and the world behind me—it all fell away. Beside me Jai stumbled and slowed, but I couldn't turn back. We were neck and neck, Tom-Tom and I, blood and blood. The sun enraged the sky and I saw them, before us, haloed in the rising dust. Their feet played the earth like an enormous drum. We ran toward them, enraged, and sweat stung my eyes but I didn't need to see TomTom to know what his face looked like. Mine looked the same.

Then we were among them, and I could barely see through the grit. Soon it blotted out the sky, and the trees, and left only a red sun and our persons. It was so beautiful, I lost my breath. My feet pounded against the ground until I could no longer feel them.

YASMIN ADELE MAJEED

The Clean-Out

FROM *Narrative*

I HAD BEEN dreading my mother's arrival all week, and now here she was, her own mother in tow. I watched their car wind up the long dirt road that led to the beach house, a cloud of dust following in their wake. Tall grass separated the house from the beach, and out of instinct I crouched in the field, out of sight. After a few days alone at the house, it was my new routine to take these evening walks along the beach, following its crest until the sand receded into the redwood forest in the distance. The forest marked the end of my walks. I was always too scared to enter the woods alone.

I held this last moment of solitude close—the sea behind me, the road in front—before the slam of the car door punctured the evening's quiet. "Teo," my mother called out. "Where is she?"

I watched her circle the car and help her mother, my Lola, out from the passenger seat. Lola looked tired. Four weeks ago, Walter—her late husband, and my mother's stepfather—had died unexpectedly. Complications from chemo, my mother had told me on the phone.

Lola said something to my mother, who did not reply. "Teo, come help," she said, sharply. For a moment I imagined myself as a petulant daughter, running away into the forest, where no one could find me. But I had never been that girl, and I felt too old to be any other kind than the one I was.

I stood up. The grass tickled my ankles. "I'm here," I said. "Right here."

Their faces turned to me in surprise. Lola's broke into a smile when she saw me, but my mother's was troubled. She didn't expect me from that direction.

The last time I saw Lola was during our annual visit to Vacaville last fall. She looked the same to me now, her cherubic face brown and lined by years spent in too-sunny places: the Philippines, Guam, California. She had worked as a seamstress for most of her life. When I visited her, she sat me down in her garage to take my measurements for dresses that, when we got home, my mother tucked into her closet, with the promise that I could wear them for "special occasions" that never arrived. Lola's garage walls were lined with shelves of pastel Beanie Babies and wispy-haired troll dolls, and I always associated her with their treacly cuteness. As she aged, she looked more and more like them—a small, overripened child.

As I helped her into the beach house, I was surprised by how strong her grip was. She had just turned eighty last year. She retired from work ten years before that and had taken to wearing elaborately decorated acrylic nails. These ones were a deep crimson with sequined bows glued to the pinkies and forefingers. I found her nails glamorous, evoking her short, youthful career as a lounge singer on the Manila club scene. But my mother, my practical mother, found Lola's nails tacky.

"Are you excited for college, Teodora?" Lola asked. Her voice was shaky, quieter than I remembered. "When do you leave?"

"At the end of August," I said. I was going to Williams in the fall. It would be my first time leaving California, and my first time leaving home. I had been counting down the days all summer.

"You're going so soon, baby," she murmured.

I didn't reply. I was too focused on my mother, who was quietly—and suspiciously, I felt—messing with their bags in the trunk. So much so that I didn't notice Lola digging her nails into my arm until I settled her on the couch.

"Oh!" she said. "Sorry, baby. That's my fault."

I examined the damage, a line of pink crescents on the inside of my wrist. "No harm, no foul, Lola," I said to reassure her.

When I looked back up she was staring at the floor blankly, as if someone had come and switched her off without my noticing.

"I'll go check on Mom," I said, touching her shoulder with the tips of my fingers. Lola did not reply.

We were at the house on a simple mission: to clean it up. I had been at my father's house in Sacramento when my mom called to dispatch me to the beach house. "I don't know what shape it's in," she said. "But I don't want to see any of his stuff." She was referring to Walter. "Are you okay?" I asked. "I'm fine, Teo," she said cheerfully. I could tell she was upset. "Everything's perfectly fine." She always hated him.

When I'd gotten to the house, there was not much evidence of Walter. He had purchased the summer house with his pension. It was a drafty shotgun, built too close to the beach, and the ocean crept closer each year. We never used it for vacation getaways the way he imagined. My Tiyo Francis lived there with his wife when he was released from Folsom, my cousin Bea stayed for a semester when she got kicked out of CSU Fullerton for dealing bunk ecstasy to freshmen, and my favorite cousin Carlina had stayed with her girlfriend when her dad finally kicked her out last year. When I was eight, I spent a blissful summer here with my mother, because, as I found out on Labor Day, she had been quietly getting divorced from my father.

Tiya Eilene had initiated a redecoration five years ago that cleared the house of memorabilia. I had gathered the remaining trinkets—the photos from Walter's Naval Academy graduation and family reunions that my mother didn't want to go to, tchotchkes from various island cruises, including a handful of tinsel leis and pressed pennies engraved with the national flora of American states, a Bush-Quayle '93 hat, and a lavender marbled urn carrying the ashes of a "Penelope 'Peggy' Williams, beloved daughter, sister, aunt, and friend to many," a collection of mac 'n' cheese boxes that expired thirteen years earlier, in 2005—and placed them in the closet of Lola's room. But in Lola's bedroom, I left the framed picture of her and Walter sitting in front of this house, their faces ruddy and happy from spending the day in the sun.

I remembered Walter as a quiet, red-faced man who always seemed both bewildered and infuriated by his strange lot in life as the ineffectual white patriarch of a large Filipino family. At the rare family gatherings my mother took me to, he usually sat in what Carlina called "his throne," a cracked leather recliner stained with his usual drink of choice, cranberry juice, a vice picked up after his turn to a late-in-life sobriety.

The chair would soon be sold, or donated, or trashed, along with the rest of his and Lola's earthly things, in this house and the other. His was a legacy of credit card debt and online poker losses, and while the rest of the siblings were back in Vacaville, my mother was tasked with watching over Lola for the duration of the clean-out, the euphemism they used for this unexpected end of Walter's life, the life that Lola came to America for.

Where Lola would go when the beach house and the Vacaville house were sold was still unclear and subject to stealthy, passive-aggressive negotiations among her children. Ever the master of high-stakes emotional poker, my mother refused to show me her cards. My bet was on Tiya Eilene, who was unmarried and the only one of the siblings who was Walter's biological child. She lived in Vegas, where she worked as a phlebotomist and played bingo on Tuesdays, Thursdays, and Sundays. Surely, she would be the obvious choice.

As I approached the front door, I heard the faint, ugly sound of a jungle bird. My mother met me at the doorstep with a regretful look and a wire cage in her left hand. An enfeebled, feathered creature peered up at me. Its eyes were circled with a familiar layer of beige crust.

They had brought the bird.

"Sweetie, I hear you," Lola crooned from the living room.

The cockatoo spat back one of the jingles she picked up from daytime TV, which Lola left on all day to keep the bird company. A running joke was that Sweetie was the best voice in the family—the joke was that listening to the bird squawk out the melody of "Mack the Knife" was an experience one could only wish on their worst enemies. Which, for our family, was often one another. My main gripe? The bird never shut up. As a child, Sweetie had terrorized me, swatting her wings in my face and nearly biting my finger off on more than one visit. I had assumed they would leave her at the house.

"Belen, bring her here," Lola directed my mother, who caught the disgusted expression on my face.

"Don't say anything," my mother said to me. "She refused to leave it behind. Besides, you didn't have to spend hours in the car with it."

Sweetie whistled another song in response, which I vaguely recognized as "The Girl from Ipanema."

"Fine," I said. "But if it bites me I'm finally killing it."

"That's not funny," she said. "Don't joke about death in front of her."

"Sorry," I said. "How is she?"

My mother placed the cage down in the kitchen. Sweetie chirped hoarsely. "What do you think?" she said. "Her whole life has been upended. Her husband died."

She never referred to Walter as her father, or her stepfather. She rarely spoke about him at all.

Lola entered the room and made her way toward us. Her short hair was buoyed by the humidity, and I was reminded of a photo she had shown me from her showgirl days, her hair done up in a careful bouffant, her face unbroken and sweet, still so recognizably her own. To me, she looked the same as when I last saw her. But what did I know about her, this woman whom I saw a few times a year—if that—for less than a week at a time? I could read little from her face, which was turned adoringly to Sweetie.

Sweetie had a strange diet. Lola liked to feed the bird Eggo waffles and wet lettuce that she stuck to the cage with clothespins. She ate a specially made mix of birdseed, which was collected in pink and blue plastic cups clipped along the interior of the cage. I rarely saw the bird eat, but Lola diligently changed her food every morning. On that first day, she walked my mother and me through the process: warming the waffle just so, washing the lettuce with lukewarm—not cold—water, and pouring out three tablespoons of birdseed, making sure to scrape off the extra seed with the flat edge of a kitchen knife. The waffles, she told us, were doled out every evening at exactly 7 p.m. for dessert.

"How old is Sweetie?" I asked Lola.

"Oh, she's old," Lola said. She handed the food cups to me so I could tip the seed in. "She's Filipino too, you know."

I laughed, thinking it was a joke, but Lola was serious. "I got her in Manila," she said. "When was it . . . 1979. In the summer. Right before I went to the US. She was an engagement present from my older brother."

I nearly spilled the bag of seed, but my mother caught my arm. The bird was more than forty years old. "How is that even possible?" I asked.

Sweetie was hunched in her cage, violently flipping her head toward us every time we said her name.

"They live a long time, these birds," Lola said. "Fifty, sixty years. She even speaks Waray, huh? Better than Belen." She whispered a phrase to the bird, who chirped back a sound that plausibly sounded like what Lola had said. Lola beamed at us, and I clapped, more for her than for Sweetie, but I could sense that my mother was annoyed.

"My Waray is fine, Mom," she said.

Lola shrugged. "Well, your Tagalog isn't good. You should practice more."

My mother snapped the food containers into the cage bars. "I'm busy."

"With what?"

"With work. With raising a daughter." I noticed that Lola was looking at my mother, but my mother would not meet her eyes. She was staring at the ground. As the daughter being invoked, I wondered if I should say something to keep the conversation from escalating further. I regretted asking about the bird's age in the first place and stared at Sweetie accusingly. *This is your fault*, I thought, illogically, and I realized that I did not know whose fault it was that every conversation we had devolved into

the airing of the same wounds: that Lola had left my mother
and her siblings with my great-grandfather so that she could
marry a stranger, that my mother did not want to leave the Philippines but was forced to when she was sixteen, that when my
mother turned eighteen she did not speak to Lola for eight
years, until one day she called to say, "I'm pregnant, Mom. I'm
having a daughter."

But if Lola was offended, she didn't show it. She flicked her
eyes coolly between us. "Well, she's grown," she said. "Now what
will you do with your time?"

The next morning, my mother went into town and returned
with a car full of boxes and packing tape and bubble wrap. We
began the slow work of packing up the house and filling the
car for trips to Goodwill or the unattended backlot dumpster
of the Safeway in town. The days passed this way, consolidating
each room into as few boxes as possible. Lola spent too much
time in her bedroom, I thought, and often, when I knocked on
her door, she would call out to say she was taking a nap. Eventually, she stopped replying, and I stopped knocking. There
were times, after the glow of dinner, Lola humming some old
show tune with Sweetie, my mother and I washing the dishes
together, the sound of the ocean outside, where I felt that this
maternal oblivion could be the rest of my life. But then, just
as quickly, I would remember that I was leaving soon and my
body would itch with the desperate need to leave the house,
to go to college, where I would not be a granddaughter, or a
daughter, but just another girl.

I still took my walks alone. From the beach, I liked to watch
my mother and Lola, mother and daughter, sitting together in
the warm light of the house. At that distance, I could see only
their shadows in the light, changing shape with each movement
of their bodies. I wondered what they would see if they were to
look out the window. Would they recognize me from this far
away?

At night, after Lola hugged me goodnight, checked with my
mother that Sweetie had gotten her waffle, covered the bird's

cage with a sheet, and shuffled into her room, my mother and I watched "Christmas in July" on Lifetime, an endless marathon of movies about white women and, what seemed to me, petty familial problems that always resolved themselves neatly in time to celebrate the holidays together. I knew that these women existed only to placate the rest of us from unhappy families in varying degrees of dysfunction. I knew my mother knew this too. Neither of us acknowledged this it remained the only TV we watched together.

"What if she lived with us?" I asked one night, during a commercial break.

My mother muted the TV. "Are you trying to be funny?"

"No, I'm serious. Why not?"

"You mean she'd live with me. You're leaving." Somehow this sounded like an accusation, although no one had been more excited about my getting into college than my mother, who had cried so intensely when I got the acceptance letter that I was afraid she was confused about which school I had gotten into.

"I'll be back, like, all the time," I said.

My mother sighed. She reached over and squeezed my arm. "I'll think about it, Teo."

I knew this was her way of saying no.

One afternoon, while Lola was napping, my mother asked me if I wanted to go for a walk in the forest. It was a mild summer day, the sun peeking through the canopy above us, lighting our way through the trees. My only pair of shoes, Vans so old that the canvas was ripping at the seams, were impractical for a hike. I kept tripping on risen roots and rotted fruit scattered along the path. My mother, however, was a woman prepared for all seasons. She had brought a waterproof hat and cargo pants whose bottoms she unzipped into knee-length shorts, and she wore her usual thick-soled boots. She loved to hike, to be in nature, and could have easily sped along intrepidly ahead. But she walked patiently beside me.

"This place reminds me of the Philippines," said my mother. "This morning I woke up, and for a moment I felt like a little girl. Something about being by the water."

I had never been to the Philippines. And since she left as a girl, neither had my mother. She claimed she had no time to travel, that it would be too expensive, but I suspected that the real cost, the one she could not bear, would be the bridging of the gap between her memory of home and the reality of it now.

"We had a forest right behind our house," my mother said. "My Lolo would never let us go in there alone."

"Why?"

"He told us different stories to keep us out. Usually ghost stories. The spirits of dead wives who would sit in the trees waiting for children to walk by so they could steal them. A curse on the forest that could turn any child walking through it into an adult who would never be allowed to return home because their parents wouldn't recognize them anymore."

A blackbird flew overhead, cackling furiously, startling us both for a moment. Then my mother continued, "Once he told us, and I think this is true, or at least based on something that happened in a forest in the province, that once they found a Japanese soldier in the woods. He had been there alone, thinking he was hiding out from American soldiers without realizing that the war had ended twenty years earlier. I don't know how he could have survived like that. Lolo says at first he was in denial, he thought it was a trick to capture him. Luckily all his ammunition had been used up by then, and he was a skeleton from living off mangoes and the occasional slaughtered cow for years, so he wasn't a threat. Even once they convinced him that the war was over, he couldn't bring himself to surrender. I think they made him, but my Lolo always said that it must have just been a formality."

"I can't imagine believing in anything enough to hold out that long," I said.

"I think he was just crazy," my mother said.

"Right."

"Lolo built me a shed to play in, since I couldn't go into the forest," my mother continued. "We would go and tell ghost stories at night. It's still there, next to the old house."

"Did Lola ever tell you stories?" I asked.

"No," she said. "She was never there."

I did not know what to say. She had told me versions of this story many times before. There was an insistence in her voice, as if she assumed that I did not believe her. I did: but I felt burdened by her confessions, which came more and more the older I got. Selfishly, I preferred it when my mother did not talk about her daughterhood. It put too much of a mirror on me, and at that age I was too much of a coward to look up and see myself clearly. Even now, I am that way.

"She wasn't a good mother, Teo," she said.

"I know," I said. "You told me that already."

Lola dug up a cardboard box stuffed with photo albums. She spread them on the dining table, and I sat with her as she flipped through the yellowed plastic sleeves. "This is your great-grandmother," she said, tapping at a photo of an old woman with horn-rimmed glasses sitting at a kitchen table. Beside her was a lanky boy leaning against the doorway. He was wearing plastic sandals, his skinny feet lifting at the heels. "And that's my older brother," Lola said. "Francisco. He was my parents' favorite."

"He's handsome," I said.

"He was," said Lola. "They could afford to send only one of us to school, and they sent him. I was so mad. I didn't talk to them for weeks. But then he ran away and got married without telling anyone. Some girl he met in the city."

Stories about our family in Leyte often followed this same narrative arc. The introduction of a family member I had never heard of, an opportunity they were given to pull themselves out of poverty, and the manifest ways they squandered what they nearly had in their grasp.

She showed me another photo, this one of her as a young woman in a secretary blouse and bouncy, curly hair. In the corner, she had signed her full name in dramatic, silver cursive letters: Reyna Cristina Atienza Camino. "After that they sent me. But I didn't finish."

"Why not?"

"It wasn't for me." She shrugged. "I'm not like you, baby. Smart, huh?"

I shrugged too. "I guess, Lola."

"Here, look," she said, pulling another photo out of its sleeve. "It's your mother." My mother as a girl—shy, black-haired, with a half-formed smile, the expression caught on film before she could complete it. Illogically, I thought she looked like me, as if I were the progenitor of our face and not the other way around. Beside her, with his arm around her shoulders, was an old man in a pale-blue barong. This was my grandfather, my namesake, Teodoro. "So dark, those two," Lola said, as if this were a personal failing they shared. "She always looked just like him. That's why they got along so well."

There were endless photos. Of the house, the land, christenings, birthdays, spare candids. Lola visited Leyte every year to see our extended family of second and third cousins and uncles and aunts who I had never met. She knew them all because she was responsible for all of them, because she had squandered everything and had everything. She had dropped out of school, had three children by a man who left one morning without a word, and a year later, at a Manila nightclub, met Walter, a young naval officer who married her and whisked her away to the US base in Apra Harbor.

The truth was that when my mother told me Walter had died, I felt relief. Things would be simpler now he was gone. But somehow, even in death, he was a pain in the ass. It was with his money that Lola helped pay for the family's schooling, weddings, and debts. Who would do that now?

The next evening, we ate a dinner composed of freezer leftovers on the terrace. Frozen pizza, steamed broccoli, hash browns. We had only a few more days left in the house. At the end of the week, we would drive back to Vacaville, where Tiyo Jose was waiting for us. I had placed my money on the wrong sibling. It had been decided that Lola would live with him and his family in Anaheim. "There are lots of Filipinos there," my mother said. "You'll never be lonely." This did not seem to move Lola, who was more interested in talking about her annual trip to the Philippines in the fall, a trip that seemed impractical given how different her life was going to be soon. On her phone, she showed me photographs from her last visit.

"This is the south side," she said. "We're thinking of building a house there for my cousin Alina's daughter. She's getting married in the fall. Isn't she beautiful?" She passed the phone to me, but my mother intercepted it. She stared at the photo of a young woman posing beachside beside the old house, the house my mother and Lola grew up in.

"Where's the small house?" my mother asked.

"What do you mean?" Lola said.

"The shed Lolo built," my mother replied, and in her voice I caught an unfamiliar note, the sound of a child whining. "The one he made me."

"What do you care about that?" Lola said. "You're not going back there. What does it mean to you?"

"What happened to it?"

"It was damaged in the typhoon. You knew that."

"You were going to do repairs."

"It cost too much. It was easier to just tear it down."

My mother tapped the phone, as if she could conjure the small house back into being. "It was my house."

Lola spoke in a tone I was familiar with, the tone my mother spoke to me in when she thought I was acting like a child. "This was my house too, Belen."

My mother's face twisted and she stood up for a moment, as if formulating a reply, but instead she swallowed it down and rushed back inside, slamming the screen door so hard that it slapped back open.

Lola lapsed into the same blank expression that she wore all the time now. Although I was still sorry for her, I did not feel the urge to comfort her, or to explain myself when I followed my mother inside the house. I found her by Sweetie's cage, the door cracked open, placing a waffle inside. When I walked up to her, I realized that she was crying. I turned to her, and she held me the way she did when I was younger, an embrace that I refused more and more because I was afraid of how much she needed me. But for that one moment, I let her hold me. When we separated, I saw Lola in the doorway, looking shocked as she turned her head away from the house. At first I thought she felt betrayed because I had gone to my mother and not to her, but when I followed her gaze I saw Sweetie, let loose, flying into the forest.

It had rained earlier that day, and the forest floor was black and wet. The trees were full of native birds: orange-breasted robins and bluebirds that traveled in pairs and black crows the size of small children and even a low-flying hawk who turned a yellow eye at us, as if to ask our odd crew of women, why are you here, so far from home? Who are you looking for?

Lola moved slowly, and I held her hand as she navigated her way through the trees. My mother walked ahead of us, moving too quickly, I thought, aggressively looking around in search of the bird. Lola played a video of Sweetie singing on her phone, hoping the bird would reply. I suspected that Sweetie wouldn't be easy to find. In her cage, the cockatoo looked frail, always on the verge of teetering over into the pile of droppings and loose feathers that formed a rank carpet along the bottom of the cage. But as she dived into the forest, disappearing from sight, Sweetie flew elegantly, assuredly, as if this whole time, traveling from one country to another, she had been waiting for the right moment to slip free.

An hour passed, and then another, and Sweetie's recording began to grate on all of us. Lola turned the volume down, and we rested on a knocked-over redwood, the bark still gummy from the rain. Through the canopy, the sun ran orange, glinting against the red of Lola's acrylic nails. My mother stood up and did a last scan of the forest. "It's getting dark," she said. "We should go back."

"Where are you going?" Lola asked.

"Back to the house, Mom," my mother said. "We can't stay out here all night."

"Why are you giving up, huh? How can you leave now?" Lola's shoulders tensed.

"I'm tired. We can look again in the morning."

Lola wouldn't stop. "How can you be tired? It's your fault she's gone."

"It was an accident, Mom."

"I distracted her, Lola," I said. "It's my fault too." But neither my mother or Lola acted like they heard me.

"You just wanted to hurt me," said Lola. "So you let her out."

"I did not, Mom."

"Yes, you did."

My mother pressed her hands to her temples. "You are so fucking stubborn."

"Ha!" The sound echoed around us. Lola's face was wild, her eyebrows raised in unexpected fury. "I'm stubborn?"

"Yes."

"You're stubborn. You couldn't even come to Walter's funeral."

My mother whispered, "You know I couldn't go." I wondered, then, if she had let the bird out on purpose. Or merely let neglect shape her actions, making the accident inevitable. But before I could ask the question, she was already walking away, leaving me and Lola alone in the darkening forest.

I took Lola's arm. "Come on," I said. "We can look more tomorrow." She hesitated, but my mother had already disappeared into the trees. She was right, it would soon be too dark to find our way home. Lola held my hand as I guided us back, pointing out the roots and dips in the dirt so she wouldn't trip. When we returned, my mother and Lola went into their separate bedrooms. Neither one could bring herself to say sorry.

At dawn I woke to a strange whining noise that I thought was the wind, but then I remembered: Sweetie. I walked through the house, following the ebb and flow of the sound, peeking in the corners behind the sofa and the fridge in case the bird had somehow found her way back in. But there was nothing there, just boxes and things soon to be placed in boxes. I was checking behind the TV when I realized that the whine was emerging from Lola's bedroom. It was the sound of her crying, a sound I had never heard before.

I wished then that a different grandchild was here in the house with her instead of me. Carlina or Bea or Ricardo or Alonso or Gigi. Any one of them would have heard that sorry sound and opened the door that separated them from the woman in the room alone. They would have bothered to ask Lola how she was feeling. They would have realized that this was the last time they would spend time with her like this, before the rest of their life began.

Years later, on one of my occasional visits back to California, I confessed to Carlina how I had felt. It was my last trip home for a long time—I was three weeks into my first pregnancy, and I had not yet told my mother. But I told Carlina, and somehow our conversation led to Lola, who was gone by then, and Carlina had taken my hand and answered the question I did not ask. My real question. "You'll be a good mom, Teo," she said. "I know you will."

Still, I did not believe her.

Lola's crying softened; soon the house was quiet. Through the living room windows, I could see the sun rising quickly over the forest. It was bright enough to start looking again.

The forest was louder than last night, and when I played Sweetie's song off my phone I could barely hear her over the birds cackling and crying and singing above me. I walked with my eyes trained on the trees, hoping to spot a flash of pink against the green. But even once the sun had risen completely, there were no signs of the bird.

Eventually, my foot settled on something soft. When I looked down, there she was, lying on her back in the brush. Her body convulsed with quick, shallow breaths. She must have hit a tree, or a telephone wire. Her left wing hung crooked behind her back, and twitched with each breath. I scooped her into my hands and held her in my lap. She was very heavy. That was how I knew Sweetie was dying—how heavy she was. There was no recognition in her eyes, no sense of my holding her. Just those quick breaths and the wings shaking the body into silence.

When I returned to the house, I realized that almost everything was finally in boxes, some set aside for storage, the rest marked for donation. The clean-out did not make the house feel new or more spacious but instead much smaller than before. It was unbelievable that everything could have fit in there in the first place. My mother and Lola were awake, waiting for me. Among what remained, they stood there united in their questions for me: Where did you go? What did you see?

I told them as much of the truth as I could. The rest, I kept for myself.

ELIZABETH MCCRACKEN

Seven Stories About Tammy

FROM *Zoetrope*

1.

"Her name is Tammy," Morris had announced ahead of time, which is what threw his family off. The imagined Tammy, his first girlfriend, first to be brought home anyhow, was a girl in a bikini he'd met in Tallahassee, a model, he told his fellow Harkins, who filled in the rest. Hair in pigtails, a vacationing Iowan, a girl who'd blow over, a girl you'd be teased over for the rest of your life. When Morris appeared, he was not with a girl but a woman. This Tammy—the actual Tammy—had thick, blonde hair she wore in a mid-neck bob whose depth could be measured with a ruler. Hair like the Sphinx. Tan like the Sphinx. A smoker's voice: ruined? No, sexy and persuasive. Morris was twenty-seven. She wasn't.

Immediately, the parlor game was *how old is she?* and Dennis, the father of them all, decided he would win.

"It's a pleasure to meet you," Tammy said.

He took her hand and palpated it. "I'm Dennis," he said.

This was years ago, in the old house, with the oak dining table on the rickety sunporch, the rumbling pocket doors and skewed everything that gave the place the feel of an ocean filled with ships, future wrecks, the white sofa with the mashed cushions, the china cabinet missing half its pulls. Soon they would move to a new house, though Dennis hadn't told them that yet: He'd come into some money. He was a family man, and his thoughts should have been plural and third person, *they*'d come into some money, Dennis and Miriam and the children. But it had been his father's money, and therefore he said to himself: *mine*. Victoria was a senior in high school, and Porter in eighth grade. Morris and Tammy were just passing through, staying in a hotel in the Back Bay, paid for certainly by Tammy, who had an air of wealth—small gold earrings; long, navy wool coat. That hair, which must have been expensive to maintain. Dennis didn't know these things, being secretly rich himself. The rich never know the cost of anything. His wife, Miriam, knew.

They'd never met anyone from Florida, only people who'd ended up there, as if by gravity. Tammy was tall and angular, stood with her hands in her back pockets—blue jeans, ironed. Morris's jeans were ironed now, too. By her? Or had she put Morris to work? She seemed like that sort of woman, efficient and ruthless, with beautiful manners. There was a moment in that first ten minutes when she might have put the lot of them— Morris's parents, sister, brother, the family beagle Albert—to work. Set them right.

Everything would have been different if they'd been obedient. Tammy might have saved them all, not just Morris, who wouldn't have drifted away. Porter wouldn't have drunk so. (Of course he would have, but maybe to more charming effect.) Their parents wouldn't have argued. Victoria's life would have been changed the most. She was seventeen then, a fool for charismatic women.

They looked at Tammy, their first stranger. They offered her the middle of the sofa. Not even Morris sat beside her. It was 7 p.m., start of November, mid-1980s. In this particular group, nobody yet understood their own properties.

"Well," said Tammy, on that white sofa. "What would you like to know?"

She gestured at her own lap, and the family realized that she meant, incredibly, about herself, and they decided they already knew everything there was.

"I'm on duty," said Dennis, and he went to the kitchen to cook and drink.

The name *Tammy* didn't suit her, but it wasn't like *Albert*. Albert was a girl dog, not a boy, and had been named after the tall, serious neighbor down the street, an Episcopalian minister with the first goatee any of them had ever seen and a heart so full of God's love the family couldn't keep themselves from making fun. *Albert* was chosen in the usual way, each of them offering a name, alternately earnest, pretentious, absurd: *Héloise, Fathead, Cora, Darling, Ladybird, Grandma, Lucrezia Borgia, Peanut Butter, Chicken Kiev, Gidget, Missy, Mommy, Albert*—the last seized in a panic when it appeared the dog might really, truly, be called Mommy. *Throw Albert to the dogs!* thought the mother, whose name was Miriam. Albert did always seem a godly dog after that. By "godly," they meant serious of expression and soulful of howl and given to eating her own shit.

Miriam looked at Tammy: soft at the jaw, unwrinkled but the threat all round her face, green veins visible at the backs of her hands. The air of money suggested that she was well-preserved, as opposed to careless in her youth. An ironing board of a woman, Tammy, articulated in some places yet not others, stiff, useful for one or two particular things. Adjustable but inflexible. She and Morris both wore white shirts with their dark jeans, as though they were a musical duo, or specialized missionaries, her collar turned up, his spread out.

"Dinnertime!" called Dennis.

The children of the family went to the kitchen. It was a dance both choreographed and improvised, the elbow to the swinging door, the laying down of mats on the table.

Tammy held back.

"No," said Miriam, in response to what? "You're our guest. Sit, sit."

"Where do you want me?"

"Anywhere," said Miriam, trying to mean it.

Tammy—handsome, elegant—looked over the table, chose a chair, failed the test, and settled into their mother's place, beside their father. When Morris delivered the last dish, Tammy directed him to the chair opposite her.

Easier to communicate silently across the table, thought Miriam, who herself had been a spy at other people's dinner tables. When you sit next to your confederate, everyone can read your code.

"Where in Florida?" Dennis said, as he sat down.

"You wouldn't know it," said Tammy.

"I know everything," he told her.

"Ah *ha*," she answered, with admiration.

But he'd wanted to demonstrate the everything he knew. Albert the dog sat on her feet.

"Hello, you," she said to the dog, under the table.

"Albert," said Morris. "Manners."

"She's all right," said Tammy.

"She just wants to be loved," said Miriam, embarrassing everyone.

Tammy said, "Oh, Albert. *I* love you." She straightened her silverware and seemed unhappy.

Morris lifted the tablecloth, grabbed the dog by her collar, and pulled her out. "Get along, Albert," he said. Roughly, tenderly, he gathered her in his arms and carried her to the back door and let her through.

When he returned, Tammy said, gently, "Mo."

"Hmm?"

"Hands," she said, and rubbed hers together.

"Ah, yes." He went into the kitchen to wash them.

Dennis had cooked dinner, seafood and béarnaise sauce in puff pastry, scallops in bacon, asparagus in bacon and butter, so much butter the air shone with it. His sauces were always breaking, and the kitchen always streaked with roux and red wine in his wake; but he loved to cook, so they agreed he had a gift for it. Miriam's own cooking ran to stuffed peppers and chili. One look at Tammy made clear she was a health nut.

"This looks wonderful," she said miserably, her fork looking for a way in.

"I'm a real butter-and-egg man," Dennis said.

"You always say that," said Porter, "and I still don't know what it means."

"It's a quote."

"Which explains nothing."

The boy, age thirteen, eyed the glasses of wine around the table. Sometimes, at dinner parties, he was allowed a drink. His father disapproved, but his mother insisted that allowance was why her family produced no drunks—they learned early on how to handle their liquor.

Porter was voracious. They all knew it, that the once ordinary, delightful child might just devour them all, not because he wanted to eat *them*, but rather the whole world in which they happened to be. The question was how to slow him down. He'd grown six inches in the past year.

Tammy said, to Dennis, "You're a real French chef."

"I dabble."

"Well, if this is *dabbling*," she said. She thought she was an invited guest. She was a contestant.

Sometimes drink made an odd encyclopedia of feeling rise up inside of Dennis, voluminous and leatherbound. He was childish, more childish the older his children got. He didn't want to be outshone or outfucked. He thought he'd like to sleep with her—he hadn't known, before this moment, that he would always want to seduce his children's . . . what would you call them? He'd just never had the chance before.

Not sleep with. Snog, maybe, as the English would say. Enrapture. Win over.

The uses of her bob were clear, the way her hair fell and obscured her face, then swung back into place. With long hair, it would have been intolerable, but she wielded the bob like a lady with a fan in the olden days, folding and unfolding it.

"Was he always such a talented actor?" Tammy asked.

Dennis pointed encouragingly at her plate. "Who?"

"Your son. *Morris.*"

"He dabbled," said Miriam.

"He's very good," said Tammy. "He's better than you know."

"I know *everything*," said Dennis again.

"I didn't know you were acting, Morris," said Miriam. "I thought you were working as a waiter."

"At a dinner theater," said Tammy. "I'm the manager. He'll be in *The Man Who Came to Dinner* next month."

"Who keeps kicking me?" said Dennis, and—in probing under the table—knocked a full glass of red wine into Tammy.

She sat for a moment. Her white shirt, formerly the bright white of a yacht's sail, now resembled the flag pirates raise to warn other boats. What would she do—take it in good humor, or weep, or wait to be rescued? And yet nobody, including Morris, was coming to save her—not even Albert, who scratched at the back door like a family curse.

Tammy said, in a flat voice, "Oops-a-daisy."

"Victoria," said Miriam. "Take her upstairs. Get her some clothing—you can go into my closet."

Miriam was short and, in those days, bosomy—she'd dressed for their guest in a caftan. Tammy gave a look that conveyed her exact measurements and personal taste. *I will not partake in a caftan,* her eyebrows said.

She reviewed the table, assessing everyone—her eyes lingered on plump Victoria—and then she said, "Porter."

"Yes?"

"You'll have something I can borrow."

"Like—like my suit?"

"Jeans," she said. "A T-shirt."

"I have those." He turned to his mother. "But what about—"

"I don't need underwear," said Tammy.

Morris went up with them, to supervise, and when they came back down—Tammy in a pair of red corduroys worn fretless at the knee, and a plaid flannel shirt tucked in, and a belt, ludicrous, resplendent—he explained that they would be returning to the hotel.

Oh, were you here, Morris? his family thought.

"She's got to be in her forties," said Miriam, once they'd left.

"No," said Dennis. "No."

"At least."

"I was sitting close-up. Thirties, though."

"Forties. I'll bet money."

"How do we find out?"

"She's not," said Porter. "It's sun damage."

"What?"

"That's what she told me. Because of Florida."

"How did that come up?"

"I don't know. She told me that. Why she might look a little old."

"Well, *that's* suspicious," said Dennis.

"She said it to the mirror, not me."

"I didn't like her," said Victoria.

"Me, neither," said Porter.

"No?" said Dennis.

"She was flirting with you, Daddy. All through dinner."

"Really? She must have been trying to make a good impression."

"She didn't," said Victoria.

"She did not," said Miriam.

"Well, we'll never see her again," said Dennis.

"Wrong," said Miriam—and then, in voice of prophecy: "That's our first child gone."

2.

They were married in a VFW hall: no dancing, not enough food, a cash bar, a handful of guests. The groom had made the arrangements. Tammy, thank God, had not worn white, but a light-brown suit with lapels that looked like clubs, the kind on playing cards. Morris wore a nice blue suit with a thick, blue knit tie that resembled an expensive sock. His best man was a little chinless guy who was from Texas and liked to talk about it. No maid of honor, no flower girl, no ring bearer. The Texan was it.

Miriam disapproved. She would have disapproved if there'd been a cast of dozens. She disapproved of the wedding, and her disapproval suffused all its particulars: the paltry crowd, the menu of spinach pie and grape leaves from the Armenian grocery store. She and Dennis had paid the bill but were not otherwise consulted. Half an hour before the ceremony, Tammy revealed that they'd been legally married the week prior at City Hall. This was just theater and revelry. The tables were square. They should have been round.

"I like Texans," Dennis told the Texan. "Texans get irony. You do understand that it's just a state, right? Like Delaware is a state." He'd taken off his suit jacket, rolled up his sleeves. The VFW hall was going to his head.

The Texan had a thin mustache and bad teeth. He was a professor of Texan literature.

"That's a thing?" Dennis asked.

"We aren't rubes and cowboys, or parochial hayseeds, no matter what Easterners think."

"Well, thinking your state has its own literature—" said Dennis, and Miriam, without planning to, said, "How old is she?"

"Who," said the Texan. "Tammy?"

"She dudn't mean Katherine Anne Porter," said Dennis, in a bad accent.

At that, the Texan smiled unhandsomely. "Couldn't say."

"Couldn't *rightly* say."

The Texan shook his head and rattled the ice in his drink.

The bride and groom had sat in the middle of the hall at their own little table, and now went table to table like royalty visiting every island in a distant archipelago. They were sober. They were always sober. Dennis and the Texan were drunk, or drunkish, and each thought the other a fool who could be put right through politeness.

"So you know Tammy from where," said Dennis.

"Texas," explained the Texan. "Corpus. *Christi.*"

"She's a Texan?"

"Sixth-generation."

"I thought Florida."

"Tammy? No. Lived there a long time, though."

"We thought Florida." Dennis turned to Miriam. "Didn't we?"

"A native Floridian," said Miriam, for the pleasure of saying the word.

"No, ma'am," said the Texan.

"How long? Has she lived in Florida."

"Who knows," said the Texan.

"You know, in Massachusetts, we don't count generations," said Dennis. "We don't even *have* an adjective."

"That's because y'all's state is so small people keep getting shoved out the back door into New York. Mo and Tammy'll end up in Texas, I bet. I'm a seventh-generation Texan myself."

Morris and Tammy still lived in Florida.

Florida—Miriam had been drinking, Miriam was not herself—Florida basically *was* Texas, wasn't it? One of those states with a panhandle and too much sunshine.

The Texan said, "Texans like to get back to Texas, in my experience."

"Back to the family ranch," said Dennis.

"Dime store," said the Texan. "Family dime store."

Dennis stood. "There should be dancing. Isn't this a wedding? Aren't we paying for a wedding? I got quarters, and there's a jukebox right over yonder. There shall be dancing, goddammit."

"You're paying for it?" the Texan said to Miriam, once Dennis had left.

"Well, it's not much. Though I always thought her family was rich."

"Tammy's? No, ma'am. That store's been near-failing since the turn of the century."

"She *seems* rich. She's got an aura of money."

"Money does not have an aura. It's money. It's a fact."

"Morris would never live in Texas."

"Well, ma'am, you might be surprised."

"'Ma'am,'" Miriam said. "You think that's charming."

"I think it's polite. Other people find it charming. Tammy! Mo! We were just speaking of you."

Here they came, the happy couple.

The Texan rose and threw his napkin on the table with a flourish, as though he'd defeated it. "Congratulations."

Where was her husband? Trying to convince the bartender to plug in the jukebox. When they were out in public and he was behaving badly, it was her job, she felt, to steer. *Do not go into the ditch, do not go into the ditch.* Her job to interrupt, to pat his arm, to remind him that he was a family man. *Think of us, if not yourself—it's not too late.* Now Miriam got up and hugged Morris, plush and handsome Morris, who didn't belong in Texas. She wouldn't let him go.

"Mother," said Morris, who'd never called her such a thing. "Thank you for everything."

"Is—have you done something to your voice?" she asked.

"What do you mean?"

"It's deeper. Different. It makes you *look*—"

"I've been working with a voice coach," he said. "On my accent."

"You don't have an accent," she said. Then she remembered it, that tiny flag of Massachusetts that had raised itself in his vowels, now gone.

"Porter's drunk," he told her. He pointed with his chin: his younger brother sat at the bar in a suit, which he'd outgrown since its purchase a month before, holding himself like a stack of books. At any moment, all his components might start sliding.

"Oh," she said. Then, "Maybe he's not." He was sixteen. He shouldn't be drunk. She was his mother and responsible, though she rummaged in her brain for a way to blame Tammy.

Tammy kissed her on both cheeks, the kind of physical affection that Miriam particularly disliked: pure obligation. They held each other's elbows.

"I love your son," Tammy told Miriam.

Miriam thought, *Jesus*. But she was the nice parent. "Thank you," she told Tammy. "Thank you for doing that."

The music kicked in—Dennis had made good on his jukebox threat, and inexplicably chosen "In the Ghetto."

Tammy conveyed unhappiness in her elbow grip, and then leaned in and said into Miriam's ear, "Of course, we hope to have children."

"What?"

Tammy's breath was as soft and insubstantial as health food. "We hope to give you grandchildren."

Miriam wanted to say, *Oh? Where will you get them?* Tammy wasn't bad for fifty, or however old she was, but Miriam didn't like being drafted into games of pretend.

"Well," she said into Tammy's ear. It was easier not seeing her face, easier to say things under the cloak of Elvis. "We'll see."

"We're praying for them."

"You're *praying*," said Miriam. She leaned back and looked at Tammy, the little swaths of wrinkles on either side of her mouth, the whole, palpable middle age of her. All this while—three years—Miriam had thought, *I can't ask her. How can I ask her?* "How old are you?" she said now.

"Morris and I are of an age."

You couldn't call somebody a liar. Miriam couldn't. If Dennis were here, he might, or he might laugh and shake his head. Across the hall, he was trying to maneuver an old lady through "In the Ghetto," a waltz to a ballad, a victory dance, though the song was already ending. Miriam could only wait for Tammy to release her elbows, to return her to the inane Texan.

"We'll go pretty soon," said Tammy. "You all stay. We have the hall till eleven."

You all. It was a con, thought Miriam. For three years, Tammy had been coming to visit; and every time, she'd sat with Albert the beagle, never helping in the kitchen, never picking up a plate, talking solely about Morris. Miriam's first born! Her favorite child, though of course that was a secret; how could he not be, she'd spent so long looking uninterrupted into his face, his eyes as they passed from pale blue to hazel brown, as his skinny legs—he'd been born scrawny, six pounds—acquired rolls, and his arms cuffs of fat. Of her younger children, she remembered mostly them saying, *Look, Mommy, look,* and she had then, she'd looked, but it was always away from Morris.

Look, here came Porter, led by his sister, plump Victoria, with the beautiful legs she knew how to show off, *look.* Porter *was* drunk. Even his hair was drunk. What nobody had told Miriam about motherhood: that the bodies of her children would feel like her own body. Not in any poetic way, not that she felt their pain or their ecstasy. Only pride and shame, vanity and self-loathing.

"In the ghetto!" yelped Porter. He seemed like he wanted to add something, but the words were coins on the floor, and if he bent to pick them up, he'd go over.

"You're leaving?" Miriam said to Tammy.

"Yes. Any moment." She touched Morris's hand—Morris! her husband! Morris, a husband!—and he slipped an arm around her waist.

"We're leaving?" he said to her. "Well, Ma—"

Was he going to run down the list of possibilities? Was this an acting thing, an accent thing: *Maman, Mutter, Mam, Madre, Mère—*

Her son was wonderful, blockheaded: If Tammy told him she was young enough to have children, he would believe her.

Dennis was talking to the old lady. He looked sweet, pacific, even as his hand rattled in his pocket for more quarters. For the moment, he'd cast off his bad behavior, and Miriam felt it settle around her shoulders. This happened sometimes. When he was away from her, she'd find herself heading straight for the ditch, full of joy and destruction and pressing the pedal to the floor.

She said, "Take Porter home on your way."

Tammy said, "I don't think—"

"It's not like it's your *real* wedding night."

Morris turned to Tammy first, then to his mother. He'd always been so easily confused. "Yes, it is," he said.

"I won't pry your father away for an hour. Porter needs to go home. You're going that way anyhow. Everyone's already been deflowered, is my guess."

"Christ," said Tammy.

"Okay," said Morris.

"Thank you," said Miriam. She sat down. Everyone was looking at her. She couldn't sort out what they were thinking, and she didn't care. "Are you a well-known scholar?" she asked the Texan. "The foremost?"

"I'm famous in Texas, which is good enough for Texans, which is good enough for me," said the Texan, and then: "I guess he's marrying his mother."

"I guess he is," said Morris's mother, and her unmarried children were terrified to see the joy shining in her face.

3.

Victoria sometimes decided to distinguish herself as the one Harkin known for her kindness, her openness. She decided to practice on Tammy.

"Look at you, girl!" said Tammy, ruining it. "So skinny! You're beautiful."

"I wax and wane like the moon," said Victoria. Which was true all her life: She gained and lost—plump, fat, slender, though never actually skinny, no matter what Tammy said. People treated you differently, depending on your size, but Victoria always felt entirely herself, the same, she just emitted different noises, like the bars of a xylophone when struck.

They were in Philadelphia, 1991. Tammy and Morris had lived in Center City for a year, in a high rise across the river from the train station. Victoria had moved to the city the month before—she was getting a master's degree in psychology at Drexel—and lived in a large apartment on the third floor of a semidetached house at Springfield and Forty-Eighth.

That morning, she'd returned from a run to find her first-floor neighbor sitting on the front steps, as he often was. He was in his fifties, blond the way babies are. "Halt," he'd said. "There's been a break-in."

From the knob up, the front door was intact and itself, but the bottom half had been shattered entirely. It didn't look like the work of human strength—more a wild animal of the folktale variety, or the sort of sudden storm that rearranges livestock in the Midwest, picks up a bunch of pigs and drops them where it wants to, not where's convenient for the pigs. "He must have really needed whatever was inside," said the neighbor, Joe, and Victoria had reflexively wanted to say, *Or she*, as was her habit. "Must have," she said instead. Turns out, all he'd needed was the hundred-dollar bill that Joe had fixed to his refrigerator with a magnet. Victoria's apartment was untouched.

She did not tell her parents this story. She didn't tell anyone. As long as she said nothing, the upper half of her was intact, still locked, like the door.

Morris and Tammy had invited her for dinner, and Tammy had answered the door and exclaimed over Victoria and led her into the living room and gestured to its floor-to-ceiling windows that looked west, over the universities of University City, and farther. That's why a high rise. Victoria understood and despised her understanding.

"Isn't it nice," said Tammy.

"Yes, quite," said Victoria, who'd been trained by her mother. The living room was one sofa and a variety of cushions on the floor, pulled up to the coffee table, which seemed to be a chunk of farm machinery topped by a giant piece of glass. These days, Tammy was an interior decorator. Morris was acting, mostly sea captains and villains at a local children's theater, though he took the train to New York for auditions, hoping for something better, and came home and cooked and did the housework. Now he brought out shallow bowls of soup. He wore a manly apron that looked to be meant for smithery of some kind, but the soup was delicate, delicious: a smooth substance of mushrooms and vegetable stock and a hint of peanut.

"It's so good!" said Victoria. This time, she'd lost the weight mostly through hours of swimming at the Drexel pool and the speed she bought from Joe, the neighbor. The speed wasn't an everyday thing, just weekends, a new habit. She snorted it. Her nose was sore. Even now it was.

"Do you want more?" asked Tammy in a friendly way.

"Oh, no thank you!" Victoria said. "I should save room for dinner."

In the pause that followed, she realized this *was* dinner. There was no further course, not so much as a cheese plate. In her head, she began to tell her mother. Mortification could be useful if you could convert it to a story, this was among the lessons of her childhood, though usually you had to sit with it first, to soften it up and fashion it into something for someone else to admire.

"I'm having more!" said Morris jovially. "You, too, Vic?"

My beautiful brother, she thought. The family spoke of Tammy as though she'd kidnapped Morris from a playground to raise him as her own child, but he'd been an adult, and clearly life with her suited him. He'd grown into a handsome man, with thick hair cut expensively by somebody—a dour, old-man barber; or a dour, young-woman stylist, Victoria guessed—who also attended to his eyebrows and beard. Even his nose looked different. Before Tammy, it had tended to the piggy—prominent nostrils, bunched bridge—and the change wasn't surgical but in the way he held his head, and how he no longer viewed the world with alarm.

"Vic? More soup?"

Victoria wasn't sure of the right answer. She grasped her bowl and tried to stand from her cushion.

Across the coffee table, Tammy accomplished this as if on hydraulics, saying, "Sit, sit," as she rose. "And then we have something we want to show you. Why we asked you here."

Victoria *had* wondered. What could they want from her? And then she was seized with fear: an egg. They wanted a baby, but Tammy was too old, so they needed an egg, one that would be family. The idea disgusted her. Also, it didn't make sense: You couldn't do that with a brother and sister. It had to be something else. They'd given her a glass of white wine that tasted green as a tree, with an aftertaste of violin. Who knows how long it had been in the fridge.

"All right!" said Tammy. "Here's what we want to show you."

She had a videotape in her hand, and she slid it into the player.

"This is important," she said. "Self-defense. Have you ever heard of model mugging?"

Victoria shook her head. "You were a model, weren't you?"

Tammy laughed and touched her throat. She was never so happy as when other people were stupid. "No," she said. "I mean, I was, but not that kind of model. You need to learn how to defend yourself. I want you to watch this."

On the television, a group of women stood beside a man wearing an enormous, padded suit, the scale of a cartoon character at a theme park. Under his arm, he held a large, blank head, which he then set atop the suit. His actual head—with its mustache and shaggy hair—disappeared, and he was no longer human. He was robot, or a zombie swollen from an allergic reaction. A series of little plays ensued. A member of the group would pretend to walk down the street, and the padded monster would follow and touch the woman on the shoulder. One by one, the other women would then attack, screaming *NO!* and *STOP! NO!* They'd knee the monster in its padded stomach, kick it in its padded groin. Victoria had always imagined self-defense classes as silent and elegant, but these women took pleasure in thrashing their enormous would-be rapist. *NO! DON'T!*

In her head, Victoria saw the shattered door of her building. Whoever had done that might do anything he liked. To be pummeled to death: At least she'd feel the hands of a stranger upon her, all she'd ever wanted.

In Philadelphia, she drank too much and snorted speed on the weekends—and the occasional weeknight between—and filled her closets with recycling, bottles of beer in one and stacks of newspapers in another, she never remembered what day or where to take them, and it had been months. It was as though Philadelphia were a forest in which she'd been abandoned; she'd never felt so alone in her life. Years later, she'd realize that feeling was adulthood. Nobody had told her she'd reached it.

Victoria then recognized Tammy among the group; in her gray tracksuit and blue baseball cap, she looked like an old lady. It was her turn. Tammy on the TV slapped at the man in the costume; and while her aim was true, her wrists were weak.

"I'm the best student," Tammy on the cushion said, beaming. "I can take you to a class."

"Maybe."

When it was over, Tammy said, "I have clothing. I was going to donate it to charity, but it'll fit you now, it'll be good for job interviews, some lovely stuff."

The bedroom had the same view: river, train station, west and more west. The curtains were open. Why not? Nobody could see in. Victoria imagined the streets filled with model muggers stalking ordinary women, nosing through the city like mice in a maze.

"Here," said Tammy, dangling a pair of black jeans and a suede blazer and a peachy silk blouse.

"All right," Victoria said, and headed for the bathroom.

"Where are you going?" said Tammy. "We're both girls, you can change here."

Neither was a girl. Victoria was twenty-four, and Tammy was— well, how old *was* she? She had a deep line between her eyebrows, and her earlobes looked ripe, like stone fruit. Victoria couldn't bear the idea of revealing herself, her various stretch marks, the unshaved and untended neighborhoods of her body, all the evidence of neglect and intemperance. So she turned her back, only to face the mirrored closet doors. Tammy's pan-opticon.

"I was fucked up when I was young," Tammy said.

"What?"

"Probably I'm still fucked up."

In the mirrors, Tammy seemed frightened for Victoria, as though this night would decide everything. But straight on, she looked like herself, acid and inexorable. "You're so beautiful," she said, and Victoria could see in her own reflection that it wasn't true. Her hair was uncombed, and her face had broken out in weird blossoms, from the swimming pool or from the speed. Epidermal confusion; her human hide. She was smaller than she had been, that was true. It seemed a mistake God had made, that you could change sizes like this.

Victoria would tell her mother this story, but it was snagged and laddered, a mess.

"Not quite," said Tammy, frowning at Victoria's hips, and with all of West Philadelphia watching through the windows and frowning, too.

4.

It seemed to Porter that he was always drunk and in the back seat of a car, Morris driving, Tammy showing her pinch-pot profile. Tammy despised Porter. He'd known that from his first back-seat ride, away from their wedding.

He's older now, Porter, older than Morris was then, and nearly as old as their father lived to be, and he must acknowledge that it was odd, his mother insisting that the bride and groom deliver the groom's little brother home. They should have driven off to their own life together, waving from a carriage. Instead, they had a teenager in the back of their Toyota, hiccuping like a drunk from a cartoon, with a red nose, tipping a crushed hat at parking meters.

"I can't believe your mother," said Tammy.

"It's not a big deal."

"It's a big deal to me. I wasn't ready to leave."

"Honey! You said you were ready."

Porter had the sort of hiccups that actually made him say *hic.*
"Hic," he said, from the back seat.

"Jesus," said Tammy.

They pulled up to the family house—the new one, which everyone hated. The bride and groom were arguing but in voices of love. Porter tried and failed to open the door. He was the level of drunk that made him wish he had a mirror, to look at himself and marvel at how drunk he was. Assess, too, but mostly marvel.

"It was a battle between us," said Tammy. She touched the side of Morris's face. He'd shaved off his beard for the wedding, a mistake. "And you let her win. On this day, this one day, you should have made clear that you're on my side."

"I *am* on your side. Who else's?"

"I'd worried about this." She shook her head.

"Oh, sweetheart," said Morris. "I am—you're right."

"I know it."

"What can I do now?"

She shrugged. Her shoulders were bare: she'd taken off the jacket and set it like a sleeping baby in the trunk of the car.

"We're here."

"We're here," she agreed.

Porter still couldn't open the door. At first, he'd thought it was the drink—one of the things he loved most about drinking, the funhousification of the stupid world, how it bent corridors and spun beds. The sense of upheaval. But he wasn't *that* drunk. He tried the handle again.

"Your mother loves you, I guess," Tammy said. "But she plays favorites."

"Does she?" asked Morris.

"She's never been to one of your plays."

"In high school—"

"I mean lately."

"She was going to. Before *Hornby* closed."

"That wasn't your fault. You were wonderful."

"Thank you, sweetheart."

"When you're famous, she'll regret it."

"Maybe."

"I mean, you're *known*. You're *known now*."

Something had shifted, Porter realized. They were putting on a conversation for his benefit, and yet he'd also disappeared, the obligatorily silent audience until this play reached its eventual end. He pulled the handle, gentled it back into place, pulled, gentled.

"*Hornby* should have been a big deal," said Tammy.

"It could be revived." Morris yawned, his knuckles against his mouth, and Porter gave an answering yawn that he couldn't keep quiet.

"Well, I'm not tucking you into bed," said Tammy.

"You're not," said Morris, hurt.

"Not you!" she said. "*Him.*"

They'd remembered him! Thank God. "Can't open the door," Porter said, joyfully.

"You fucking *baby*," said Tammy, in a mild voice. She said it for the same reason she might to an actual baby: What were the odds he'd remember?

She undid her seat belt and reached across him. Her bare skin was fragrant, almondy. Porter felt like he should do something. Lick it. Bite it. Her upper arm went past him. He was suffused with love for her, he understood why Morris adored her, her bossy anger. Yes, he was a fucking baby. Her fingertips caught the handle. Nothing. He kissed her shoulder, and she withdrew as though spring-loaded, both all at once and inch by inch.

Was it the kiss—a joke to himself: What's the dumbest mistake you can make in this moment with the materials at hand—that sealed his fate, that convinced Tammy to convince Morris to convince his parents to send him to a summer camp in Idaho for wayward boys? Rehab, said his first girlfriend, a few years later. Oh, god no, said Porter, punishment. I was sent away. Poor kid, said the girlfriend, who didn't want to hear anything more, lest it change her feelings about it. It was the worst time in my life, he said. I can't bear it, said the girlfriend, and she was telling the truth.

Tammy's face made clear his mistake.

He fiddled with the handle. This time, he let it thunk. "Child lock's on," he told the roof of the car. "Somebody'll have to get out to help me."

5.

Things happened over the Tammy years. Albert the beagle was middle-aged when Tammy appeared; they loved each other. Albert knew they were both likely to be put in the backyard. The Harkins would say, of either of them, *Well, of* course *you're a member of the family,* but it wasn't true. Neither Albert nor Tammy *wanted* it to be true. The fur of Albert's belly was white when they met, a loose rug, a pleasure and a catastrophe as she slid on it. But her hips grew rusty, and her mind forgetful. She couldn't be left outside; she wore a little red coat for walks in the cold, and then boots; her eyes turned to opals, and she barked at shadows. She refused all food but hot dogs. She peed on the sofa. She died. She was replaced, infuriatingly, by a large ginger cat called Colonel Pickering.

Dennis was middle-aged, too; a professor of psychology at Lasell Junior College; then, once the money from his family came in, a former professor who believed he'd find his destiny. Any day now. Perhaps *he* was meant to be an actor. Or a playwright. Or an author of books about self-actualization who'd become—something. He had a heart attack and reformed all his bad habits for six months. One of his retinas detached, and in the course of surgery, the doctors put a bubble of gas in his eye, which required him to keep his head parallel to the ground while the eye healed. He drank red wine through a straw and listened to talk radio so he could disagree with it—or so he told his wife, who suspected he didn't. One spring day, his children asked him about a living will, and he waved the notion away, saying, "I mean, I don't want to be a *vegetable.* But anything short of that . . ."

What did he mean? What's short of a vegetable?

"Anyhow," said Victoria, "I don't think you're supposed to use that term anymore."

"To avoid offending carrots, no doubt," said Tammy, who was flattered by people who told her she was offensive. Offensiveness was one of life's reliable pleasures: You couldn't make someone love you, or fear you, but—with wit and a scalpel—you could always offend.

Time passed, and no great destiny materialized, and Dennis came to think that the only way he might change the world would be by leaving it: The world would miss him. So he did. The next heart attack was so sudden he fell through the floor of existence without a chance of rescue. Was not replaced.

6.

Porter and Elena spent eight Christmases at home, in San Luis Obispo—at first, just the two of them, then with their twin daughters. Elena was an only child, and Porter longed to be. Twins were a joke and a relief, sparing them the decision. Elena's parents were dead. Porter's were—not estranged, that was too strong a word for it. Not part of the equation. Unforgiven but not unforgivable. Elena had met them three times.

A grown-up way to live, thought Elena, to be, in your thirties, already at the head of the table. But also childish, as though you were pretending. Then Porter's father died, and he returned from the funeral saying, "Christmas, I think. All together."

We're always all together, Elena said, to herself.

She was pregnant again, two months. Their friends with kids had parents and siblings who babysat, for as much as a week at a time: Perhaps there were upsides to making nice with the family. They would gather in Rhode Island for the holiday, in a house Porter's mother had rented with a view of the ocean, bedrooms and bathrooms for everyone, an attic under the eaves with room for the children—meaning the twins, Leah and Samantha, who were six. Victoria's Millie was only three months old, and Morris and Tammy were childless.

"Childless, except for each other," Porter said.

"What does that mean?" said Elena, who had met Morris but not Tammy.

"You'll see," said Porter. "They're each other's little biddle baby."

On the drive from Logan, Porter worried over which room they'd get: Everyone else was already at the house. "They'll put us all in the attic," he said.

"They won't."

"When I was a child," he said, "I got the worst room. It didn't even have central heat."

"What?" she said. "In *Boston?*"

"'We have divided in three our kingdom,'" said Porter. "But bedrooms, I'm Cordelia. Luckily, there's an ocean nearby, so I can drown myself."

The girls hadn't slept on the red-eye and were now unconscious in their car seats, would be off the entire week.

Elena said, "That's Ophelia. Who drowns. Not Cordelia."

Porter said, "*I* would have liked to be an actor, too."

"You're an artist," she said, and he was: an illustrator and cartoonist. Elena taught dance at a fancy private high school.

"I would have liked to be an actor," he said again.

The house was brick and ivied, up a hill. From the street, you couldn't see the promised ocean view, though you could hear the water.

Morris met them at the door. He had a mustache, a recent acquisition but already belonging to the ages: lush, piebald. "You remember your Uncle Morris, don't you?" he said to Leah and Samantha. "No?"

They'd been three when they met him in California.

"It's the mustache," he said to Elena. "How are you?" He kissed her cheek. Porter leaned in for a hug, and Morris caught him by the shoulder, stopped him, pushed him back, assumed an expression of fondness. "Hey, kid. Merry Christmas. Let me take your bag."

Morris led them to a room on the second floor with a view and an attached bathroom. "This is you, and the girls will be upstairs, right overhead. Get settled in, and join us downstairs."

The house was on a cliff. Ocean filled the frame of the window, magnificent, sick-inducing. Elena was from Omaha. She had never thought to be frightened of the ocean, was relieved to find that the bed was parallel to the shore, and her side—an inviolable organizing principle of their marriage—inland.

Downstairs, you couldn't get away from the ocean, though the effect was less dire, being lower, with a visible deck. The house was old—there would have been walls down here at some point, rooms, order. Now the first floor was an open space: fireplace at one end, kitchen at the other, dining table between, windows onto the water.

Victoria sat in a blue, floral armchair with Millie in her lap; Morris was at the sink, handling a bouquet of kale so large he resembled an allegorical figure illustrating Plenty, or Wealth; their spouses were elsewhere. Their mother was wiping the kitchen island with a dirty sponge. Porter and Elena's arrival didn't seem to change the energy at all, as though they were ghosts. As though the other Harkins were immune.

"Did you give us the best room?" Porter asked.

Victoria shrugged and kissed the baby's head. "Where are the girls?" she asked.

"They'll be down," he said, and she told the baby, "They'll be down."

The attic bedroom had a pony-size billiard table and a stack of board games and two sets of bunk beds, so each twin could sleep aloft. To sleep in a new place, for a child, was to live an alternate life, as significant as a Halloween costume.

"Hi, Ma," said Porter.

His mother gave him a distant smile that grew no closer when he kissed her cheek. But then she touched his jaw. "I'm glad you're here," she said, with a hopeless look in her eyes that seemed to belong to a younger mother.

They didn't hear Tammy come down the stairs. She was too elegant and sheer, and bracketed by the twins, who—though ordinarily given to galumphing, Samantha particularly—seemed to absorb her quietude. Dressed in a long, white shirt and white jeans, Tammy had her arms out, fingertips touching the girls' shoulders, displaying them like angels. She and Morris lived in Wimberley, Texas, now.

"Porter," she said, warmly, warningly. "And you must be Elena." She took Elena's hand. Her fingers were spigot cold.

"Tammy," said Elena. "Of course."

Morris had set down his kale, his mustache fretful. "Did you sleep, darling?" he asked her.

Tammy shrugged. Elena felt the shrug in the clasp of her hand—a charge of attention, or interest. Tammy was the only person in the room who gave off anything like it. "Your children are lovely," she said. In her white clothing, she seemed like a benevolent cult leader—early days of the cult, before things turned mad and all about money—and Elena thought she might do anything Tammy suggested.

"Is that true?" Porter said to the girls, herding them away. "Are you lovely? Come on. Let's go find the beach." He turned to the room—his mother, sister, brother, Tammy, the baby, not his wife—and said, in a voice of disbelief, "It's good to be back."

Tammy had been described as wicked, peculiar, who knew what actual age, so Elena had not been prepared to feel tender. All week, Tammy wore white, in a variety of fabrics—wool, denim, gauze, silk—one of those older women who follow a sartorial plan as though a prescription. Perhaps she wanted to look tan, in absence of tanning. She wasn't well. Her bones asserted themselves, she'd turned the corner from slim to skeletal. Her elbows were wider than her forearms; her wristbones shone like ornaments; her cheekbones, always high and forbidding, gave her the air of a patient with a wasting disease (life is a wasting disease), though around her eyes seemed padded with fat. Even her brassy hair had greened like a bell. Perhaps they should have bundled her up and put her on the porch so the cold could clear her lungs. When she'd first come to the family, she'd been in her fifties, surely, and now she was in her seventies, surely, though Morris was a youthful forty-five. She spent most of the time in their room, the door closed whether she was in or out. When occasionally she did appear, she doted on Leah and Samantha.

"Come talk to me," she'd tell them, perched in a corner of

the vast sectional sofa at the far end of the main room, the part with the footrest. "I can hold a conversation. Unlike a *baby*."

"You don't like babies," Leah said.

"Not much," said Tammy, patting the cushions on either side of her. *Come, come.*

"She's just a little *baby*," Samantha explained, as they slipped under her arms, left and right.

"A baby isn't an interesting person. *You*, on the other hand, are interesting people."

They nuzzled against her.

She could be off-putting, too, of course. "Leah and Samantha," she said. "What a funny combination of names." And, "Well, you're certainly not *identical* twins." They weren't: different heights and shapes and colorings; and from the way she said it, they could tell that one of them was preferable, looks-wise, probably Leah.

"Oh, the baby's in a strop again," said Tammy. "Don't listen to her, girls. *We* don't have to wait on her."

Millie, the baby, was serious when she wasn't wailing, in the period of infancy when she could shape-shift from pink and fresh-bread sweet to covered to the neck in soft, yellow shit in an instant. She had a bumpy rash on her face, and visible cradle cap, as though she were turning to wax. Leah and Samantha watched her the way they watched the fire: with respect and fascination, until they leaned too close and were batted away by grown-ups. They snuck their hands to her cheeks when nobody was looking. They talked baby talk to her. Everyone had expected them to be jealous of the baby, but they weren't the ones.

No, it wasn't that Porter's mother was unforgiving, thought Elena, just that she had the quiet dignity of somebody whose memory had started to rub away at the edges, who trod carefully to avoid the precipice. "Hello, darling," she'd say to Leah, Samantha, the baby. She smiled doubtfully from the head of the table at every meal.

"She's still mad at me," Porter said to his sister, as Elena chopped garlic. It was Porter and Elena's turn to cook that night, Victoria had drafted a schedule. Porter was on shrimp-deveining duty.

Victoria's husband, Ben, said, "That's a lot of spice for the baby."

The baby was going to eat scampi?

"No, but *eventually*," said harmless, bland Ben, who couldn't utter the word *breast* or *milk*—*milk* was worse, when it was human, and you were surrounded by in-laws.

"She's not mad," Victoria said to Porter.

Tammy stood a foot or two from the counter in a pale canvas smock and wool leggings. She looked ready for martyrdom, a wheel, a cross, a cell to be walled into. She said, "Why would she be mad?"

"She's not mad," Victoria repeated.

Tammy tapped her temple and said, "Early onset."

"Early onset *what?*" said Porter.

"I wouldn't call it *early*," said Victoria. "She's seventy." Then, "Her memory's not what it was."

Porter had lost track of the bowls: the one with the shrimp ready to be cleaned, the one with the shells and guts, the one with the gleaming, finished shrimp. What was he holding? Where did it go? He emptied his hands onto the counter. "Can she still live alone?"

"She doesn't," said Victoria. "She lives with us."

"Since when?" said Porter.

"Porter," said Tammy. "It's high school all over again."

"What do you mean?"

"You haven't done the reading. You can't bluff your way through."

Whatever he'd done wrong, his mother had forgotten. Whatever she'd done wrong, too. It was too late for everything.

Christmas Eve, Elena stood on the deck. Tammy joined her. Even her down coat was white, segmented like a caterpillar. The morning was sunny and cold. Elena squinted and looked up at the house.

"Nice house," said Elena.

"It is," Tammy agreed. She sat on one of the built-in benches. "Sneaking outside makes me want to smoke a cigarette."

"You smoke?"

"Oh, not for years," said Tammy. "I mean, occasionally. But I wouldn't here. Or around you." She gave Elena a knowing look. "You're expecting." She indicated her own jawline. "I can always tell." Then, "I think it's terrible, what Victoria and Ben did." There was pleasure in her eyes, in-law to in-law.

"What did they do?"

"They always do it. Took the best spot." She pointed to Victoria and Ben's room at the corner on the second floor, with its double exposure.

Elena had known all along, was full of love for her husband, the dummy, who'd convinced himself otherwise. They all kept their doors closed. "You have a balcony," she observed.

"No," said Tammy. Then, "Yes. But Ben and Victoria rushed in and took the best room." She pointed again. "Best view. On the corner. They said it was the only one with space for the baby."

"We have a good view," said Elena. "They're all good views."

"It's terrible," said Tammy, not so confidential now. She wrapped herself tighter in her white coat, her white shawl. "I'm going in."

She stayed in her room for the rest of the day, the door closed, right through dinner.

The next morning, Christmas, Tammy came down in her pajamas—white silk—and her robe—white wool, with satin piping—nicer than anyone else's clothing.

"Wine is flowing," she said, nodding at the champagne glasses.

She sat by the fire, built with great competence and noise by Morris. Porter was drawing pictures for his girls. Ben watched. "Impressive," he said.

"Thanks."

The picture was a bear wearing a monocle.

"You should write a children's book," said Ben.

"Maybe."

Say it, thought Elena. But she could see he couldn't: It would cost him too much. "Porter sold a couple of illustrations to the *New Yorker*."

"Great!" said Ben. "Porter, that's great."

Tammy said, "You know, Morris is very good at drawing, too."

"All my children are good at drawing," said Miriam, uniting three long-divided things. She was sitting at the dining table, her fingers playing fretfully, musically, along the edge.

"Morris could have been an artist," said Tammy.

Elena wanted to stab her with a comb. Why a comb? Because they were in a women's prison together, and that's how it worked.

Tammy had given the twins vintage kimonos and remote-control animals—one dog, one cat—and no other gift could compare. Samantha in her kimono said to Elena, "Look, Mama, look!"

"What is it, honey?"

"I got a robot."

"Sorry," said Tammy, as though she'd bought the girls cartons of cigarettes, then to Samantha, "Do you like it, sweetie? I saw it in the store, and I knew you had to have it."

"Why apologize?" Porter asked.

"I hope it's not too much. Is it too much?"

Porter had thought that the children would win him the love of the family: his mother, his siblings. But the girls received the love directly. Elena saw. It flowed over and around him.

Being sent away was the story of his life, one of the first things he'd told Elena, and he'd thought, finally, he might have a conversation with his mother about it. But it was too late. It would have been too late even if she remembered everything. They'd read his absence as carelessness. They believed he'd never done anything deliberately in his life.

"Mom," he said to her. One of the flaws of the house: long benches instead of chairs, the better to cram people in. He threaded his legs in to sit beside her. "Come to California."

"Oh," she said. "Why would I go to California? No. I don't—" She waved her hands to dismiss the things she'd forgotten, as though they were cluttering the table in front of her. "No more travel. Not capable. I'd like a glass of wine, I think." She looked hopefully at the bottle in front of her.

"Red or white?" said Ben.

"I've got it, Ben." Porter poured some of the left-out wine into one dirty glass for his mother, into another for himself. "You could live with us."

"Live where?"

"In California," he said.

She took his hands in her own and looked at them. She smelled, as she had since his childhood, of over-ironed clothing. He'd imagined she'd be lighter after his father's death, she'd be one of those terrible words applied to old women: *sprightly, spry.*

"I only know one family in California," she said. "I know lots of families here."

Then Porter took a sip of wine. Nobody but Elena could have realized what that meant—he'd been sober fifteen years. Elena nearly tasted it herself, the particular darkness of stolen drink. Nostalgia, unhappiness, the belief that if he put himself in peril his mother would emerge from wherever she was to untie him from the railway tracks. She'd done that for years, before he was sent away. And then she stopped.

He said to Tammy, suddenly, "I was a child."

"Yes," she said. "We all were."

"When you sent me away."

"I didn't do that."

"Porter," said Miriam, "it wasn't—" and Morris interrupted her. "Porter, knock it off," he said, deploying his big-brother voice.

"I saved your *life*," said Tammy. "Don't forget it."

"You didn't. You put me in *more* danger, and then I saved myself."

"So it worked."

"Did it?" said Porter.

"Look at you."

"It wasn't Tammy," said Miriam. "It was us."

Tammy sat across the table—it took her nothing to step over the bench, she was a wraith, she manifested.

Maybe everything that happened afterward—Porter's self-destruction, the collapse of his marriage, the tragedy of Leah, the long unhappiness of Samantha—perhaps it all grew out of Porter's spite. Or maybe it had been written in his DNA, or in the stars, the two things now indistinguishable, and Tammy had only delayed it a while.

She said, "It was me, Porter. And I'd do it again. I'd do it for any of you."

Morris and Tammy left soon after. "To get a jump on traffic," Morris said jovially. His eyes twinkled; his new mustache drooped.

Ten minutes after they pulled away, Elena stood and said, "I want to show you something."

Solemnly, she led everyone up the stairs and swung Morris and Tammy's door open to reveal a room twice as large as any other, with a bay window, a bathroom with a balcony, a tub with a view.

It didn't make sense to be jealous of a room—especially in a house altogether so lovely. And yet.

"They have two trash cans, and I don't have *one*," Miriam said, and then, "I'm taking a bath in this glorious tub."

"Me, too," said Elena. "You first, then me."

Each in turn, they did, put their healthy, joyous, petty bottoms where her bony one had been; and from water, they looked at water. Even the baby.

7.

"She seems peaceful," said Victoria.

"She is," said Morris.

He was holding Tammy's hand. She'd fallen down their stairs a week prior, but she'd been dying before that. She was in bed, unconscious—but whether asleep or blanketed by morphine or in an actual coma, Victoria didn't know and couldn't ask. Beneath the navy-blue quilt, Tammy looked like a reliquary for her own broken bones.

Morris had pulled out all the scrapbooks of Tammy's life, of their life together and Tammy's life previous to Morris, and Victoria missed her mother with foolish passion. The answer to the enduring question of Tammy's age could be found here, surely. Miriam had died two months earlier, just shy of eighty.

Victoria picked up one of the books. Young womanhood: Tammy as a dancer, before she'd adopted the bob, her blonde hair to her shoulders, her body liquid, from the *Corpus Christi Caller-Times*. The date torn off. All the dates torn off, and Tammy blossoming and beautiful. Victoria regarded Tammy in the bed, and she was beautiful now, too, in the same way, everything that had ever constricted her face, the competition and the pride, gone. "She's so full of herself!" Victoria once said to her mother, and Miriam had said, "No, it's a lack of self-esteem that makes her act that way. People who hate themselves make such a lot of noise to hide it."

Victoria knew that was true, and it made her furious. Why should she feel sorry for the bullies and braggarts of the world, when she had her own one-layer self-loathing to attend to? Worse, what if that was her, too?

"Darling," said Morris.

"What?" said Victoria.

"Ah!" said Morris. "No. I—would you get me a glass of water?"

They were the closest of the siblings, despite the age difference that meant they hadn't been young together. He'd had a whole upbringing as an only child. What had their parents been doing in the ten years between them? Doting. Deliberating. Suffering the slapstick tragedy of human reproduction. Victoria longed to ask Morris, but didn't, out of love for him, out of guilt.

Her entire life, she'd wanted to love Porter, and she did, but she could never take his side, because he kept changing sides. His wasn't the only temper in the family, though his wildness was his own. With Tammy gone, what would she and he have to talk about?

"You should take a break," said Victoria.

"Oh, no thank you!" said Morris, in a pleasant tone of voice.

"It's hard," said Victoria.

"It's not," said Morris.

She walked down the stairs of their house, whitewashed, which Tammy would not walk down again, nor touch the mahogany banister. She went out the front door into the cold. She would call her husband and chat with Millie, now nine, whose voice always sounded so high and strange on the phone, then Porter, and they would worry over Morris and talk about Tammy, and they wouldn't be nice: They'd revive their parents' various grudges against her, examine her unhappiness, which she'd always been so generous with—she was still alive, they could be unkind—and what a fool henpecked Morris was, and what a fool she was to believe that at any moment he'd have his long-awaited lucky break and become a successful actor, and in the end Porter and Victoria would have the same thought, though they couldn't say it aloud, not even to each other, and they wouldn't know that it was Morris's thought, too, and Tammy's last thought, flowing down her spine and out her fingertips with her soul. For once, they would all understand one another, the absolute astonishment: *To love another person like that! To have been loved!*

CARRIE R. MOORE

Till It and Keep It

FROM *Sewanee Review*

IN THE BEGINNING, there was her sister's breathing. Which meant neither of them had died.

It was faint, a slip of sound in the truck's stillness. But it reached into the front seats and nudged Brie awake. She lay over the console, an ache in her ribs, sweat on her eyelids. Against her wrist, morning light fell in a thin orange beam. So she could see colors again, which meant the illness was fading. She'd been smart to pull off the road—sometimes, rest was all you needed.

"Harper," she said, "wake up. We're still a long ways out."

Her sister's breathing quieted. Brie felt behind her, arms weak, neck too stiff to turn. If she could just touch Harper, surely she'd wake, too?

This was hardly the worst they'd been through—unlucky as they were, born into prolonged summers and floods rushing deep into the coast and dwindling federal relief. There was the land they'd worked in Low America for years, the trees more branch than fruit. The miles of brown fields after they'd fled Randall's farm and the masses of white tents clustered outside silver cities and along freeway exits. On more than one occasion, thin-hipped walking men eyed their truck as it sped past, but who knew if they carried viruses or meant them harm: Any kindness had to be carefully doled out. When the sisters had long passed the health inspection at the Arkansas line, they'd stood in a shallow creek while Brie shaved Harper's deep honey curls. The green city lights wavering in the distance made Harper's hair shudder on the water's surface. "I don't care what it looks like," Harper had said, gripping Brie's elbow. "Just so I don't feel his hands in it."

"I got you," Brie murmured, tying a wrap, red as a caul, over her handiwork. "It'll look good." She finished just before the outage drowned them in darkness.

In the truck, Brie finally twisted to glimpse Harper in the space between the passenger seat and door. The wrap fell over her sister's cheek, flattened against the backseat. Who knew anymore, how a virus would go. Some filled your lungs with fluid and made your muscles go liquid for weeks; others made your skin ache even in moonlight. This one had made Harper break out in hives once they were well into Tennessee, then start asking why the sun looked brown as the trees. As she drove, Brie said, "Just hang on. We'll stop soon," and passed her sister a silver canister of tea leaves to chew. But whatever was ailing Harper hit Brie too. As the hot pressure spread through her skull, she eased off the road, into woods blurry as gray flames. She cussed. Then prayed: *Lord, cover us.* It was different from her usual prayer: *Lord, let us get the chance to taste something green.*

Brie repeated her sister's name. They hadn't survived so much for her to lose Harper now.

Then she saw the orange and green shapes just outside the window. The orange globes, dimpled and striped pink. The green, a sharp tip. It took her a minute to recognize them, long as it had been since she'd seen such fruit.

"Harper," she said. "There's peaches out there."

As if he'd heard, a man appeared at the window, the peaches vanishing behind his brown face. He opened the door, cool air rushing in. Then he lifted her against him, and her whole body split with pain. Her neck couldn't hold her head, which tipped over his arm. "God almighty," he said. "There's two of you."

She sank her teeth into his shoulder. Held tight until she felt his skin break.

He cussed. She felt him grip her thighs, trying not to drop her. Then his grip was gone, and so was everything else.

*

She woke in a wooden shed that smelled of grass and sweat. In the bed beside her, Harper slept curled against the rose-patterned sheets, her fingernails gray in the moonlight falling through the window. When Brie woke again, it was to the sound of splashing: The man stood at the sink, scrubbing her patchwork jeans with a bar of soap. She yelped, fearing her own nakedness before him. Then he was moving toward her—or toward Harper—the lone lightbulb swinging above his low curls. She aimed her fists at his forehead, striking once before he caught her wrists. His hands were cool and damp, and this brought her back to her senses. Someone had dressed her in a thin blouse.

"Nothing's going to happen to you," he said, though he didn't let go. His shirt had slipped in the tussle, exposing a white patch covering his shoulder. "Go on back to sleep, and I'll get Lauren in here soon as I can." But Brie didn't sleep, not for a while. She studied the scythes and rakes hanging on the door he'd closed behind him. Beside her, Harper's fingers twitched once.

She woke the third time to a white woman bent over her, kneading her calves. The woman had a gray braid that swept Brie's thighs, her knuckles bony and blue-veined as mountain ridges. When Brie moved, the woman adjusted the bandanna over her nose and mouth, then turned to two steaming mugs sitting on a crate. She offered one to Brie and moved to the bed's edge, far from where Harper slept with half-parted lips.

When Brie sniffed the rim, the woman said, "It's just tea. And it hasn't killed you yet."

After the woman introduced herself as Lauren, Brie asked, "You live here?"

She shook her head. "Got my own to take care of."

Her own, Brie thought. It could mean a sibling, spouse. So many ways to have a family. She took a careful sip, the brew bitter and piping hot.

"Mind if I work on your friend while you drink?" Lauren asked.

Brie let Lauren massage Harper's thighs, thin above the sheets. "Who lives here, then?"

"You took a bite out of his shoulder. May want to apologize

for that. He took a lot of risk, letting you stay here. And quarantining you." Lauren's hands pushed and pushed against Harper, stuffing life back in. "Seems like whatever you had makes a real mess of your nerves. But I figure you're out of the woods now."

Brie lowered her mug to her stomach. "My sister—" She breathed deep and touched Harper's shoulder. "Will she be all right?"

Lauren's eyes flickered. Of course she'd doubt they were siblings, comparing Harper's yellow skin to Brie's mahogany. Lauren was older than their mother had been, old enough to remember a time before most people were brown, either by sun or by blood. "She's—making it," Lauren said, and lifted Harper's arm toward the ceiling, working her thumbs into flesh that went pink under the pressure. "Between the two of you, you got the stronger genes."

Brie felt for Harper's free hand. When they'd been girls in east Texas, she'd gone under the floodwaters, dry leaves plugging her nose. Harper had yanked her into the boat by the armpit, the skiff swirling in the chaos: "You're not allowed to die, you hear me?" Water streamed down her sister's face. Then she rowed the two of them to something like safety, to drier ground some twenty miles from the government complex where their mother had died with her lover.

"Don't worry," Lauren said—and when she patted Harper's arm her hand was hot with her exertions—"You're both safe here."

The whole place was a dream of green. The farmhouse with its clean white panels and long windows, the surrounding shrubs like woolly-haired children. That evening, she took dinner on the porch steps, a plate of venison and beans on her knees. In another time, she'd have avoided the meat—who knew what it carried?—or eaten slowly to disguise her hunger, but there was already so much her mind couldn't swallow. The trees bending in the breeze, threatening to drop their fruit. The soil dark and loamy enough to hold a footprint. Even the men on the far edges of the porch relaxed as they ate. They sat with their backs to her, dirt settled on their shoulders. Had she not known she and Harper were somewhere in Tennessee—and had it not been for the cloud of heat—she would've thought they'd made it to Maine. Which meant Harper had been wrong when she said Low America was finished, that—if the cities would not let you in—you had to get north to have a home that would flourish and last.

Behind her, someone said, "You looked better passed out."

When she turned, the man with the patch on his shoulder was toweling off his face. "Calmer, at least," he added. He must've come from around back, too close to the shed where Harper slept. It was thirty seconds away. Twenty, if she didn't let her full belly slow her down. She kept her hand on her fork. Said, "Only a crazy person would say somebody looks better passed out."

"Bad joke. Didn't mean anything by it."

He flopped the towel over the railing, then leaned on it with one elbow. The men behind him murmured greetings, gratitude for the meal. Had this happened on any other farm she'd worked? The owner feeding them? The men called him Colton.

"Where you two headed?" he said, when his attention returned to her.

Brie, chewing, kept her eyes on her plate.

"Fine," he said. "It's none of my business."

She looked over his shoulder. Up the dirt road, a few mares grazed, their tails flicking in the air. Their black coats were so shiny it made her eyes prickle. "How'd you come by this farm?" she asked.

"My parents, who got it from theirs. Prices weren't so high, once."

And it had survived all the storms. "But how do you manage to keep affording it?"

"We treat the soil right. Grow no more than we can handle and shield during freezes. Take help, if the right sort of people come along." He glanced at the men behind them, still intent on their plates. "Not saying we don't get trouble like everyone else. Or god-awful weather. But we get by."

He moved closer, and his shadow touched the knee of her jeans. She tightened her grip on her fork. "I won't hurt you," he said, brows relaxing. "I just want to sit. Right there, next to you."

She didn't protest. He smelled the kind of clean that meant a bath every day or every other. *Waste of water,* Harper would've said, but Brie let herself enjoy it for a few breaths. The money some people had.

"You know," he said, "my shoulder's kept me out of the picking three days."

She ate a sliver of deer so fast her fork barely met her tongue.

He sighed. "Listen, we won't get anywhere like this. Your truck's still on the edge of the farm, 'bout a mile off. Maybe you've got ten miles of fuel in there. Been forever since I've seen anything not electric."

"Didn't really have a choice."

"Not judging you. I know a guy with a fuel reserve. In town. I can get some for you."

Around her, these trees, bursting with life. A man could be tolerated, if he had all this. "We'll work for it," she said. "I'm guessing those peaches'll rot if you leave 'em too long."

His whole body became an apology, head dipping down, smile hanging off his face. The spots on his forehead put him anywhere between twenty-five and thirty-five, given how Momma once said people aged faster than they used to, the sun being what it was. "I wasn't asking for anything. The guys'll haul a few gallons over tomorrow, so you don't have to worry yourself. You and your friend—"

"My sister. I'm telling you, I'll work. 'Least 'til she's awake."

Her eyelids lowered. *Imagine.* Time spent on this place as rich as something out of Momma's old photographs, the previous century with its regular crops, its more manageable seasons. Just wait until Harper saw it. Maybe Maine could wait, a little while.

When she looked back at him, the dark color in his eyes gave way, like the earth easing beneath her boot.

On the first day of work, she waited in the orchard, calves quivering. She'd arrived earlier than anyone, before the sun would drain her further, and she thumbed the bark of a tree as she tried to contain herself. Then she gave up and grabbed a low-hanging peach. It burst in her mouth, its juice stinging her tongue. When she turned, Colton was a few feet away, studying the trail on her chin. She wiped it, clutching the rest of the fruit. Then he approached with a small jug and rinsed off the peach's remains until her hands were soaked. "You've gotta clean 'em," he said. Then he grabbed a peach from a branch near her cheek. Rinsed that one off too. Bit in.

The second day had all the hard work of the first. It was May, and the laborers had long developed their routines, leaving behind families in camps to pile into electric sedans or ride three to a horse or bike the full five miles to Colton's farm. All eleven of them went right to work, reaching into the trees. Because her legs were still weak, Brie stood below Colton and made a tent out of a blanket, catching the peaches he tossed down and carefully lowering them into crates to avoid bruising. His wound bled through its dressing and onto his shirt.

On the third day, they traded places. He had to steady her on the ladder, his thumb pushing into the back of her knee, his flesh a damp circle beneath her stiff shorts. Imagine being hungry for touch, of all things. "You know," he said, "for a while, there was just my family to help out with all this. Either we killed ourselves or a lot went wasted."

He was waiting, she knew, for her to ask more. But she wouldn't. When she was fifteen and Harper twelve, their mother had begun whatever-you-wanted-to-call-it with the new water monitor. Sex. Convenience. Love. William had appeared out back of the government complex, where Momma pinned a sheet to the community clothesline and Brie and Harper played cards on the AstroTurf. He knelt beside the filtration unit and installed new canisters, all the while looking back at them. Above her playing cards, Harper rolled her eyes, though she went still when he said to Momma, "Decades ago, I had my own house around here. Though I have to say, you look better than my memories of that place." "That might not be saying much," Momma said, though the lines in her face went softer than they'd been in years. Nights later, from the bedroom allotted for the teens, Brie and Harper heard Momma and William laughing in the den, louder than the other adults. Beneath the door, candlelight flickered. "Didn't they assign him his own unit?" Brie whispered, and Harper answered, "Who cares. Momma promised we'd head out before the next hurricane anyway."

Against Brie's knee, Colton's thumb sweated. Or she did. In the distance, she saw Lauren heading toward the shed, preparing to tend to her sister.

"I can manage," Brie said, and he let her go.

On the fourth day, Lauren returned to cook for the workers. Three miniature chickens and corn hash stewing over a fire, which stretched toward the sunset like it was kin. Brie had learned by then that the men never stayed late, wanting to get home to their families before full dark. By the time the sky turned pink, they'd stacked their empty plates in neat piles, and the ones who had to walk plunged their faces into the water buckets so they'd be cool for the journey back. She watched from the front porch until Lauren's laugh floated through the house's open window. Brie turned. Lauren stood with a man in the kitchen, his mouth mashed against her neck. So her family *was* her husband. His hair was gray, and his red-spotted hands pulled her against him. No wedding band, but then again, it was smarter not to. In the complex, everyone crammed together on their assigned floors, anything valuable could become someone else's. Once, when the mess hall had run out of proteins, she and Harper had slipped a silver necklace out of a newcomer's backpack. Easy, to bribe a café worker with something so flashy. "We might have the chance to pay her back for it," Harper had said as they picked at their hard-boiled eggs, icy from the back of the fridge. Though of course the newcomer had been gone days later, already checked out of the complex and on her way elsewhere.

"What you thinking 'bout?" Colton said, sitting beside her. She shook her head, and he said, "Hey, now. Your sister'll be fine." Her heart pounding, she let him maneuver her into the tender pad of his shoulder. His breath caught. Could've been pain. Or the closeness.

The fifth day, she saw the damage she'd done. She'd knocked at his front door, waiting for the usual breakfast of eggs and toast, and he'd come out with his shirt half askew, his wound exposed. Bridges of skin stretched from one raw side to the other. "Come in?" he said. "Cool off?"

Four chairs at the kitchen table, only one pulled out. A pair of leather boots, about his size, by the door. It was already marvelous, that landline plugged into the wall, a sign of what else he could buy. Probably he had a cell phone stashed away somewhere, one of the nice, expensive ones from a company that could afford to keep its data centers cool.

But God, this air-conditioning rushing over her. So long since she'd been in a real house, not a shed or barn attic or truck.

She allowed herself to sit in one of the chairs, slow. If she leaned against its pillow, would she smear it with grease? No matter how many times she scrubbed herself, dipping her sponge into the bucket of soapy water outside the shed, she was dipping into her own filth. He placed the eggs before her and took his own cup of coffee near the stove. She asked, "You live here alone?"

"If I answer that, you'll answer one for me?" When she nodded, he said, "Yeah, alone."

She let her fork break the yolk of her egg. Finally, he said, "Where'd you and your sister come from? And where you headed?"

Two questions, but she let him get away with it. "Left Texas after Hurricane Bev. Spent a few years working farms in Mississippi. Just earning what we can 'til we get to Maine."

"What's in Maine, aside from crazy winters?"

Permanence, she thought. Water. Greenery. She said, "Well, what's here?"

He twisted toward the window, and something in her knew his body often leaned against the sink this way, waiting, his gaze on the road. After a beat, he said, "What's not?"

On the sixth day, when she returned to the shed, her body reeked of peaches. There it was: Harper turning on the mattress at the scent. All the fear that had clutched Brie's heart uncoiled.

"You?" Harper murmured. "You were gone?"

Brie rushed toward her sister. With her cleanest fingers, she pulled back the sheets, then retreated.

Harper's chest rose and fell. "Why are you way over there?"

"I don't want to get anything on you."

"Like . . . I care about that."

"I'm filthy. You just can't see."

Harper squinted at her. Then said, "I can see it," and closed her eyes.

By the time Harper fell asleep again, everything was bright, everything a peach, even the sun, half crushed against the horizon. Brie closed the shed door behind her and walked toward the house, limbs alight. The men were gone when she mounted the stairs. There was only Colton, sitting on the railing, reading a big leather Bible. "Thought you were in for the night," he said.

"Harper's awake. And I want to hug her but—" She looked down at her hands, then the rest of her body.

"Oh," he said, lowering his Bible. "I see."

The bathroom was far nicer than the ones in the complexes, the tile mint instead of gray, the shower so hot it burned off her dry parts, flakes of skin and dirt swirling down the drain. She could feel the soap foaming on her scalp, lifting the crusted sweat so her hair fluffed. She showered for as long as she could stand it, half-wondering if he would come upstairs to remind her about the water regulations. But he didn't.

On the doorknob, he'd left a black dress with four pockets and a bra a size too big, like hands hovering over her breasts. Leftover from some cousin or sister or somebody else? A wife? A woman who had *things*. Brie clothed herself, then sat at the top of the stairs and tucked her chin on her knees until the sun went down. In its fading light, she could see the hairs curling on her arms. When Colton appeared beneath her, at the stair's foot, she sat up to regard him. They remained there, considering each other in the gathering darkness.

"I have to go up now," he said. "To bed."

She said, "Show me."

When they lay beside each other on his mattress, not yet naked, he touched his shoulder's ruined skin and said, "I'll have this scar for the rest of my life."

"Guess it'll match the others." So hard to be sure of him or of this long-suppressed heat inside her. But there was no denying this mattress. It was even softer than his chest.

"You mean this?" he asked. "This one's from where a dog nipped me. And I've got this one near my ear from when I was out on a delivery. This desperate kid with a knife." As he spoke, she pressed her ear to his heart, letting only half his words enter her. She shouldn't have mentioned the scars; she didn't need to know about them.

"Can I?" he asked, his fingers tilting her chin toward him.

They kissed and she thought, *This too, is rest.* Soon, he removed her dress so she was naked and clean against his own clean body, and she remembered how she'd purposefully forgotten this: to have somebody other than Harper.

On the morning of the seventh day, she returned to the shed and found Harper standing beside the bed, both her arms outstretched, like two wings, for balance. Brie wiped the grime from her sister's forehead.

She thought: *Well, I guess we have to go now.*

She said: "Harps, I tried. But we're low on fuel, and we can't leave 'til we can pay for it."

To be safe and headed nowhere, for once. The illness left Harper's skin stiff with sweat, and Brie helped her shower with the bucket outside the shed. With the towel, she made a fuzzy curtain, shielding her sister from the house and its fields.

"Shit, shit, shit," Harper said, laughing, her blonde eyelashes damp, "promise when we get to Maine we'll make sure our farm's got warm water. No more freezing like this."

"You want to shower in the house?"

Harper shook her head. Cleaned herself furiously, cold water flying off her hands and slapping Brie's feet. Harper's body was all bones and caverns. Like some long, slender rodent lost to time, the hairs on her legs like quills. "I must look god-awful," Harper said.

"You should've seen yourself before."

"At least you look good." Harper exhaled, scanning the rows of peach trees. It was Sunday, no picking, and maybe this would make it easier for Harper to appreciate the beauty.

"You see the colors?" Brie asked. "How bright the peaches are?"

"Sure." Harper shrugged. "I see them."

They ate Lauren's chilled sunflower soup, which did nothing to stop them from sweating. Then they walked, Harper's body sharp as it leaned against her. Brie talked about Colton and the harvest schedule, keeping her voice neutral. Almost two weeks they'd been here, and maybe two more would get them what they needed. It was about a quarter mile to the dirt path that ran right up to the house, then another quarter mile on the other side. By the time they'd finished, Harper was panting.

"God, I'm sorry," Harper said. "I wasted so much of our time."

"You didn't." Brie wiped her forehead, felt a drumbeat of shame. Being here was the best time she'd had in a while—and what did that say about her? "If the High checkpoints are as strict as they say, you wouldn't have passed, sick like that."

"Still, if he'd hand over the fuel, we could be on our way. But somebody's always bargaining."

Brie pressed her lips together. Colton was coming out of the house. He paused on the porch and pulled at his collar, the heat getting to him all at once.

"That him?" Harper asked.

"Yeah." She squeezed her sister's shoulder. "You know I bit him? At the truck, I thought he was coming after you, so I took a chunk out of his shoulder."

"Look at you," Harper said. Then she shook her head and laughed until it sounded like crying, so loud you could believe it—and not the wind—stirred the trees. She quieted only when Colton approached.

"Glad you're feeling better," he said to Harper. His hand hung in the open air between them. "We both worried about you."

"Well, *you* wouldn't know, but I always make it."

"I believe it. House is ready, whenever you are. I've got extra rooms."

Yes, Brie's body said, but Harper went, "We're fine in the shed," and tugged her away.

They had the whole afternoon before them, all the laborers

having remained home with their families in the camps. Possibly, the bright emptiness was even better than being permitted into the cities, because inside Dallas or Little Rock or Nashville, you would have reliable water systems and sturdier infrastructure and your own space, though it would not be this much. Brie and Harper lay on a blanket in the orchard and let the peach trees shelter them from the heat. Colton hung around, standing over the blanket so they were in his shadow. He was trying to win Harper over with talk of how his family had been Tennessee natives for centuries—slaves, then sharecroppers, then farmers, then Low America nationalists, and, blessed, for now, from disaster, though when Harper kept complaining about the gnats, he quieted. "And your family?" he asked. Neither Brie nor Harper answered. He picked at his shirt, mumbled something about dinner, and retreated into the house.

"What makes him think we want to know about his life?" Harper asked. "His family didn't have the sense to move north, and he doesn't either, apparently."

"I don't know. This farm's not nothing."

"It's peaches, Brie. And who knows if they'll even grow next year."

"Not *just* peaches. Sweet potatoes on the other side. Okra. Tomatoes. Not to mention the chickens and everything Lauren's got at her place."

"He still eats chicken? Gross."

Brie folded her hands across her stomach, which rose fuller than it had in years. She couldn't admit that she'd eaten chicken alongside him. Pork, too, with everyone else, and no one had gotten sick. But it was always Harper who did their imagining: Leave the complex. Take the electric trains. Get work on farms when they could. Save and work and save and learn until they could get to Maine and buy land at least worth the impossible price, until they could choose a life that gave them a chance. Even the uncertainty of High America had to be better than here, which was always hot and had the tornadoes and floods and mosquitoes and viruses to prove it.

"Place is nice, I'll give you that," Harper said, grabbing her hand. "But even Randall's was nice, at first."

*

The next morning, when it was time to resume picking, Harper refused to join the others. "Tell Mr. Man I'll be with Lauren in the kitchen today," she said as she shrugged on her denim overalls, newly washed. The color in her face was returning, though she'd eaten around the pork on her breakfast plate.

Brie didn't tell Colton. Instead, they spent the day at opposite ends of a row of peach trees, keeping all the men between them. Was he being sensitive to what she needed, letting her wear out her fingers like everyone else? Only days before, when they'd lain together, he'd mumbled into her ear, "I think I might love you." Which felt absurd, unless he meant he could see his way to something like love. With her. Even her own body opened to pleasure around him, some ancient room inside her unlocked. Though—it was also like they fit only because he was a man and she was a woman and they were in this beautiful place.

Her sister would say, *One room ain't a whole house.* Or something like that. Once, at seventeen, a boy from the complex had been assigned to plant onions beside her in the communal garden. He wasn't special, aside from the fact that he hadn't been sick in the past year and didn't let his temper get the better of him in the heat. It was one shiny coin of a moment: rocking with him in that storage facility. When she told Harper, her sister paused sewing the arm back onto a jacket. "You know what they used to do centuries ago, when they wanted to keep slaves on plantations?" Harper said. "They let them get married. Or let them call it that anyway." Her sister had never taken to William, whom the other women couldn't lure from Momma's bed for long.

Brie descended the ladder before her allotted tree, then wiped her brow with the back of her hand. The day was ending, and when she turned, Harper stood in the house's doorway, that wrap on her hair, her body a red-tipped match at the edge of the fields.

Come dinner, they ate with Lauren in the kitchen, the men outside. Lauren and Harper had made soybean casserole with pepper and dehydrated herbs, which they ate at the kitchen table. *Don't you miss this, Harps?* Brie thought. It had been forever since they'd eaten someplace that didn't require sitting cross-legged in a dry field or in a truck's cramped cabin. But Harper only nibbled, leaning toward Lauren, which was always how Harper got with women. "Your place must have a lot, too," Harper said. "You don't come here every day."

"I wouldn't say a lot." Lauren smoothed the cap of her hair to where it tightened into a braid. "It's only the two of us."

"At least you don't have kids." When Lauren laughed, Harper blinked. "What? There were so doggone many in the complex."

"It's nothing," Lauren said, and her newly soft voice made Brie press her foot over Harper's; you could never tell what people had lost. "You'd manage, if you had them."

"Maybe we want more than managing." Harper freed her foot and cleaned her plate. Brie wondered if there was more casserole. It'd be careless to ask for meat in front of Harper.

"How long you two planning on sticking around?" Lauren said as she skinned a peach.

"Just 'til we earn fuel," Harper said. "Get our truck going."

"Who's got fuel?"

"Colton knows somebody," Brie murmured. "We're just working off the cost to him."

The peach skin Lauren pulled away wrinkled like her mouth. "He's honest. He'll make good on whatever he told you." She said nothing else for a while, and Brie felt caught in the net of her stare. "But in the meantime, I'd appreciate help with the canning. We'll wrap up harvest soon, and whatever doesn't get sold in town will need preserving. Think you'd be interested?"

"We could be," Brie said. Harper studied an ant wandering over her plate.

That night, as they faced each other on the shed mattress, Brie said, "There's a lot we can learn in a place like this, if we both work."

Harper curled her fist under her cheek. "We been working and learning for years. At some point, you just have to go."

Brie rolled onto her back and stared at the ceiling. There had been cobwebs in the rafters that morning, and now they were gone.

"I don't think peaches grow in Maine," Harper said, her voice softer. "But maybe apples? Potatoes? Would that make you happier, staying through the canning?"

Brie did not return to Colton's room that night, but she thought about it during that third week, as she and Harper joined the others in the peach orchard. It felt wrong to think about his shower, his plush bed. Anybody else would be making sure their sister didn't tip over during the harvesting, given how Harper yanked the fruit hard enough to snap branches.

Colton didn't approach her in the fields until midday, the sun overhead a white, unflinching eye, the others taking lunch and Harper gone to use one of the outhouses. His knuckles brushed the loops of her jeans. "You've done enough now," he said. "I'll get the fuel tomorrow."

"Still too much to do. Like the canning. And probably more."

His shadow nodded on the tree in front of her. "You know you're welcome to anything in the house. Whatever you want. Whenever."

That night, as Harper slept, Brie went to him. She showered and slipped into a strawberry-print dress he'd left for her, though she ignored the bra. From Colton's bed, she imagined the woman it once belonged to moving down this hallway, her feet gentling against the floorboards. Brie sat on the bed and looked out at the pristine dinner plate of the moon. When Colton crawled in beside her, she chose to stop thinking about anybody else.

After, she asked him to show her around, and he obliged. A series of rooms: an office with piles of papers, a bedroom with a blue gingham comforter and sewing machine on a round table, one entirely empty room that he closed the door on, quick. The hallway had a long table covered in a yellow quilt and glass figurines of animals she couldn't identify, ghostly in their long-necked translucence. A photograph of a grinning, gray-haired couple stared back at her, their arms extending from the frame as they angled the camera toward them. Behind them, a city of canals.

"My parents," he said.

"You must be ancient."

"I wouldn't say that. A lot of people wouldn't."

She lifted a teacup, its trim curving silver in the moonlight. In the complex, what little she and Harper owned had been lost. They'd waded knee-deep through the partially drained floodwaters, where everything shelved had been coaxed out: the R&B records their mother inherited from her parents, Brie's baby shoes curling with pink ribbons, the framed photograph of their family eating quesadillas at the canteen on Harper's twelfth birthday. All of it ruined.

"Yours," Colton said, and closed her fingers around the teacup. "If you want." She nodded. In the distance, she heard a horse's wet neigh. "Will you tell me how old you two are?"

"I'm twenty-four." She wouldn't tell him Harper's age. *No part of me is any of his business,* Harper would say.

"That's about what I thought," he said. "Though I wish I hadn't needed to spend so much time guessing."

She didn't ask how old he was. Nor about the woman who had lived here before. "I'm thirty," Colton murmured, releasing her fingers. "I need you to know I'm not ancient."

They'd been there six weeks when the picking ended. By mid-July, the summer fleshed out and the laborers had fleshed out too, growing partners and children who appeared on the horizon for the final, celebratory dinner. Lauren and Harper had spent hours on the knotted rolls of bread and creamed potatoes and the pig, slaughtered and then garnished with peaches, though this last task had made Harper vomit on the back steps. A mess of a gathering, at first. The cast-iron pots and pans jumbled on the table. People knocking against each other as they filled their plates. The children working their way from lap to lap, only to scramble back toward their parents. These families, vibrant under the string of yellow lights buzzing on and on.

They'd figured something out, something different from the thrown-together families of the complexes, where everyone belonged to everyone, no room for it to be any other way. But here a laborer with hair only a shade redder than his face had two wives, their trio occupying one corner of the long wooden table. A pair of men in identical plaid shirts, who arrived and left together daily, lay on a blanket, the taller man's arms around the shorter one. And then there were the endless man-to-woman couples, chasing their children down the dirt road, dust coating their hair.

On the porch, Brie watched as Harper's wry half-smile settled into wary amusement. Even in Brie's earliest memories of her sister, Harper was this watchful. Eleven years old and studying their mother parting the pale, heart shells of the crabs that washed up after Hurricane Sharunda, her callused hands exposing their tender pink flesh.

"Makes me think about William," Harper said. "That night he taught us how to do that dance from the cities." They'd never known why Momma attached herself to him. He couldn't find a crab on a doorstep. He took most of the money for who-knew-what and ate more than his share of their rations. Maybe he was simply a source of warmth that first winter. And he did dance.

Brie remembered: the four of them in the common area, her own voice providing the bass of the old music, Harper's soprano carrying the melody, their mother and William harmonizing as they rolled their feet against the floors and wound their arms in the air. But she couldn't speak about it, not with how much she was already holding inside. One of the laborer's wives, a sunkissed woman with brown curls haloing her face, began singing, "My old man sleeps with one hand on his gun, the other 'round my heart."

A surprise, when Harper started singing too, her voice unfurling like a cool mist. The woman smiled at them, and Brie thought for sure Harper would stop, but no, Harper rose, swaying, her wrists fleshier, her fingers pulling the air's invisible strings.

The woman moved her hips, raised her fingers too. But Harper closed her eyes, her lashes a veil to another world inside her: their old bedroom shared with the other teens, the sketches of the solar-assisted cities copied from the common room television, the packed classroom where they wrote out their plans for something better. Brie closed her eyes too, let the swirl of lights fill the darkness. Maybe Maine will be like this, she thought, when we get there.

By the time Brie opened her eyes, the woman had lost interest in Harper, settling against a man in a wooden chair, his grin lost in the tangle of his beard. Across the yard, in a huddle of other men, Colton's eyes met hers, as if Harper's dance, the arc of her arms, plucked a taut string between them. He mouthed something: *Stay*, maybe. Or, *Wait*.

Her sister was turning, dragging one boot in a circle through the dirt. She stopped. "Just dance with me," she said. "For Momma?"

When they were back in the shed, they splashed water on their faces. Harper unwound her head wrap, and Brie fought the urge to even out her hair, which stood up in spikes and looked so much worse than it had that night at the river. Harper picked at the flyaways as she studied the teacup resting on the windowsill. "That's pretty," she said, and Brie splashed the water harder.

"Something's on your mind," Harper said when she was combing out Brie's tight kinks.

"You seemed happy tonight."

"Guess I was."

"You ever think about just staying here? Even beyond the canning?"

The comb met a knot. Harper pulled hard, then gentler. "Hey," Harper said, and the brightness in her voice wasn't what it should've been. "Don't ask me that again, all right?"

Brie dug her nails into the mattress. Stupid, to forget the point of all this. In the silence, the laborers called out last goodbyes.

"You remember that little garden snake we found in the complex that time?" Harper asked. "I would've fed it forever, if Momma hadn't made William kill it."

"She was afraid. Can't really blame her for that."

"That's what I'm saying," Harper said. "You were scared too, at first. But you got over it."

She supposed so. Harper's fingers were in her hair, tentative, searching.

A few nights later, when Colton pressed his own fingers to her scalp, she shrugged off his touch. She'd snuck out and lost herself under him, but now his sheets felt thin, her shoulders cold. He rolled toward the other side of the bed.

"I wasn't telling you to go away," she said.

"Truth be told, I've got no idea what you want, half the time."

She sat up. Slid both legs over the bed and toed the tops of her boots.

"See?" he said. "There you go."

When she turned, his face was more crushed than she was expecting, his wrinkles drawn out. "I'm trying," she said, and he set his chin on her shoulder and said, "At least tell me what happened to you two. The whole story."

She made herself inhale. What rushed into her body felt like a flood itself: William saying, "There's no better place to be," even when they were the last ones in the complex, the common area empty after the calls to evacuate. They had a shaky peace those first hours, playing cards on the concrete floor until the power went out, then quietly wondering where everyone else had hunkered down, until the wind outside grew louder than their voices and Harper shouldered her emergency pack and said, "I *told you*," and climbed the stairs to the adult quarters on the second landing, then the teens' on the third. "Just get some rest," William said, as they each took a bunk, the gray walls around them shuddering and Momma, beside him, pulling the blankets overhead. Hours later, sleepless, Brie twisted on the mattress and her arm draped over its edge and met warm water, already rising toward her shoulder. Her scream was silent inside her, and she would've sat inside that silent scream forever if Harper hadn't pulled her away, leading everyone through the hollering wind and the waist-high water up the next flight of stairs to the storerooms with cans scattered over the floor, then up the escape ladder to the roof, where the emergency boats were chained. "You can't release it 'til after you're in it," Harper shouted to William and Momma through the fury of rain, but either William didn't hear or he'd grown desperate because the second boat was loose and slowly sliding away from him and Momma, then blown out of reach and over the edge, the way their bodies would've blown over if they weren't on all fours. Where, Brie whispered, had her attention been at the moment of William and Momma's vanishing? The water rose too high too fast, already dragging her from Harper, then sealing her beneath. And out of that black water and screeching wind, Harper reappeared, grabbing her wrist and hoisting her into the safety of the boat, which rocked against its chains then shot away the instant Harper unclipped them, away from the patch of roof where Momma and William had once been. That roof soon vanished entirely, just like the other roofs across the development, the lightning flashing against the black water hell-bent on clearing the earth.

It did not make her feel better to tell Colton. Nor did it make her feel good to explain what came after: The government acknowledging that, despite the flooding it would cause to adjacent regions, they'd had no choice but to release the water from the reservoir, which could not keep up with the rainfall. The promise she and Harper made never to depend on anyone but each other, to get all the way north before settling down. Still, she talked. Of the farm work that bent her back like a blighted tree, the money dwindling from the cost of food and water. Of the viruses that didn't kill them but took them out of commission for weeks. Of how Mr. Randall's farm hadn't been so bad, until Brie saw him pull Harper against him in the cornfields, one large, pale-knuckled hand gripping the hair long and wilting as wheat. They disappeared into the stalks. Brie raced to his truck, which was parked outside the barn, and after gunning the engine, raced toward the bodies in the field, honking the horn until Mr. Randall leapt up, his glasses lost in the dirt. "Enough," she'd yelled while Harper climbed in, covering her face in the swirling dust. In the rearview mirror, Brie could see him shouting after them as he ran, obscured by the dust until he was out of sight. Brie's hands shook as she drove, swerving out of the fields and onto the road. "I was supposed to kill him," Harper said, and it was the first time Brie had ever heard her sister sound unsure. "I told myself I would, the next person. You grow up, you get older, and you think—" Brie clutched Harper's hand, and the two of them drove, drove, drove into distant states, none as far as they wanted to be.

Brie stopped. How long had Colton been holding her arm?

"Let me come with you," he said. "Make sure you get to Maine all right."

"Why would you leave all this?"

He pulled her against him and squeezed. She closed her eyes. God, to love her sister and still want this comfort. When she looked out the window, she saw that the land was still green, even after its trees had been picked clean.

The next morning, Brie couldn't look her sister in the face, as if, in telling their story, she'd removed all their clothing. She stood with Harper on the porch, her mind aware of Colton watching them as he fixed breakfast in the kitchen. She'd let Harper borrow her teacup, but it was hard not to read into her sister scowling at the gray haze over the farm and its promise of rain. It came as they sipped their tea. So did the woman on horseback.

She was a white blouse and straw hat in the distance, a ghost floating on the horse. Brie, alert, noticed Harper stiffen. The woman was too tall and dark to be Lauren, and anyway, she did not wave. Instead, she reached the front of the house, slid off the horse, and hauled a drenched canvas bag over the dip in the animal's back, before it shook rainwater from its mane and trotted off to a soggy patch of grass. Only then did the woman's gaze flicker over them—then return once more. She opened her mouth, slow, a tiny hole appearing at the very center of the world. Finally, she called, "Col," and the intimacy of the sound made something in Brie tip over completely.

From inside came Colton's approach: a collection of footsteps, the fumble of the doorknob. Brie breathed in deep; Harper's brows furrowed over the teacup.

When the door opened, he said, "Alice," his hands flexing beside his thighs. The woman stood on her toes and kissed him quick on the mouth, and Colton went still.

Brie thought: *I let you all the way in.*

"This," he began, not looking at her. "This is my . . ."

But Brie knew. She stepped away from him, deeper into the porch's shadows. The woman tipped back her hat and studied—what? Her outfit? That strawberry print dress, the fruit dark with rainwater.

"Looks good on you," the wife said.

Brie thought: *How did I ignore it?* In the kitchen, Alice took off her hat and laid it on the table. Shook out the short, fuzzy dreads that jutted over her ears. Kicked off her boots and left them in the middle of the floor. She went through the cabinets and pulled out bread and a jar of peaches Lauren had canned only the day before. As she ate with her fingers, she said, "These are better than I'd have expected."

Colton couldn't decide who to angle his body toward. The four of them sat at the kitchen table, a kettle of tea at its center. Because Brie couldn't look at him—everything, after all this time, belonged to this other person—she turned toward Harper, who, for once, was relaxed, even inside and even without Lauren. Harper rested one wrist on the table, the other against her face. Brie's mug burned her fingers.

"You tired out your horse," Harper observed.

"Had to, with every camp leader flagging me down for water packs."

"Where were you?" Colton said. He still hadn't touched his mug.

"Outside Etowah," Alice said. Then, more quietly: "Then outside Valdosta. Hillsborough. 'Bout a four-month trip."

"More like two years," Colton murmured. And Brie felt his words hum in her ears. He meant them for her.

"I meant this leg. I was checking on some farmers we knew." She pushed one of her dreads out of her face. "Before that, I . . . spent some time in Nashville."

"You survived their so-called 'quarantine'?" Harper asked. Her lips failed to hide her smile. "How'd you get them to let you in?"

"They're trying to grow peaches inside their nursery." Alice smiled a little, a warmth rising through the wrinkles in her face. "And a few other things I could help them out with."

"You didn't leave here 'cause you wanted to help out somebody else," Colton said.

"No. I suppose I didn't." Alice pursed her lips. "Don't worry, I just need a place. At least for a little while."

Colton pushed away from the table, and the tea shook in their mugs. He'd almost made it to the stairs when he paused and said, "What do you mean by 'farmers we *knew*'?"

Alice folded her hands. "Know. The Rogers stuck around. And the Tanners."

"Jesus." He pulled hard at his chin. Then his eyes said to Brie, *Come?* And he went upstairs.

Brie didn't move. Alice leaned back in her chair and licked her perfect, yellow teeth. "How long you two planning on staying?" she said.

"At this rate," Harper said, and leaned in, "who knows?"

How long would she have to stand it? Sitting there listening to Alice talk about how much rain there had been near Bristol, how much harder it was to find a hotel with reliable power? Harper goaded Alice on: How far north have you traveled? How strict were the state checkpoints in High America? Why would you ever leave a city, given its resources and healthy populations? "Even those won't last forever," Alice said, and inside, Brie felt some seedling wilt within her.

When Alice had finally gone upstairs, Harper following and asking more questions, Brie rose, her ankles loose. She thought of how much she'd told him, this man she'd only known seven weeks, and this was what he'd held back? She was almost outside when Colton grabbed her arm. "Please," he said, his hand a band of heat. "I never even thought I'd see her again."

She yanked her arm away and stomped down the porch steps. In seconds, she was soaked.

"How was I supposed to know?" he shouted.

Later, the shed where she lay beside Harper was boxed with the scent of rain.

"She's lovely," Harper said. She sat on the mattress and picked at the hairs on her legs. "No idea why she's with *him*. If they are together."

Brie grabbed the sheets beneath them. "It's been a long time since I met somebody who talked that much."

"Is that all you have to say?"

Brie turned so her hair, dense from humidity, covered half her face.

"Wow," Harper said. "I don't think you've ever tried to hide anything from me."

The rain didn't stop for five days, a sheet of water walling them in. The phone rang, and when she answered, Brie could hardly make out Lauren's voice: Will come when—. Rain too—.

"Wait 'til the connection's better," Harper said, and padded barefoot into the living room.

Since Alice had arrived, Harper had stopped asking about the fuel. When Colton appeared in a room to find Brie, he'd speak her name. If he caught her alone, he asked questions: Will you just come back upstairs? Don't you know that she's not even sleeping in my room?

In the meantime, Brie scalded, sliced, and jarred the peaches, using instructions pieced together from Lauren's calls. At some point, she let Colton stand beside her. He stirred the syrup, then poured the finished mixture into sterilized jars. There was the prolonged, quiet gaze of their shoulders. *Don't*, Brie thought. *Don't you dare.* She was wearing her old jeans and the plaid shirt she'd worn upon arriving. Only once had she been alone with Alice. The two of them were making breakfast together, and Alice touched her back and said, "Oh, honey, he's just a man," and flipped a pancake.

Harper always curled up with Alice on the couch, propping herself on one elbow. Or else she sat across from Alice on the ledge of the living room window, swinging her legs side to side. What happened, Brie thought as she looked at her sister, to our own talking? Then again, people needed . . . some shining link to other people. Or at least they told themselves this.

Halfway through a Tuesday that turned the fields to lakes, the crops covered, Alice nodded at Harper's head wrap and said, "You must get hot under that."

"Not the hottest I've been." But Harper untied the wrap, and that awful hair emerged.

Alice tugged at her own locs. "I'm thinking of cutting mine that short. Practical."

"Yours isn't so bad. Not so long you'll waste water getting it clean."

To Brie, Alice said, "How do you keep yours from tangling?" and Harper answered: "Me."

It was the kind of comment that used to make one of them touch the other in affection.

At the end of the rain, the sky a thin gray, Alice and Harper made their way into the flooded fields, heading toward the empty peach groves. Brie watched from the kitchen window, how Harper kept covering her patchy scalp with her arms. Alice caught Harper's elbows and brought them down, until the tufts of hair were exposed. Which was maybe all right. Maybe Alice could make Harper understand how easy it was to long for certain things. Even if it made you foolish.

She felt Colton behind her, a coolness that pricked her neck. "Did I say it?" he asked. "That I was sorry?"

Brie watched Alice and Harper pause near the trees. Fireflies circled their shoulders in a queasy green. She and Harper would have to go soon. Nothing here belonged to them.

Colton breathed above her hair, the strands rushing from his mouth. "Alice is just one of those people," he said. "You know what I mean? They never have enough, and so they go and you let them. That's not my fault. This whole time, I've never lied to you."

Standing here with him. In this house. All the water out there. For so many nights, before they came to this place, she'd shivered under such weather, and for a time, the truck cabin felt like enough—was dry at least. If she and Harper had left for Maine already, they'd have been caught in this torrent, the cabin smaller than ever.

Her body surprised her, turning toward him: *Touch me now*, it said. *While there's time.*

*

Because she and Harper had gone so long without speaking honestly, Brie did not immediately worry about Harper's absence a few days later, when the fields had dried. She woke in the shed with room to spread out, Harper's side of the mattress empty. When Brie did not hear the splash of the water bucket outside, she assumed Harper had already started the day's work.

She began her own tasks, packing the jars and listening as Colton talked to men who'd come in from town, gray-suited government suppliers who wanted to know about getting some chard. True, Harper's head was absent from the orchard, but Alice was gone too, and there was Colton to think about, how they'd lain together three times since that evening the rain stopped.

Harper's absence alarmed her at lunchtime. Even the cool pleasure of the kitchen couldn't dispel the strangeness of the empty chairs.

"She'll be back," Colton said when he saw her face. "Alice probably took her on a walk."

They both heard it from the house: the low growl of a truck with too many miles on it.

Brie went out to the porch. Their truck, that old blue beast, plowed down the dirt drive, growing louder as it approached, as if eager to move on. She felt Colton behind her and spun around. His eyes were already widening to hold hers.

The driver's door shot open and Harper hopped down, legs steady. In the passenger seat, Alice made a visor of her hands.

"We got the fuel," Harper said. She walked up to Brie, her gaze so intent it was like their foreheads were touching. "Alice traded the horse in town. And got enough to get us a long way."

"To Maine?" Brie asked.

"Or close." Harper looked over her shoulder, past the house. She licked her mouth's dry corners. "We can head on now. Don't even think I have much to pack."

Harper walked toward the shed; Brie did not realize she'd followed until they were inside. "I think," Harper said, sweeping her backpack over her shoulder, "we can at least make it near Richmond today."

Brie looked around the shed. So many things were hers now: the dresses, the extra underwear, the teacup. Slowly, she filled her backpack until it no longer drooped. Her wooden comb rested by the sink, and when she didn't move to collect it, Harper dropped it inside her backpack for her.

When Brie got to the truck, she expected Alice to climb down from the passenger seat. But Alice didn't. She leaned over a map on the dashboard, whispering to herself.

Brie hesitated. Tried to understand what it meant for the three of them to be going. Maybe Alice knew the checkpoints or had ways of getting into places. Or maybe Harper simply pulled people along. In Brie's hesitation, her backpack dangling from her fingers, Colton lifted her from behind. He crushed her upward into him, so her feet left the ground. Like he was trying to say goodbye. Or to lift her into the truck himself.

She said, "Hang on."

Harper tossed her own backpack inside. Extended a hand for Brie's.

"I can't," Brie said, and clutched her sister's hand. "Go yet."

Harper gestured with her fingers, impatient. Alice looked up from her map, eyes fluttering. "Brie," Harper said. It was not a question.

Colton lowered her to the ground, one inch at a time. Her toes pressed into the soil. "Later," Brie said, and stepped back until her head met Colton's neck. "I'll meet you later."

Harper's face flushed. She opened her mouth, closed it again. "What about one more night?" her sister said finally. "And we leave in the morning?"

"We can come back for her," Alice said. "Some other time."

"Come back and get me?" Brie asked. "I'll be ready, by then."

Harper didn't answer. And that look on Alice's face: the boredom everywhere but the tight mouth. Brie rummaged through her backpack and pulled out the old tea canister, the teacup sharply silver in the sunlight. "Take these. In case you get sick again."

Colton walked up to Alice, who shook his hand, then bent to whisper into his ear. After a moment, he said, "Yeah, you too."

Alice said something like, *Don't I always.* Or maybe it was, *It's a long way*. Brie couldn't tell. Harper pulled her into an embrace. "I'm not watching this happen again," she whispered. "Don't be fucking stupid."

"I'm not," she said. "No hurricanes here, right? And maybe—you'll find a good phone. In the meantime." She kissed Harper's shoulder so hard it hurt her teeth. Then she pulled away. She pressed her backpack to her chest, over the warmth Harper left.

She stared down until Harper's boots vanished and the truck door slammed and rattled. When Brie turned to face Colton, she saw his relief.

Though she might as well have looked behind her. When Harper and Alice drove off, the truck was louder than anything.

Inside the house, Brie was alone with him. She wobbled as she walked into the kitchen and set her backpack on an empty chair. *I live here*, she thought, looking at the white cabinets.

Colton put his hands on her arms. Then let them fall. "Your sister," he said.

"She was—" She sat down in one of the empty chairs. It was like the backs of her knees had been scooped out. "We found her. At the complex. This group brought in from another part of Texas, this town that had run out of water. Momma and I, we'd gone to pass out food and Harper had nobody. Was just sitting in a tire with her knees up. And so we kind of made her ours. But she was never—" Her fist loosened. She couldn't even believe the sentence enough to finish it. Harper had refused food for days, snarling at the adults, throwing dirt at the children. But not at her. She'd approached Harper with an onion. Polished it on her shirt and took a bite before offering it. Harper watched her. Then held out her fingers.

"Oh," Colton said, his shoulders relaxing. "So you're not really sisters then."

When he saw her face, he stepped back. "Don't look at me like that," he said. "We can't start like this, with you looking at me like that."

For the long months after, when the phone rings and she hears the inhale on the other end, she waits for the caller to speak.

"I'll swing by?" Lauren will say. Or one of the laborers will go, "Y'all need somebody?" She tells them to come on. Surely, if someone can call, Harper can too, whether she got ahold of a phone in some city or reached a Maine cell tower not destroyed by a storm.

For now, Brie thinks, there's the work of living for the life she has. Going into the fields, sometimes with Colton and sometimes without him, all the crops to rip up or plant anew. Evenings with Lauren and her husband across the kitchen table, bellies delightfully warm from roast or nauseous from the latest vaccine, the power flickering around them. Nights where Colton thumbs her navel and talks about the land surviving, bountiful forever. She wonders about children. She has never had to have her own answer, about whether or not to have them.

In other moments, her mind reaches elsewhere. She'll twist from the kitchen sink and study the phone, always waiting to be called to life. *What if it were the very beginning of the world?* she imagines Harper saying. *You'd choose me then?* Easier to think of that than the days after Harper's leaving. She'd gone walking, and something crunched in the dirt beneath her boot. She'd stooped. Found a piece of the teacup, a jagged slice of white and silver, her gift hurled against the trunk of a peach tree.

Maybe Harper would ask nothing, would return with no warning at all. The truck kicking up dirt. Harper leaping down, her hair grown back and landing around her shoulders. She'd holler across the green space. Come rushing toward her so fast the wind would meet her before they collided.

It's hard not to come up with such stories. The waiting, long as it is. It's long enough to remember how eternal a love she had once. How difficult a time it'll have finding a way back.

Angelo

FROM *Ploughshares*

EVENINGS I MEET Angelo in the parking lot behind Whataburger to get high. This has become such a ritual that we don't even talk about it anymore. We just meet up in the same spot right behind the dumpster, a small patch of creosote bushes that shield us from any onlookers. It used to be that we'd drive over to Angelo's apartment afterward and watch the news or watch the Spurs, but Angelo is married now—he's been married almost six months—and so we don't do that anymore. Instead, we just pass a joint back and forth, sit in his car for about an hour or so, listening to music and occasionally talking, but mostly just sitting there quietly, a ritual we've shared since high school, since longer, probably, than either of us can remember.

In the early days, long before the two of us had jobs or high school diplomas or any sense of what we wanted to do, Angelo used to drive us down to the south side of San Antonio, to an area of the city called Southtown. This was where a lot of the artists in the city lived and where the cheapest studio spaces were. During the summer between our junior and senior years of high school, Angelo had actually rented a space down there himself, a modest twenty-by-twenty-foot room with high ceilings and central air conditioning and a small metal cabinet in the back with a lock on it where he could store his work. There was a round window on the west side of the room that looked out on the courtyard and that brought in nice natural light in the late afternoons, and there was a small refrigerator that Angelo had bought earlier that year to store his iced coffee and the sandwiches that his mother made for him and the beer that his older brother occasionally bought for us. It was a nice arrangement overall. On the far side of the room, Angelo had set up a wooden easel and a daylight lamp and a long table for drawing, and next to that, he had a smaller table where he kept his brushes and his palette scrapers and his other paint supplies. In the late afternoons, when both of us were tired and dizzy from the turpentine fumes, Angelo would eventually put away his work and turn on some music and open up the window and the door to let in some air. It was always hot that summer. There'd been a drought for over a month—forty straight days without rain—and the temperatures were often in the triple digits by late afternoon, sometimes even as high as 108 or 109 by evening. Still, Angelo would always insist on airing out the studio, opening up the window and the door, claiming the fumes we'd been inhaling all day were probably going to kill us, then walking over to the mini fridge and getting us both a beer, tossing me a bottle from across the room, then motioning for me to go outside, into the sunshine and the heat.

Out across the courtyard, there were several other small studios, all of roughly the same size and most rented by other young artists—none as young as Angelo but many in their early-to-mid twenties. As we sat outside in the midsummer heat, sweating under the shade of the studio's steel awning, we'd often stare out across the courtyard at these studios, waiting for the other artists to emerge. There were other places we could have been, I suppose, other things we could have been doing, but both of us liked the quiet camaraderie of this little studio community, especially in the early evenings, when the other artists would begin to come out of their own small studios and open up their own beers, sometimes starting up a little fire in the circular stone fire pit in the middle of the courtyard, throwing on a marinated skirt steak or some poblano peppers, some tortillas wrapped in tinfoil. As for Angelo and me, no one ever seemed to question who we were or whether we were old enough to be drinking with them or why we were out there with them instead of home with our families. I'm sure they must have known that we were underage, but they never said a word about it, just as they never said a word about the fact that I showed up each day alone, simply to hang out with Angelo in his studio while he painted, even though I didn't paint myself, even though I mostly just sat there writing in my journal, or reading a book, or scrolling through the internet on my phone.

There was only one time I can remember the subject even coming up. This was an evening in early June, a few weeks after we'd started going there regularly. This sculptor named Michelle, a beautiful woman in her late twenties, came up to me as we were sitting around the fire pit drinking—a small group of us, just sitting there talking quietly and listening to music—and she just touched my arm lightly and leaned into me, leaned into me in a way that made me think she was going to kiss me, but instead she just said, "You two going out, Cole?"

"Who?"

She nodded across the courtyard at Angelo, who was standing with another group of people, passing a joint.

"No," I said. "We're just friends."

She nodded, then smiled, as if to herself.

"What?"

"Nothing."

"What," I said again. "Why are you smiling?"

"I'm not," she said. "I mean, it's nothing." She looked away. "It's just that if you were, you know, you'd be a pretty cute couple, that's all."

I nodded but said nothing to this, and then a moment later, she stood up and walked away and that was the last time anyone ever said anything about it.

Still, I knew how it looked to some people and knew what other people were probably thinking and saying. I knew that what Angelo and I were didn't make a lot of sense, even to us, that we weren't something that was easily defined or categorized, that we weren't something that was easily explained or understood.

Later that night, as we were lying in our sleeping bags in the studio—we often slept there when we were too drunk to drive—I told Angelo what Michelle had asked and he looked over at me in the darkness and then propped himself up on an elbow.

"So what did you say?" he said.

"I said we were just friends," I said. "Why? What would you have said?"

"I don't know," he said. "Probably the truth."

"Which is?"

"Which is who the fuck knows?" he said and laughed and then he eased over next to me in his sleeping bag and wrapped his arms around me, pulled me toward him. I could smell the beer on his breath, could feel the strength of his lean arms as he squeezed me tighter, as he pressed his lips to mine, then eventually released me, rolling over onto his side again, and then facing the wall, his head turned away.

When we woke up the next morning, we said nothing about this, just as we never said anything about what happened in the darkness of his studio late at night whenever we'd been drinking. It just wasn't a thing that we did.

These days, when I think back on that time, when I think back on those long, quiet days in Angelo's studio, I see only fragments, fleeting images that skip across the surface of my mind like sunlight. I see Angelo sitting at his table, mixing paints in his palette or cleaning off his brushes with a rag. I see him sipping on a bottle of Modelo, or Shiner Bock, or Budweiser. I see the toes of his sneakers always covered with paint, the holes in his too-loose jeans, the tightness of his T-shirts. I see the angle of soft light coming through the west-facing window on the far side of the room, the dust motes suspended in midair, swirling in slow motions, and I see Angelo himself looking over at me from time to time, smiling, both of us in a kind of trance, a daze, and then later in the day, I see Angelo cleaning up his palette and brushes, running everything under hot water in the stainless steel sink on the other side of the room, then turning on music finally, putting on a fresh T-shirt, combing his hair, coming to me.

I have no idea, even now, how Angelo managed to pay for

that studio that summer—it wasn't something he liked to talk about—but I knew that the money hadn't come from either of his parents, and I knew that it hadn't come from a job, because he hadn't had a job, a real job, since that past winter when he'd worked weekends as a waiter at El Mirador. In the beginning of the summer, we'd both talked about the possibility of getting jobs but ultimately decided against it. This was going to be a different type of summer, we decided, a summer of self-reflection, a summer of growth, and for Angelo, a summer of serious work, as he was still planning to apply to undergraduate art programs in the fall.

He didn't talk about this much, but every so often he'd pull out his folder of brochures and pamphlets and other materials for his college applications and look them over. He'd talk about how he'd need to have a strong portfolio, a strong body of work, then he'd look off kind of listlessly and cross his arms, as if bracing himself for disappointment. I knew that the school he had his heart set on at the time was RISD, but whenever I'd bring this up, he'd quickly change the subject or cut me off mid-sentence and say something about how RISD was a fucking lottery ticket, a long shot, *a pipe dream, dude,* and then he'd go back to doing whatever it was he was doing. Still, I could tell he was hoping for it secretly, was hoping for any of these programs, really, and whenever I'd think about this, I'd feel a little panging in my chest, the knowledge that in a year from now, he'd likely be gone from here—off in California or Massachusetts or Rhode Island—while I'd still be here, doing who knows what, living who knows where. Unlike Angelo, I didn't have the grades for college, not for the types of colleges he was looking at, anyway, and my mother didn't have the money to send me either, had never set up a college fund for me or anything like that. Ever since my father had moved back to El Paso two years earlier, any talk of the future—mine or hers—was off the table. We were in survival mode now, as she often liked to remind me, just trying our best to get through each day.

Still, as much as it saddened me to consider my own situation, and as much as it saddened me to think of Angelo leaving, I still wanted it for him, still knew that he had both the grades and the talent to make it happen—to get scholarships perhaps, or other types of funding, to get help.

I remember one evening in mid-July—this was right in the middle of the drought—sitting with him outside under the steel awning in front of the studio and talking to him about it, sitting there quietly as he looked through all of the program brochures he'd collected, all of these colorful pamphlets and glossy folded print-outs, photographs of students huddled around their earnest professors, their blue jeans speckled with paint, their hands clutching sketchbooks, as they looked on eagerly at the painting the professor was critiquing, the studio background advertising an atmosphere of both seriousness and calm, of erudition and peacefulness.

"It looks nice," I remember saying to him at one point. "I mean, like, really nice, you know?"

"Yeah." Angelo nodded and then shrugged. "No way I'm getting into any of these places, though."

"Why not?"

"I don't know," he said, looking out at the courtyard. "Some things you just know, right?" He rubbed his legs. "I mean, these kids are just, like, really impressive, for one thing."

"And so are you," I said. I looked at him. Then I reminded him of the art contest he'd won the previous year, a citywide competition that involved all of the city's school districts, which was judged by a panel of renowned local artists and was even written up in the *San Antonio Express-News* alongside a photo of Angelo and the other two finalists.

"Yeah man, but that's local shit," he said. "No offense, but that's San Antonio, you know? No one cares about what's going on down here."

Angelo had grown up in Austin, had lived there until seventh grade, and liked to distance himself from San Antonio by saying things like "no offense" to people like me, who'd lived here all our lives.

"I don't think that's true," I said. "There's a lot going on down here." I motioned around the courtyard at the other studios, the other young artists working inside.

"Yeah," he said. "A lot that nobody knows about."

He reached into his pocket then for a pack of cigarettes, lit one, then passed the pack to me.

I knew these things he was saying were just a kind of defense mechanism for him, the way he protected himself from hoping too much, but sometimes it grew exhausting, having to reel him back in, having to pump him back up, having to reassure him that he wasn't as deluded as he thought, that he wasn't wrong for believing in himself.

After a while, he put out his cigarette on the ground and then leaned his head on my shoulder, a rare display of public affection. I looked around the rest of the courtyard to see if anyone could see us, but the courtyard was empty now, no one in sight.

"Plus," he said, "if I left, I'd probably end up missing you too much, you know?" He tapped his leg.

"We could write letters," I said, "like in the olden times."

"You mean like the 1980s?"

"No," I said, "like the 1880s, with a quill and shit."

"I think you're thinking of the 1780s," he said and laughed, shaking his head.

"See," I said. "That's why I need you to stick around, to keep me from saying dumb shit like that."

"Yeah, that's my point," he said, shaking his head again. "That's my point exactly."

He leaned forward then and looked out at the courtyard, at the small cacti and the bougainvillea growing along the far wall, the hibiscus and Mexican bush sage and, beyond that, at the sun just beginning to set along the tree line in the distance. It was a quiet night, everything in its place, everything still.

We sat there for a while quietly, just looking out at the courtyard, and then after a few minutes or so, Angelo turned back to me and looked at me more seriously.

"You know, I think my mom might be sick," he said.

"What do you mean?"

"I don't know," he said and shook his head. "I don't even really know."

"Like really sick?"

"Yeah," he said. "I don't know, maybe." He stood up then and started back toward the studio door. "I don't want to talk about it, though," he said, and then he went inside and closed the door, and I let him stay in there by himself for a long time, until I finally saw the light go off, and then I went inside myself and got in my sleeping bag and waited for him in the dark, waited for him to come to me.

It wasn't always like that, though. There were some days when he barely talked to me, days when he was so caught up in his work that it was like he wasn't even there, like he was in his own private world, a world that didn't involve me, and even when he finished up his work, he'd still be there, lingering in that world, his eyes so distant that it was like talking to a ghost, like a person who had left the world of the living.

I remember one evening in mid-July finding him sitting out by himself on the edge of the courtyard, smoking a cigarette and looking through a book of photographs by Robert Frank, his eyes glazed over from a lack of sleep and weed and a long, six-hour session in the studio that day. All summer he'd been working on a series of modest-size oil paintings in various neutral tones, lots of grays and whites, and he'd been looking more to books of photographs for inspiration, specifically books of black and white photographs, than he had been looking to books of paintings. Earlier that day, I'd gone with Michelle and her boyfriend, Trevor, to get some beer at one of the local grocery stores, and when I got back, Angelo was gone, the studio clean, and a small note taped to the door saying he'd be back later. Now, I could see that he'd gone somewhere to find weed—maybe smoked out with some of the other artists behind one of the studios—and was clearly off in another reality. I'd been lonely for him all day. He'd barely said a word to me since lunch, since we'd gone out for tacos at one of the little taquerias in the neighborhood, but I could tell that he wasn't in the mood to talk now.

I sat down beside him on the wrought iron bench and leaned my shoulder against his. He didn't move. In front of us, people were starting to come out of their studios, and somebody had started up the music and lit the fire pit, and some other people

were opening up beers. It was a small gathering that would become much larger in the next hour.

"Why don't you come down and join everyone?" I said, nudg-
ing his arm, but again he didn't move. He was still looking down
at the photos.

"How much did you smoke?" I said after a moment, but again
he said nothing.

In the distance, I could see Michelle sitting down on one of
the chairs around the fire pit and lighting a cigarette and then
looking up at us and waving. I waved back.

But when I turned back to Angelo, he wasn't looking at Michelle. He was looking straight at me, his eyes suddenly concerned.

"Why are you crying?" he said, touching my hand.

"I'm not," I said, reaching up to touch my own cheek, just to
be sure.

"You are," he said, squeezing my hand tighter, looking even
more concerned, and then he looked back down at his book.

Later that night, in the darkness of his studio, he came to me
for the first time in nothing but his boxer shorts, his back sweaty
from the hundred-plus temperatures, his body lean, wiry, the
small muscles of his arms tensing beneath his soft skin, the stubble on the edge of his chin rough against my own.

Afterward, as we lay there in the still darkness of his studio, he talked again about his mother, only now his voice was
calmer, more measured, his thoughts more lucid. He said that
the following week she'd be beginning her first round of chemo
and that he didn't know what would be happening after that. It
was all so up in the air.

I looked at him. "What type is it?"

"What type of chemo?"

"No, what type of cancer?"

"I don't know," he said. "The bad type. All I know is that it's
everywhere now." He looked down at his hands.

I said nothing to this, and he nestled in closer to me, let me
hold him. "I think that joint I smoked was laced with something," he said.

"Yeah," I said.

He was quiet for a moment. Then he said. "Yeah, I don't think I should be smoking that shit anymore." Then he turned over on his side slowly and drifted off to sleep.

The next day when I woke up, he was gone. No note. Not even a text message of where he'd disappeared to or when he might be back. Days later, I'd find out that he'd gone back home to be with his mother and to look after his little sister as his mother went through her first cycle of treatment, but at the time, I had no idea. All I knew was that he was gone, that he wasn't responding to my text messages or phone calls, not even to the lengthy email message I'd written him earlier that week.

In the meantime, I was still spending my days hanging around the studio and the courtyard—Angelo had made me a key earlier in the summer—still sleeping there, still drinking beers in the evenings with Michelle and Trevor and the others. At home, there wasn't a whole lot waiting for me. My mother had started working double shifts at the ICU in the evenings, which meant that even when she was supposed to be home, she usually wasn't. Once or twice a week I'd go home to do laundry or pick up fresh clothes or grab some food from the refrigerator or the pantry, but for the most part I tried my best to stay away from there.

There was still the residue of my father lingering in every room, the remnants of his life with us. Throughout the summer, I'd been trying hard to get rid of any evidence of him from the house, selling off his records and DVDs, his books, the expensive set of tools he'd left in the garage. This was not only my primary source of income those days—the selling off of my father's life—but also an exercise in exorcism, an eliminating of all the bad energy he'd left behind.

One afternoon during that week when Angelo was gone, I remember my mother coming home to find me sitting on the floor of our living room, going through a box of my father's old military things—various patches and photographs and pins, a couple of baseball caps with insignia on them.

"What are you doing?" she said.

"Getting rid of his shit," I said.

"And what are you going to do when he comes back to get it and it's not here?"

"He's not coming back," I said, and though I hadn't meant for it to come off as harsh, I realized that it had. My mother winced and thinned her lips and then went over to the fridge to grab a beer.

"Where have you been all summer, anyway?"

"About."

"About?"

"Yeah, as in out and about."

"Uh huh."

She took the top off her beer and took a long sip. She was still dressed in her nurse's uniform, a pair of mauve surgical scrubs.

"Well, if you're really looking to get rid of his stuff," she said, "why don't you take that ugly workout bench in the garage so we can park the car in there again. I'll actually pay you to get rid of that thing."

"Can I use your car?" I said.

"You can use whatever you want," she said, and then she turned around and walked out of the room.

When I got back to the studio later that night, two hundred dollars richer from having sold my father's workout set to a pawn shop on the south side, I found Angelo sitting around the fire pit with the others, drinking beer and laughing. He looked up at me when I arrived and waved, smiling, as if he hadn't just disappeared for five days, as if he hadn't just ghosted me.

"What's up?" he said, as I walked over and sat down beside him in one of the iron chairs.

"Where have you been?" I said.

"Home," he said, and then looked down, his smile fading. "Sorry," he said more quietly.

"It's okay," I said.

"It's just been really heavy at home, you know?"

I nodded. The others around the fire pit had moved on to a conversation about some new band they'd all seen at one of the clubs on the south side earlier that week. I looked over at Michelle who gave me a plaintive smile, then went back to the conversation.

"I've actually been working on some new stuff already, though," he said. "Some stuff I started today."

"Oh yeah?" I said. "Different?"

"Way different," he said, and then he smiled at me in a way that told me he was probably stoned. "I want to show it to you later, okay?"

I nodded.

"Great," he said and smiled, and then patted my hand.

But by the time "later" rolled around, he was too messed up to even stand, let alone show me his art, and I ended up having to carry him back to the studio myself, laying him down on his sleep mat and taking off his shoes and then sliding him into his sleeping bag with all his clothes still on.

At some point later that night, I heard him getting sick in the bushes behind the studio, and when he came in a few minutes later, he was holding his T-shirt in his hands, and I could see he'd gotten a large tattoo of something serpentine and dragon-like on the side of his body, right beneath his armpit.

"When did you get that?" I said.

"Long story," he said, and then he walked over to his sleeping bag and climbed back in, closing his eyes.

Did I fall in love with Angelo that summer? It's hard to say. It's hard to put a name on it. All I know is that I wanted to be around him constantly. I never didn't want to be in his presence, or near him. And even when he went home to check up on his mother, as he did periodically, I'd feel the need to check in with him constantly, just to hear his voice, just to be assured that nothing between us had changed.

Meanwhile, Angelo himself became more focused on his work, churning out five or six paintings a week, not all of them of the same quality, but many of them quite stunning. These were very different paintings than the paintings he'd been doing earlier in the summer, more abstract, more colorful, almost

as if he was working against the bleakness of his current life, the
tragedy that was unfolding at home, by throwing color back into
it, by pumping energy back into the world. Often, at night, he'd have other people from the compound
over to look at his work. In the past, he'd always been shy or
evasive when it came to showing his work, but I could tell he
was proud of these latest pieces. Beers in hand, the other artists would wander around quietly, sometimes smiling or nodding in approval or glancing over at Angelo and giving him a
thumbs-up. None of them were ever particularly effusive, but I
could tell they respected him. All of them agreed that he'd have
no problem getting into at least one of the programs he was
applying to, and probably several.

"He's good," Michelle's boyfriend, Trevor, said to me one
night, as we were standing outside the studio, smoking. "No
one here will ever admit it, but he's probably better than most
of the other artists here." Trevor was more of a conceptual artist than a traditional one, and he didn't feel the same type of
competitiveness the others did. He was a tall guy, unassuming
and lanky, his blond hair perpetually pulled back in a bun.

A moment later, Michelle emerged from inside the studio,
holding a beer and smiling.

"Did you tell him?" she said to Trevor.

"Tell me what?" I said.

Trevor looked at her and shook his head and then drew on
his cigarette. "They're bulldozing this place," she said, looking
around the compound. "The whole thing. Putting in condos."

"When?"

"I don't know. I think December. Or maybe earlier."

"December." Trevor nodded.

"Shit," I said and shook my head, looking around the compound myself. "So where's everyone going to go?"

"I don't know," Michelle said quietly, looking over at Trevor
and taking his hand. "That's what we're all still trying to figure
out."

Later that night, as we were lying in the quiet of Angelo's studio,
the lights dim, I thought of telling Angelo about what Michelle

had said but ultimately decided against it. I could tell he'd been preoccupied all day, distant. All night, he'd been texting someone on his phone, staring at the screen distractedly, putting it back in his pocket, then taking it out again a moment later, repeating.

Now he had turned it over, so that the screen was facing the floor, and turned it off, pushed it a few feet away from him. He leaned back on the mat and closed his eyes, sighed.

"I need to go home again for a while," he said after a moment, crossing his arms.

"Okay," I said. "How long?"

"I don't know."

There were only a couple weeks left in the summer, only one full week, really, before classes started up and we'd have to leave this place.

"She needs me," he said. "My sister, too."

I nodded. "Where's your dad?"

Angelo looked at me and then just shook his head and shrugged. "That's a good question," he said. "A really good fucking question."

At some point later on, as I was drifting in and out of sleep, I heard Angelo get up and leave the studio. When he came back a few minutes later, he was holding a joint, which he lit as he sat at his worktable, the daylight lamp turned to face the wall, casting his jaw in silhouette. A moment later, when he noticed me staring at him, he came down to the floor to join me, passing the joint to me, then taking off his shirt.

That would end up being the last night we were ever intimate with each other, the last night we'd spend together at his studio, but I didn't know any of that then. All I knew was that he looked good that night, smelled good.

"I think he's at my uncle's," he said, as I took off my own shirt, then took his free hand in mine. "My father. I think that's where he is."

"Why's he at your uncle's?"

"I don't know," he said. "Can't deal with it, I guess."

I nodded.

"These fathers," he said, looking at me and shaking his head, then smiling slightly in a way that told me he was including my own father too. Then he put out the joint on the floor of the studio and came closer to me, kissing me softly on the lips, the neck.

"One day we're both going to be far away from this place," I said quietly, as his lips moved lower.

"The compound?"

"No," I said, shaking my head. "This city. This state."

Angelo pulled back for a moment and looked at me, squinting, as if wanting to believe me, then finally, he shook his head. "Not me," he said. "My family. We never get out."

Even now, I sometimes still think about those words—not necessarily the words themselves, but the way he said them to me, the certainty in his voice, the gravity.

All summer, he'd been saying the opposite, planning for the opposite, and yet now it was obvious that something had shifted, changed, and even as we lay there together that night, holding each other, it was clear that part of him had already disappeared, vanished.

Still, I remember the quietness of the studio that night and the softness of his skin as he lay there beside me, shirtless, one arm wrapped around my waist, whispering to me until we both fell asleep, the smell of his thick hair, the rhythm of our breathing, and I remember later, long after we'd both fallen asleep, that shock I felt upon waking and seeing him standing at the doorway, looking out, not saying anything at first, and then turning to me in an almost-frightened way and shaking his head. It was still dark outside, still dark in the studio, and I could hear the faint sound of sirens in the distance, some muffled shouting, and then it hit me—the thick, ashy smell of bonfire smoke, only the smell that was coming into the studio right then was much thicker than bonfire smoke, much harsher.

I stood up and walked over to the other side of the room, where Angelo was standing in the doorway, looking out, and we both stood there for a while, staring out across the courtyard at what I could now see was a burning studio unit—a studio unit that had formerly belonged to an artist named Noel but that was now empty—and I could see the flashing lights of two police cars and a fire engine about fifty yards off in the distance, and I could see everyone else who had slept there that night, just standing around the courtyard, stupefied, confused, taking videos with their phones, calling friends. In the end, we would never find out who had lit that fire or what had caused it. Had it been an act of arson? An act of protest? An accident? There would be lots of speculation, but never any clear answers, not even months later, when the compound itself was getting prepared for excavation, when everything else was being torn down.

"What the fuck?" Angelo said, as we stood there staring at the burning building. "What the actual fuck is wrong with this place?"

I said nothing because I had nothing to say. I was still half asleep, still disoriented. But Angelo was already moving back toward the back of the studio, packing up his palette scrapers and brushes, collapsing his easel.

"We need to get the fuck out of here," he said and stared at me. And that was all.

How does an artist stop being an artist? I'm not one, so I can't really say, but it doesn't seem possible that it could be as easy as simply turning off a switch, moving on to something else. This is a subject I've often broached with Angelo, and every time I do, he always says the same thing: that it wasn't about what he wanted to do at that time; it was about what he needed to do, what he had to do.

By the end of that summer, there was no longer any talk of RISD or Cal Arts or his college applications, and by the time his mother died in late November, Angelo had all but stopped thinking about college at all, had withdrawn his applications from even the few local and in-state institutions he'd applied to—all but UTSA, which he'd eventually end up withdrawing from in March. With his mother gone and with his father still mostly absent, he felt he had no choice but to stay home and look after his little sister—at least until she was a little older, at least until she was out of high school. As for me, I was mostly on autopilot by that point, just trying my best to get through the end of senior year. At the end of that next summer, my father would come home for a short time, and I'd move out and into an apartment by myself, and then a few years after that, when Angelo's little sister graduated from high school, we'd get an apartment together, the two of us, though it would never again be the way it had been that one summer between our junior and senior years of high school, that one summer at the compound. By that point, Angelo was only dating women, was only even considering women, and I was dating nobody at all, not knowing even then what I wanted or who I wanted. Then, about two years later, Angelo met Vanessa, his current wife, and I could tell the first time I met her, the first time I saw the two of them together, what would be happening, that any chance of what we'd once had returning was now over.

Angelo and I don't really talk about this very much anymore—there's not much to say—but every once in a while, when he's really high, he'll talk about Vanessa, he'll talk about how she knows all about him, how she knows that he's bi, how he's told her this from the start. I'm not one of those guys who erases himself, he says. She knows who I am. But sometimes I doubt it. I know for sure he's never told her about us. If he had, she wouldn't be so welcoming to me every time I came over, wouldn't kiss me on the cheek every time before I left, wouldn't call me on my birthday, as she did this past year, just to check up on me, just to make sure that I was fine.

I want to tell you one other thing, though.

That painting Angelo made that won the citywide competition—it was incredible. Full of vibrant colors and frenetic motion and this weird sort of energy that made it seem like it was moving, even when you were just standing there, staring at it. I still ask him about that painting sometimes, ask him if he ever still looks at it, but he doesn't like to talk about it, just as he doesn't like to talk about anything having to do with art, or anything having to do with that summer.

The last time he even mentioned anything about that time was a few months ago—one of those rare moments when we were sitting in his car behind the Whataburger, reminiscing about high school. He'd only been married about two months at that point and was still getting used to their new apartment, their new living situation, and I could tell he was looking back a lot lately, trying to orient himself in his new life by working out his past, and I could tell also that he was pretty stoned, more messed up than usual, and so I took the opportunity to ask him something I'd always been wanting to ask him, something I'd suspected for years but never had the courage to bring up, and he surprised me when I did bring it up by admitting right away that yeah, he'd been the one to set fire to Noel's studio unit that night, that it had been him and him alone. He said this very calmly, as if he assumed this was something I'd always known. Then he drew on the joint I'd just passed him and looked out the window.

It was early evening, the sun descending beyond the small office buildings across the street, the Whataburger parking lot empty.

"They were going to bulldoze it all anyway," he said.

"You knew that?"

"Yeah, of course."

"So why burn it down, then?"

"I don't know," he said. "If I knew the answer to that, I wouldn't be thinking about it so much."

"You still think about it?"

"For some reason, I do," he said. "For some reason I still think about it all the time."

He was very stoned, as I said, and he looked out the window lazily then, dreamily.

"You were in a lot of pain back then," I said.

"Yeah," he said and nodded. "You and me both."

And I remember some other things too, like I remember how strange the world felt that night, that night we left the compound, and how quiet the streets of Southtown were at 3 a.m., how it felt like no one else in the world was awake, and I remember Angelo playing this mellow electronic music, this European synth pop, and leaning back in the passenger seat and closing my eyes as

he drove, taking in that familiar scent of mineral spirits and turpentine and oil paints, all of his paint supplies piled in the back
seat and the trunk.

"We'll go back tomorrow and get the rest of the stuff," he
said. "Okay?"

But if Angelo ever went back, I never knew about it, and he
never talked about that place again, really, not for a very long
time.

Instead, we went into our senior year of high school and kept
our heads down, tried our best to push through, to get our diplomas, but that night—that night we left the compound—that
night was about something else, I think—it was about saying
goodbye to something, moving on, and I remember having that
feeling even then, as I sat there in the passenger seat with my
eyes closed, the quiet synthesizer music, the smell of Angelo
smoking out the window, the soft hum of the air from outside
coming in.

I knew he was taking me home to my house—I knew that—
but at that moment, gliding through the quiet streets of south
San Antonio, this beautiful man beside me, it didn't feel like we
were going anywhere at all.

NATHAN CURTIS ROBERTS

Yellow Tulips

FROM *Harvard Review*

THE WEEK THE novel coronavirus came to Utah, a series of earthquakes rattled the Salt Lake Valley. On the tallest spire of the church's flagship temple, the angel Moroni stood holding a clarion to his lips. The statue was more than twelve feet tall, made of hammered copper and coated in gold leaf. His purpose was twofold: He celebrated the foreordained spreading of the restored Gospel throughout the world, and he announced the immanence of the Second Coming of the lord Jesus Christ. And then the plague found us even here in our Rocky Mountain Zion, and a series of earthquakes struck, and the angel himself chattered, and the golden trumpet—which had been pressed to Moroni's lips for almost 130 years—fell clattering from his grasp. This was a much clearer signal than God customarily sends, or so my son believed.

By that time our cul-de-sac was already in disarray. Old Bill Nilsson, who was the neighborhood's beating heart, had died on Valentine's Day. Bill was the homeowner association's capo, consigliere, and enforcer. Bill Nilsson was the man who pruned and fertilized the rose bushes in the community bowery; who would fix a family's sprinkler system before they even realized it was broken; and who would babysit a near-stranger's great-grandchildren, or a friend's mentally impaired son, on a moment's notice. Rumor had it he perished on February 14, at an unofficial reunion of college friends, the very moment he finished bearing his testimony. Bill Nilsson was a saint, and he had a death befitting such. Out in the world there were rumors of an impending epidemic. In our cul-de-sac we spoke only of the growing legend of Bill Nilsson's departure: It wasn't just his testimony; he had told his friends how much they meant to him, and then he said a heartfelt prayer, and finally he looked at his wife of fifty-five years and recited a love poem. Then his heart quieted and he was dead before his head hit the floor. At the funeral, his eldest daughter described this as a "badass" way to go. It wasn't a word we were used to hearing inside the chapel of a Latter-day Saints meetinghouse. But after her eulogy the daughter sang "I need Thee Every Hour" with such sweetness and clarity—"ev'ry hour I need thee"—she could have gotten away with saying far worse.

I was thinking about how nice it would have been to have married a woman who could sing. My boy and I were seated on folding chairs in the overflow area at the back of the chapel. Better Mormons with larger families occupied the pews, with Bill's own brood taking several rows at the front. All the way in the rear—so far back we were practically in the multipurpose room, a basketball hoop overhead—my buttocks were growing numb. Next to me Brigham, my boy, sang along with the soloist. Full volume, he cried out: "I need thee, oh, I need thee!" Plaintive and yearning, as if the boy believed what he really needed was Bill Nilsson's eldest daughter. For a wife or for a mother, I cannot guess.

"Cram it," I said. "Knock it off."

"Tan parsons lose their prowler," the boy sang. He had lost command of the hymn's lyrics. Brig was nearing thirty, but he had ever been a child inside his mind and heart, and he would never be anything else. The boy took pride in dressing himself for church. He had four suits that were nearly identical, but it was important to him not to have to double up except in a month with five Sundays. Yet he would go nowhere without his camouflage fishing cap, which he was allowed to wear inside the chapel because the entire ward knew the sounds Brig made when he was upset. There used to be another "boy" like Brigham in our ward—the same age in mind and heart, at least a decade older in body—and the two of them usually occupied each other during services. At the worst, we could keep them quiet by daring them to see which of them would remain reverent the longest. It's a powerful friendship that's forged in such commonalities: similar disabilities, single fathers who were not too good to deploy a manipulation now and then.

Balding pate, unpredictable vanity, ubiquitous fishing hat. I clenched my fist and pressed a knuckle into the flesh of his leg, threatening him with a charley horse if he wouldn't pipe down. Brigham squirmed. "Peach me I try rich porpoises my belly fill," he sang. "Need thee now, I need thee oh!" The numbness in my ass was spreading downward. Several feet in front of us, seated in the last row of proper pews, was Sister Meghan Palmer. She twisted around to fix us with a gaze and shush us both. I saw it coming before I ever heard it. A generation ago, Sister Palmer's face would have been stretched to translucency like strudel dough. But we were in the age of injectables, and she had the skin that was common among affluent women of her era, frozen fast and subtly plumped, as if inflated with cold baby fat. Meghan Palmer's hair was chin-length, sharp, a shade of yellow that suggested hair sometimes turned gold after it had gone silver. A booth-tanned complexion that was deepened with bronzer. Lips painted bubblegum pink, a color only the elderly ladies of our ward could have gotten away with—a younger woman would have been taken aside. The sound she made stunned us both, my son and I, into boyish shame. A shush like a serpent's hiss that carried at least as far as Brig's singing ever could have.

Then the earthquakes. The trumpet. Quarantine, canceled church services, teddy bears in windows. The entire neighborhood went inside; when it came back out a few weeks later— every hand carefully scrubbed, every body distanced by six scrupulous feet—it was spring. For Brigham and me, the transformation was not sudden. We witnessed the geometric progression of the window bears (two, four, sixteen) and we saw the nickel-size crocuses herald the coming of the hyacinths, which announced the daffodils, which summoned lilacs out of the dead land, by which point the blossoms were on the cherry trees and the irises were making themselves ready. Bill Nilsson was three decades my senior, but he had completed the St. George Triathlon at my age, and again when he was fifteen years older. I got winded taking the garbage out. Bill had seemed as eternal as the three Nephites or the Wandering Jew. His mortality became my own mortality. The day after his funeral, I told Brigham we were going for a walk. A walk where? "Grab your hat, let's go." But where to?

Nowhere in particular. The first week we walked to North Canyon Park, about a mile each way. The following week we added the short paved trail that was the park's hidden feature. Then we walked that trail twice, three times, four. The third week one of my toenails fell off. But it was the nail with the fungal infection, and it was for the best because it grew back clean. Chalk art began to appear on the sidewalk. Bubble letters that were as likely to say "Hang in there" as "Trust in Him." When we were ready to take on the mountain, we first tried Eagle Ridge Drive. The view on that side was of the refineries of North Salt Lake. Two thirds of the way to the bottom of the hill, there was a house with a life-size statue of Christ in its front yard. Brigham was moved to pay his respects, tramping through the neighbor's lawn to kneel at the Savior's feet. I wondered where he learned this kind of enthusiasm. Not from me. Certainly not from his mother.

Even in Utah a statue like that was a strange sight; it gave an ordinary suburban home the look of a meetinghouse. A gleaming white Jesus standing next to the front porch—I thought it was excessive. What were these people trying to prove? Was it not sufficient to simply worship a deity; did we also need to decorate our yards with Him? I said a prayer every night and over most meals, the hot ones at least. I attended sacrament meeting nearly every Sunday and priesthood meeting sometimes, if the boy wasn't acting up. I paid 10 percent tithing. Why did my neighbor need a six-foot statue in the yard? For that matter, why did the church need a twelve-foot one on a spire? "Brigham," I said, "come away from there!"

"I need thee now, I need thee," he said plaintively. Not to me, of course, but to the statue.

"Come!" I said. I slapped my thigh loudly. I was glad nobody was around to hear me speak to my son like a disobedient pet.

So we avoided Eagle Ridge and instead walked down and up the other side of the mountain. It appeared the deer were also quarantining, because the tulips in our bowery, and on Eaglewood Drive, were allowed to bloom that year—but only the yellow ones. I've long felt resentful of yellow tulips. They're redundant with daffodils, which are more resistant to disease and deer. What tulips are good for is their variety of colors, and for getting eaten up as buds, before they have a chance to present themselves. Meghan Palmer's house had a whole patch of them, yellow tulips in among yellow daffodils. One week I saw her watching us from her window. I waved, but if she waved back I never saw it. The following week the streets were full of human life, and Meghan Palmer called out to us. "Abraham Sorensen, look at you!" she said. "And Brigham too. You two have gotten so fit. I've seen it! When I first saw you boys doing your hikes up and down the hill, I thought, 'Now there's something.' I couldn't imagine going all the way down and back up again! But now the thing I marvel at is how you can hike for hours every morning and still hold on to those potbellies!"

It was important not to let on that her words bothered me. "I'm not a vain man," I said. "These walks are about feeling better, not looking better." I'd lost fifteen pounds in six weeks, but I wouldn't give her the satisfaction. The boy's belly did have a way of protruding. Someone, a special education teacher or a psychiatric nurse, explained it as a side effect of his fitting into the world differently from most. It never occurred to him to feel self-conscious, so he never bothered with sucking in his gut, which is apparently something the rest of us are doing so often we no longer notice it.

"You have such a pragmatic mind. That's lucky for you. Brother Palmer is always buying us spa visits, and the latest treatments, but he does have money to burn. It's wise for someone like you to remember walking is free."

"Isn't it wonderful?" Brigham asked.

"What's wonderful, dear?" Sister Palmer said.

"It's wonderful," Brigham said, "because the whole world is ending!"

Every morning we took our walk. When it snowed, when it rained, when the hot wind blew over the desert and came to parch our lips. Brig wore his camouflage fishing hat and a long-sleeved thermal shirt, even after the weather grew warm. He called out to everyone he saw, got as close to them as they (or I) would allow. "Isn't it wonderful!" he said. He knew every neighbor by name, even folks I wasn't sure I recognized.

"My heart is joyous!" he said.

"Lead me guide me walk beside me! Jesus wants me for a sunbeam!" he sang.

My job at the Office of Tourism was already work I usually did from home. Brig was in no position to look after himself, and I didn't have the means to hire someone more than occasionally. With little to do besides posting cancellation notices to the website, I spent more time watching television with my boy. His favorite was a Japanese toy show called *Kamen Rider*—a commercial with occasional commercial interruptions. He also liked the Hanna-Barbera and Looney Tunes cartoons, which were already old when I was young. They were far more violent than I remembered. I was horrified to see a child (or anthropomorphic animal) punished by being given castor oil. When I was a kid, I assumed castor oil must taste very bad. As a grown-up, and a parent, I understood that castor oil is a powerful laxative and that the children of the past were punished with stomach aches and explosive bowel movements.

One afternoon I found Brig missing from his post in front of the TV. He wasn't in the bathroom or anywhere else that I could see, and I almost ran barefooted into the cul-de-sac, screaming his name. But I found him in the storage room downstairs. He'd gotten into the provisions Mormons are all but commanded to keep, eating Nutella and Marshmallow Fluff from their jars. I was relieved and exasperated. "Brig, we put these things aside for the apocalypse."

He grinned gleefully, sugary goo smeared across his lips and fingers. "It's an apocalypse now!" he said. I didn't think this was true, but we were certainly experiencing some of the features of one. I brought some toilet paper and canned ravioli upstairs, these being the things that were now impossible to find at the store.

It was his mother who chose the name Brigham. I would never have. The person who gives her son such a name is at the far end of a pendulum swing, and it's inevitable that it will come hurtling back the other way. Some folks, especially in our religion, are given to extremes extreme belief, extreme disbelief. Wendy tried both several times, and finally settled on disbelief. We were introduced during our senior year of college by the bishop of our singles ward. He could only have been a few years older than us, but back then I regarded him as mature, authoritative, and pleasing to the eye. "You two have the same problem," he told us. "I believe you might be able to help each other out."

Wendy and I had sex six times. The first time—the night of our wedding reception, after we were sealed in the temple— barely counts because we were so confused as to the procedures. The second resulted in an eventual miscarriage. We spent four attempts making Brigham, after which it seemed unlikely we would ever try again. Wendy claims she knew immediately that Brig was different. But she never said anything at the time, and how could she have known? No one else suspected it until he would not learn to speak. I was disappointed. It's not what any parent wants for their child. Wendy was devastated. She spent her days thinking of new things she would now be unable to do. I had never heard her mention a desire to travel, but our meals started to fill with Europe and Asia, and all the sights there we'd never see. I also thought those places sounded interesting. God had created an awful lot of world. But my home was wherever Brigham was, and he was in Utah. We put him here ourselves.

Wendy took a job doing marketing for a place that packaged and resold essential oils and herbal supplements. There are many such businesses in Utah; we are the multilevel marketing capital of the world. Eventually she joined a book group of Latter-day Saints women who wanted to read about topics unrelated to the gospel. That evolved over a decade into a wine-drinking group for women who never wanted to think about Mormonism again. Through work she met some women who belonged to a cooperative that grew rosemary and lavender on a farm in Oregon.

Early in the pandemic she called us. She wanted to know how her husband and son were—a reasonable curiosity, though I hadn't heard her voice in over a year. "Do you want to speak to Brigham?"

"Really, Abe, what would be the point? He won't remember it tomorrow."

"You'll remember it tomorrow," I said. After that she called us every week.

The nature of our marriage was surely a subject of gossip in our ward. An open secret, at the least. The more tolerant the world becomes, the easier it is for even the most cloistered to recognize the signs. In 2015, when the church forbade the children of gay couples from attending services, the people of the ward watched Brigham and me with concern and apprehension. But that restriction was for the kids of practicing homosexuals. I'd had sex only six times in my life, never with a man. Brigham was too simple to have been baptized into his own religion, but I was confident he would still be allowed inside the chapel doors. A cooperative lavender farm in Oregon: Was anything ever so lesbian in its signifiers?

Columbine, bleeding heart, forget-me-not—spring.

Daisy, coneflower, coreopsis—summer.

Meghan Palmer called to ask that we no longer use the sidewalk in front of her house during our morning walks. There's a type of audacity only a Mormon lady can muster. She might bear and raise six children while keeping an immaculate home, remaining behind her husband as a silent partner and helpmeet. Yet she could be as fearless and confrontational as any feminist when warning someone to steer clear.

"Sister Palmer," I said, "the sidewalk is public property. It's for everyone; you don't own it."

"In fact, Brother Sorensen, I think it would be for the best if you didn't use Eaglewood Drive at all. Not when you have Brigham with you."

Her words took me unawares I was nearly speechless. "Are you banishing us from the neighborhood?"

"Listen, Abe, I know you think I'm just a mean old lady. But he's upsetting people. He wants to hug everyone when we're supposed to be keeping six-foot distance. He's happy about all the things that make the rest of us terrified—myself included. I couldn't be more afraid. You know people my age are vulnerable, and my husband is diabetic on top of it. Everything that makes the rest of us nervous gives Brigham the thrills."

The next morning we took our walk down Eagle Ridge. The refineries in the valley filled the air with their fume. At the home with the life-size statue of Jesus they seemed to be having a sort of revival meeting. There were a dozen people out in the yard and at least that many inside the house. Folks were chatting and laughing. One of them had a guitar, but he wasn't playing it at the moment. I considered that a mercy.

I never stood a chance of stopping him: Brigham was halfway to their porch before I realized it. They welcomed him—it's always difficult to guess which way that's going to go. A few of them motioned for me to come join in, but I figured it was better for all of us if I remained on the sidewalk. Brigham started singing "I Need Thee Every Hour." I couldn't blame him. It was still stuck in my head too. Some of the others joined in. The guitar player started strumming.

Only six months had passed since Bill Nilsson and I had had a conversation about the tulips. He'd been out at the community bowery, planting bulbs along the edge. Brig was in someone's yard, playing in the leaves. "Daffodils?" I asked.

"Some daffs," Bill said. "Mostly tulips. I always put some daffodils in with them hoping it will throw the deer off the scent. It hasn't worked yet."

"They'll all get eaten. What's the point?"

"I'm expressing my optimism!" Bill said.

Brig had been making a mess with the leaves. I called his name and slapped my thigh. I didn't always have the patience befitting a Christian father. Bill watched us both with a look of mild amusement on his face. "What colors?" I asked him.

"Yellow, red, and pink. Those are the colors you want to see in the spring, don't you think?"

"If you planted all daffodils, you'd at least have yellow. What's the point of a yellow tulip? Daffodils are more resilient. And they proliferate more readily."

"Don't you think tulips have a right to exist? A right to try to exist? Even the yellow ones! They might not make it through to blooming, but imagine how much more beautiful the world will be if they do. We owe it to them to let them try. We owe it to ourselves." He was delivering a homily, that much was obvious. But what mystical old-man wisdom was he trying to impart? That everyone deserves a chance to thrive on their own terms? At the time I assumed he was referring to Brigham. I realize now he was talking about me. Or Wendy. Or both of us—we had the same problem, as the handsome young bishop said.

My boy stood clapping and laughing with these Mormon revivalists, welcoming the end times. The latter days. But there would be no Second Coming, not that year, probably not in our lifetimes. Eventually we would carry on living as if nothing had happened. The people of Utah would remain at home—quarantining from a virus many of them thought was a conspiracy—and with two hunting seasons skipped, the deer would descend from the mountains, a plague unto themselves. Dry summers, near-snowless winters, record heat and ongoing drought, rangales of famished deer colliding with cars and scything gardens. Daylily, allium, lavender. They would eat rose-buds from off their thorny bushes. They would eat tomatoes, summer squash, hot peppers—not just the fruits, but the plants themselves. They would devour vegetation they otherwise would never have touched. They would eat the petunias, the gerani-ums, and the marigolds, annuals laid down to celebrate the on-going world, an expression of optimism. But first they would eat the tulips: yellow, red, and pink. But also paisley, pinstripe, polka-dot, plaid. Rainbows and rainbows of tulips in colors still unknown.

JULIAN ROBLES

Third Room

FROM *The Drift*

IN NOVEMBER MY landlord and her family left the city to celebrate the abrupt cessation of her husband's paralysis. They planned to visit Durango, where she had grown up, and Quintana Roo, where their daughter's godfather lived. The family was feeling hopeful. All of us were. Before leaving, the landlord had halved my rent and given me a spare key to the private terraza on the building's top floor. I kissed their baby on the head, hugged the husband, and wished them luck.

In response to her husband's paralysis, which began shortly before I moved into the apartment in July, the landlord had purged a number of habits from her life and replaced them with healthier alternatives. She encouraged me to do the same. To show my solidarity with her or with the sick man, or maybe with the two of them, I stopped listening to podcasts while making breakfast. I practiced yoga and taped my lips shut before bed. There were other changes: I cut masturbation out of my life entirely. I stopped reading novels with nameless protagonists. Instead of poking and counting the benign lipomas under my ribs, I plucked the outer edges of my eyebrows.

The night before they embarked on their trip, the landlord invited me to dinner. Her family lived in the apartment directly above mine. The husband was Honduran. She was Mexican. Their two-year-old daughter was, I supposed, Honduran-Mexican, or perhaps Mexican-Honduran, or simply Mexican, since Mexico was the country we lived in. She was white, like her parents.

We ordered Italian food from the restaurant around the corner. The landlord's husband now healthy, I judged it appropriate to at last bring to her attention certain features of the apartment in need of repair: low water pressure in the shower, a loose doorknob, flickering lights, and, naturally, the issue in the third bedroom. But out of respect for their solemn dinnertime recollections of the husband's illness, and after witnessing their elation in describing the morning of his recovery, I again postponed broaching these issues.

I sent a couple of courteous text messages the day after they left, which, because she was a relatively benignant landlord, received prompt responses in the form of animated stickers and GIFs. Her favorite animations tended to mirror the tone of my messages or the mood of the conversation: clips of conga lines and dancing racoons when my rent payments cleared, a meme of a terrified chihuahua the afternoon I locked myself out of the apartment. Rarely did she reply with words. That morning, frantic baby pandas spun beneath my list of grievances.

At the top of the list was the man who had been living in the third bedroom of the apartment since at least September. To explain both my delayed discovery of him and my tolerance for his extended presence, it is probably necessary that I describe the layout of the unit: the main apartment consisted of two bedrooms, a bathroom, a living/dining room, a balcony connected to the living/dining room, and a kitchen. Adjoining the kitchen was an exterior walkway that faced into the building shaft. This exterior walkway led to a third bedroom otherwise unconnected to the rest of the apartment. Its size and orientation relative to the main unit suggested that it had once functioned as a servant or maid's quarters, or as the dwelling of a young boarder. The room sat at an oblique angle to the kitchen, which provided a view into its two windows. I recalled from my initial tour of the apartment a twin-size mattress on the bedroom floor. Opposite the mattress was a desk and a leather swivel chair, both partially visible from the kitchen. The third room was perfectly livable and functional, but extraneous to my own living purposes and to my purpose for being in Mexico. Thus I had ignored it since moving in. As a result of this neglect I can't say for certain when the man arrived. One week the room was empty; the next he was seated at the desk, his hand moving from left to right, apparently writing.

My reaction upon spying him through the kitchen window was less fear and more akin to fatigue—yet another chore. I was in the middle of cooking breakfast, and I had an omelet to attend to. Then I had to clean the bathroom. And later that afternoon I had an appointment with the archivists at a rare book library. *I'll deal with him later,* I thought. When I came home that evening, he was still in the room, still seated at the desk, and still writing. The only difference in the scene was that the bedroom's overhead light had been turned on. The third room suffered from poor exposure to natural light; its solitary bulb had likely been emitting that dull, whitish glow since the early afternoon. These seemed like reasonable grounds for confronting the uninvited lodger—financial grounds, I mean—but I remembered that the landlord covered the utilities, and despite my close relationship with this landlord in particular, I was opposed, at least ideologically, to the existence of landlords in general, and for the man at the desk, who had never been invited to dinner or heard stories of the illness that had paralyzed her husband, my landlord would likely represent a general case of landlordship—i.e., a rent-seeking immorality that I did not want to appear allied with by suggesting that he was adding to the electrical bill. I closed the kitchen curtains and cooked my dinner: Chilean salmon marinated in homemade teriyaki sauce.

The following morning I walked into the kitchen and was surprised to see the third bedroom's light already on and its new inhabitant seated in the same spot. Had he slept at all? Light didn't reach the third room until almost noon, and by the early evening the room would begin to darken. One fluorescent bulb running nineteen hours per day represented a negligible contribution to the electrical bill, which, as I had already decided, was really none of my business. It was his devotion to his work that had begun to irk me. I couldn't imagine him writing anything so important as to compel him to remain seated at all hours of the day.

I described this scene in a message to my landlord the day

after her departure. My Spanish had become rigid after living outside of the country for several years; in casual conversation I could come across as stilted to the point that people struggled to understand me, and I reasoned that the landlord may have misinterpreted my initial messages. I emphasized that the man had been in the apartment—her apartment—for a month and showed no signs of leaving. Her reply: a GIF of an orangutan running in circles with its hands on its head. "I'll get to it as soon as I'm back," she added. She didn't plan to return until February, at the earliest.

The only other person aware of the man's presence was my girlfriend, who was living in Querétaro. From the beginning she had been of little help; after three years of dating, these kinds of stories simply didn't interest her. "Don't tell me about people trapped in apartments anymore, please," she had said when I called to inform her of the man's sudden appearance. "I don't want to know about their broken hearts and their storied vanities."

I had at the time assented while silently observing how she maintained an interest in novels about families across generations and literature vaguely to do with history—history as a process meant to induce sympathy and, in certain, directed cases, antipathy. In that regard my girlfriend wasn't different from any of my friends. I didn't bore her, and she didn't bore me, exactly, but the relationship bored both of us—that was clear. It was something I had come to accept. I would never again be excited about love, but I wouldn't be discontent, either, except in fleeting conversations in bars or in flirtatious gazes from across the room at parties—circumstances that induced not a feeling but rather memories of a feeling that had become inaccessible.

Instead of calling my girlfriend I met a writer for coffee. This writer was fifteen years older than me, spoke little Spanish, and had recently moved to Mexico for reasons that remained unclear. The writer was from New York and had written books about nameless protagonists who abandon their lives and flee to comfortably defamiliarized places. Their sites of refuge weren't exotic in the traditional sense of the word—they were cities where everyone spoke English and that people from New York recognized at least in name, in the instances where names were provided. The idea was that the characters lost their identities upon entering these uncanny realities, or arrived at them with aspirations of nonexistence—meant to comment, I supposed, on a pervasive homogenization and disintegration of identity in our, the readers', lives. But the settings of these stories were so plainly removed from the world of economic and political exigencies (and by no coincidence invariably devoid of non-white characters) that they became, paradoxically, comfortable and familiar to New York literary audiences, and thus I often fell asleep reading this writer's books.

Nonetheless, given his experience in matters of people willfully disappeared, nameless, or otherwise effaced, I thought he might have suggestions for how best to rid myself of the man in the third room. I described the man's arrival to the writer, who listened patiently and occasionally interjected to ask me to clarify certain sequences of events. After reaching the end of my story, I began silently questioning the fundamental nature of the problem. Could I reasonably argue that the man was doing any harm? His presence—at once discreet and obtrusive—unnerved me, that was clear, but part of the reason I was in Mexico was to investigate material conditions and social organizations that my peers had, so far as I could tell, ignored in their own art. In material terms, I didn't use the third room. Wasn't the real problem my willingness to allow a second and third room in my apartment to lie fallow? And in material terms, the man had no effect on my daily life. There was only one bathroom in the apartment, for example. That must be where he went to relieve himself. But even so, the man left the bathroom immaculate, and he must have only used it while I was out of the house or asleep so as not to disturb me. The same went for food. If he was eating my food, he replaced whatever he consumed, down to the crumbs at the bottom of the bread box. In this regard, he *took* (if I might hazard the rhetoric of plunder) far less than any previous guest had. A number of friends had visited me since I'd moved back to Mexico, and I had always refused their offers of payment or reimbursement, saying, "My house is your house. Any food, anything you need, don't worry about it." More than once I'd even hosted strangers—Central and South American migrants headed to the United States. Hadn't I told all these people to stay as long as they needed? The New York writer asked if I had tried confession. "Religious confession?" I asked. At the time very little weighed on my conscience. One or two deeds from childhood, nothing major. "With the man in the room. Have you tried sitting him down and telling him about yourself."

"Why would I need to make things about me?"

"In a way, you already have," the writer replied. "The man in the third room could make for an interesting audience. I've been exploring monologue in my work lately."

I admitted to the writer that I hadn't entered the third room more than a handful of times, and not once since the man's arrival. To be frank, it was an option I hadn't considered. In fact, it wasn't an option: To enter the room was as implausible as trapping oxygen with my hands. Why? Because the man was in the room and I wasn't. It seemed obvious. If he had invited me in, then perhaps things would be different, but for the time being he was inside the room and I was outside.

"You've only seen the man from a distance, then?" the writer asked.

"Through the kitchen window," I replied. "The window isn't far from the third room," I added at the sight of the writer's furrowed brow, his mouth twisting into a smile. "Really, it's just outside the window," I repeated. In that instant I had trouble recalling the man's features. I had seen him only from behind. I knew that his hair was short and black, and that he wore a green flannel shirt nearly every day.

"How do you know it's a man in there, or anyone at all? Maybe you left the light on," the writer said, his smile now undisguised. These were possibilities I had already considered and discarded, I explained. But, no, if I was being honest, I hadn't ventured a closer inspection.

I invited the writer to come see for himself. I had already decided not to see this writer again, and I had little desire to have him in my apartment, but his demure self-assurance had precluded any possibility of a courteous farewell. Better to prove him wrong than to shake his hand. It was a thirty minute walk from the café to my apartment. The writer spent most of that time outlining the plot of his latest book. He planned to return to New York the following month to attend a conference, or maybe to speak on a panel, or it was possibly the case that he was receiving an award. The details were unclear, because the writer had transitioned so abruptly into descriptions of his winter plans that for several minutes I thought he was describing deeds accomplished by the narrator of his novel. This new novel's narrator would have a name—the writer's name—and his deeds would unfold in familiar, fully-realized cities. Gone was the speculative wound across the material flesh; the warped mirror had been righted; the skyline openwork of tarpaulin and scaffolding would be overlaid with steel and history—so went the writer's explanation of his book.

We arrived at my apartment. I led the writer into the kitchen and pulled back the curtain to show him the man in the third room. For a fleeting instant I worried that the man wouldn't be there. I had never shown him to anyone before. If he were gone, or if I saw him but the writer didn't, it would mean I was at last losing my purchase on reality. All my life that had been a possibility, and indeed I considered it an inevitability. I had come close a number of times before returning to Mexico, and it was part of the reason I had moved back—to lose my mind alone, away from family and friends. I looked out the kitchen window, and into the windows of the third room. The man was seated at the desk, the fluorescent light glowing above his head.

"There," I said to the writer, who was out the kitchen door before I could say more. I took a step after him, hesitated, and then came back inside. Through the kitchen window I watched the writer knock on the door to the third room, enter, and close the door behind him.

I waited. The writer was standing in a spot that obscured almost my entire view into the room. It was just possible to make out the seated man. He hadn't stood to greet the writer or to expel him from the room. It appeared as though his hand was still moving across the desk. If I knew anything about the man after nearly six weeks living together, it was that his work ethic

was unwavering. The writer could blabber for hours about defamiliarized cities and nameless characters, and the seated man's
hand would continue moving, filling the pages before him at a
rate nearly equivalent to the rate of his breath or the beat of his
heart. Was his project circumscribed by cadences as intrinsic,
and as expansive, as these? Was I witness to an exhaustive tran-
scription of the totality of a single life—each page a record of
his thoughts at that exact instant, each paragraph a digression
into the texture of each of those thoughts, and each sentence
a description of the shadows cast by the texture of every varie-
gated vanity and anxiety; and the next paragraph an account of
the sensation in each limb, every finger, the simultaneous activ-
ity of every cell of his being? With the arrival of the writer in the
room, the relative homeostasis of his work (which I caught myself referring to as a *literary* project) was likely to be disrupted.
Now he would have to account for two bodies, or at the very
least he would have to account for the influence exerted on his
body by an additional, foreign body: the room had become a
chaotic system, subject to distortions in time and space. Would
his project survive such a cataclysmic event?

 Night fell and the writer hadn't returned. No sound escaped
the third room—the writer wasn't screaming for help, nor was
he arguing with the man at the desk. This wasn't a hostage situation. It was a case of two adult men in a room, plain and simple.
Better to let them be, I thought. The writer could show himself
out when the time came, and maybe by then he and the man at
the desk would be on such good terms that they would exit my
life together.

 That night I dreamt of the third bedroom. I dreamt that
I had followed the writer's advice and entered the room to
tell the man about myself, but the man sat there without responding. His face was simple and familiar. It was the face of
any person in a crowd, anonymous and inoffensive. He blinked
and breathed, turned away from me and continued writing. I
looked over his shoulder to read the text, surreptitiously at first,
and then blatantly after I saw that he made no effort to hide
it. The papers were covered in Oulipo nonsense: words continu-
ously reorganized in adherence to the dream's fickle logic. Next

I tried narrativizing a bit. I hung a rope from the piping and told the man how inevitable this moment was. "This rope reminds you of your uncle," I said tearfully. "Remember, the one who used to hide under the bed and scare you as a joke, and who later hung himself in his shed?" The man at the desk continued writing. "All ropes remind you of that uncle," I shouted, "and now that you have tied this rope, this is the closest you will come to imitating your uncle's act." If I let him be, he continued writing like a robot on a circuit, but when I lifted his hand or turned his head, his body yielded without any resistance. It wasn't difficult to remove his clothing. I cupped his penis and testicles, I took photos of him nude and threatened to ruin his reputation if he didn't leave my apartment. At the last second I refrained from placing his testicles in my mouth. I dressed him in a rush, ashamed. I apologized and told him to stay as long as he needed.

The doorbell cut my dream short. My phone was also ringing. I looked at its screen and saw several missed calls from my girlfriend. In my concern for the man in the third room, I had forgotten that her boss had granted her a few days' vacation. I ran downstairs to let her in. On the walk up I explained the latest developments with the man—now *men*—in the room, to the extent that she was interested in hearing about them. I pulled back the curtain in the kitchen and pointed to the broad back of the writer from New York. He was standing in exactly the same position as the night before. Through the gap between his midsection and arm, I spied the man at the desk, writing away.

One man, I explained to her, was manageable. But the addition of the writer complicated my responsibilities to the third room. I wasn't sure what he would need, materially. For example, should I bring him meals and toilet paper? The man at the desk had shown himself to be self-sufficient; he attended to his bodily functions without disturbing anyone. The writer, by contrast, was only a writer—a New York writer at that, meaning he was accustomed to a certain style of praise and luxury. Luxury behind a facade of working-class grit. I wasn't sure how much grit I had to offer. It had been several years since I'd been truly poor, and over the last decade I had come to accept the conspicuous luxury of my labor: sitting at home all day, reading, annotating, doing "work" not much different than that of the man in the third room; in that way I was similar to him, albeit far less productive. I was Mexican, that's true, and on the tanner side, which lends itself to interpretations of impoverished grit. Maybe that would suffice.

"When will you stop worrying about this?" my girlfriend said, turning from the window and continuing down the hall to my bedroom. I followed her into the room and apologized. She sat on the bed and undressed. I lifted my shirt over my head and then unbuttoned my pants. She watched me, shrugged, and left the room wrapped in a towel. It was her ritual to take long showers after the three-hour bus ride into the city. I lingered outside the bathroom to advise her in her battle against the low pressure and unpredictable water temperature, secretly hoping for an invitation to enter. But today she was in a rush to meet friends for lunch.

"You've been so busy with research lately, I didn't think you'd want to come," she said. It's true she hadn't arrived at the most opportune moment, the men in the third bedroom aside. The Mexican government was funding my work. The selection committee had called the research "very promising," and its members expected a stellar mid-year report. That was the condition of my return to the country: A report of merit on peculiar industrial patterns I had identified at the city's outskirts—what I had argued in my proposal were critical to understanding the country's "narratological imperatives." But I was having trouble finding the information I needed. I worried about the months to come. I worried they would make me leave Mexico again.

My girlfriend dressed and rushed downstairs. From the balcony I watched her cross the street and hail a cab. She waved up to me before getting in. I returned to the kitchen to watch the man in the third room. I sent another message to my landlord. In it I explained that my girlfriend—whom the landlord adored—was visiting, and that it would infinitely improve her stay if we could resolve the issue of the man in the third room. In less than a minute the landlord replied with a GIF of two hearts spinning spirals around one another. She followed this with a clip of an audience applauding and another of a news reporter slipping on a mound of loose dirt.

I drafted a long response accusing her of breaking the terms of the lease, and then I deleted it. The apartment was too good to lose. It was fully furnished, in an enviable location near major transit lines, far but not too far from the hip areas populated by tourists and rich Mexicans—and I paid half of what anyone in the neighborhood paid. I also couldn't deny that there were pleasant memories between us, the landlord and me. The German vacuum cleaner, the king-size bed—both gifts from her. Her daughter's godfather was a software developer-turned-shaman based in Quintana Roo, and in the fall they had involved me in a ceremony in their apartment meant to bring good fortune on the landlord's then-paralyzed husband. It would be childish to abandon so much comfort on a whim, I told myself.

In the evening I left to join my girlfriend and her friends for dinner. On the bus ride to the restaurant, I read a short essay on my phone written by the writer who now inhabited the third room. The essay, published that very week, discussed the writer's relationship to Mexico and the country's influence on his upcoming novel. Prior to his arrival in Mexico, the work had been a disordered mess of shapeless characters and ideas. Now it had direction. He all but repudiated his previous four novels as amateurish drivel. The essay's publication had been timed to the release of his book, which was receiving advance praise from critics and peers alike. The only voice missing was his. No one had heard from the writer for a couple of days, although this wasn't yet cause for alarm; he had a reputation for entering into periods of monkish solitude after finishing his novels.

We returned from dinner just past midnight. I showered, then spent some time spying on the third room through the window in the kitchen. Everything appeared as before—the man seated at the desk and the writer standing above him, rocking just so on his feet, from ball to heel and back. Perhaps the writer and the seated man had become each other's most trustworthy collaborators and confidants. Maybe they needed each other now. For the first time since the man's arrival I felt happy for him. Had this been what he'd sought all along? I didn't believe that my girlfriend, or anyone I knew, would ever offer me that kind of companionship. She praised and supported me, but I was certain that she couldn't be counted on to fight to her last breath to preserve my work if I were to disappear suddenly and forever from the Earth. I had posed this question to myself a thousand times: Would she rescue my papers from the fire and smuggle them onto the last train out of Prague? The answer was no. Before falling asleep I asked her if I should alert anyone to the writer's whereabouts. My girlfriend said there was no point drawing so much attention to myself. We were lying in bed with the lights off. I wasn't sure what she meant by that statement. She rolled to her side with her back to me. I touched the nape of her neck and waited.

"Remember when we used to tell secrets before bed?" I asked.

"We were younger then," she replied. She was facing the mirrored closet. At the last second I suppressed the impulse to reach over her and turn on the lamp, to see her face, to gaze upon the expression that carried those words. The next morning she was gone.

I've written here exactly what I told those who came looking.

Her bags and clothing were exactly where she'd left them. There was still a small depression in the pillow where she'd rested her head, and scattered around that depression like trampled foliage were little tangles of her hair. I went straight to the window in the kitchen. The man at the desk was no longer visible. I saw her, my girlfriend, standing next to the writer. Her shoulders rounded forward and a braid unraveled down the line of her neck. The rest of her body was hidden from sight. Like the writer, she faced the seated man. They fully obscured my sight of him, but I knew.

In the days that followed I asked myself what could have compelled her to enter the third room. My initial guess was uncreative, reductive, and debased. An inventory of her clothing left in the bedroom led me to conclude that she had entered the third room with what little she'd worn to bed—a thong and a loose tank top. The three-hour bus rides between cities were becoming exhausting, and for several months we had been in an open relationship. I suspected she had waited for me to fall asleep and then crept into the third room to seek the affections of the two men, her apparent disinterest in the room a ruse all along. "Fine, you can have her," I shouted into the building shaft. I abandoned my plan to race into the room to save her, a plan that I must admit was only a delusion of bravery. That very day I fell back into old habits. I didn't leave my apartment for a week. Each morning I undertook a head-to-toe inventory of my body's asymmetries. Along the right thigh had arisen two new ingrown hairs, and on the left shoulder a small lipoma. I prodded the lipoma until the skin bruised.

Twice a day I looked out the window to check on the third room. Initially I left small plates of food in the exterior walkway outside the kitchen door. A week had passed, and it appeared through the window that my girlfriend was losing weight. Maybe that wasn't the case. Maybe I wanted a reason to believe that she was suffering and that I could end that suffering.

Given the security situation in the country, her disappearance soon caused a minor media sensation: Another young woman missing after decades of so many others lost—and a foreign, upper-middle class woman at that. One day her phone rang nonstop, as did mine. The calls were so insistent that the phone batteries eventually drained. The writer's book, meanwhile, was being discussed as a major contender for several literary awards.

I asked myself who would arrive first, my girlfriend's parents or the police. As it happened, they arrived together. When the doorbell rang I was lying in bed prodding a small mole on my scalp. My girlfriend's mother was in tears. She and my girlfriend's father were just off a twelve-hour flight. I was determined to remain civil; I answered everyone's questions and gestured toward the third room. One police officer stayed with me while two others escorted the parents into the room. When he saw that they weren't coming back, he unholstered his gun and charged out the kitchen door. I remember thinking that he looked like a hero in an action movie.

Since that day the number of people in the third room has increased far past a point permissible by the physical bounds of the space. First more police arrived, and eventually government officials and members of the military. This attracted protesters and counter-protesters, whose disappearances hastened the arrival of volunteer organizations devoted to searching for Mexico's missing. The ranks of the vanished grew, but I couldn't stop counting my lipomas. Within a month journalists arrived to interview the writer. I'm not sure how they found out he was here. Later a friend of his came to present him a medal awarded for his novel. Then his ex-wife showed up with his twin sons, followed by a string of old lovers.

Despite increasing disruptions to civil services as more people in the country disappear, the committee funding my work still expects a progress report in March. It is now January. Every so often I return to the kitchen window and gaze out at the third room. I assume the light is still on and the man continues writing, although within a week of the police's arrival the room had become so full that the windows went completely dark. This hasn't brought me the relief I would have expected. The man has disappeared from sight, but I can never be certain of his definitive departure. His writing task has become gargantuan, perhaps impossible. For the time being I've holed up in this, the apartment's second room, to focus on drafting my report for the committee.

I've kept the landlord abreast of the situation. Earlier today I informed her that a Cuban reggaeton star had entered the third room to shoot a music video. She replied with a GIF of a man in purple pants gyrating beneath a disco ball. Then my rent payment cleared and she sent another video of rosy, joyous people linked in a conga line.

WILLIAM PEI SHIH

The Masterclass

FROM *Los Angeles Review*

NOT SO LONG ago, when I used to play the piano, a well-
respected Record Producer approached me at the Music Festival in New England to say that they had heard of my name,
and some good things about my piano playing, and asked if I
would like to sit down for coffee in order to discuss the prospect
of signing me and recording an album together—a debut album: The Rach 3rd. Few pianists were attempting to record the
piece at the time, and the Record Producer had already heard
of my interpretation of the Rach 2nd and not to mention, the
Rach 1st, and also my performance of the *Rhapsody on a Theme
of Paganini,* the collection of Rachmaninoff's *24 Preludes* and
the *Études-Tableaux,* and so on. "It sounds like you've done some
fascinating work so far with Rachmaninoff," they told me. So of
course, I said yes.

I had recently graduated from the Conservatory, where I
had studied with my Piano Teacher, whom I had chosen to
study with because I was enamored by them—a once stellar
prospect of a career, and who had made some good recordings
on Mendelssohn, but was now Head of the Conservatory, and
who was renowned in their own right, and known to be a "star-
maker." And because we had come from that same lineage
of piano performance (the Russian School: Pletnev, Yablon-
skaya, Kaplinsky)—I had hoped that they might understand
something of my own piano playing, and more importantly,
the intentions of that kind of performance, and where I might

be headed with such similarly played music. But that was the problem. And I was only to find that my Piano Teacher understood all too well what this meant, perhaps much better than I could have understood what our kind of piano playing actually entailed, and the nuances of all the obstacles required to play and perform it, especially in the context of the music world's status quo—another kind of mediocrity that was also the most difficult to convince.

I was working on Rachmaninoff. The *3rd Piano Concerto in D minor, Op. 30.* Other piano teachers along the way said that it was typical of someone like me to be working on something like Rachmaninoff—especially the 3rd—known to be the most technically difficult of all the Rach concertos. But in truth, I knew that the Rach 3rd was thought to be *too* difficult for most, and that many other peoples' imaginations at the Conservatory had faded in a way that mine was only beginning to burgeon. This is not to say that I thought myself to be a superior pianist. On the contrary. It only meant that I was younger and not yet overwhelmed by such heights and conquests. My muscles, still limber. My mind, still fresh, and still unaffected by the culmination of the minuscule and social media. It was what I had to work with, and work with it I did. Again, that was then.

Now we were all at the Music Festival together in New England, and my Piano Teacher, that well-known and widely respected pianist with long fingers that cast even longer shadows—who I had wished in all my time at the Conservatory to notice me in the way that a coach might notice and pass along their expertise to a budding younger athlete—must have seen me and the Record Producer talking together. And from the corner of my eye, I watched as my Piano Teacher made their way over across the verdant lawn (as it was the height of summer) toward us, and come to say hello to me, and I was nothing short of—elated. Up until then, my Piano Teacher's schedule had been too busy or full to spend any meaningful time with me—at the Festival, and even during our three years at the Conservatory together. In fact, in the three or so years that I was their student, they canceled many of our lessons, so much so that I came to suspect that they didn't want to teach me any longer, for fear that I might learn *too* much. But each instance we passed each other, each instance we nodded our heads and said "hello," whether in a hallway of the Conservatory, or at a concert hall, or practice room, they would always say how important it was that we should make some time when we could, in the near future, in order to catch up. Though I always got the impression that they were only paying me a kind of lip service, in order to wave me away, get me off their plate, so to speak. Now I introduced my Piano Teacher to the Record Producer—though of course, they both already knew of each other, as the Classical Music World is a small and dwindling world, becoming gradually more claustrophobic with each passing year, especially for us pianists and those shrinking listeners of instrumental music—with the exception of blockbuster film scores of movies like *Titanic*, that is. But even that was limited.

My Piano Teacher then saw that we were going to sit down for coffee, and to my utter delight (and even excitement)—which I had to find the strength in me to suppress—asked if they could join us. It was shortly before the Masterclass that my Piano Teacher was about to give at the Festival, and since we had a few moments to spare, I said, "Of course," because in truth, in all of my time of studying with my Piano Teacher, for one reason or another, the music of other people (other more important and promising students), kept getting in the way. And it had occurred to me that I rarely ever had the opportunity to talk with my Piano Teacher in any authentic nor meaningful manner—as naturally, there were always one too many talented pianists at the Conservatory who not only craved the same kind of attention from my Piano Teacher that I did, but also sought to impress upon them their own talents, as a means of advancing their own careers in the small world that was known to be concert music. And so there were other factors that came to play, so to speak. For instance, those who were beautiful went to the front of the line. Then there were those who were well-connected. Or those with already famous last names like Lang or Gbala or Ferrandez or Jones, also moved ahead. Those who were rising stars, especially those who my Piano Teacher believed might provide a favorable review in the near future, riding on the tail ends of such comets, because my Piano Teacher was actually foremost, a pianist—in want of an audience.

At the table, my Piano Teacher took a seat directly across from the Record Producer, an appropriate place, I rationalized, for someone of their influential stature—for which I even pulled out their chair as a reflex of respect: a hangover from my days at the Conservatory—a kind of Stockholm Syndrome that I myself and many former students of the Conservatory would be unable to shake in the years following our graduation. I look back on that time now and think how young and uncomplicated I must have appeared, and worse, someone with nothing that could be gained, as I was not from a wealthy family, or someone well-connected, which mattered very much to my calculating Piano Teacher, especially in terms of future donors to the Conservatory. Nevertheless, I took a place at the side of my Piano Teacher, the only seat that was left, and I watched on, as at first, they spoke of the weather, which had been mostly sunny, and then of the solar eclipse that had passed the previous day like an omen.

"Hopefully a good omen," my Piano Teacher noted.

Then they both spoke of their children—also aspiring pianists. In fact, my Piano Teacher said that I was skilled, quite skilled, at instructing children the piano—as I had previously given lessons to their own children as well, and how I had a way with kids as if something about me would always be stunted and left to the realm of the childish, whereas they themselves couldn't even bother to get their own children to sit still, let alone play Mozart, etc., etc.

The Record Producer seemed impressed.

I thought back to how when I was teaching my Piano Teacher's children on their Steinway & Sons Model D: The concert grand (the kind of piano that conveyed what you asked it to), and how I endeavored to become the teacher that I had always wanted, but never had for myself. Of course it would then dawn on me that my Piano Teacher's children had already had all the best teachers at their disposal and all the opportunities to excel (no doubt brought about by my Piano Teacher's influence and platform), and were already being set up for success in a way that I myself would never have known to exist, had it not been for my little bit of inspiration and the secondhand upright piano that I practiced on in the decade or so before I entered the Conservatory (I had auditioned with the Rach 1st). And maybe a part of me had wished that my own Piano Teacher would have been that symbol of a teacher for me, for I could have really benefitted from the kind of mentorship and advocacy during my time at the Conservatory, while I was feeling my way through each progressive chord of the Rachmaninoff 3rd. Instead I had been met with more discouragement, more disillusionment— another kind of lesson to learn. And they were again, always very busy, as someone in their position would no doubt be, and would be obligated to save their time and attention for more lucrative opportunities—the best of them, schmoozing with the likes of so and so, who had just delivered a series of concerts at Carnegie Hall, playing the Tchaikovsky Concerto No. 1 in B♭ minor, Op. 23, and who might one day, in the not so distant future, become a judge of a competition that my Piano Teacher may enter themselves, and would endeavor to win. So besides teaching myself the Rach 3rd, I had also taught myself how to be understanding—how to wait my turn, even if that turn would never seem to arrive. And how to savor the hope that I would one day be noticed for my meticulous music. It didn't matter that I had moved across the country in order to study at the Conservatory, and to study with my Piano Teacher, and then having to wander in a kind of purgatory of thought or hope that a friendship between like-minded pianists with the same lineage of piano playing such as us might blossom. Of course I didn't realize then that being like-minded was actually *too* much the issue here, too much the problem, for my Piano Teacher sought to be the only one of our Rachmaninoff-playing kind. And I suppose, the fewer that existed, the better. Or none at all, so they could be the only one to stand out in the relief of other players.

But now how my Piano Teacher's face lit up when they went on to speak to the Record Producer of other prominent students at the Conservatory, other people who they'd taught throughout their lengthy teaching career—that their long fingers had carefully caressed and guided, and made to be in their debt, those who had gone on to cast their own shadows in the music world—many former students who were already superstars in their own right, who no longer felt the need to thank my Piano Teacher as they were nominated for numerous Grammy Awards and American Music Awards, and the like, playing in such venues like Carnegie Hall, and Lincoln Center, and the Royal Albert Hall in London, and in cities like Prague or Tokyo or Cairo or Lagos.

Then there were the students who were already rising stars— for example, so and so who was coming out with an album on *The Goldberg Variations*, which was likely to be very good, a "game changer" for how *The Goldberg Variations* had been currently perceived for the last four centuries, since the time of Johann Sebastian Bach. Another so and so who was coming out with an album of Schubert *Impromptus*, also likely to be very good— because these were students from the Conservatory, the school, already famous for producing wondrous instrumentalists, along with stellar recordings of classical music, most notably debuts— performances that were given the benefit of the doubt and raved about, most notably for their potential. Did anyone expect anything less? Another so and so who was working on a collection of miscellaneous pieces by Debussy and Ravel, in conversation.

At this point, I could see that the Record Producer was beyond enchanted with what they were hearing, and even knew of the other record producers that many of these debut pianists had been signed to and were currently working with, and even went on to ask my Piano Teacher if they might let them visit the Conservatory, in order to see for themselves some of the talent that was being developed, and perhaps recruit a few more instrumentalists or vocalists to their own roster, as all record producers (whether they admitted it or not) were constantly on the lookout for new talent: debuts—to which my Piano Teacher only smiled and said with what I thought was a tinge of bitterness, "Of course—debuts." Then, "But surely, there is room for more seasoned performers?"

"It depends."

"I understand. After all, I am the Head of a well-known Conservatory."

Still they would exchange numbers. "Have your people call my people," my Piano Teacher said. They shared a laugh.

The Record Producer then said, "Well, *I* am my people."

More laughter ensued.

Then my Piano Teacher noted what they themselves were working on—a fantastic piece of music, something unimaginable, perhaps underrepresented in this day, this age, and lo and behold, when the time came, they might be in search of a record producer as well, someone new, and sooner rather than later, because, "Well, you know, it's almost complete."

"Oh, I see."

"That is, if the right Record Producer came along, I could be persuaded to switch. If I had the right offer, that is."

"I *see*."

And yet, my Piano Teacher didn't volunteer the information outright. Up until then, my Piano Teacher had already made a series of recordings: a collection of Mozart Sonatas, a Robert Schumann album, a collection of duets from the Romantic era that was rereleased for its 25th anniversary, since its own debut. In reality (and it took me some time to realize this), many of the people who listened to these recordings were mostly prospective students (including me)—those who had dreams of attending the Conservatory and making recordings of piano music themselves one day. And they listened thoroughly to my Piano Teacher's albums and found every nugget of a good thing that they could elaborate upon in order to tell my Piano Teacher as if they were reenacting "The Emperor's New Clothes." And it was easier for my Piano Teacher to believe them, even if people would overdo it sometimes, for in reality, most listeners outside the world of the Conservatory did not know of my Piano Teacher's albums. And if they did, it was only that they were the albums by the Head of a well-known Conservatory, and not quite the work of a craftsman, let alone, a genius. But I knew that my Piano Teacher deserved much more credit than this—for they studied intensely the performances of Cliburn and Argerich, and even Rachmaninoff too, and when I listened carefully to these recordings by my Piano Teacher, I could see that this was no doubt true. Too bad it was evident of so many other pianists as well, including myself, a dime a dozen.

The Record Producer then asked my Piano Teacher what it was that they were working on, and my Piano Teacher could no longer hold back: *Rachmaninoff*—a reinterpretation of the 4th Concerto: redone, and perhaps, better than ever. "And hopefully to be recorded with a first tier orchestra, like the Philharmonic."

"Oh! The 4th!" A look of surprise, even awe, crossed the Record Producer's face. My Piano Teacher reciprocated. "People don't usually record the 4th, do they?"

"Exactly."

"Well we certainly need more Rachmaninoff recordings these days, more than ever, I suppose."

"Don't we?"

"Otherwise Rachmaninoff will run the risk of being forgotten one day, overshadowed by the likes of Taylor Swift and Ariana Grande."

"I do agree!"

Finally, the Record Producer turned to me and asked what *I* was working on. And it felt like the moment of truth, one that I had been waiting for all my life. The hours that I had combed through each beating heart of the Rachmaninoff 3rd, the late nights (several of them flashed before my mind's eye). Then our lessons together, where once my Piano Teacher had been moved enough by my playing to say, "not bad," before gathering themself up and becoming all the more withdrawn again. I thought of my lessons with their children, too, even teaching them the opening theme of the 3rd Rach Concerto, and giving them a break from Mozart's *Twinkle Twinkle Little Star*, as if I was preparing their fingers for other, more interesting and difficult prospects to come.

My Piano Teacher seemed taken aback by what the Record Producer was asking me, but then they cut in to say, as if I was no longer present, "Well if I'm to be honest, they're really all over the place. That is the problem. They're playing everything these days—Bach, Beethoven, Brahms, Gershwin—and

I'd have to say, they're still a work in progress, and not quite ready to record an album, especially a Rachmaninoff album." My Piano Teacher then turned to look at the Record Producer, and into their fading gray eyes. "But, but, but . . . if you need a piano teacher for your children, this person right here, is the one to ask."

"Is that so?"

"Very much *so.*"

At that moment, I remembered that a few months before I'd graduated from the Conservatory, my Piano Teacher stopped me after one of our lessons. I had played for them a section of the second movement of the Rach 3rd, the *Intermezzo.* It was the slow movement. After I was finished, I braced myself for my Piano Teacher's criticism. They had a way of criticizing— "bludgeoning," was the word that they used. They were proud of it too. But, in fact, they didn't "bludgeon" me as I had expected. Instead, they were momentarily silent, lost in thought. Dare I say, they looked "bludgeoned" themselves. Or was it age? In fact, the last notes that I had played on the piano still seemed to linger in the air, as if refusing surrender. Outside, I could see that one of my classmates had been peeking in, listening curiously all along to the lesson, and right then and there I knew that I had done something more significant than I could even comprehend at that very moment. And then, after what felt like its own eternity, my Piano Teacher said to me, "It's good. Really good." Then after a breath, "But it's *too* good." And I learned that there was a problem in being too good, like what was supposed to be music would all too easily tread into the territory of cacophony, if I wasn't careful. If I was too much. Too soon. Too able to eclipse an already dying star.

They then told me what they wanted to tell me—that ultimate lesson of my life: that not every pianist who graduated from the Conservatory could go on to become great pianists. "One only notices the brightest of stars, and from them we make constellations of meaning. But don't you see? None of it's real. None of it exists. Only an illusion, and for an ephemeral amount of time, at that. And still, most of us spend the rest of our lives chasing after this initial mirage. In the end, it is like chasing after the fountain of youth—and you learn soon enough that you can't catch up to things like that. No, you can't." There was something wistful in their eyes as they said this. Then there was the reality of other things to consider too: "Many of us go on to teach. Some of us even go on to be the heads of conservatories, especially now since there are many more conservatories than ever before. Others go on to accompany singers and violinists. More still, many of us quit playing music entirely, which is fine. And do you know why? Because we are all, first and foremost, listeners—and that alone in itself is a gift, perhaps even the greatest of gifts." My Piano Teacher leaned in to make sure that I had heard the finality of what they were telling me: "And it should be enough for *you*."

It felt like a curse that they were trying to place upon me. Or was it an omen? I felt my muscles begin to tense. My mind, becoming tainted. And though I did all that I could do to resist it, I couldn't. I was trying to hold on, to not let go. I sat there in the silence of the music room, too powerless to contradict my superior, because somewhere, deep within, I still harbored a hope that things would take a turn in another, more fruitful direction. Though it didn't.

What I didn't understand at the time was that it wasn't true: that my Piano Teacher couldn't have any Record Producer that they wanted, and that they couldn't be nominated for all the Grammys and American Music Awards and other awards of the like, because in short, they weren't considered, even though they certainly wanted it to happen for them—despite the institutional prestige, despite the platform of the Conservatory, despite the network of nepotism. But I saw that in the end, the institution was against them as well, teaching them its own lesson: there were no shortcuts over the mountain of longing. And the audience that they kept tapping into was only an audience of future pianists—which wasn't actually an audience at all, only a symbiotic experience until it was no longer symbiotic, whereupon each party would go on to seek out another relationship to massage. Therefore, the possibility of those days were over now, and all that was left for my Piano Teacher was a kind of foreplay of those earlier days of potential, when they them-self were the student. And yet, like a contradiction, my Piano Teacher still wanted it all and *them* all—every listener, every ear, the kind of listener who almost didn't exist anymore, who gave the performer the benefit of the doubt, as opposed to cav-ing to a reflex of criticism, those who were scarcely able to do it themselves—perform. But exercising their power of opinion, instead, which was another kind of performance. An opinion that was amplified by social media and popularity, and not to mention, fervor, giving off the appearance of fact.

"Oh my, look at the time," the Record Producer then said. "Isn't your masterclass about to begin?"

"Oh, yes. I believe that it is." My Piano Teacher downed the last of their coffee. "Don't worry, I've been around the block more than once."

"I bet. Well, I'm looking forward to hearing you play."

"I'm glad of it. Because I'm definitely a player."

Of course, the Record Producer had heard all that they needed to hear—music or not. And they didn't ask me about recording that album again. Nor did they ask me about teach-ing their children the piano, or anything else. The main event at the festival was about to begin—the Masterclass, which would be given by my Piano Teacher. Later that evening, my Piano Teacher would say something to the effect, "Not all people who graduate from the Conservatory are meant to perform." I wish I could say that it was the last time that I saw my Piano Teacher, as we all went our respective ways after the Music Festival in New England. But rarely is my dignity as strong as I desire it to be. Afterward, I admit that I was heartbroken, in a way that could not be rectified. And then one day, the recitals dwindled for me. One day, something in me dried up and recoiled. Everything else, buried by a kind of ash.

Only I sometimes email my Piano Teacher. I do so from time to time. I don't know why. The remnants of Stockholm Syn-drome, perhaps. It is like the last strip of land that I have yet to go down. Now that I am no longer a problem, my Piano Teacher will say that they miss me. *Who else is there to water the flowers? Who else is there to alphabetize the scores in my office? Speaking of which, my children say hello, though they've recently quit the piano in favor of the cello, but thank you for all your help, anyway.* [😊 😊]

My Piano Teacher never asks if I am still working on the Rachmaninoff 3rd—or if I am still playing the piano, for that matter. *Because I had heard that you quit.* I don't read the rest. There is music in silence.

Then one day, it is my Piano Teacher who emails *me* to say that their new recording is finished—the Rach 4th in G minor, Op. 40 (with a second tier orchestra) and that it will come out soon and how they wish that there is a review in *The Times,* though there isn't, which can only be an early indication of how the recording is going to be received by a fading listening audience with misconstrued opinions. Or rather, how it is going to be ignored. And that my Piano Teacher had searched me up on Google (perhaps in an effort to placate their insecurities), and had half-expected to find a recording for myself, if even one that I might have uploaded on YouTube, but there isn't. I learn that my piano teacher is right, as they had been trying to teach me the lesson of all lessons all along, the lesson that I had fought so hard not to learn. But they had come across an article that I had written about—*The Masterclass: Why I Quit Playing the Piano?* (The short answer is you lose the joy.) And then they finally ask me what they want to ask, "Were you talking about me? Am I the reason?"

This is a fantasy at this point. And I even go so far as to imagine that I will not meander or hesitate to write back to my Piano Teacher, just like the many times when my Piano Teacher will not reply to me. Or how they might ghost me, though at the same time, haunt me in every other aspect when I think back to those days when I had played the piano with such a fullness in my heart, as if at any moment, it were about to burst. I imagine that I would have the courage to say yes. I imagine that I would say, "Yes, it was you, it was always, of course, you." I imagine that I would be a problem once more.

JUSTIN TAYLOR

What About This

FROM *Harvard Review*

BROTHER, I HIT my limit of being alone. Of the empty bed, the lonesome bender. Also of video games, Kierkegaard, Only-Fans, the *Atlantic* monthly magazine, which now publishes just ten times a year, scenic hikes, the cooking channel, YouTube, pour-over coffee made properly at home, courteous neighbors, God's silence, Spotify, fearless deer grazing front lawns in the gloaming (also dawn), every newsletter, the local supermarket's bruised bananas and BOGO ground beef deals, two-factor authentication, Delta-8 gummies, open mic night, wing night, NPR, letters from ex's lawyer, various attempted nutrition shakes, tension rod sliding down walls of bathroom in miserable efficiency apartment, app-based therapy, Spiritual Gifts quizzes, the very concept of podcast, and the Book of Common Prayer. In 2 Kings 5.13, Namaan's servants counsel him to follow the guidance of the prophet Elisha on the grounds that he came expecting a hard task so why turn away in anger just because he's getting off light? Grudgingly Namaan accepts this and is cured of his leprosy. Try-ing to remind myself of something, maybe, in recalling this, but also I was enrolled in Homily 101 and a draft was due. Is due. I had copied out longhand the passage of my exegetic interest:

> And his servants came near, and spake unto him, and said, My father, if the prophet had bid thee do some great thing, wouldest thou not have done it? how much rather then, when he saith to thee, Wash, and be clean?

KJV of course; I don't do NIV. Anyway, I taped the page to the wall above the kitchen table in the miserable efficiency and had been staring at it, hoping to shake something loose, but drawing blank beyond the observation that some people are just desperate for punishment, which was God's point, and at any rate not personally applicable. I was only errant and on the verge of knowing why.

I defected to div school because two good women in Cincinnati had hit their limit: one blocked my number and the other changed our locks. Suffice to say it served me right and my thought at the time was that learning to serve might set me right, and it might have, but I was proving an at-best-indifferent exegete and am frankly frightened of the prospect of shepherding a flock. I came here in a blaze of self-abnegation, but these people were always trying to get me to stand up and declaim.

I got in my car, cranked the radio too loud to hear my thoughts—sick unto death of my own namby heresies and underbreath bitching—and Jimi was hollering Dylan and I decided to drive seven hours south toward the ocean, okay Gulf, to wash and be clean.

Almost got there, too.

I sailed clear through the hearts of Huntsville and Birmingham. Would have made Montgomery as well but for a sudden desire to spite my Siri, her limpid efficiency and Xanax affect, her Episcopal rectitude—that's what I was fleeing! All that savorless salt. They dress like Bostonians bound for the Cape and talk like Colonel Sanders between juleps two and three. They drink hot tea with lemon, or nothing, or copious dry gin. They are mellifluous carolers, some at the helms of family foundations, all possessed of a savage restraint that raises up my mania, for which I'm nearly grateful but also afraid because where will it go? Where *can* it go? The Living Christ don't want it. Nor the women of Cincinnati.

Which only leaves the road the road the road.

Highways forsaken, I cruised through gone-brown cotton fields sprawling both sides of some two-lane, the final white bole dregs blowin' in the wind, and let's chant names for local savor—Vredenburgh, Buena Vista, and Beatrice; Tunnel

Springs, Monroeville, and Repton—Repton, shortly after which I was of necessity back on I-65 but off again as soon as I found State Road 113 and shortly thereafter elated to hit Flomaton— what a name!—which turned into Century when I crossed the Florida line.

A while goes by, ears ringing, no phantom faces flashing, nobody says anything except for rock 'n'rollers and they are perfect, perfect, says the juggler to the thief. Headlights and the yellow line, engine of my Mazda 3 bleating out its pitiful 1 AM.

Finally low on gas and having largely outrun misery, I risked turning the volume down. Also it was near to midnight, so after filling up in a Panhandle town by the name of Brine (which, by the way, is nowhere near water) I chose the first open bar I came across, though it was also the only one, so maybe "chose" isn't the word.

One way or another, brother, I intended to accomplish fate.

The bar had nothing on tap and a blue neon wall skull paying homage to tequila: no particular brand, just the general proposition. Marty Robbins on the juke and sitting alone in blonde splendor was a clear-eyed woman with a high-set ponytail plunging down her straight broad back. Medical boot on her left foot, cowboy boot on her right. She had a tightly puckered smile from the tequila she'd just knocked back in a shot glass shaped like a cowboy boot.

So three boots total but none to make a pair.

It could have been one of Christ's parables, like talents and mustard seeds, though I guess in His telling—if He'd told it—it would have been sandals.

Marty still yarning as I stood there. You forget how "Big Iron" has eight damn verses. I sure could go for "Cool Water" next, or "The Master's Call." Anything except "El Paso."

I liked this bar.

After all that time strung up in Episcopal rectitude, I was hot for hedonic apostasy or advanced Catholic mortification. Tit sweat down my chin or the knotted strop; I didn't care. Any of it would have been to the purpose, stern reminder that the word is flesh and to dust we shall return but, hey—not yet. Not yet. *Sufficient unto the day is the evil thereof* spake my KJV when I'd tried my hand at scripture cracking—where you open to a random page and line and heed the wisdom, i.e. take the hint. Six days running I hit Matthew 6 and on the seventh day I burst. I broke free, I mean if you can call this freedom, which—again—was what I was out to discover. What were the right words to name my life with? What is the nature and aim of prayer? But enough backstory, brother, for there are no backstories in Heaven. If you're pleading out how you got there, it's the other place.

I was in Florida, a stranger, basking in blue-skull glow, getting eyes back from the splendid blonde boot gal. Full smile, now unpuckered. Her medical boot chunky and black, her cowboy boot well-scuffed tan leather, her small glass boot empty. Marty had given way to Jerry Jeff, and Cinderella here had a drugstore cane hung by its crook from the back of her chair.

I knew I had some road stink about me but also knew this was not a deterrent, necessarily, for a certain breed of woman. Or maybe it's any woman if you catch her in her certain mood. I cut a figure handsome enough for midnight on what might have been a Wednesday. At forty-one, I had all my hair still, gray at the temples but barely, and temple gray can be attractive, I have been told, repeatedly, in fact, in Cincinnati, before I was blocked and locked out and defected to the Cumberland Plateau to go insane heeding the call amidst sweater-vested men with weak handshakes and perfect teeth. I had come to think of my gray temples as a down payment on incipient silver foxdom, an inheritance I would come into like a trust fund, and that would make me a more effective priest besides, assuming an effective priest was still what I wanted to be. I had a day's good stubble on my cheeks and chin, cash to spend, nobody left to betray. I wanted a lot of the right things for a lot of the wrong reasons, and some of the wrong for right. This is what the whole Bible's about, basically, which belief had led me wayward and late to priest school only to find out that it was the one belief that none of the priests at priest school shared with me.

But, hey, we're risking more backstory, and I don't want it—*Don't look back!* as Lot and Bob would say.

I sent the woman a round and got one for myself and sauntered over. Horrendous yet apt word, "sauntered." I was pea-cocking, but how can you not, sipping Cuervo from a glass boot in Northwest Florida? I stood before her. We clinked and drank—no toast—and only then did I infer permission to sit. I could feel our fast agreement blossom, some mysterious prom-ise passing between us, knee to knee beneath the table, heat to heat. We left the bar together and went back to her place and I relieved her of her dress and underthings but left on the medi-cal boot and the feeling of that firm plastic pressing my backflesh as I ate her is one thing I'll cherish forever. I had wanted to feel something different and now I had.

Brother, I was full of feelings now.

Celeste and I spent a week together, torrid, twice involving the cane so smooth and cool and remorseless against my throat that I saw fireworks and when restored to breath took to my knees by the side of the bed to thank God for hiding. For leav-ing me be.

I will find you again, I prayed, adapting the famous passage in Augustine. *I will find you again but not yet—please not just yet.*

We made halting progress along America's third coast, all those shrimp basket towns, here's more names if you want them: Gulf Shores, Fairhope, Spanish Fort, Biloxi, Gulfport, Bay St. Louis. I had thought we'd end in New Orleans, but we never even made Louisiana. We tacked north instead for a day trip to Richton, Mississippi, which is a nothing town, some thousand souls and a NAPA Auto Parts, north of the De Soto National Forest and due east of Hattiesburg, which is not a nothing town but rather a town where there is nothing, unless your dream is a box of Raising Cane's tenders and to see the horrid gates blocking the private drive to the McMansion of local demiurge Brett Favre.

We went to Richton to see the former orphanage—now a private home—where the poet Frank Stanford was born to a widow and out of which he was adopted mere months later by a divorcee, which surprised me to learn, that they'd give an un-wed woman a baby. Pretty forward-thinking, or desperate, for Mississippi in '48. The woman married soon enough and so the poet got the name we know him by, not that I had known his name. I like poetry fine, but today I was merely wheelman; this was Celeste's deferred dream coming true. Stanford moved to Memphis, later Mountain Home, Arkansas, married young and cheated some, shot himself just shy of his thirtieth birthday—twice in the heart with a pistol, which is something—with his wife downstairs. He left behind near a thousand poems about death and the moon, plus one epic poem near a thousand pages on its own, also about death and the moon. Celeste's long wanting to make this trip and my having been the one to take her seemed more and more evidence of the substance of things hoped for, etc. Of our having accomplished fate. The blind promise we had made on that first night was in fruition now, the text of the vow unsealed so we could see what we'd sworn.

She had her eyes closed. I beheld her in her solemn blonde splendor and let the silence accrue. We were strangers to each other, and everyone in this whole world is an orphan, not just orphans. We are weak in the face of a simple command when we would have preferred a great one. Impossibility is freedom. Only the doable can be demanded. I would add this to my un-finished sermon, should I ever return to that efficiency where the smudged pages lay.

We had our silence, but the world was far from silent. Yard life of grass and insect and breeze and trees, a mower some-where. Some wilderness rose up and took dominion, like Mr. Stevens and his jar (as mentioned, I like poetry fine), and I saw that there was an end for Celeste and me, which meant a new blank page to face alone, only not yet—not just yet.

She dozed and I drove with the radio off, thinking about how Namaan starts out in 2 Kings 5 as a victor in war, but within a few verses is reduced to some freak refusing the very cure he's been begging for.

Captain of the host of the King of Syria, was Namaan.

And the next day who even gives a fuck?

Not God!

It was late in the day when we made Perdido Key. The pure luck of a forlorn beach, so we stripped down. I helped her get the boot off and watched her hop to the clear green water, calmer and warmer than I'd dared hope, our double luck, and, as we were alone there in easy waist-high surf and I was already stiff from having watched her hop, I took her while she floated on her back, splayed like a snow angel, and I wept some, the tension release of my last exegetic chains breaking (not to mention the other), but really it was her, her blondeness darkened with seawater and the feeling of her weightless weight in my hands, as I held her by the hips to keep her close, my well-scratched back stung by the lapping swells.

In time we repaired to the sand but did not dress. We sat on our respective piles of garment to keep our nethers clean and in our shamelessness watched the sun set on the Gulf.

Dinner at Margaritaville and a short drive back to Brine, and then it was fare thee well.

What wondrous love it was: abrupt and unprecautioned, all in brackets. Some man could have been hot on our trail, big iron on hip, looking to kill me over her or her me, but none was. She could be full with my child now. Or I could describe a line of sweat down her taut neck as I tightly held her hair, but I cannot tell you what she did to her foot to warrant that boot. I learned all about her dead genius poet and we took perhaps twenty meals together and sang along to many rousing choruses in the car and shared sexual particulars and small talk and that final sunset, quenchless fire diving like the dove down past the red-gold rim of the world, but for all that I never did ask about the boot, and she never offered. It just seemed like part of her. Like if I were to drive back through Brine this time next year and find her again, she would still be wearing it, perhaps dandling progeny, mine or someone else's, perhaps alone and waiting without knowing what for, and not minding that not-knowing, a saint of patience and craving, as on the night we first locked eyes and accomplished fate.

If God had wanted me to know about the boot He would have told me.

If you don't believe I believe that, brother, then you really haven't heard a word I've said.

My route out of Brine did take me back over the plateau I had started from, but I did not stop there. My efficiency rental and whatever was stacked and piled inside. Let the junk man come.

I kept going. I keep on. I live in hotels, not nice ones. Check the version of the book in the drawer, swim in pools chlorinated too much or not enough. I know humility of spirit and when to stoppeth one of three. I have seen men die. I am gone gray. I still meet women glad to have me, and likewise, but Celeste is yet and ever where I make pilgrimage. No more idolatrous than Dante, I don't think. Phantom pressure of black plastic; eye of my storm; soft pale hairy shin and calf rising out of boot in damp sand. I check every town for extant bookstores and scan the poetry section under "S." Many of these stores don't even have poetry sections. Morgantown, Stillwater, Golden, Gassville. Wallace, Idaho, and Whitefield, New Hampshire. Tullahoma, Provo, Mountain Home. You can buy a book of crossword puzzles or a souvenir candle, but you cannot have death and the moon. This is a sin and outrage but finally no concern of mine, for I was not put here to save every soul, only to do the great and simple thing that I am bid. To keep watch for high signs of the next blind promise. I press pedal flush to floor and say, *What about this?* to God, who says nothing, nothing yet, fine by me. I am homeless and homeward bound and I am listening.

I am nowhere near running out of road.

Aishwarya Rai

FROM *Granta*

THE FIRST MOTHER Avni brings home is too clean. She wears white at all times, perpetually a mourner, and roams the two-bed flat with a feather duster tied to her slim wrist. "Don't I look just like Aishwarya Rai?" she asks, and pours bleach into the bathtub and onto her body. Scrub-a-dub-dub. Avni asks her no questions and takes her straight back.

At the shelter, they lead her to the back and shoot her. "She's had multiple placements," they explain. "Sometimes, this is the humane option."

The second mother is mean, and very, very beautiful. This one actually does look like Aishwarya Rai, Avni thinks. A star. She buys a weighing scale and makes Avni stand on it and watch the numbers wobble.

"Too high!" she decides when they steady.

"Let's play a game," Avni says, stepping off the scale. She crosses her arms over her body and watches as she shrinks in the mirror. "Would you rather have a fat, happy daughter, or a daughter who is thin and sad?"

The second mother doesn't hesitate: "Thin."

"And sad."

"Yes," she agrees.

Avni nods. "How do you sleep?"

"Too well," she confesses. "Like a baby."

The shelter people take her back, no problem. She has a

highly desirable look, they say, and will find another home quickly. And does Avni want to take another look around?

Avni does.

The third mother is sad. All she talks about is the village she came from, where she'd had cows and babies who all died one by one. She'd longed for a living child her whole life, she says, but Avni has never been to a village, nor once felt the urge to milk cows.

"Did you love your husband?" she says, and when the third mother nods, asks why.

"My choices were to love him or not," she says. "And loving him seemed easier."

"That's a good answer," says Avni, and decides to keep her, at least for a while.

They learn each other slowly. Third Mother wakes each day to make kadak chai and drink it on the two by two foot balcony with a wrought iron railing that Avni never uses except to dry her underwear. Third Mother drinks several cups of chai a day. Third Mother cooks in the late afternoons for dinner and next day's lunch. Third Mother packs tiffins and sends them to Avni's office with the neighborhood dabbawala. Third Mother puts too much salt in her food, but Avni's tastebuds adjust. Avni starts to crave salt. Avni likes having a hot lunch every day. Avni likes having a hot dinner. Avni likes that Third Mother snores because she can hear it through their shared wall. Avni has panic attacks when she tries to sleep. Avni gets cold all over and her legs twitch like the limbs of a dying insect. Avni feels frightened and lonely and frequently lightheaded. Avni needs company in the nighttime but Avni doesn't like men.

"How old are you?" Third Mother asks one week into living together. She's opened the small kitchen window for ventilation while she fries bhindi in hot mustard oil. Through the metal bars, Avni can see the alley, and past it, into the balconies of the building next door. In the early mornings they are parrot perches, and in the afternoons, drying racks. In the nights, smoke spots for fathers, sons, rebel daughters.

"Twenty-three," Avni replies. "You?"

"Thirty-seven," she says. The bhindi crackles.

"You look much older," says Avni, surprised. "It must be all the grief."

Third Mother wears salwars on weekdays and sarees on weekends and tries on short dresses from Avni's cupboard when Avni isn't home. She marks her parting with sindoor and has long, butt-length hair that Avni pulls from between her teeth at mealtimes and out the shower drain each week. Her eyes are deeply lined.

Avni panics on a Saturday night and doesn't know why. Her arms and legs spasm, stop being hers. She clenches her muscles for ten seconds, breathes in, breathes out. She wants to call her mother but they haven't talked in nearly six months. She folds her knees under herself and leans forward in child's pose. She lets her belly hang between her thighs. She tries to rest her forehead on the floor but fails. She times her breaths to Third Mother's snores and makes it through the night.

"How did you sleep," Third Mother asks the next morning, and Avni lies.

"Fine."

Third Mother hums but doesn't push.

Avni had thought that she liked that about her. She doesn't say anything. She says, "Do you need anything washed?"

Third Mother brings her a basket full of clothes and cotton panties with lace trims.

Avni's bedsheets are soaked in sweat. She strips them and throws everything into the machine. She sits, watches soap bubbles form and froth and go round in circles. The day is a wash. Scrub-a-dub-dub.

"Why did you choose me?" Third Mother asks one day while Avni is making coffee.

It has been nearly a month since Avni brought her home. The knobs for the stove stopped working years ago, so she turns the dials until she hears the click of the gas then holds a lighter to the burner until it catches flame.

"You looked like all the mothers on TV," Avni says.

All the mothers on TV look tired and sad and like they are singularly holding their families together.

At work, Avni adds subtitles to ads for shampoo and Knorr

instant soup mixes. Her desk is infested with roaches but the view is good. Sixteen floors high, the Arabian Sea a kilometer away. Aishwarya Rai tosses her gorgeous, bouncy hair over her shoulder and says, "Total Repair 5: Because we're worth it." A little boy says, "Mom, do we eat or drink this?" and his mom replies: "Knorr Soupy Noodles! Swallow how you like."

The noodles make Avni hungry. She sneaks away. Outside the front of the building, there's a Starbucks and a Crêpe Suzette. To the back of the building, under big swathes of tarpaulin stitched together, a khao gully. She buys a vada pav for thirty rupees and asks for extra salt, extra chillies, extra bhajji. Her mother had never let her eat street food growing up. She breaks off small bits of the soft buttered bread and feeds them to the calico on the corner.

Her job bores her. The cat accepts crumbs from her hand then sets to work with her rough tongue. Scrub-a-dub-dub. All detergent ads are the same. A child comes home from school dripping in mud. A mother says, "Ay-hay!" But she isn't angry. She knows she can fix this. Avni remembers this from her own childhood. Laundry's an easy thing to fix. Her mother calls. She doesn't pick up and she feels guilty about it. She doesn't want to fight.

They'd fought frequently when she was young: about Avni's weight and her face and her body and her birth. They were very good at fighting—they always said things that were mean and true. Avni would say something mean and true, like, "You're just a mother," and Mother would say something meaner and truer, like, "I was going to leave your father but I got pregnant with you." Then Avni would run away to the terrace and pretend that Aishwarya Rai was her real mother, that any minute she'd show up in a white stretch limousine and take her away.

Avni strokes the cat's white patches. The cat blinks at her, and she blinks back. She'd heard that slow-blinking is a way of saying "I love you."

When the cat wanders away she goes back upstairs. Dating apps. Wellness drinks. Travel agents. Paint. Bridal lehengas. Coffee. Gold. Food delivery. Dabbawala delivery. Third Mother sent mooli ke parathe and thecha. The parathe are soft and flaky. The thecha is sour and spicy and tingles all the inside walls of her mouth. Her coworkers buy food from the trolley like she used to, but she finds it bland now. Lacking salt. She cries on the bus home. There's the salt. She licks her stinging lips and thinks of Mother.

"Tell me about her," Third Mother says, when Avni explains why she's been crying.

"She was a size four her whole life," Avni says. "Except when she was pregnant with me, and then she was a size eight. She was a bad cook but a good baker. She never let me lick the spoon. Her Victoria Sponge was so soft you hardly had to chew. She didn't love my father until she had me, and then she had two choices, and loving him was easier. She loved yoga and she could carry her whole body on the palms of her hands like a crow. She didn't have any friends except me. I was her only friend. She thought Saif Ali Khan's voice was sexy. And she sang to me most nights."

"She sounds nice," Third Mother says.

They hug for the first time. Third Mother's arms circle her shoulders loosely, cautiously. Avni finds it lacking.

In the morning they brush their teeth side by side, spit-spit-gargle-spit. The Colgate is minty-fresh and the shower is freshly wet and the bathroom smells like mehndi. They drink chai on the balcony, then Avni drives Third Mother back to the shelter.

In the car she whites and wilts and asks what she has done wrong. Avni notices newly the way her hair catches a copper tang under sunlight, like Aishwarya Rai in 2008. She doesn't know what to say.

The shelter people fuss over Third Mother and give each other knowing looks. "Perhaps," they suggest gently, "you might try an older mother? One with more training and experience?"

The shelter houses 150 women who used to be or long to be or have no choice but to be Mothers. They live in small double rooms with identical furniture. They cook together in a common kitchen and grow tulsi plants on the windowsill. On Sundays they sit in a long line that winds its way past the rooms and around all the living room furniture. They oil and braid each other's hair. Avni did high school community service hours here. They seem happy enough to her.

"All right," she decides. "I'll give it a shot."

They bring out a tall, unsmiling woman with white hair pinned behind her ears.

"Avni," they say. "This is Nazneen."

And so Nazneen becomes the fourth mother. She is significantly older than all the other mothers. Practically a grandmother. She is stern, but when Avni drives them home she rolls her window down and sticks her head out to feel the breeze. Then she laughs and laughs like a child.

Nazneen makes different food than Third Mother had. Lots of meat, cheap cuts but perfectly cooked so they fall off the bone. She is from Hyderabad and she buys whole chickens straight from the butcher. She makes Avni learn how to clean and cut.

"It's gross and sad," Avni says. "I don't want to do it."

"If you want to eat you will cook," Nazneen replies, unfazed. "You have got yourself a mother, not a maid."

She places the chicken on a wooden chopping board. "See," she says, indicating where with her big knife. "If you can, always cut through the joints instead of the bones."

Avni watches as she makes clean lines across the body of the chicken until it is disassembled and what's left looks less like bird and more like meat.

"This knife is not sharp enough," Nazneen observes. "Got it?"

Avni nods. Her mother calls and she hits ignore.

Nazneen's face softens. She cuts breast, thighs, drumsticks, wings into small, fairly even pieces. "This is called karahi cut," she says. "Your mother never taught you?"

"No," Avni says. "She must have thought other things were more important."

"Like what?"

Avni shrugs. "I don't know," she says, picking up a piece of raw chicken and squishing it between her fingers.

Nazneen thwacks her hand with the hilt of the knife and she puts it back down. Nazneen says, "Tell me more."

"There's nothing to tell," Avni says, pressing her damp, sticky fingers together. "My mother never really cared for food. And I think I was a disappointing child."

She was not a beautiful child. The last time she had spoken to her mother, she had been on her knees. They were doing yoga together in her mother's spare room. Child's pose. Avni couldn't fold herself forward far enough for her forehead to touch the floor then, either. Her stomach got in the way. Mother had been genuinely sad. She had said, "You look nothing like me."

The chicken karahi has less salt than Avni is now used to, but it's moist and delicate and she hardly has to chew. She swallows; Nazneen pretends not to see her tears. It goes down easy, and there's the salt.

They do dishes before bed. Avni scrubs, Nazneen rinses.

Nazneen doesn't snore, so Avni feels extra alone in the nights. She can't sleep again. She paces the flat and tries to regulate her breathing. Over and over, she counts down. Five things she can see, four things she can feel, three things she can hear, two things she can smell, one thing she can taste. She watches people smoking from the kitchen window. She chews on ice; she throws away the weighing scale.

"I heard you," Nazneen says in the morning. "Do you often sleep badly?"

"Yes," Avni says, stirring instant coffee into her bubbling milk.

"Does anything help?"

Avni shakes her head. "Nothing you can do."

"Something for another mother, perhaps?" Nazneen guesses.

Avni takes her coffee to go.

At work she gets to observe a shoot for the first time. She is tired and jittery and building a booth with thick black cloth in the lobby of an ugly high-rise near Atria Mall. She stands in for the model while the cameramen set up their lights. She moves as instructed to. She flinches at the flash. She closes her eyes when the lights get too bright.

"You, move!" someone yells.

When Avni opens her eyes, there, two feet away, surrounded by hair and makeup ladies, dressed in all-white with strings of pearls wrapped around her swanny neck, wind machine blowing her hair dramatically back, is Aishwarya Rai.

The shoot takes hours. Aishwarya turns this way and that, offers long, slow, catlike blinks to the cameras. She is selling "Volume Shocking Mascara" and it is shocking how beautiful she is. Avni tries to lock eyes, tries to slow blink back at her. They break for lunch and someone brings around chutney-cheese sandwiches for the crew. Aishwarya sits on one of those high makeup chairs and feeds herself a Caesar salad. Avni watches. The pieces of romaine are too big. Oh no. They're smudging her perfect makeup. Her personal assistant is putting on a pair of disposable gloves. Her personal assistant is ripping each romaine leaf into smaller bites, one by one by one.

"Chai?" someone says.

Avni takes it without shifting her gaze. She drinks without shifting her gaze. She spills chai on her white shirt and says, "Shit!"

Aishwarya hears; Aishwarya sees.

Avni doesn't know what to do now that they are actually holding eye contact. She slow-blinks. Aishwarya's eyes narrow, but she does not blink back. From somewhere else in the room, the director claps his hands loudly and Aishwarya disappears under a fluster of people armed with cotton pads and makeup brushes and bobby pins.

Avni dabs at her shirt but she only makes the stain worse.

Her boss's boss's intern, a skinny man in skinny jeans and a ganji, comes up to her and says they don't need her anymore. She can leave.

"But what if I don't want to leave yet," she protests, holding the shirt away from her body and squeezing. A few drops of chai fall to the floor.

"Sorry," he shrugs. "Aishwarya Ma'am wants you gone."

"No," Avni says, letting the fabric go. It falls back onto her body, sticks wetly to her stomach. "Why?"

The intern tugs at his own ganji uncomfortably. "She said you scared her?" he says, like a question.

In Avni's head, an image reverses: a white stretch limousine pulls up outside a middle-class apartment building in Panvel,

Aishwarya Rai inside. The passenger door opens, then closes. The limo speeds off. A young girl picks herself up off the ground and watches as it disappears.

"Aishwarya," Avni says, while the intern tries to tug her away. "Aishwarya, I'm sorry!"

From the middle of all the makeup artists and hairstylists, a long, pale arm extends outward and rises up like a kind of deity. It offers a graceful red carpet wave. Goodbye.

Avni drives home in a very regular size Maruti Suzuki.

When she arrives, Nazneen is at the dining table. She has found Avni's old photo albums and is looking through them carefully.

"Hey," Avni says, reaching for the book. "No."

She flips, unrepentant. "Is this your mother?" she asks. "It must be. You look just like her."

Avni sucks in a breath. She sits down. "I don't want to talk about her," she says.

Nazneen closes the book. "I do," she says. "Do you want to tell me what's wrong?"

"Not really." Avni gets up and moves to the kitchen. Nazneen follows her in. She takes off her shirt and stands over the sink in her bra. The Vim is running out, she notices. She drips what's left onto the top and turns on the geyser, then the tap. Scrub-a-dub-dub. When she bends over she feels her stomach curve and expand over the waistband of her pants.

"Why don't you call her back," Nazneen says.

"I can't let the stain set," she replies.

Nazneen takes off her dupatta and drapes it over Avni's shoulders. She says, "I would like you to take me back to the shelter."

"What," Avni says, dropping the shirt. "Why?"

"You should be using Surf for this. Never mind." Nazneen takes over. She switches off the geyser and turns the tap to the coldest temperature. She soaks the stain. A few minutes pass. She says, "I don't think I am the right mother for you, Avni."

Avni laughs. "What a shit day this is," she says. She pulls the dupatta over her body and covers herself.

"I am sorry to upset you," Nazneen says, switching off the tap and wringing the shirt with all the ferocity of a TurboDry until the excess water has sweated out. "But I don't think you will find what you are looking for in a new mother."

Avni says, "Let me put on a shirt."

The shelter people are tired of her, Avni can tell. What is wrong this time, they ask, and why has she returned, and does she understand adoption is a serious lifetime commitment? Avni says she is very sorry for troubling them and lets Nazneen go.

Nazneen doesn't try to hug her. She takes her hand and holds it just long enough for Avni's to feel warmed.

"You must have been a good mother," Avni tells her.

Nazneen smiles. "You say that because you are not my daughter."

In the house, Avni finds her white T-shirt drying on the balcony that has been unused since she took Third Mother back. It is spotless, as if the stain was never there. As if the chai had never spilled. Somehow she knows that she could have done exactly what Nazneen did and still made everything worse instead of better. Something-something mother's touch.

She goes to bed without eating and she can't sleep. Her stomach feels like it is being wrung dry and her head is on a spin cycle, being vigorously washed. Scrub-a-dub-dub. She draws her legs up to her chest. She clenches her muscles, she breathes in, she unclenches her muscles, she breathes out. She picks up her phone and calls her mother back.

"I didn't call you to fight," she says as soon as Mother picks up.

"I know why you called," Mother says. "I can always tell."

"Sorry," she says, and feels better already.

"You can't do like this," Mother tells her. "Calling me only when you need me."

Avni closes her eyes and decides to say something mean and true just one more time. "If I call you when I hurt," she says, "you make it better. If I call you when I'm not hurting, you make it worse."

Mother says, "Well," and blows her nose loudly.

"Sorry," Avni repeats. The breath on the other end of the line tells her Mother is still there. She pictures her, in bed at this hour, in one of those thin cotton nighties she buys from Love

Lady every spring. For better or worse, she knows Mother as well as Mother knows her.

"Do you want to hear about my day?" Mother asks finally. "Do you want me to sing for you?"

"Yes," Avni says. Her head slows down. She uncurls her legs slowly and evens out her breathing. She stretches out so her whole body is flat against the mattress. "Please."

And Mother starts to speak, and Mother starts to sing.

An Early Departure

FROM *Five Points*

IT WASN'T THE best time for me to be out of the office, but my niece asked so of course I went. The train ride to New York took four hours. For quite a few years when my niece was little, we used to meet up there, all of us, on a Saturday in autumn—my sister and her two children, my mother and me—arriving from different places by train and having a hectic stand-up lunch at Penn Station before checking into our hotel. We'd go to a show, eat at John's Pizza afterward, then walk through Times Square with us grownups flanking the kids, though looking back I wonder how much protection we could have provided if anyone really wanted to get at them; we were only three women, with not that much weight among us. Still, we would have had the advantage of our investment in the children's safety, which counts for a lot.

My sister and I look alike, and my niece looks like both of us, and I knew that anyone seeing me hold Tanya's hand back then as we strolled down the street might easily take me for her mother. I savored this more than I should have, but I figured it didn't hurt anyone; nobody else had to know.

Before bedtime on those Saturday nights, we hung out together in one of the hotel rooms, just catching up and watching the kids goof around. One year, my sister booked a hotel with a rooftop pool, and how much fun was *that!* Watching my niece and nephew laugh and splash under the stars. Another year we arranged the trip around my fortieth birthday, and they sang to me over a red velvet cake from Magnolia Bakery. I got the impression that they all made a special effort to give me a nice time, knowing how I might feel turning forty with no children of my own. Nobody said this out loud, but they were right that I felt a certain way, and the celebration helped in the moment even though it made me sadder when I was alone on the train back to Boston the next day.

Back then I liked to read quotes from successful women about not having children. Like Jennifer Aniston, who said, "You may not have a child come out of your vagina, but that doesn't mean you aren't mothering." *I'm mothering,* I told myself, whenever I spent time with my sister's kids. *So they didn't come out of my vagina. Is that such a big deal?*

On Sunday mornings of those weekends, we ate brunch together before we all headed back to Penn Station for our rides home on three different tracks. They were short visits, sometimes not even a whole twenty-four hours, but they were the most alive and comforting times I can remember—the kids so captivated by the novelties they saw around them (pretzels the size of their faces, horse buggies in Central Park), and so eager to join the scene. The year my nephew Henry was nine, I bought him a stuffed frog from a street vendor, and Henry promptly named the frog Hoppy, placed it on his head, and proceeded to walk around that way the entire day. My mother was healthy enough to walk long distances with us, from the park all the way down Fifth Avenue to where we always stayed near Rockefeller Center.

Tanya works there now, apprenticing to writers for a comedy sketch show. It's her dream job, straight out of college, the one she'd told us she wanted when she was eleven and we all took the NBC backstage tour. The others of us smiled and said *of course* she would get a job like that, though none of us really believed it.

But we should never have doubted her. Once when she was three, we went to a minor-league baseball game, and our seats were across the stadium from a pop-up carnival. Tanya caught sight of the Ferris wheel, pointed to let us know she was headed there, and took off. My sister and I followed the whole way, keeping her safe without her knowing, and we were amused but more than a little unsettled when the baby never looked back.

Tanya asked me to come see her in the city, and followed this up with a second request, which was not to tell her mother. This was tricky, because she wouldn't say why, but I convinced myself it had something to do with wanting to surprise her mother somehow. My sister's birthday wasn't for another six months, and it wasn't a big one, but in this way I allowed myself to honor Tanya's request, and to book my train tickets without mentioning it to my sister in our every-other-day text exchange. Why Tanya herself didn't just tell me whatever she needed to in a text or email, I couldn't guess, though it would become clear all too soon why she wanted to see me in person.

My niece apologized for not being able to put me up, but of course I understood—this was New York! She shared a two-bedroom walk-up with two friends from college; one of them paid a little less and slept in the dining alcove. I remembered such arrangements from being young myself, though in Boston, not New York. When I got older, I would never have wanted to live in the same circumstances, but at the time, it was fun.

Besides, I could afford a nice hotel room. I checked in early, then met Tanya at one of the subterranean restaurants at 30 Rock. It was January, and from our table we watched the skaters on the rink outside. I hadn't seen her in half a year, since we'd all gotten together in the place my mother lived to celebrate *her* big birthday, but I was glad to see that my niece hadn't changed much since then. One of my favorite things about her had always been her sweetness, and I admit that when she first told me she was moving there, I was afraid the city might turn her hard.

"How's Grandma?" she asked. "I wish she could still make the trip down here. But she seems to be doing better than a lot of people her age."

I agreed, and kept myself from reminding her that she could always inquire of Grandma herself how Grandma was doing. I didn't want to start off on a rocky foot.

I'd speculated a lot, of course, about why Tanya had asked

me to make the trip down. Did she need money, and hesitated to ask her parents? Had something happened she didn't want them to know about? Was she pregnant and sought my advice?

I can't deny it made me feel special, to have been summoned. My niece said she needed me, so I dropped everything and went.

"It's about Henry," she said, after the server had left the table. I knew she'd ordered the least expensive item on the menu because she expected me to insist on paying, which I would. "He's in trouble."

"What kind?" In the moment before concern hit, I felt surprise. Her brother, a senior in college, had always been a quiet kid, not afraid to go his own way but not interested in ruffling any feathers, either. At least, that's how it always seemed to me. It was hard to tell, because of the quietness. He spent a lot of time on his computer—to the extent that I knew my sister sometimes worried about his eyes—but he seemed to enjoy our family visits, never hiding in his room or otherwise retreating when we were all together. I couldn't imagine what sort of trouble my niece might be talking about.

He'd gotten himself involved in a hacking scheme, Tanya told me. There were plenty of kids at his school who knew how proficient he was at finding his way around various systems, and plenty who needed their grades boosted and would pay to have it done.

Slowly, I repeated Tanya's words aloud: *gotten himself involved.* "You make it sound as if he couldn't help it. As if he had no choice." I noticed that my hand was trembling as I reached for my water glass. Tanya saw it, too. "And I wouldn't call that 'getting in trouble'—I'd call it committing a crime."

She sucked her breath in, barely audibly, and sat back in her chair. "I didn't expect you to be so harsh," she said. "This is *Henry* we're talking about."

"I know." It chilled me to see the look of distrust in her eyes. "You think I'm not upset?"

And then through the sense-channel that connects women in a family, our mutual mind's eye, I could see we were both remembering the day her brother walked around New York with his new favorite stuffie balanced on top of his head. Oh, Hoppy! I put a hand to my throat.

She leaned closer, and I could see she was wearing the butterfly necklace I'd given her on her sixteenth birthday. My immediate response was to feel flattered, but this was followed by a flash of insight I wished I could ignore: She'd worn the necklace to butter me up. "It's not like it was a crime," she said.

Somehow I managed not to exclaim. How delusional was she? How willing to ignore what she knew—never mind common sense—to believe what she wished to be true? "Yaya," I said, then waited for her to look directly at me. "Hacking into somebody else's database and changing the data is *absolutely* a crime."

"No, I *know*," she said, not bothering to hide her irritation, "but it didn't start out like that." She went on to recount the story of a crush her brother had, on a girl who seemed to like him back. "But it turned out she only made nice so he'd change her civics grade." I could tell how hurt Tanya had been to hear this, on her brother's behalf. And I remembered the kick it had always given me to hear her use old-timey phrases such as *made nice*.

"So she dumped him afterward?" I asked. "What made her think he wouldn't just go into the system again and change it back?"

"Because," she said, "she knew him enough to tell what kind of guy he is."

"So where does it stand? Did somebody expose him, is there an investigation?"

Tanya nodded. "The college's disciplinary board. He's afraid he's going to be expelled. And after that, the dean said, they might involve the police."

"He hasn't told your parents?"

"No. And he doesn't want them to find out."

The server came and put our lunches in front of us. Neither of us reached for a fork. "Why are you telling *me*, then?" I asked, though of course I already knew.

It chilled me again to see how much, in that moment, she hated me for making her come out and say it. "We thought . . . because of your job . . . you might be able to . . ." But she couldn't finish. Instead she dropped her face toward her chest and began to sob. "I'm sorry, Aunt Kim, I should never have asked you. I know it's shitty, I know it's wrong, and trust me, Henry does, too. But he begged me. He didn't think you would do it if *he* asked, but he knows you're like a second mother to me."

Ah, those magic words: "a second mother." They are meant to be a compliment—one of the highest—but the person they are addressed to, the person so named, understands all too well how far the second mother falls short of the first.

My sister had often referred to me as a second mother in relation to her own children, especially Tanya. I knew she meant well and wanted to make me feel good. And I would have felt touched by my niece using the phrase now, except that I realized she was doing so in an effort to get what she and her brother wanted.

So: she had become a little hard, after all. I knew she would not have relished this task of trying to secure my help, but she had her priorities in order, and her brother came first. I had to admire it, in a way. She was still the girl who set out for her destination with no intention of letting anyone stop her along the way.

"I'm sorry, Yaya," I told her (and there *was* a considerable part of me that was sorry, the part that should have done what any mother would do), "but I really can't intervene. Not that I think I actually *could* help, even if I did."

"Yes, you could. They'd listen to you." She was pleading. I saw that her eyes were dry, and concluded with a tumbling crash inside me that her sobbing had been fake.

Knowing I had to find a way to steel myself, I pretended I was speaking to a potential client I'd never met before, instead of my beloved niece. I told her that matters like these had nothing to do with the ones I dealt with in my job. Even if the college did contact the police and press charges, my reach—my jurisdiction in a different kind of agency, and a different state—wouldn't come close.

But it wasn't only that it wouldn't work or that I might get exposed, I told her. It would be the wrong thing to do. That I had to say this made me feel like crying myself, and the truth was that I said it even before I'd finished mentally running through the sequence of people I might conceivably call to make life easier on my nephew.

"I know it doesn't seem like it right now," I said, "but even if I did try to help, it wouldn't be the best thing for Henry."

"Why not? He's learned his lesson. He'll never do anything like this again."

"But he did it this time. And it wasn't a momentary lapse of judgment—that kind of thing has to be thought out. It has to be planned. It's better for him to face the consequences, in the long run. Trust me."

She had zero intention of trusting me; this I could tell from her face. "So you're not even going to try?" Her eyes pricked like points of glass.

"Oh, honey." In that moment I understood that the most rewarding and significant aspect of my existence, the role that had sustained and buoyed me for more than twenty years in an otherwise lonely life, had just come to an end. "I can't."

Before I arrived, I'd hoped she'd bring me back to her office and show me around—she'd mentioned something, on the phone when we made arrangements, to this effect—but it became clear after I paid the check, after we took the escalator back up to the lobby, that she intended for us to part ways. I hugged her, I hugged her, not wanting to let go even though I knew she'd already slipped away from me to a place I'd not be allowed to enter, even if I did ever manage to find it again.

I'd booked the hotel room for that night expecting that Tanya would let me treat her and her friends to a dinner they wouldn't have been able to afford on their own. I confess I had fantasies about how proud she'd feel of her cool and generous aunt, and the way all the girls would hug and thank me when we stepped out of the restaurant.

But now I didn't need the room, on top of which I wanted only to get away from the city. I canceled at the hotel even though it was too late to get a refund, then wheeled my bag to Penn Station where I changed my return ticket, which cost me a fee. But it was worth it; Amtrak would not be able to hurtle me home fast enough.

Home? Well, no. But back to where I belonged.

On the ride to Boston I sat on the side that gave a view of the water, when there was water to see. In New London, a young mother got on with a boy who was about two years old and miserable, crying not for any particular reason but for the sake of crying; it's easy to tell the difference, if you've spent any time around kids. I helped her collapse his stroller, and offered him the bag of crackers I'd bought at the station but not yet opened. The mother fell all over herself thanking me, and the crackers distracted him for a while, but when the bag was empty he threw it on the floor and started crying again.

I couldn't change my seat, not only because the train was full but because the mother would know why I moved, and I didn't want to make her feel bad. I pulled out a folder and tried to look at some work, but it was futile. Partly this was because of the boy's whining, but mainly it had to do with how sick I felt about the scene I'd just had with my niece.

At one point I sighed and let my glance fall across the aisle. The mother seemed to take this as an invitation. She leaned over and whispered, "It gets easier, right?" in a tone that attempted lightness but couldn't conceal the desperation it contained.

I understood instantly what she assumed about me, and perceived the familiar, shameful thrill of passing. "You'll be *amazed*," I said, and something about the way I pronounced the word must have intrigued the boy, or tickled him (the buzzy Z sound!) because he paused in his crying to look up at me and smile. I smiled back. The mother jumped on it, grabbing first one toy and then another out of the diaper bag at her feet, and these distractions finally took hold. Her son became immersed in a handheld pinball game, and stayed quiet for the rest of their ride.

I felt a wave of pride I knew to be ridiculous, but it blunted the despair I'd boarded with. Only later, pulling into my station after they'd gotten off a few stops before, did the truth set in. Clutching my workbag tighter than necessary as I stepped onto the platform, I realized that of course I hadn't fooled the boy as I had his mother. Didn't I understand children better than that? He'd smiled at me not because I'd charmed him, but to let me know he recognized a liar when he saw one. Jennifer Aniston could pretend all she wanted, but this kid wasn't about to let me get away with offering a promise that wasn't mine to make.

Contributors' Notes

Other Distinguished Stories of 2024

American and Canadian Magazines Publishing Short Stories

Contributors' Notes

LAUREN ACAMPORA is the author of the novels *The Paper Wasp* and *The Hundred Waters* and the linked story collection *The Wonder Garden*. She has won or been nominated for the GLCA New Writers Award, the Center for Fiction's First Novel Prize, the Story Prize, and the New England Book Award and has received fellowships from the New York Foundation for the Arts, MacDowell, Ucross, Art OMI, and the Ragdale Foundation. Her writing has appeared in publications such as *The Paris Review, New England Review, The Missouri Review, Guernica,* and *The New York Times.*

• When I was a child in Connecticut, a classmate's father arranged for a Bengal tiger to visit our elementary school. I believe it was the mascot of the company where he was an executive. The strangeness of that wild animal in the orderly environment of our school, with its desks and bells and lunch monitors, left a deep impression on me. Years later, my family visited the sprawling estate of a retired financier who kept a menagerie of exotic animals. As my young daughter stood near the chain-link fence of the African serval enclosure, she must have triggered the prey drive of one of the wildcats, because it suddenly sprinted toward her, stretched its leg through an opening in the fence, and clawed at her torso. As luck would have it, she was wearing corduroy overalls that day, and the claws caught in the fabric. She was unhurt and unfazed, but it could easily have gone a different way. These two episodes together inspired "Dominion." I wrote it as part of a collection of stories about human-animal dynamics—all the ways we love, fear, fetishize, exploit, and identify with other creatures, depending on context and species—and how we ourselves are governed by animal instincts. The character Roy Fox also appears as an anti-hero in my novel *The Hundred Waters.* But "Dominion" is his moment in the sun, a glimpse into his view of himself, not as a villain but a self-made man who's earned his power and pleasure, a benevolent steward of beasts, sharing his bounty with others. It's also a dive into the Biblical idea of dominion and the notion of entitlement at the root of human behavior.

SARAH ANDERSON is a recent graduate of the Helen Zell Writers' Program at the University of Michigan. Her fiction has been published in *Epiphany* and *Joyland*, won two Hopwood Awards, been nominated for a Pushcart Prize, and received support from the Barbara Deming Memorial Fund. She is currently at work on her first novel. Find her at sarahwanderson.com.

• "Take Me to Kirkland" initially grew out of two main fragments. The first piece to arrive was the scene of the narrator meeting Chloe and the intensity between them. My own breasts came in late, and one of my clearest memories from teenhood is the obsessive, desperate way I looked at other women's bodies, like at any moment someone might jump from the bushes and announce a winner. That moment of sizing up by the mailbox was my way into the scene, and then the friendship came in a series of images: the cutting of the lemon, girl underwater, the trampoline.

The second piece was the section about childhood misunderstandings. I was a deeply anxious child, and that anxiety was made so much worse by all the things I didn't understand about the world. I just had this vague sense of how much I didn't know, and it terrified me. Perhaps because of this, and having made it to the other side, I take a particular joy in collecting other people's stories of the misunderstandings they had well into adulthood. Like the narrator, I truly believed for a long, long time that Al Gore was only his last name.

It eventually became clear to me that the two fragments were connected, and I spent another year figuring out how to stitch together a narrative around them. Once it started to take shape, the story became a vehicle for a collection of other strangenesses, things that used to or still unsettle me in ways I struggle to articulate, all the ways the world never does actually make sense even after you grow up, and all the stories we tell each other and ourselves to try to understand it.

A huge thank you to Michelle King for helping this story arrive at its final form, and for publishing it.

EMMA BINDER is a writer from Wisconsin. They have received a Stegner Fellowship in fiction from Stanford University, an Elizabeth George Foundation grant, an Institute for Creative Writing fellowship from the University of Wisconsin, and a Vermont Studio Center fellowship. Their work has received an O. Henry Award, the Gulf Coast Prize in Fiction, the Indiana Review Fiction Prize, and a Wisconsin Writers Award, among other honors. Their stories have recently appeared in *The Kenyon Review, Michigan Quarterly Review, Electric Literature*'s Recommended Reading, *Gulf Coast*, and elsewhere. Currently based in Wisconsin, they are working on a novel.

• One of my obsessions, both artistically and in life, are the stories of queer and trans people who come from rural places and small towns, who may be omitted from the acknowledged social fabric of these communities but still shape them and are shaped by them. Queer and trans people are everywhere, so if their existence is not visible in a certain place, that erasure has been somehow designed. I also wanted to write a story about the feeling of freedom, and how some environments allow us to feel free while others are designed to constrain us—perhaps we experience that constraint through fear, shame, self-hatred, or an ambient hunch that we need to hush some vital part of ourselves in order to make our lives simpler. And maybe we love and miss those places regardless. So the emotional and thematic context was very clear to me, but the actual events of the story—Cody seeing a man falling through the ice, saving him, meeting him and his friends at the bar—took shape slowly and organically, during a warm winter when I was taking a lot of walks past ice fishermen.

I started this story in 2022, amid what I already thought was a harsh political climate for queer and trans people in the United States. Looking back on this story in the even darker and more oppressive landscape of 2025, I feel compelled to say that the ability to live in environments where we feel free, and where we can experience self-determination and authenticity, is literally lifesaving; it allows us to move past raw survival and access deeper, human, complex modes of living. It allows us, as Cody says in the story, to experience such essential things as "love, family, peace." That is true for trans people and for every person on this Earth.

SARAH BRAUNSTEIN is the author of the novels *Bad Animals* and *The Sweet Relief of Missing Children*, and her short fiction has appeared in *The New Yorker*, *Joyland*, *Playboy*, *Harvard Review*, and other places. She lives in Maine and teaches at Colby College.

• Some years ago, my elementary-aged child went for a jog in the neighborhood, promising to stay alert and to avoid strangers. He returned with a telescope a stranger had been throwing away. The man, he said, had told him he could buy a new part for it on the web. My son and I ordered some plastic mirror thing for $3 on eBay, but we could never get it to fit, and the telescope now sits in the basement wrapped in cobwebs. From the day he came home with it, the telescope radiated with meaning. It felt like the set-up of a short story on my front stoop, the kid and the object. The telescope lets the child see the cosmos, a world beyond the household, beyond what the mother knows. I imagined a mother who would feel threatened by this, who would wonder about the man . . . who might even go to his door to complain. She would be lonely, half-aware of her motivations. When she knocked on his door and I saw the entryway to Marco's living room, his reading glasses, I realized this might be a story about real estate, or friendship, or love . . . the narrative opened up to me, a Venn diagram of these elements. I began to imagine a daughter who is prickly and tart, always one step ahead of her mother. She has a band on her wrist that counts steps, another device Toni did not give her, and downloads apps without permission on Toni's phone. Poor Toni! It began to make me laugh, the Sisyphean task of controlling a young adolescent with a burning mind. Well, what about her own burning mind? Toni as a former creative person came into focus then. I wanted to write about so many things, to say something about grief, creativity, doubt, fear . . . finding my way to the end of this story was a challenge. At one point Toni says she stopped writing because she never could figure out how to end things. "Abject Naturalism" sat in a file for a long time until I could understand what its ending needed to do. I am grateful for the editorial eye of Willing Davidson, who helped me see what did not belong, and I am honored that it has been chosen for this volume.

SOPHIE MADELINE DESS is a writer living in New York City, with fiction and non-fiction in *The Paris Review, The Atlantic, The Washington Post,* and more. Her debut novel, *What You Make of Me,* was published with Penguin Press in February 2025.

• A friend of mine is getting his MD, and from him I learned of the existence of the Gynecological Teaching Assistant—a person trained to use her own body as a teaching tool to instruct medical students on administering breast and pelvic exams. I was immediately obsessed by the thought of this job. To bring "performance" into the exam room; to be probed and prodded, to pretend. The job struck me as perfect for a voice that had been floating around in my head, the voice of Izzie in "Unfathomably Deep." Izzie's passion, grief, and spunk all took shape as I imagined her as a GTA, lying on an exam table, surrounded by handsome, untalented medical students. Eventually that career choice became secondary to the main thrust of the story, which is to do with allegiance, violence, and fate. It is a story born of the question: What forces and passions possess us in the wake of grief?

LYN DI IORIO is from San Juan, Puerto Rico. Her novel *Outside the Bones* was shortlisted for the John Gardner Memorial Prize. Her short stories have appeared in *The Georgia Review, The Kenyon Review, Review: Literature and Arts of the Americas,* and elsewhere. She is a recent New York Foundation for the Arts NYFA/NYSCA artist fellow in fiction and had a "distinguished" story in *The Best American Short Stories 2021.* She studied at Harvard, Stanford, and UC-Berkeley and teaches literature and creative writing at the City College of New York and CUNY Graduate Center. She is currently completing a novel and short story collection.

• "Maritza and Carmen" is part of *Let Me Take Care of You,* a collection I'm writing set in Puerto Rico. At the heart of these stories are kaleidoscopic encounters following Hurricane Maria—moments of connection between people who might otherwise never have met. The storm, followed by institutional collapse, cruel neglect, and the arrival of stateside billionaire profiteers, paradoxically led to a strengthening of bonds and a collective determination to regroup and regrow. This shifting landscape shapes the world of my characters.

The inspiration for this story came when I realized a character I had killed off in a previous piece might not be dead after all. That earlier story follows Taína, a teenager angry about being uprooted from the States to the town of Vega Baja by her mother, Carmen, a police officer and over-bearing striver. Their conflict escalates as Hurricane Maria arrives. When the river overflows, eventually swallowing Carmen's police cruiser, Taína has a vision of an indigenous chieftain said to have drowned in that very river. In that moment, where she once felt alienated, she starts to experi-ence a profound connection to both the island and her mother.

When I finished writing Taína's story, Carmen seemed beyond saving—claimed by the river, dead as could be. But just as Taína had her epiphany, I began to wonder: What if Carmen needed one too? Inspired by Addie Bundren's ghostly voice in Faulkner's *As I Lay Dying*, I imagined Carmen's final thoughts as she drifted away, burned by her own taser.

Then I asked: What if Carmen didn't die? What if, instead, it was parts of her identity—her roles as mother and policewoman—that died? Where Taína finds a new sense of belonging, Carmen loses hers entirely.

While writing "Maritza and Carmen," I often thought of my own mother—like Carmen, from Vega Baja—and a cherished cousin. Both, in different ways, were women whose identities as mothers overshadowed everything else. The more I explored Carmen's survival, the more she seemed to want to abandon the rage and reactiveness that had defined her—even if it meant leaving behind her role as a mother. It fascinated me that rule-obsessed Carmen might have another chance. And that's when Maritza—elusive, unpredictable, and perhaps more interesting—was born.

ISABELLE FANG is a writer from Toronto and Taipei. Before making her debut in fiction with McSweeney's 75th anniversary issue, her essays ap-peared in *Catapult*. She graduated from The New School with a BA in liter-ary studies. She's currently at work on a collection.

• "Gray, Cotton, White Lace Edges" started with just its ending: A man returning all the used panties he bought from a woman over years and years. That ending sat in a list of ideas until I began drafting a story about reality TV that felt lacking, needed a personal tension to inform the reality TV gimmick. It may sound cliché but the idea to combine the two came to me in the shower when I wasn't thinking of much at all. Once I had the two ideas together, it became about exploring what it even means to try and return something like that. In having so many characters to play around with, I started writing toward the unspoken needs and wants we have hidden in all our relationships. I wanted to write about people who, somewhat by accident, end up meaning more to each other than they first bargained for.

I'm forever grateful to Eli Horowitz and the whole team at *McSweeney's* for taking a chance and gifting me my debut in fiction. I'm honored Ce-leste Ng and Nicole Lamy chose "Gray, Cotton, White Lace Edges" to ap-pear in this year's anthology. Finally, I owe all my fiction to the late great

David Burr Gerrard, who taught me from Introduction all the way to Advanced Fiction at The New School. Even now, David's feedback from my freshman year is the voice of my better judgement as I write first drafts and persist through rejection.

BRET ANTHONY JOHNSTON is the internationally bestselling author of the novels *We Burn Daylight, Remember Me Like This,* and the collection *Corpus Christi: Stories.* His work has appeared in *The New Yorker, Esquire, The Atlantic, Virginia Quarterly Review,* and elsewhere. *Encounters with Unexpected Animals,* a collection of short fiction in which "Time of the Preacher" appears, will be brought out by Random House in February 2026.

• One way—maybe the only way—that I'm remotely useful to friends is my ability to identify (and, if needed, catch) snakes. They'll text me photos and ask how dangerous the snake coiled under their garden hose or sunbathing on their deck is. Sometimes they'll ask me to please come remove said snake from the premises while they lock themselves in the car and enjoy a panic attack. They tend to think I'm doing them some giant favor, but in truth the prospect of seeing, let alone holding a snake, is so thrilling that I'm always fighting to mask my giddiness.

So, about a year into the pandemic, when my buddy called to say he and his wife were pretty much sure they'd just seen a small snake slither under their refrigerator, I was in my truck and heading their way long before I'd actually been invited. They didn't know what kind of snake they'd possibly glimpsed, so they were understandably worried it might be poisonous. Further, their young son (hi Bowen!) would absolutely freak the f*%! out if he got wind of a possible snake, so we came up with a cover story that good old Uncle Bret was just stopping by to help find a "leak" under the fridge. Fortunately—read: unfortunately—after hours of searching, we never located the leak. Driving home, I had the fleeting thought that my buddy might've invented the snake out of—what? Camaraderie? Kindness? Cabin fever? We were all longing for connection during that sad and surreal period. He didn't invent the snake, of course, but I started wondering who would and under what circumstances. I wrote "Time of the Preacher" to find out. It's safe to say I was as surprised as anyone by what the characters do and don't find in that house.

I'm deeply indebted to everyone at the almighty *Virginia Quarterly Review,* especially the peerless Allison Wright, and to Nicole Lamy and Celeste Ng for giving the story such lovely homes. Thank you, too, to Bowen and his parents. If the fridge springs another leak, I'm here.

HANNAH KINGSLEY-MA is a writer and audio producer. Her work has appeared in outlets like *The Drift, The New York Times, The New Republic, Zyzzyva,* and *The Believer.*

• I've always been interested in where pockets of privacy exist in our closest relationships—and how many different strains of intimacy there are within our wider social constellations. I'm also interested in seeing how these different kinds of intimacy collide. The prime setting for a collision seemed to me to be someone else's family vacation. When I was revising this story and thinking of potential scenes to add, I jotted down a series of incomprehensible notes, including the phrase: "dog stink / fear dream." Many thanks to the fearless editing team at *The Drift* for taking on this fear dream story, and to Nicole Lamy and Celeste Ng for including it here.

WILLIAM LOHIER is a PhD student in English at UC Berkeley. Prior to this, he worked at Scribner and received his master's from Oxford and his bachelor's from Harvard. His work has been published by *One Story* and *The Harvard Advocate*. He received the 2020 Ecker Short Story Prize and was the 2018 NYC Youth Poet Laureate.

• I learned about the term *drapetomania* in a class on Morrison, Ellison, and Faulkner. Halfway through the semester we were sent home because of the pandemic. I began the story as part of the final paper for the class, since the term seemed to connect much of the historical violence we were reading about with the horrors of the present. The characters all struggle to negotiate agency within an apocalyptic scenario, and running, in the story, speaks to that negotiation. The running mania hijacks bodies and becomes a horrific worlding in its own right, but by the end of the story, the running comes almost as a relief. To me, this relief runs parallel to the relief of writing, of turning the incredible pressure I felt as a teenager beginning to write this story during the pandemic and Black Lives Matter protests into something generative, beautiful, that spoke literally to the various movements I was witnessing and experiencing.

YASMIN ADELE MAJEED's stories appear in *Narrative, Joyland, Guernica, American Short Fiction*, and *Best Debut Short Stories 2022*. A graduate of the Iowa Writers' Workshop, she lives in New York, where she is at work on a novel and a story collection.

• I started writing "The Clean-Out" in 2021, and for a long time, all I had was the opening image of Teo hiding in the grass, watching her mom and Lola arrive at the beach house. From there, I slowly sketched out each woman, uncovering who they were to one another. In much of my work, I am interested in the debts that immigrant daughters are born into, and their creative attempts to pay them off. These characters are both daughters and mothers, and what they owe each other, and what they believe they are owed, drives the story. I wanted to capture the force and complexity of the women on the Filipino side of my family, and through the lives of these characters, consider the contradictory narratives that can exist within a single family.

I'm indebted to a few writers in the making of this story. The first is Edward P. Jones—the use of the retrospective first person and prolepsis were inspired by his work. The second is my former teacher Madhuri Vijay, who read an early draft in my first workshop in graduate school and gave me some ruthless and much-needed advice: Kill the bird. And finally, another one of my teachers, Anthony Marra, brought this story to the editorial team at *Narrative*, all of whom thoughtfully shepherded "The Clean-Out" through to publication.

ELIZABETH McCRACKEN is the author of four novels, three collections of short stories, and a memoir. Her ninth book, *A Long Game: Notes on Writing Fiction*, will be published by Ecco in December 2025.

• A few years ago, I wrote the first connected stories of my life, not out of artistic imperative but necessity: I'd forgotten about a book deadline and had to compose some stories quickly to meet it. Easier to run a pentathlon, I decided, than five unrelated races, and so in a matter of weeks I wrote five stories about the same two characters. The experience was exhausting and exhilarating, my favorite writerly state; the stories felt more comprehensive and less conclusive than either standalone stories or a novel. Was I done with these people or not? The writing seemed akin to knowing human beings in real life, with moments of both closeness and estrangement.

"Seven Stories About Tammy" is the third story I've written about the Harkin siblings, and is itself a kind of speed collection of connected stories. The anthology form of the story owes a debt to Denis Johnson's "The Largesse of the Sea Maiden," one of those debts I didn't recognize until I picked up *The Largesse of the Sea Maiden* after I had already written it.

My grandmother was a dogged fabulist when it came to her age, and so were her sisters. Two of the Bernstein sisters—there were six—performed as folk dancers in New York City in the fifties and kept scrapbooks of clippings with the dates torn off. I've always been fascinated by this particular piece of vanity, which has never made sense to me, and have long meant to write about somebody who lies about her age over decades.

CARRIE R. MOORE is the author of *Make Your Way Home*, a collection of short stories featuring life in the American South. Her fiction has appeared in *One Story*, *New England Review*, *The Sewanee Review*, *Virginia Quarterly Review*, *The Southern Review*, and other publications. She earned her MFA in Fiction at the Michener Center for Writers, where she won the Keene Prize for literature and was the inaugural fellow at the Steinbeck Writers' Retreat in Sag Harbor. Much of her work explores Black interiorities, particularly Black women's longings and dreams.

• As a writer, I'm interested in intimacies, in the people we love and why. I tried for three years to write about chosen family, and earlier versions of this piece featured a woman moving out of her mother's home and into her partner's. Then, I got married, and this story's current iteration took shape. I spent that newlywed summer building a life with a man I never had any doubts about marrying: couch-shopping, taking walks in our city of evergreens, learning each other all over again, now that we shared an apartment. Time passed quickly. In my mid-twenties, I was happily settling into what my life would be.

Yet part of me knew I'd foreclosed some other way of being. I'd now never share a dwelling with my best friend, with whom I chatted regularly on the phone. She lived halfway across the country, which didn't matter for our emotional closeness, our friendship that felt as real as any romance. Still, I'd always thought we'd be roommates, someday. I'd imagined us moving to some walkable city and filling a cozy apartment with books and talking over tea until the middle of the night. The story stopped being about a woman and her mother. It began to feature a woman and her best friend, whom she called a sister.

I kept thinking about household structures, how we join our lives to others. As a practicing Christian, I thought of the Book of Genesis and the story of Adam and Eve. Those scriptures serve as the structural backbone of this story: a woman meets a man, who's been in the world slightly longer than she has, in an Edenic landscape. And outside of that Eden, the world is full of horrors.

The story gained momentum. Then—the COVID-19 pandemic happened. My writing grappled with my worst fears, exaggerated by hours of doomscrolling: inexplicable virus symptoms, division between red and blue states, the climate change that plowed ahead, regardless. I read articles about the difficulty of entering the administrative region of Hong Kong, and I wondered what would happen if American cities adopted a dramatized version of quarantine. By then, my husband and I were living in Texas, and I was also reading local coverage of Hurricane Harvey and its aftermath. All of that has shown up in this fictional setting.

Still, nine years after its first draft, the core of this story is a relationship between two women. I kept wondering what life Brie and Harper would choose, if their world required a new genesis.

ANDREW PORTER is the author of four books, including the story collections *The Disappeared* (Knopf), *The Theory of Light and Matter* (Vintage), and the novels *In Between Days* (Knopf) and, most recently, *The Imagined Life* (Knopf). A graduate of the Iowa Writers' Workshop, he has received a Pushcart Prize, a James Michener/Copernicus Fellowship, and the Flannery O'Connor Award for Short Fiction. His work has appeared in *One Story*, *Ploughshares*, *American Short Fiction*, *Narrative*, *The Southern Review*, *The Missouri Review*, and on Public Radio's "Selected Shorts." Currently, he teaches fiction writing and directs the creative writing program at Trinity University in San Antonio, Texas.

• I wrote the opening paragraph of "Angelo" several years before I wrote the story. This isn't that unusual for me, as I have dozens of documents saved on my computer filled with opening paragraphs, opening scenes, sometimes just a single opening sentence. Every so often, I'll go back and look through some of these documents and see if one of these forgotten openings still speaks to me, and that was the case with "Angelo." When I came across that opening paragraph a couple years ago, I knew there was a story there, and the story itself arrived fairly quickly soon after—in about a week or two—which is unusual for me.

At its heart, "Angelo" is a love story, but it's also about that period in one's life when so much seems both possible and impossible, when your vision of your own future changes daily.

And because I wrote the opening paragraph of the story first, I knew all along what the future would hold for Angelo and Cole. I knew where they'd end up. I just didn't know why. So, that's what the story was about for me: going back to the beginning to discover why.

Special thanks to Laila Lalami for selecting this story for the issue of *Ploughshares* in which it first appeared, to Ladette Randolph for her kind support of my work over the years, and to Celeste Ng and Nicole Lamy for choosing it for this year's anthology.

NATHAN CURTIS ROBERTS was born, raised, and educated in the San Francisco Bay Area. His stories and essays have appeared in *The Atlantic*, *The Threepenny Review*, *River Teeth*, *New England Review*, and many other publications, some of them lost to time. He lives in Utah.

• When I started writing the original version of this story, the COVID-19 pandemic was at its peak. I was living in a neighborhood that felt alien to me, sharing a roof with my family for the first time since I was a teenager, feeling frightened about my own future as well as the state of the world. The earthquakes really did happen, as did the trumpet falling from the statue, and there was a small but visible contingent of Uthans who were excited to be at the beginning of The End. My next-door neighbor died on Valentine's Day, leaving his eighty-year-old widow the sole caretaker of their disabled son. Material for a story was all laid out for me, but I started off with some foolish ideas. I felt like such an outsider in suburban Utah, I couldn't imagine myself in the place where I really did live. So I started writing about someone who fit in: older than me, different in worldview, temperament, and sexual orientation. The narrator was a retired police officer; I might regret admitting that the working title was "Assigned Cop at Birth." I struggled for months to get anything worthwhile onto the page, aside from the story's basic scaffolding. I took a long break from the manuscript, and when I came back to it, the problems seemed obvious. The story wanted to be about a misfit. The narrator needed more of me in him. I made the character younger, queerer, funnier, and a more alert observer—with these changes, the first draft of what would be "Yellow Tulips" came together in a few days. I can't say I ever grew to feel like I "belonged" in the neighborhood; it was more like the community and I achieved détente. The process of crafting this story helped me find some beauty and grace in a religion I hadn't believed in since I was sixteen, one that rejected me before I ever had a chance to reject it.

JULIAN ROBLES is a Mexican (-American) writer raised in California. His work has been published in *AGNI, The Drift, Post Road,* and *Washington Square Review.* He is managing editor of poetry.onl.

• The apartment where I began and finished this story belonged to a psychologist. She offered me the place on a handshake after a five-minute conversation during which she complimented my aura. This was five months before I saw a different psychoanalyst in Del Valle who described my dreams as "suffused with atavistic fear." At the start of our first session, the psychoanalyst drew my attention to the sound of a bird nesting beyond the window. He sent me home with a gabapentin prescription and advised me against reading or writing before bed.

I suppose I followed the psychoanalyst's advice, because I wrote this story over the course of an afternoon in the last sunny month of the year. I composed it at the dining table in an apartment far too large for a life willingly circumscribed to a kitchen, a bathroom, and a bed where I spent hours reading Shakespeare's sonnets and feeling guilty for not reading enough Latin American literature.

I had spent the month, and the preceding rainy season, searching government archives for business records that didn't exist. My research notebooks were empty, the apartment was empty—so I filled the apartment's rooms with friends, friends of friends, cousins, siblings, a dog, parents, and strangers. It was only a matter of time before I filled it with heartbroken hallucinations.

The psychoanalyst never learned what kind of bird sang beyond his office window—a storm overturned the bird's nest; the textile worker joked that I was CIA and denied my request for an interview; the labor activist broke into sobs before she could finish telling me about the shadow in the car in Chihuahua; the psychologist who lived above me moved before I could lend her a book of William Goyen fiction translated to Spanish.

This story holds and hides a Mexico I fled from, incomplete. Names, titles, birdsong—the word for things: I relinquish these to the man in the third room.

WILLIAM PEI SHIH's stories have been published or are forthcoming in *The Best American Short Stories 2020* and *The Best American Short Stories 2025, The Georgia Review, Virginia Quarterly Review, McSweeney's Quarterly Concern, Joyland, The Southern Review, Michigan Quarterly Review, Boston Review, The Los Angeles Review, The Southern Humanities Review, Crazyhorse, F(r)iction, Catapult, Ursa Short Fiction, Asian American Literary Review, The Des Moines Register, The Masters Review, Reed Magazine, Carve, Hyphen,* and elsewhere. *Longreads* included his story "Happy Family" on its list of Ten Outstanding

Stories to Read in 2023. His stories have been recognized by the John Steinbeck Award for Fiction, the Flannery O'Connor Award for Short Fiction, the Raymond Carver Short Story Award, the UK Bridport Prize, The London Magazine Short Story Prize, the Granum Foundation Fellowship Prize, among others. His stories have been nominated multiple times for the Pushcart Prize. He has been awarded scholarships to the Sewanee Writers' Conference, Bread Loaf Writers' Conference, Sun Valley Writers' Conference, Kundiman, the Napa Valley Writers' Conference, and the Ragdale residency. He has served on the admissions board for the Bread Loaf Writers' Conference for several years. A graduate of the Iowa Writers' Workshop, he was a recipient of the Dean's Graduate Fellowship. He is the fiction editor at *Guernica* magazine. He currently lives in New York City and teaches at NYU. For more information, please visit williampeishih.com.

• "The Masterclass" originated as a cut from a novel that I was working on, but over a summer in Paris, evolved into a piece of its own, encapsulating themes of mentorship, the struggles within artistic communities, and the complex interplay between ambition and disillusionment. I saw the story in conversation with Franz Kafka's parable "Before the Law" from the novel *The Trial*, and Jacques Derrida's essay of the same title, while also exploring the hardships that accompany the pursuit of excellence in the dwindling and anti-intellectual world of the story. I wanted to follow characters who harbor secrets and are faced with impossible choices, and who lose themselves in the trivialities of vanity. At the same time, this story also reflects the intricacies of mentorship—when it goes awry and the layers of conflict that arise when resources are scarce and competition is seemingly fierce. I wanted to capture some of the complexities of gatekeeping and nepotism in artistic spaces, revealing how such dynamics can often undermine the creative process and distort genuine connections. Ultimately, this is a story about how we treat one another amidst these pressures, and it reflects my ongoing fascination with the human condition, the lessons born out of unequal relationships, and the necessity for preserving kindness and generosity in an often unforgiving landscape.

My heartfelt thanks to my editor K.K. Fox and the team at *The Los Angeles Review* for publishing this story, and to Celeste Ng and Nicole Lamy for choosing this story for this year's *Best American* anthology.

JUSTIN TAYLOR's most recent novel, *Reboot*, was named a *New York Times* Editors' Choice and Notable Book of 2024, as well as a Best Book of the Year by *The Washington Post*. He is the author of three previous books of fiction and a memoir, *Riding with the Ghost*. His fiction and nonfiction have appeared in *The New Yorker*, *Harper's*, *Granta*, *Forever*, and *Bookforum*, among other magazines and journals. He is a contributing writer to the *Washington Post Book World*. He has been a fellow of MacDowell, the Virginia Center for the Creative Arts, and the Vermont Studio Center. Since 2020 he has been the director of the MFA program at Sewanee, the University of the South. Originally from South Florida, he now lives in Portland, Oregon.

• I wrote the first draft of "What About This" longhand at a coffee shop in Winchester, Tennessee, on December 1, 2022, during the last days of a difficult semester spent far from home. I'd been given a generous teaching fellowship that I worried I had squandered. Back at the beginning of the term, a screenplay I'd co-written had generated some of that fabled "Hollywood interest," resulting in one Zoom meeting after another in which a fit smiling person in a sunlit home office heaped praise on my and my co-writer's heads for a breathless hour then disappeared from our lives forever. At one point, we were invited to develop a detailed pitch deck for a reboot of a major sci-fi/horror franchise whose name I'm still not sure whether I'm allowed to say. All this took time and energy, not to mention hopes and dreams, and resulted in exactly zero deals or dollars. By Thanksgiving I was desperate for something—anything—to show for the university's investment in me, and my own time. Thus to the coffee shop, where I bought the biggest latte they'd sell me and proceeded to pour four months' worth of writerly anxiety and existential vertigo into a voice suggested by the innocent seminarians-in-training who, in reality, it was my privilege to live among in the little university housing village on Roarks Cove Road. Thank you to my colleagues at Sewanee, the University of the South, for their ongoing camaraderie and support. Also to Emily Adrian, for sharp notes on the manuscript and for telling me when it was done. Last but not least, my utmost gratitude to Christina Thompson and the staff of the *Harvard Review* for giving this story of spiritual homelessness such a good and loving home.

SANJANA THAKUR is a writer from Mumbai, India. She is the 2024 winner of the Commonwealth Short Story Prize, a Bread Loaf Environmental Scholar, and Best of the Net nominee. Her fiction has appeared in *Granta*, *Michigan Quarterly Review*, *The Rumpus*, and *The Southampton Review*. Her poetry has appeared in *The Adroit Journal*, *Booth*, and *Pigeon Pages*. Sanjana is a graduate of UT Austin's New Writers Project and Wellesley College.

• At some point a few years ago, in the long list of ideas and scrapped lines I keep in my Notes app, I wrote: "Too many mothers - a store to rent or buy a mum. Many different kinds to choose from." Later, in my second year at the New Writers Project, I was gaining my sense of self as a writer but also feeling a kind of fear and frustration. For years, through college and through my MFA, I had written stories about mothers and daughters. I'd begun to wonder if I would ever be able to write anything else.

I've always been someone who writes with urgency, pushing up against deadlines. I had a story due for a fiction workshop in a couple of days, so I went through my scraps document and stumbled upon that idea. I decided, then, to write a story chock-full of mothers—so full that I would hopefully satiate my obsession. That's how "Aishwarya Rai" was born.

My obsession was not satiated, but I do think this story, with all its different mothers, allowed me the space to explore how variable and complex mother-daughter relationships are, and how impacted by cultural and societal standards of womanhood and beauty. What are the expectations mothers and daughters have of each other? What happens when you fall short? Can you find the perfect mother? Does such a thing exist?

I am grateful to the Commonwealth Foundation for recognizing this story, to *Granta* for being its first home, and to the incredible teachers who had a hand in shaping this story and shaping me as a writer: Edward Carey, Lauren Holmes, Megha Majumdar, and Elizabeth McCracken. I am grateful to Nicole Lamy and Celeste Ng for finding this story a second home. Finally, I am grateful to my mother—for trying, and for letting me be an imperfect daughter.

JESSICA TREADWAY is the author of four novels and three story collections, including one that received the Flannery O'Connor Award for Short Fiction. "An Early Departure" is part of her fourth collection, *I Felt My Life With Both My Hands*, forthcoming next year from Cornerstone Press. She is a longtime faculty member in the creative writing program at Emerson College in Boston.

• When I start writing a story, I usually know what it's about but not what will happen in it. I begin with a relationship, situation, or memory that holds emotional resonance for me, because as a fiction writer that's my most natural and valuable resource. For "An Early Departure," I was remembering those sweet days when my nieces and nephews were little and my sisters, our mother, the kids, and I would meet up in New York City the way my characters do here. One of those nieces does live in New York now, though the only thing she has in common with Tanya is that they both set off for the playground without once looking back. I have always cherished being an aunt, and I know better than to think it's like being a mother, but it was easy to imagine my way into the heart of a woman who makes that mistake because she needs to.

The stories in my new collection are all narrated by fictional, ordinary women who experience shifts in their perspectives about themselves or the world or both. Because they are ordinary and because these shifts aren't visible to the people around them, it's tempting sometimes to believe I'm not writing about important enough things. But my own favorite stories are the ones that invite me to inhabit characters during those private moments of discovery or transformation, so I'll probably keep aiming to render variations on that theme.

Other Distinguished Stories of 2024

DeVita, Randy, "This Window Does Not Open" (*Bellevue Literary Review*, Issue 47)

Eggers, Dave, "Keeper of the Ornaments" (*American Short Fiction*, Spring)

Fishman, Lillian, "Isabel" (*Granta*, Issue 166)

Freudenberger, Nell, "Attila" (*The New Yorker*, August 5)

Galchen, Rivka, "Crown Heights North" (*The New Yorker*, January 1 & 8)

Goodman, Allegra, "Ambrose" (*The New Yorker*, September 30)

Goyette, Marie, "Freefall" (*StoryQuarterly*, no. 56)

Groff, Lauren, "The Ghosts of Wannsee" (*The Atlantic Online*, September 28)

Halliday, Devon, "Nothing That Counts" (*One Story*, Issue 317)

Hebdon, Nicole, "The Fish King" (*December*, vol. 35.1)

Holladay, Cary, "The Living, The Dead, and Those at Sea" (*The Los Angeles Review*, May 10)

Homes, A. M., "The Walker" (*Zoetrope*, Summer)

Hunt, Laird, "The Kings of Christmas" (*Zoetrope*, Summer 2024)

Jackson, Greg, "The Honest Island" (*The New Yorker*, November 11)

Kalu, N. Jane, "The Lucky Bastard" (*Narrative*, Winter)

Kapur, Kanak, "Long Sleeves" (*Sewanee Review*, Spring)

Katz, Ariel, "Negative Space" (*The Missouri Review*, Winter)

King, Lin, "Yellowpeople" (*One Story*, issue 312)

Kingsley-Ma, Hannah, "Working Life" (*Zyzzyva*, no. 127)

Klam, Matthew, "Hi Daddy" (*The New Yorker*, October 14)

Krouse, Erika, "Eat My Moose" (*Conjunctions*, no. 82)

Kunkel, Benjamin, "Prairie Dogs" (*Granta*, issue 167)

Leichter, Hilary, "Double Shift" (*Conjunctions*, no. 82)

Lemann, Nancy, "The Oyster Diaries" (*The Paris Review*, no. 248)

Lemoine, Sanaë, "The Egg" (*Harper's Magazine*, March)

Lemus, Jared, "Saint Dismas" (*The Atlantic*, April)

Lesmeister, Keith Pilapil, "Fish & Rice" (*December*, vol. 35.1)

Lewin, Trent, "The Reach" (*Boulevard*, Vol. 38, Nos. 3 & 4)

Lewis, Terri, "Alien" (*Chicago Quarterly Review*, vol. 39)

Livesey, Margot, "The Letter Writer" (*Colorado Review*, Fall/Winter)

Lorentzen, Christian, "The Accursed Mountains" (*Granta*, issue 167)

Lou, Angie Sijun, "Reincarnation Waiting Room" (*Bomb Magazine*, September 16)

Malcangio, Tori, "Invasive Species" (*The Missouri Review*, Spring 2024)

Manghnani, Shivani, "Island Girl" (*Craft*, October 11)

Marra, Anthony, "Countdown" (*Zoetrope*, Spring)

Martin, Andrew, "Lovefool" (*Harper's Magazine*, August)

Mason, Daniel, "Mare's Milk" (*Harper's Magazine*, December)

McCracken, Elizabeth, "Howard Johnson's, Late Spring" (*StoryQuarterly*, no. 56)

McFarlane, Fiona, "Hostel" (*The New Yorker*, March 4)

Nathan, Olivia, "Anachronisms" (*Sewanee Review*, winter)

Neville, Susan, "The Wind Phone" (*The Sun*, December)

American and Canadian Magazines Publishing Short Stories

Electric Literature
Epiphany
Event
Exposition Review
Failbetter
The Fairy Tale Review
The Fiddlehead
Five Points
Flash Boulevard
Flash Frog
FlashFlood
The Florida Review
Foglifter
Forge Literary Magazine
Fractured Lit
Full Bleed
Gargoyle Magazine
Gemini Magazine
The Georgia Review
Gold Man Review
Gordon Square Review
Granta
The Gravity of the Thing
Grist
Guernica
Gulf Coast
Harper's Magazine
Harvard Review
Hawaii Pacific Review
Hayden's Ferry Review
The Headlight Review
Hemingway Shorts
The Hopkins Review
The Hudson Review
Hyphen
Image
The Iowa Review
Iron Horse Literary Review
Isele Magazine
Jabberwock Review
The Jewish Fiction Journal
Joyland
Kaleidotrope
The Kenyon Review
Lady Churchill's Rosebud Wristlet
L'Esprit Literary Review
Lilith
The Limberlost Review
Lindenwood Review

The Los Angeles Review
Lowestoft Chronicle
Lunch Ticket
The Malahat Review
The Massachusetts Review
The Masters Review
McSweeney's
Meridian
Michigan Quarterly Review
Mississippi Review
The Missouri Review
Mount Hope
Mukoli: The Magazine for Peace
The Muleskinner Journal
Mystery Tribune
n+1
Narrative
Nelle
The New Chicagoan
New England Review
New Letters
New Ohio Review
New World Writing Quarterly
The New Yorker
Nimrod International Journal
Noema Magazine
Noon
North American Review
North Carolina Literary Review
North Dakota Quarterly
Northern New England Review
Notch
One Story
Orion
Oxford American
Oyster River Pages
Pacifica Literary Review
Pangyrus
Paper Brigade
The Paris Review
Passages North
Passengers Journal
Peauxdunque Review
Pembroke
Permafrost
Phoebe
Pioneer Works Broadcast
Pithead Chapel
Ploughshares

The Point
Porter House Review
Propagule
Pulphouse Fiction Magazine
Quarter After Eight
Raritan
Red Rock Review
River Styx Magazine
Room
Ruby
Salamander
Salmagundi Magazine
Salt Hill
San Antonio Review
Santa Monica Review
Saranac Review
Saturday Evening Post
Scarlet
The Seventh Wave
The Sewanee Review
Shenandoah
Short Story, Long
SmokeLong Quarterly
Solstice
The Southampton Review
South Carolina Review
South Dakota Review
Southern Humanities Review
Southern Indiana Review
The Southern Review
Southwest Review
Spaceports & Spidersilk

Split Lip Magazine
Starlite Pulp Review
Stone's Throw
Story
StoryQuarterly
Subtropics
The Summerset Review
The Sun
swamp pink
Swing
Tahoma Literary Review
Terrain.org
Texas Monthly
The Threepenny Review
Transition
TriQuarterly
Vestal Review
Vincent Brothers Review
Virginia Quarterly Review
Vita Poetica
Washington Square Review
West Branch
Western Humanities Review
Whale Road Review
Whisk(e)y Tit
Willow Springs
Witness
The Write Launch
The Yale Review
Your Impossible Voice
Zoetrope
Zyzzyva

ABOUT
MARINER BOOKS

MARINER BOOKS traces its beginnings to 1832 when William Ticknor cofounded the Old Corner Bookstore in Boston, from which he would run the legendary firm Ticknor and Fields, publisher of Ralph Waldo Emerson, Harriet Beecher Stowe, Nathaniel Hawthorne, and Henry David Thoreau. Following Ticknor's death, Henry Oscar Houghton acquired Ticknor and Fields and, in 1880, formed Houghton Mifflin, which later merged with venerable Harcourt Publishing to form Houghton Mifflin Harcourt. HarperCollins purchased HMH's trade publishing business in 2021 and reestablished their storied lists and editorial team under the name Mariner Books.

Uniting the legacies of Houghton Mifflin, Harcourt Brace, and Ticknor and Fields, Mariner Books continues one of the great traditions in American bookselling. Our imprints have introduced an incomparable roster of enduring classics, including Hawthorne's *The Scarlet Letter*, Thoreau's *Walden*, Willa Cather's *O Pioneers!*, Virginia Woolf's *To the Lighthouse*, W.E.B. Du Bois's *Black Reconstruction*, J.R.R. Tolkien's *The Lord of the Rings*, Carson McCullers's *The Heart Is a Lonely Hunter*, Ann Petry's *The Narrows*, George Orwell's *Animal Farm* and *Nineteen Eighty-Four*, Rachel Carson's *Silent Spring*, Margaret Walker's *Jubilee*, Italo Calvino's *Invisible Cities*, Alice Walker's *The Color Purple*, Margaret Atwood's *The Handmaid's Tale*, Tim O'Brien's *The Things They Carried*, Philip Roth's *The Plot Against America*, Jhumpa Lahiri's *Interpreter of Maladies*, and many others. Today Mariner Books remains proudly committed to the craft of fine publishing established nearly two centuries ago at the Old Corner Bookstore.

Explore the rest of the series

bestamericanseries.com